EXTRA EXTRA

This book is a work of fiction. As a novel such things as names, places and incidents are products of the author's imagination. Any resemblance to actual events or persons is entirely coincidental. The dog TYPO was indeed a member of our team. The Boston classical music host was a real person. The Boston Globe is a real newspaper, but the Globe events mentioned in this novel are fictitious.

Powdermill Publishing Company
PO Box 267
Hancock, NH 03449
typodog@gmail.com

Typesetting by FormattingExperts.com

FIRST EDITION 2017
ISBN: 978-0-9988540-0-7

EXTRA EXTRA

by Edward R. (Ted) Leach

Powdermill Publishing Company
Hancock, New Hampshire

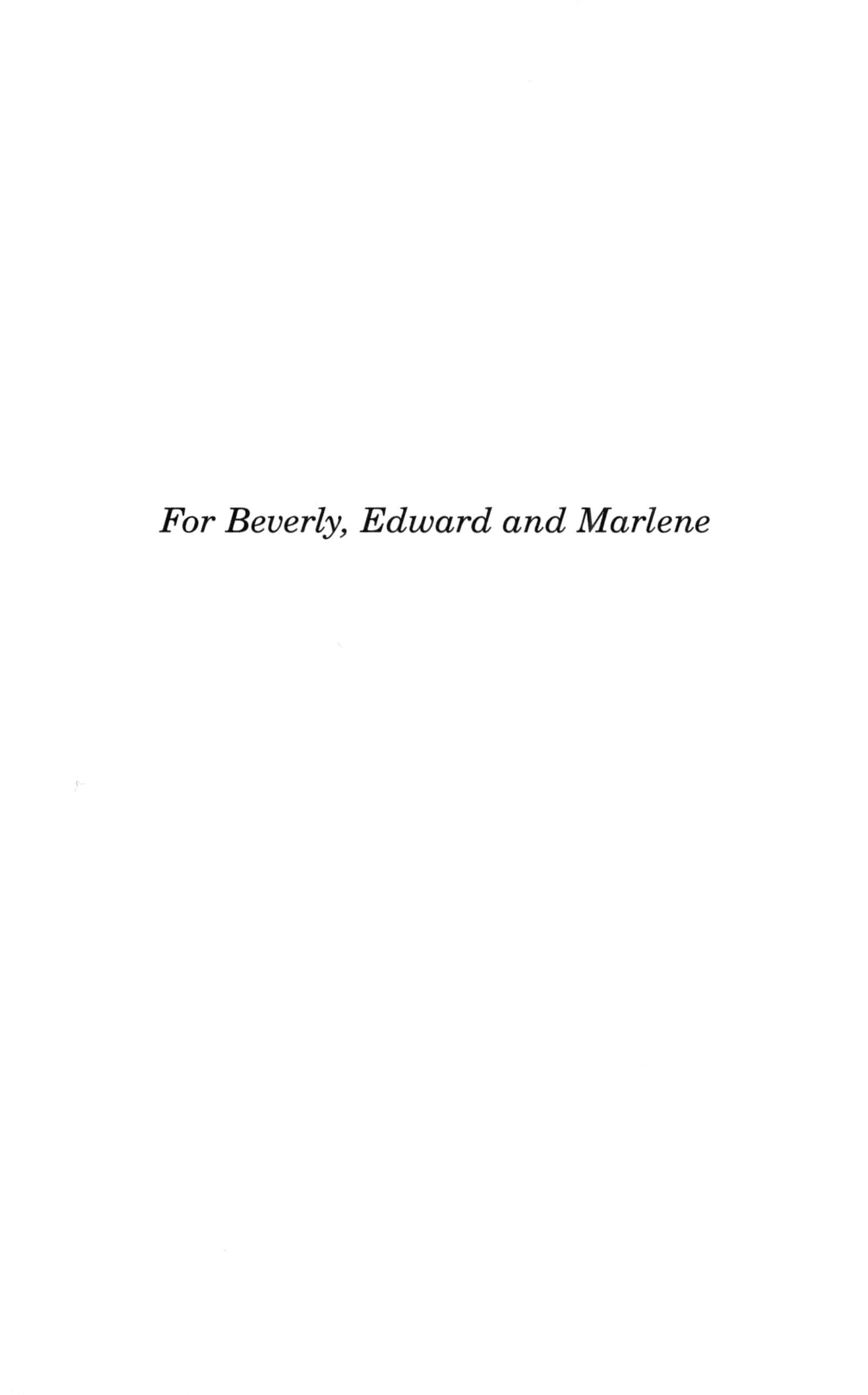

For Beverly, Edward and Marlene

PROLOGUE

News is often described as – *Newly received or noteworthy information, especially about recent or important events.*

Expanding on that definition, the label of news depends upon how it is perceived by the reader. While a report of a ham and bean supper at the local church may not be thought of as news by many readers, it *is* news for the people involved with staging, attending and benefiting from the supper. The general definition above stresses new information about recent or important events, and that new information can pertain to past, current and even future events. The community newspaper presents this palette to its readers who can mine it for information – news – of importance to them.

There are thousands of community newspapers in the United States. They are not there to boost the town, they are not there to write stories in exchange for advertising. They are there to gather, assemble, and present, as their first mission, the news – all of it – in a fair and responsible way.

This book is dedicated to the thousands of people who, over the years, have published weekly newspapers. Often these are mom-and-pop operations. Some are pretty fancy-looking productions, others are fairly basic.

And through their pages beats the pulse of America.

Their publishers do it purely for the love of the profession. They do it out of a sense of community, and they do it week in and week out. The news does not take a holiday. Rarely would you find a weekly newspaper that shuts down for vacation. If the owner's compensation was divided by the number of hours spent, it would rank right at the bottom of any chart.

But the rewards are many, and frequent. They are usually small, but they add up. You quickly learn that you can make a difference – you can be a help, and you can also be a hindrance. And the truly good publishers quickly grasp that with freedom of the press comes responsibility – lots of it.

Beginning

I hadn't even stopped and the cop was making a U-turn.

Now what do I do? Innocently go about my business or sit there and wait until he arrives?

I decided to push ahead, and climbed out of the car with a copy of the latest edition of the *Elgin Eagle* under my arm. I walked up to the front door of the car dealership, then realized that I'd forgotten the most important item, a short note attached to the paper.

I'm dead, I thought. Any hesitation now and the cop will arrive with gun drawn. What else can he do? It's 5:30 a.m., the town is asleep, and a strange car with out-of-state plates has stopped in front of a local business. A tall, dark figure emerges and quickly walks up to the front door. There, in the shadows, he remains.

But to leave the paper on the stoop without a note was a waste of time and a waste of a paper to boot. Yes, small-town publishers think about things like that twenty-four hours a day.

So I dug into my pocket, pulled out a business card, and scrawled on the back, "Jack – hope you like the look of your ad on page five. Thanks for allowing the *Eagle* to be a part of your growth. Sincerely, Ed Remington."

I was about at the "like the look" portion of the note when the bright spotlight hit. I felt like Steve McQueen caught in the glare of the searchlights in *The Great Escape*. An air of total innocence was required and I turned around so the light could illuminate the card and continued to write.

The light stayed on me as I finished the note and clipped it to page one. I shoved the paper through the mail slot, turned, and walked toward the police car. Then I realized that I'd just violated a cardinal rule of selling: Never direct an advertiser to a page in your newspaper unless you are 100 percent certain of what he is going to find.

Was Jack's ad on page five?

I thought it was, but it had been about twelve hours since I last saw it. Maybe it was on page three or page seven. And was the print job crisp and clear, or was this one of those pages where a pressman's ink-stained hands had smeared the ad in question? Crap.

The whole scenario had lasted all of thirty seconds, but it seemed like hours. It was time to fold'em and trust that my memory of Jack's ad placement was correct.

I approached the police car and said to the young cop, "Hey, thanks for the light. I'm Ed Remington, publisher of the *Elgin Eagle* up in Elgin."

"So what are you doing here?" came the cool response.

"Delivering a newspaper to Jack Harris, he's one of our advertisers."

"What's the name of the paper again?" he asked, with just a hint of warmth in his voice.

"The *Elgin Eagle*. Here, let me get you a copy."

I fully expected to be stopped as I started walking over to my car but my way was lit by the roving spotlight. As I opened the door, the spotlight entered first.

I was home free.

The light illuminated the station wagon full of 4,800 copies of the *Eagle*'s latest edition. The cop saw it and things were back on track.

I slipped an issue out of the opened bundle on the front seat and walked back to the patrol car.

"Here, have of copy of the best weekly newspaper in the state," I said, trying not to sound cocky. "I think you'll find the story about bass fishing on the front of the second section real interesting. Do you fish?"

"Whenever I can," came the response.

And with that, one more of a never-ending series of weekly crises was history.

It was 7:15 a.m. on Thursday; the weekly edition of the *Elgin Eagle* was being distributed to newsstands throughout its fourteen-town readership. The largest town, Elgin, had been at the front end of the distribution and many had already had a chance to read the paper, or at least skim it. The phone was ringing. One could almost count on the phone ringing in the newspaper office at about this time each week, and the call was either going to be a complaint about something that had been omitted from the paper or something that had been included. The posted and published office hours for the *Eagle* were eight to five Monday through Friday, but that never stopped the phone from ringing.

"Good morning, *Elgin Eagle*," I said into the phone, trying to mask the fact that I had been up and working straight for the past twenty-four hours.

"Hi, Ed, this is Bill Sauer of the Elgin PD. I can't talk right now but I was wondering if we could meet someplace so I can discuss a few things with you." Bill's voice sounded tense.

"Sure, Bill," I replied, trying not to sound too eager. Something was going to come out of this. "Where and when?"

"How about tonight? I'm on duty tonight. Maybe behind Value at midnight?" he said.

Midnight! No way, I thought, but my mouth was faster than my creature comforts and I said, "See you then, behind Value Foods."

I knew there was dissension in the police shop. I also knew that this was not rare. Like any bureaucracy, Elgin's PD has a lot of entry-level personnel who are fresh out of the police academy. They have some definite ideas as to what constitutes good policing. But these ideas soon run head first into an omelet of bureaucratic reality and real life – and then the meltdown begins. In this instance, however, I knew that we were headed into deeper water. I had seen Officer Sauer's illusion bubble burst almost a year ago. This call, coupled with lots of street talk, alerted me to the fact that we were heading toward the "separation phase" where the astute newsman tries to separate truth from everything else.

"I've got three bundles here that don't have second sections," hollered one of my drivers, "and I need more rubbers."

I wished he would call them rubber bands. But for the moment the priority crisis is three "unrubbered" bundles of newspapers that are missing second sections. That constitutes three hundred newspapers, and that was outside of our weekly print overage. Simply put, we have no way to compensate for this printer error. Now we have some newsstand juggling to do. But before that charade commences, I am wondering if our second driver is out there delivering three hundred papers that have two second sections. If that is the case, I have double trouble.

When you are moving fast and trying to make thirty or forty stops in less than two hours, you just may not have that necessary light touch to ascertain that the paper bundle doesn't feel right, that some bundles of fifty feel heavier than other bundles of fifty.

But there is no time to worry. I'll see if I can track down the driver on the road and I tell my other driver to go ahead and short Value Foods by one hundred papers. We sell out at the Value every week, but we also leave them more than six hundred newspapers. And they don't *ALL* sell on Thursday. That will buy me some time to sort things out.

"Good morning, Ed," comes the melodic tone of Lana, my office manager, as she waltzes into the office with her usual positive outlook. When her voice sounds like that, she means it. Little does she know that I am about to dump the missing-section problem right in her lap.

"Good morning, *Elgin Eagle*," she says. The phone saves her from being the recipient of the missing-section problem. "I believe so, may I say who's calling?"

Oh, hell, I don't want a call right now; I need to get some coffee.

"It's Mrs. Ely," says Lana.

"Hi, Joanna," I say, knowing that we had a story about her daughter's engagement in the paper. What have we done to deserve this call? Wrong name? Wrong headline? Misspelled names? Wrong dates? Or worst of all, wrong picture? Over the years we've managed to accomplish all of the above.

"Ed, I just got the *Eagle* and the picture and story about Deborah's engagement are just wonderful!" she exclaimed.

Wow, we won one for a change.

"Glad you liked it, Joanna. She's a great kid," I said.

"Ed, I was wondering if you could save about five copies for us. We'd buy them at the Value but I suppose that after the week is up you would have no use for them anyway," stated Joanna, who was suddenly sounding mighty cheap.

"Joanna, if you want five copies, I suggest you get down to the Value Foods as fast as possible, because the press run was screwed up this week and three or four days from now you won't be able to find a copy anywhere," I said, trying to add as much urgency as possible.

"Oh, thanks, Ed, that's good to know. I'll get right down there," she said excitedly.

Two bucks more for the good guys, I thought. What a cheap call. But why did I send her to the Value Foods that is already short a hundred papers? And they don't advertise with us either!

"Where do you keep the rubbers?" hollered Dan, my seventy-year-old, sixth-generation New Englander.

I had a good answer for that one but figured that if one posed a question of that sort, a witty answer was a waste of breath.

"Right in front of you, inside that cabinet, on one of the middle shelves," said Lana, and before he could open the doors she was there to assist. First of all, she was a most helpful person. But she was also a pragmatist. She knew that if Dan didn't get his butt out that door quickly and get those newspapers onto the newsstands, that one Edward Rogers Remington, running on no sleep, with distribution problems showing their ugly head, was going to lose it. And since she was going to be the only employee in the office until after lunch, she was going to be the target recipient of whatever crap I was ready to sling.

I headed over to one of the local hash houses for a good breakfast and some coffee. One would think that I would head home, but giving birth to a newspaper each week is just like directing a play. The adrenaline gets pumping and it takes a long while before things settle down.

Experience had taught me that Thursday, the day the paper comes out, is a day that must be spent awake. Small fires are more easily extinguished than infernos, and many small fires ignite on Thursday.

Early to bed Thursday night, a late (nine a.m.) sleep-in the following morning, and I was as good as new. Admittedly, Thursday afternoons were always an adventure, but I was truly excited about each and every issue of the newspaper, and when you get pumped up like that, you generate considerable bonus miles.

I entered Freda's Restaurant and there was the usual contingent, each occupying his or her customary chair, stool, booth, or table. The coffee-stained carpet, the aroma of bacon and dog hair, and the low murmur of the customers as they chomped and slurped their morning fare. Each booth held four or six customers and no booth was ever co-ed, except when strangers entered the place. The stallions sat with the stallions and the mares had their own separate huddles.

I moved to my preferred seat, and Barbara, the waitress, met me with a cup of coffee. Out of the corner of my eye I could see Morgan Mather heading my way. Morgan was a member of the school board, and he and I rarely saw eye to eye on school issues.

"Where do you get this crap that you print?" he said loud enough for everyone in the joint to hear. He then slapped the back of his hand against the newspaper he was carrying.

"Pardon?" I said in the most French accent I could muster. I had heard him but I wanted to test his degree of irritability. If he came back with the same accusation, I knew he was really steamed. Often, however, he would back off at this point.

"This is crap," he said, this time sort of addressing it to everyone in the place more than to me. "Where do you get this stuff?" he bellowed as a wisp of scrambled eggs flew out of his mouth.

"Usually, Morgan, we just make it up," I replied. With that I leaned across the counter to grab a little creamer. This act, I knew, would infuriate Morgan, who loved being the center of attention. To be dismissed in favor of a creamer was sure to stir him up.

He was a big blowhard whose views on education might have worked in the eighteenth century, but were totally out of touch in today's world. And he had a very difficult time separating his own brand of morality from most decisions.

I didn't dismiss most complainers as I did Morgan because we weren't always right. If you learn to listen, you will quickly put out a much better paper. But in Morgan's case I knew I was right because I had a person inside every school board meeting, whether public or private, who brought me everything. And he was not a reporter for the paper. In fact, my reporter did not know the identity of my mole.

My mole had approached me many months earlier, upset with the fact that some members of the school board were trying to "legislate morality," as he put it. They were discussing books that should be removed from the school library. Books that they felt were "inappropriate." These discussions took place both in public and private meetings of the board.

The banned-books chatter at the school board meeting about six months ago was page one in the next edition. We quoted individual school board members on both sides of the issue and we ran a stinging editorial on the subject.

That story was carefully scrubbed so as not to reveal that we had "ears" inside their private meeting. Having that inside track often allowed for a carefully crafted question in public and that brought the truth, the intent, to the surface. We were able to play that card in such a way that no one suspected that we knew more than we were divulging, and that nifty book-banning idea was DOA at the next school board meeting.

But the public backlash on the book-ban issue was so fast and intense that it drove the board farther underground. They started going into more "executive sessions," which meant all reporters were free to go home.

So Morgan was yapping about something that he thought he had engineered in secret, and voilà, he was reading it on page three.

"Morgan, my only regret is that I didn't have more space to really get into that issue," I said as I stirred my coffee and looked him as straight in the eye as possible. Morgan had one glass eye, so someone trying to "look him in the eye" has to decide which eye. The good eye was the natural choice, but you couldn't help peeking at the glass eye just to see if, this one time, it too had joined the discussion.

No doubt about it, he sensed that I knew everything that had gone on in that meeting, both public and private, and he wasn't about to have it displayed in the quasi-public arena he had just created.

Peter Richards inadvertently came to Morgan's rescue. "What books are on your hit list this week, Morgan?"

And with that the discussion turned to the Red Sox.

Pete was a salty old Yankee who had no use for "flatlanders" like Morgan. He'd no use for me either, for years. I was an outsider to Elgin and Pete and many others weren't ready for any outsider to ride into town and start "telling us what to do." Fortunately that was one thing that I did not do during my first few years in Elgin. It was a time to listen, to absorb, and to try to get a finger on the pulse of the community. So I lay pretty low and slowly brought in a new look and some new features that started to expand readership. This would have been a great time for our competition to strut their stuff front and center, but they had already started to flame out.

The old Yankees like Pete weren't so much against me as they were not for me. In fact, if one ever so much as returned as a "good morning," it was a major breakthrough.

Miles Atkins, the guy who ran the local hardware store, never accepted me or the paper. He also would scorn any failure to speak "hardware." A nail wasn't a nail, it had to have "penny" attached to it. A screw had to have a number assigned. If you wanted a wrench, you had to say precisely which one. If you said, "I need a wrench," he would dress you down with a recitation of various types of wrenches, none of which made any sense to me.

"You want a double-box, open end, combination, socket, pipe, torque, allen? What do you want?" he would snap.

At first I thought it was just plain rudeness, then I began to understand that it was a Yankee way of doing things. I still think that they could lighten up a bit. Maybe it was something we ran in the paper, but I suspect that he just didn't trust outsiders, coupled with the fact that he was isolated in his store for eight plus hours a day. He never said hello, but I always went out of my way to pop into his store whenever I was in that part of town. Eventually he began to acknowledge my presence when I entered his store. One day I handed him a copy of the *Eagle*. He wasn't quite sure what to do with it, so he put it aside and said something like, "Ok, I'll get to that later, got chores to do." But the look on his face as I handed him the paper told me that his standoffishness had run its course and Miles was bobbing across the Rubicon. He ran one ad each year, at Christmas, and totally ignored our paper. His Christmas ad was always the same, a piece of clip art showing a happy community standing around a town square exchanging presents and cheerfully singing together. I presume newspaper publishers weren't included in that happy tableau. He eventually went out of business.

Two years later, Miles, a widower, suffered a debilitating stroke and his kids plopped him into a local nursing home in Ripley, a little town to our west. It was just short of a snake pit, but was probably a step above the old poorhouses. His visitor log, I was told, was zero, so I decided to adopt him. Periodically I would stop by the home. We had an instant breakthrough on my first visit, when I showed up with an antique tool that I'd borrowed from my neighbor. It was a handled tongue-molding plane, about a foot long. My neighbor used it for a doorstop and he briefed me on it and its history before I took it to Miles. I figured it might be a great ice breaker or would kindle something from his earlier days. It worked like a charm, the sight of that tool blotted out the character who was holding it. "Miles, what in the world is this?" I said, and the door was open.

A couple of months later I mentioned in my column one of my antique-tool conversations with Miles, and that opened the floodgates for many others who wanted to share their finds with Miles. A steady stream of visitors started making a pilgrimage to the nursing home, and Miles probably had more social interaction during the final eight months of his life than he had experienced in the previous twenty years. I still don't know what a ten-penny nail is, but I do miss Miles.

The alarm went off like a cannon. I awoke in a sea of drool as I always do when exceptionally tired. The little red numbers on the clock face said 11:30. For a moment I had no idea what was happening and then the television could be heard and I realized that it was nighttime.

As well as I knew that the rendezvous with the cop was probably going to lead to a good story, I was tempted to blow it off. I have reporters who are supposed to get this kind of stuff, but my Elgin reporter had been on the job for all of two months. She had neither the background nor the perspective to step into this kind of simmering cauldron right now.

Sally is a very bright young woman, editor of her college newspaper and full of energy and ready to prove herself in the real world outside of academia. But to throw her into this development would be unfair right now.

On the way down to Value, I decided to swing past the police chief's house just to make sure he was there. His cruiser would be parked in his driveway. That in itself infuriated me. I'd fought his being allowed to take the car home, but he countered with the argument that he needed it to respond to police calls.

"They don't just come in from eight to five, Ed," he grinned at a selectman's meeting one night. It was the right argument to use in front of that panel of town fathers. The area had many different trios of selectmen and, with few exceptions, they all threw themselves heart and soul into the task. But the current panel was the *crème de la crème* of morons. Two of them squeaked in at one election, due to a prior selectman moving to Florida and another not running for reelection. The holdover selectmen was a conscientious guy, but was hesitant to venture an opinion or weigh in on anything. I think he had some sort of phobia about dissension, and that resulted in a governing panel of two loudmouths and one shadow. Any sort of vitriolic argument was readily accepted by this troika, and no sort of follow-up was needed. The response to the chief's argument should have been, "When was the last time you had to leave your house in the evening in order to attend to police business?" The chief would have concocted some phony answer but the fact was that he never did any police business at night other than scheduled meetings. There were plenty of police calls at night, we heard them on the scanner, but the chief never responded.

I turned onto Outer Park Drive and my headlights caught the reflection of the chief's car neatly parked in his driveway. There were no markings or decals on this car, it was solely for the chief and no one was going to use it to haul some upchuck-ing DWI suspect downtown for a little toot on the breathalyzer. Just the sight of it sitting there pissed me off. What a waste of taxpayer money.

OK, the chief is present and accounted for. I was ready to swing around Value Foods and find Officer Sauer. As I ap-proached the road leading to the rear of the store a car came around the corner so I kept going straight. I didn't want to be observed driving back there. A minute or so later I came around for a second attempt and again there was a car right there and I waved myself off again. The third time was a charm and I neatly slipped around the corner of the building and drove to the wide portion of the rear parking area. There was no Officer Sauer.

Oh, no. Again I was going to pay a price for keeping my appointment calendar in my head. I had the wrong date. Damn.

Then I assured myself that I was at the right place at the right time. I remembered thinking that a Thursday night was not a good night to be doing anything other than sleeping. Maybe it was next week? No, it was tonight. Just cool it, he'll get here. Maybe something came up that detained him. I started the engine and decided to head down to the cop shop to see if maybe his patrol car was there. I then realized that if I left and he showed up, then the whole thing was probably off. I turned off my engine, slid down in the seat, turned down the radio, and waited.

Within a couple of minutes Officer Sauer came around the corner from the other end. I had anticipated that he would come in from that direction and by merely pulling over to where I was, we could talk driver's door to driver's door. That is exactly what he did as he pulled up and killed his lights.

"What's up, Bill?" I asked, hoping that he would get right to the point.

"Ed, I hate to ask you this but I have to. You are alone, right?" he said.

"Right," I answered.

"And you aren't recording or going to take notes, OK?" he asked.

"Whatever you want," I answered, quite aware that my trip was going to be worthwhile.

"Ed, you gotta promise me that you will never tell anyone about this conversation. I could lose my job or even worse if any of this gets out," he said rapidly. "Promise me that all of this is just between you and me."

That bothered me a bit, so I sought to clarify that statement. "Bill, I will never reveal to anyone that this conversation took place, but I can't promise you that I won't pursue some of the information if I feel it is warranted. That's OK, isn't it?" I added with a reaffirming nod of my head.

"Just as long as it can never be traced back to me," he said.

I agreed and then thought to myself that it was pretty ridiculous because whatever comes out of this is not going to be earth-shattering stuff. This was a little podunk police department with an above-average quotient of employee dissatisfaction, but that was about it as far as I was concerned.

The police radio inside the cruiser had been sputtering since Bill arrived, but this call was much more clear and distinct. A state trooper was in the process of breaking up an altercation at a nearby rest stop and had requested help.

"I gotta go," said Bill. "I'll get back in touch with you, Ed." He grabbed his microphone to respond.

I thought about suggesting that I would wait there for him, but that might be a long wait and I was dead tired.

"Sounds good, Bill. I'll talk to you later," I said. The clandestine midnight rendezvous was over.

Crap. I drag myself out of a near-death sleep, come all the way down here to get a dynamite story, and some state cop is busy confiscating a twelve-pack of Miller Lite. Crap.

I decided to stop by the office just because it was on my way home. I rarely drove by without stopping in. I have no idea why, but that was how it operated.

I parked in front of the building and went inside. Rather than turn on one switch and light twenty or more ceiling lights, I switched on Lana's desk lamp, which gave me enough light to see my way back to my office. Turning on lights is expensive and those little things mount up.

As I entered my office, the phone rang.

"Good evening, *Eagle*," I said instinctively.

"I'd like to place a classified ad," came the response.

I took the ad over the phone, figured out the amount due, and informed the caller that it must be prepaid by the following Monday at 5:00 p.m. She said she knew that, because she ran lots of ads with us. "And when's the last time you placed one at 12:30 a.m., sister?" I wanted to say, but I didn't.

"Is this Mr. Remington?" said the voice.

"Yes, it is."

"I thought it sounded like you," she opened up. "I met you at the Fourth of July fireworks. This is Helen Delano."

"Of course, Helen, how are you?" I said, regretting the fact that I was extending this call.

"We're all fine, Mr. Remington," she said, "I really didn't expect anyone to answer the phone at this hour. Do you always work this late?"

"We were just waiting for your call, Helen," I said. "Now we can all go home."

"Thanks so much, Mr. Remington," she chirped.

There were half a dozen or so notes sitting on my desk. I decided to ignore them and deal with them in the morning, but I glanced at one that simply said, "network down."

Our computer network had crashed again and most of the staff hadn't a clue how to fix it. Dammit. No sleeping in late, because no one can write a word until the network is up and running.

I decided to take a look at it right then. More often than not the problem occurs in the same places. If I could find that now, I could get that much-needed sleep. Usually the reason for the network failure was a loose plug from a computer connecting to our multiplexer. Fortunately, I found it right off the bat and reconnected the plug. I launched a reboot, confirmed that everything was back online, and left the building. As I started my car I glanced up at the building and realized that the desk lamp had not been turned off.

To hell with it.

Chapter One

God, I love this business, I thought as I watched three people in a row exiting a local mini-grocery, each with a copy of the *Eagle*.

It appeared that two of them also had copies of our competition. What the hell were those morons thinking? But we were making progress – three years ago it would have been the other way around.

I tried not to make eye contact with anyone, because I needed to get some things done at the office before an 11:00 a.m. appointment with a prospective new reporter. This was an ongoing procedure at the *Eagle*; we had an exceptionally high rate of turnover, but, I believe, for the right reasons. I had decided from the beginning that I would definitely consider hiring local talent, or even quasi-talent to supplement a more professionally trained nucleus of reporters. What locals lack in journalism skills they make up for in their knowledge of the local scene. They also supply an important thread of continuity for the paper, providing new staffers with the spin on the local infrastructure.

The downside is that the neighborhood talent pool is quite limited, and locals are usually very reticent about getting into a heavy-hitting story. But I don't push them. If they will cover the community as it goes about its day-to-day life, I will assign one of our bright young Turks to do any stories that might tend to ruffle local feathers.

I walked into the office to hear Lana say, "Here he is now. Ed, this is John Patton of Bartlettsville."

I knew that John Patton was an attorney, but I had never met him. I could tell that this was not a courtesy call. The stiffness in his stature, the rigidity in his handshake, and the oh-so-momentary flicker in the eye contact signaled that he was on a more somber mission, and wished to hell he wasn't.

"Some coffee, John?" I asked.

"No, thanks," he replied.

I filled a half-washed coffee cup with our overheated concoction of sheep dip. "Well, what can I do for you, John?"

"I sent you a letter to the editor last week concerning your story about the Bartlettsville planning board," he said as we headed over toward my office. "I mailed it on Friday morning, and I think that is ample time for the post office to get it to you. I even came into Elgin to mail it."

"Seems like enough time to me," I said. I removed a stack of newspapers from a chair and motioned for him to sit down.

Perhaps I was being a little short with him but my personal credo says, "If you make an appointment with me, I'll be on time and give you whatever time you need. But if you drop in, you are now infringing on my schedule, and if I see you at all, it will be on my terms." And at that moment, my schedule called for coffee.

"You say you wrote a letter to the editor and mailed it, in Elgin, last Friday?" I said, wanting to make certain that my facts were correct. "I haven't seen such a letter, John, but that doesn't necessarily mean that it didn't arrive. It would probably have been in Saturday's mail and one of our reporters picked up the mail that day. What he or she might have done with it is anyone's guess, but I will certainly inquire and get back to you. Do you have a copy in case the original doesn't show up?"

What came next caught me off guard.

"I wish I could believe what you just said, Mr. Remington," said John coldly, "but I'm not buying. I made some very valid points in that letter, points that clearly showed a bias in your reporting, and it appears that you conveniently lost it." He started to get up.

"John, that is just simply not true. We have no qualms about publishing letters that are critical of us. We wish we didn't get them, but we do and we run them. I have told you the truth about your letter, insofar as I know the truth, and I told you that I would look into it."

My phone intercom rang and I said, "Excuse me just a second, John" and pushed the intercom button. It was Lana. "He's full of crap. One, we didn't run a story about the Bartlettsville Planning Board last week, Sally [the reporter who covers Bartlettsville] was off that day. Two, I have a copy of last week's paper right here and there is not one freak'n Bartlettsville story in it. Want me to bring it over to you?" she said.

"No, keep it there," I said. Lana got going again. "Three, I picked up both the Saturday and the Monday mail and there was no letter. The jerk read the story in the *Banner*. I looked it up and it sure as hell is in there, in the goddam *Banner*, page twelve. The stupid turd has walked into the wrong paper!"

The *Banner* was the other paper in Elgin – just *Banner*, no other identification as to what it was all about save for their subtitle under their flag that declared they were "Dedicated to Elgin, New Hampshire and the United States of America." I mean, who in the hell thought up that slop pile of jingoistic jerky! The *Banner* had been owned and operated by the Calloways for several generations. In the mid seventies it was sold to some poorly managed group of newspapers with headquarters in St. Louis. That management didn't have a clue what New England was all about and within three years they had totally decimated the *Banner*. The wizard management in

St. Louis rotated in a publisher and editor about every twelve to eighteen months. Elgin was like a farm team for them, a training ground. None of the Calloways remained with the *Banner* after the deal was signed.

The editorial staff rolled over like a hamster on a tread-mill, and no one seemed to really care about much of any-thing. They couldn't attract good people and thus relied on lo-cals and gossips who never wanted to offend anyone and would never ask a tough question. But a slug of local advertisers still dumped chunks of their advertising budget into the *Banner* each week because "we have always advertised with them."

The few members of the original *Banner* ownership who re-mained in town didn't recognize the newspaper that had been in the Calloway family for generations and often would call me with a tip or suggestion, conversations that I never shared with anyone.

So Lana has just gone ballistic on the phone and I told her, "OK, thanks a lot, I'll look into it," I said as I hung up the phone, hoping that Patton hadn't figured out that my phone call was coming from the other side of the room.

I could string this guy way out right now and then chop him up, but I had lots of items on my agenda to cover and so I decided to let him off the hook as quickly as possible.

"John, the story you refer to was not written in this paper. We did not cover the Bartlettsville planning board two weeks ago. The story was in the *Banner* and that is also probably where you sent your letter," I said without trying to accuse him. Then I cut him a little slack by adding, "I understand the confusion, John, but you are barking up the wrong tree."

"I am not mistaken," he insisted. "It was in your damn pa-per."

Damn paper! Now those are fighting words! But the case was won. It was time to hit the ejection button and send John on his way. I stood up. "John, you are mistaken. I am going to send you out of here with a copy of last week's edition. If the story is in there I will stand corrected, but I'm telling you that the sloppy journalism you allude to was in the *Banner*. And I doubt that you will ever see your letter published there."

I picked up the copy of the previous week's edition that Lana had neatly laid out on her desk and handed it to John, who said nothing as he beat a hasty retreat.

"Want some doughnuts?" asked Lana, grinning from ear to ear.

"Why not?"

* * *

For a weekly newspaper that is published on Thursday, the amount of work accomplished on Friday morning is the secret to its success.

My job was to make sure my young reportorial staff showed up on time and got to work. It was a huge task. They were still drained from the rush to get out the current edition, and there didn't seem to be a great sense of urgency to get things rolling on Friday. But there were people to call, people to see, appointments to be made. And as Friday wore on, more and more of those resources disappeared.

It sounds simple, but getting that through to young, and even seasoned, reporters was a never-ending task. It took me years to grasp it but once I figured it out, I knew that I had hit upon the key to a smooth-running operation.

"Good morning, Ed," hollered Sally as she shot into the room. What a great find she was, I thought over and over. I had hired her straight out of college. Young, aggressive, gung ho, eager to please. Eyes wide open, looking for direction, taking it all in. Hard worker, deadline maker, and fact checker. In short, a near-perfect reporter.

The down side was no experience, easily sidetracked, and often thought of follow-up questions twenty minutes after an interview ended. And, of course, short on life's experiences. A young reporter.

"Have you had a chance to read my story about the kid who did watercolors?" she asked as she grabbed some coffee. "Want a refill?" she continued as she started over toward my desk.

"Yeah, thanks." She topped off my cup. "That was a nice story, Sally," I said. "I wish I had told you that before you had to ask."

"That's OK, I know you're busy. I really enjoyed doing the story and he and his parents were so nice," she said.

"I thought the photos were excellent too, Sally. Did you use your camera?" I said.

"Yes, my new Nikon with a twenty-eight millimeter lens!" she proclaimed proudly.

Sally had duplicated my camera outfit. I felt like a proud teacher. I was particularly pleased that she had picked up on the twenty-eight millimeter lens. What a sharp kid, I thought. I guess we always think that anyone who agrees with us is pretty sharp.

I asked Sally what was going on with the Bartlettsville planning board. I told her that John Patton had been in earlier and was upset about a story in the *Banner*.

"John Patton, the attorney?" she said.

"Same one," I said, "What's his connection or tie to the planning board?"

"I don't exactly know," she said, "but I think that stink over the granting of an exception might have something to do with land that he owns. Or maybe a client of his. I don't know but I can find out."

"It's not a big deal, but if you can find out I would be interested," I said as I headed back to the coffee machine for a splash of cream. "Don't make a big deal in finding out,"

I added, "but this story might have stronger legs than we now realize."

"I'll check it out!" she said enthusiastically.

"Quietly," I added.

"Quietly," she said, holding her index finger up to her lips.

"What do we do about Christmas around here?" she asked.

It all depended on what day Christmas fell, I told her. We usually worked like hell the weekend before and tried to get the new edition buttoned up early. We would hope that we could keep a reporter or two around for last-minute assignments, but it was always sort of a work in progress.

Sally and I looked up Christmas and found that it was going to fall on a Monday, the worst day possible. I told her that we would probably put out the Christmas issue on Thursday as usual. We would then use Thursday and Friday to pull together a New Year's edition. Then everyone could leave on Saturday and not need to be back until the following Thursday.

The bottom line of the scheme was the fact that most of my young staff had never been away from home for the holidays. Many were straight out of college and thus were accustomed to heading over the river and through the woods for Christmas. Sadly, news doesn't go on hold for the holidays, or weekends, or nighttime. It is a twenty-four-hour-a-day cycle that repeats itself three hundred and sixty-five times a year. Staffers had to learn someday that every holiday is not going to be spent with the family. I toyed with the idea of offering unpaid time off and also double pay for those who stayed to cover. At first that scheme seemed to make sense to me but I could see it oozing into other moments during the year when someone was eager to disappear for a day or two and forfeit their pay in the bargain. It foreshadowed a potential fissure in the staff and a nightmare for preparing the biweekly payroll. But I'd end up with a much more contented staff if I could work things out so they could get at least a part of the holiday period off.

That, naturally, left the bulk of the work to me, but it was a good trade and, if properly planned, it really wasn't that much of a stretch. It was funny, though, that this young reporter was thinking about Christmas in July. Oh, the wonderment of youth!

"Good morning, *Elgin Eagle*," said Sally as she answered the extension sitting on my desk.

"Hi, Mr. Robertson, this is Sally Herron. How are you?"

A few seconds passed. "I beg your pardon, Mr. Robertson?" Sally said.

I watched the color drain from her face. I had seen this look before. Sally was getting an earful from Thomas Robertson, a local blue blood who had never done anything in his life except squander his inherited fortune, ride the cocktail circuit at full gallop, and pontificate on everything without knowing much about anything. Because he had money, he was invited onto numerous boards and committees, in hopes that he would keep his mouth shut and his wallet open.

Tears began to well up in Sally's eyes, and rigidity moved across her soft facial features.

"No, sir, you did not," she said emphatically, her voice rising a few decibels. "I'm sorry, but you never told me anything of the kind."

"He's right here." Sally shoved the phone at me.

I covered the mouthpiece and looked at Sally and shrugged questioningly. But she was too upset to respond so I decided to dive right into this newly developing saga.

"Morning, Tom," I said, aware that it was going to be the last pleasantry of this conversation.

"Ed, I was just telling your girl there —"

"Sally," I injected. To this pompous ass, anyone not a member of his country club were gals or guys. Their names were unimportant. They were stepping stones along his stagger through life.

"I was just telling her that much of what she wrote in today's *Eagle* was given to her *off the record*," Robertson boomed, ignoring my correction. "I really don't appreciate being treated like this. I thought you ran a professional organization there, but this is *National Enquirer* tactics," he added, sounding pleased with his dumb analogy.

"*National Enquirer*?" I said. "What do you mean by that?" I knew this would momentarily break his rhythm, and it did.

He 'ahhed' and 'uhhed' for a few seconds and then started up again. "You know, getting people to talk off the record, and then ambushing them by going ahead and publishing everything they say," he huffed.

"Well Tom, I don't know if that is how the *National Enquirer* does things or not, but I do know that is not how the *Elgin Eagle* does things," I said in the most level tone I could muster. I didn't want to joust with this dweeb because it was impossible to ever break through. It was always his way or none. No one had ever successfully said no to him and that was why the family inheritance was flying out the window. I was about to explain that I would discuss the situation with Sally and get back to him, but he interrupted.

"That's how they do things and that's what your gal did to me," he said, with considerably more anger in his voice.

"Her name is Sally, Tom, and I can tell you right now that she didn't *do* anything to you," I said. "There may have been a misunderstanding here, but I can assure you right here and now that nothing was done deliberately."

"I told her specifically that this was off the record and she went right ahead and printed it," he said.

"What did she say when you told her it was off the record?" I inquired.

"I don't remember," he snapped.

"Tom, when something is so important to you that you want it off the record, surely you wouldn't proceed until you had some sort of confirmation that your wishes were going to be honored, would you?" I said, knowing that such astuteness was not even remotely within the range of his capabilities.

"All I know is that I said we were off the record and she went ahead and printed it. And I'll tell you right now that I will never talk to anyone at your paper ever again," he bellowed, and abruptly hung up.

"Ed, I swear he never said anything about off the record," blurted Sally through a torrent of tears. "You've told us exactly how to deal with that, and I know how to handle it."

"I know you do, Sally. Relax, it's OK," I said trying to settle her down. "The guy is bent out of shape. It isn't the end of the world. I want you to think back on your interview with him and see if there is anything that he may have considered an instruction that he was going off the record. Maybe he said something which you just misinterpreted. Maybe he said nothing. Maybe ..."

Looking me straight in the eye, Sally said again, "There was no mention of 'off the record' in any way, shape, or form. It never came up. I promise." The waterworks started spilling over again. She said it so resolutely that I knew she was telling the truth, or the truth as she remembered it. I decided to let the matter drop, but I could tell that she was feeling like she had not convinced me.

I was blindsided on the issue because I hadn't read Sally's story. It was about a planned expansion at the local hospital, and my senior editor had handled it. I told Sally that I thought she was a peach, and not to let this upset her. I told her that things like this happen a lot in the business and just continue to push ahead. She nodded, came over for a reassuring hug, went over to her desk for a minute, and then shot out the door for what I was sure was a cool-down stroll around the block. We all did that – a lot. In fact, we each had a set route.

I grabbed a copy of the paper in order to read the story for myself to see what was so esoteric that Robertson wanted it off the record. As I read the story, no single thought or idea jumped out at me. Robertson was quoted about the need for the expansion, and he outlined a rough timetable. Other than that, there was nothing of any great significance that I could see.

My direct line rang. This was an unpublished number that only my kids, my senior editor, and Lana had. It was the best investment I ever made, for a multitude of reasons. Lana is in the office, my kids are living out of state and have never called this number, so this must be Karen Jacobus, my senior editor, or else a wrong number.

"Hello," I said cheerfully.

"Hi, Ed," said Karen. "Just wanted to warn you that you are about to get a bitching call from –"

I didn't let her finish. "Sir Thomas Robertson," I said.

"He's already called," she said without a hint of question in her voice.

"That he did," I said. "But apparently he rang your chimes as well."

"I screened him on my answering machine," she said coolly. "You really should hear it, Ed, the guy rambled on and on until the answering machine cut him off."

"Smart machine," I said.

"I listened to a lot of that interview last night and I never heard any mention of 'off the record,'" said Karen.

"What do you mean you listened to it?" I inquired, and then I realized that Sally often recorded her interviews in addition to taking notes. "Ohhhhhhh, volley interesting," I said. "I hope Sally still has the tape."

"Oh, she does," said Karen, "in fact, I think her tape recorder is still on my desk. See if it's there."

I set the phone down and walked over to Karen's meticulous desk. There was no tape recorder visible. I walked over to Sally's desk and couldn't find it either.

I went back to the phone and told Karen that I couldn't find it but we would discuss this when she came in. "I'll be there in about thirty minutes," she said.

Karen was a dynamite senior editor. We called her senior editor because I was editor and publisher. We didn't want to make her a managing editor because we felt that a lot of additional baggage was often associated with the title. She was a premier wordsmith and we decided her title would be either executive editor or senior editor. We settled on executive editor, but through a set of internal miscommunications, it was printed as senior editor in her first issue. She decided to let it stay that way.

That was exactly how Karen was in the newsroom. She knew when to get excited and when to cool it. She didn't get hung up on the little things. Senior editor, executive editor, it didn't make a damn bit of difference to Karen as long as she had the authority to massage words and direct our brilliant young staff. She had previously been a copy editor with a major Midwestern daily.

Her husband, Hal, had been transferred to Elgin and Karen found her way to our door. Within six months, her husband had lost his job and I feared we would soon be losing Karen. I made a lot of phone calls on behalf of Hal Jacobus. He was a graphic designer, but had zero ability to sell himself. One day Karen announced that Hal was going to go into business for himself.

Not good news, I thought. I had been through this before with employee spouses and that usually signaled the beginning of the end.

I told her that we just might be his first client. I wanted to do some basic design work on the paper's logo, letterhead, and business cards. I knew exactly what I wanted, but needed someone to pull it all together. Hal came in, we talked, and I launched him on the project. That would buy him a little time to get his new business started.

His work was mediocre at best, but he was the only person in town doing what he was doing and within a couple of weeks after completing our job he had landed a few new assignments. It had sort of been that way for the past three years. I knew it wouldn't last forever, but they were making ends meet.

He was particularly valuable as an on-call typesetter, and became quite proficient at it. He was thrilled not to have to go to work every day, and I held onto the best weekly newspaper senior editor in America.

* * *

John, our sports editor, shuffled into the office, carrying a cup of exotic java that he had purchased at the exotic java joint which had recently opened in town. What an incongruity. John was constantly moaning about being underpaid, yet he would buy a $1.25 cup of coffee instead of drinking the free swill at the office. It wasn't a case of gourmet taste buds, it was a case of cross-wired priorities.

"What a great game last night," he said to me as he looked for a place on his desk to put the coffee.

"You went to a game last night?" I said. Thursday night was the night the entire staff used to recuperate.

"Well, I went out for pizza and on the way home I passed the ballyard and noticed that the Texaco service station team was playing the Wattnots" (a team from a local company which made electric components of some kind). "There's a lot of bad blood there and I stopped to watch."

He then laid out one of his patented "pregnant pauses." This was how John demanded attention. The name of the game here was for the listener to ask John the logical follow-up question. In fact, if the listener did not perform at this point, John would go into a funk and the story would never be completed – which was often a wonderful option.

I obliged and offered the perfunctory, "So what happened?"

"No brawls," said John, "but the game lasted seventeen innings and was finally called a four-four tie! Unbelievable."

"How are they going to score that tie?" I asked, interested in how this might affect the season's standings.

"That's the big unknown," said John. "They are meeting this afternoon."

"Does the *Banner* know about this meeting?" I asked. We might have a slight edge here.

"Not yet," said John, "and I think Charlie [the town recreation director] isn't going to call them either. He was really impressed that I was there last night."

Don't hold your breath, I thought. Charlie Borders has never done us any favors. We have done a lot for him, but he has never reciprocated. He talks a good game, but has never delivered.

"He'll probably call the *Banner*," said John. "He's a turd about things like that."

John was getting it.

"Your reporter prospect is here," said Lana on the intercom.

Actually I had seen him walk in, but let him go through the process so that Lana could get a slight read on him. "First impression, Lana, on a scale of one to ten?"

"Oh, about seven, maybe higher," she said. Lana was the only person in the office who could pick up on a question like that and shuffle back the answer while looking and sounding completely innocent.

"I'll be right over," I said, heading across to the reception area. I thought it was important that if you had invited someone to your office, you should get up off your duff and escort the person into your office. Just one of those hangover protocols from an earlier life in corporate America.

"Hi, Dennis, Ed Remington. Thanks for coming all the way up here today," I said.

Dennis was a Boston boy, a Northeastern graduate who worked for an entertainment throwaway newspaper in Boston.

"You've met Lana, let me introduce you to John Sedlak, our sports reporter, and, coming through the door, Karen Jacobus, our senior editor. This is the editorial area of the building, over there is the administrative area, back there is typesetting and, of course, the big boards there are the composition area. Through that door is our darkroom, the johns are over there, the morgue is on that table, and the supplies are kept in that cabinet. It's quite a large space for a weekly newspaper, but we are growing into it very quickly."

"How fast are you growing, Mr. Remington?" Dennis asked.

A great question for two reasons. First it showed that he was concerned about growth, and that usually accompanies a go-getter. And second, it allowed me to unfold our track record in response to a question and not just throw it out there on my own, which I was prone to do.

"Our circulation has doubled in the past three and a half years," I said, trying to make it sound matter-of-fact. "Our reportorial staff will likewise have doubled when we make our next hire, the position you are here about. Our ad staff has grown by sixty percent in that time period and our administrative staff by one half."

"And the production staff has grown too," put in Lana, who never missed a thing.

"Our production staff has probably doubled," I concurred. I wasn't sure how much it had grown, because it was laced with part-timers who came around only once or twice a week.

The bottom line, though, was that the *Elgin Eagle* was on a royal roll. Circulation was climbing every week. We were working our butts off, and I loved it. I couldn't get enough of it. The growth, the responsibility, the shaping of this widening enterprise – it was everything to me. A big part of that secret came in hiring exceptional people. I don't know how one becomes a "good hirer," but somewhere along the way I was blessed with that gift. I have hired some losers, but the batting average for successful hires is way up there.

So now it was time to peel back Dennis's facade and see if I could find out what is in there. Conversely, he would be trying to do the same for both the *Eagle*, and for one Edward Rogers Remington. I was going to do everything I could to present the *Eagle* exactly as it was. No spin, no false impressions. I wanted Dennis to know exactly what he would be getting into and exactly what my expectations were. Then if we hired him, he'd start on the right foot. If he didn't like what he heard, then he wouldn't want to work here and we'd all be better off.

For the next two hours Dennis was grilled, his clip file was perused, his questions were answered (I'm told in excessive detail), and we had ample opportunity to take each other's pulse. I sent him off to a late lunch with Karen. She usually did the primary interview for reporters but had asked me to start this one. She hated interviews, but felt comfortable chatting over a grease burger. If there wasn't a good professional and personal chemistry between Karen and a prospect the deal was off, regardless of how I felt. This reporter would be a part of Karen's team, and he had to be a good fit.

When they returned I asked Dennis if he had any questions. He said no, he felt everything had been pretty well covered, and asked if he could take a few more back issues with him. I asked Lana to give him the last eight consecutive issues and a copy of our first extra. I told him that we had three other prospects to talk to and that we'd make a decision at the end of the following week. I also told him that we would get back to him whether or not he was the successful candidate.

I had been in Dennis's shoes when a company was considering a proposal but never had the decency to let the result be known. I really hated it when a company would just leave you out in the cold. You would interview, or pitch an idea, and then never hear from them again. I considered the practice bush league and vowed never leave anyone hanging like that.

As I was returning to my desk, I glanced over at Karen and she gave me a thumbs up. I nodded. This was a super candidate. I was already making my short list shorter – I thought we had found our person. The phone rang. "Up two points – a nine," said Lana.

As I sat down, the fire whistle sounded. That is one of the old New England traditions. When there is a fire, a whistle blows and everyone in town knows it. That is followed by a radio call and that can be picked up on a scanner – and everyone in town has a scanner.

We had a huge one in my office and speakers on every reporter's desk. Scanner news is action news and for a large segment of readership, action news is what newspapers are all about. I turned up the scanner to catch the radio report, and grabbed the portable scanner out of its charging unit.

"Alarm is for Elgin, reported structure fire at fourteen Willow."

All I needed to hear was "structure fire" and I knew we had a potentially big story. There were no reporters in the building at the moment. All had portable scanners, as did our photographer, but structure fires are not an everyday occurrence.

"I'll get it unless you want it," I said to Karen as I grabbed my camera bag and the portable scanner. I knew she didn't want it. Karen liked the more cerebral news, but I thought I would offer it nonetheless. She raised both hands together and waved them toward the door as if to say, "Of course I don't want to go. Why are you wasting time even asking? Get a move on!"

I bounded across the room and was heading out the front door as the radio crackled again with a repeat of the same message. From the time of the whistle, to my exit from the building had taken about ten to fifteen seconds at the most. I dashed toward the parking lot, passing Dennis.

"Want to cover a fire?" I shouted.

"Sure!" he said, and joined the sprint down the street.

I opened the car door and threw my stuff onto the back seat and reached across to unlock the passenger side. Dennis was aboard in a flash, grinning from ear to ear.

"We try to do these with all interviews," I said as I blindly backed out into the oncoming traffic. A horn blared and I gave a little wave out my window trying to suggest that I was aware that I'd done a really dumb thing. It irritated me to have done that, I'm usually cool under pressure. I pulled a U-turn and shot down the street toward the west side of town.

"This is a situation where you have to be careful," I said to Dennis, already playing the tutor role. "We're way ahead of the fire department and we want to make sure we don't park in their way. If we stay out of their way, they have no complaint. Well, the chief appears to be upset when we arrive before they do, but he also appreciates the fact that we cover what they do regardless of the hour." I threw that in to alert Dennis to the fact that yes, we answer three a.m. fire calls too.

I took the longer but faster route to the scene of the fire. I swung out onto the highway and gunned it. I was climbing a hill when I saw a car approaching at a hell of a rate of speed

and the emergency flashers going. Must be a fireman reporting directly to the scene rather than to the fire station. All
of our fire personnel are volunteer except for the chief. When
a fire alarm sounds, they all rush down to the fire house from
every direction. Each has his own set of flashing red lights
and some, in fact most, have sirens. There is an unspoken
competition among many of the fireman to see who can boast
the most elaborate set of lights and sirens. There was obviously a certain perceived machismo to it. The two women fire-
fighters calmly drove to the station when there was a call. No
lights, no sirens, no horns. They were also usually among the
first to arrive.

I pulled over to let the speeding car pass and to my surprise,
our photographer was at the wheel. He gave me a casual wave
and shot past like a bullet. "That's Chris Bourbon, our photographer," I said to Dennis, concealing my delight over this
virtual tour of how the *Eagle* covers the news. I commented
that Chris probably didn't know the back way to Willow Street
and was risking getting caught up in the parade of emergency
vehicles that would be responding to the scene.

Another car was coming and I waited for it to pass. Lo and
behold, it was John Sedlak. I could tell that John had not seen
me. I know that because I could not see John. He was leaning
across his front seat apparently trying to retrieve something
from the floor in front of the passenger seat.

"That's our sports editor that you just met," I said to Dennis,
who was now being ensnared by the *Eagle* work ethic. "He
doesn't know the back way either but he will probably be way
ahead of any first responders."

We swung onto Willow and I could see smoke – lots of it. The
house was set back and not visible but I knew we were close
enough. I did a quick check to make sure I wasn't blocking any
fire hydrants, turned off the engine, and then realized that
I might get trapped by fire equipment. So I fired the engine

back up and moved the car to a side street. Flames were visible near the rear of the house. The fire department refers to that as "totally involved" but I suspect that they mean "engulfed."

This was a big story – definitely next week's Page One photo and story.

As I got out, Jack Thomas, a volleyball acquaintance hollered to me, "Come on through here, Ed, you can see it a lot better." I took off after Jack. With Dennis right behind us we cut through a few backyards, ran down through a ravine and up a little rise. My God, the entire back of the house was ablaze.

I pulled out my camera and started to shoot. I had only one more roll of film but I'd soon have two other shooters on the scene. For now, I was the only camera on this side of the house, the flame side.

"The poor family," said a voice. It was Sally.

"How long have you been here?" I asked.

"For about five minutes," she answered. "I was on my way over to Anniston when the call came in. I just turned off of the highway and I was right here. The poor family," she said again.

"Who lives here?" I asked.

"They do," she said, gesturing toward a small huddle of people about twenty feet away.

I stepped back and motioned for Sally and Dennis to do the same, giving me a clear shot to the family with the house in the background. Not the perfect shot because they weren't facing the camera, but we would certainly identify them in the caption. The pictures of the family would tell it all. There was no need to talk to them just then; we had six days to get whatever background information we needed. Right now the task was to get photos. Chris was quickly working his way around the side of the house. That was one of the advantages of jumping on things early. When the cops arrive they throw up a police line around the scene, and then all photos will look the same.

Sally worked her way over to Chris and I know she was telling him that the group next to me was the family. Chris had an arsenal of lenses and gadgets and he would be able to get a good shot of the family and the house.

A huge explosion emanated from the house, followed by another and another.

"What the hell is that?" I exclaimed out loud to no one in particular.

"My son's fireworks," replied one of the women in the family pod.

"How much does he have in there?" I asked.

"Lots, and they're big stuff too," she said.

"What do you mean, big stuff," I asked, figuring that if she wanted to talk I was a willing participant.

"He works for Skyshow," she said, "and every now and then he'll bring one or two home."

Skyshow was a huge fireworks company about twenty miles away. I assumed she was telling me that the guy had a room full of aerial shells.

"How many big ones?" I asked.

"Maybe fifteen or twenty."

This presented a little bit of a dilemma. I was sitting on a huge news story, but I had some vital information that the fire chief would most likely want to know. I told Sally to keep shooting. I knew Chris was in a great position and John was somewhere out there. The *Eagle* had enough cameras to get the job done.

"Where are they stored?" I asked her. "That looked like it went off in the garage."

"They are all in the garage, on a shelf on the back wall."

That was good information. I set out to find the chief. I walked around the side of the house as the first two Elgin fire engines arrived. I could see the chief's car but couldn't find him. He had to be on the other side of the house. I started to walk around to that side and knew that I had to pick my words very carefully because he had a million things on his mind and talking to me was not one of them.

He came around toward the front talking into his radio, all the way. I stepped in front of him and said, "Listen to me, chief. I just talked to one of the house occupants and she said that there are a bunch of shells from Skyshow inside that garage. A couple just blew up."

"Where are they?" he said.

"On a shelf at the rear of the garage," I said.

"Tell Deputy Summers," he said, gesturing toward Summers.

I walked across the lawn to Frank Summers and by the time I had gotten there, the Chief, via radio, had already briefed him on what I was going to say. He motioned for me to confirm for him where they were. I pointed out to Frank what I had been told about where the shells were and he apparently was relaying the information back to the chief.

At that instant another explosion was heard and then three or four more in rapid succession. At this rate, they would all be detonated within the next few minutes and the job of fighting the fire could begin in earnest.

I figured the *Eagle* was well represented and decided to head back to the office.

"Ed, Ed," I could hear through the cacophony of radios, fire crackling and loud engines. "Ed," it came again.

I felt a slap on the back and turned to find Kurt Stockman, our Carlisle reporter, looking concerned.

"Ed, got any film?" he said. "I just had one roll off the spool, and like a jerk, I opened the camera and probably ruined everything I had shot. I know I should always travel with three or four rolls, but I didn't and I'm out of film."

"No problem." I handed him my one roll of film. "Shoot judiciously," I winked. I didn't think I had to volunteer that I too had violated our "always travel with film" rule.

"Have you seen anyone from the *Banner*?" I asked.

"No one," he said. "It's after noon on Friday, they are probably all gone for the weekend." Kurt detested the *Banner*.

"See you later, Kurt. I think we're pretty well covered here," I said as I threaded my way through a labyrinth of fire hoses.

I was stowing my gear in the car when Dennis said, "That was phenomenal, Mr. Remington! What a story."

"All in a week's work," I replied. I had completely forgotten about him, and would have driven off without him had he not spoken up.

Chapter Two

I really like Saturday mornings. It's the one time during the entire week when I can get out and take the pulse of the community. I use different restaurants for customary Saturday breakfast.

The Pines was sort of a dump, but the food was fairly good. Two things kept me out of the joint. The owner never advertised with us except for a Christmas greeting ad, and even then the ad was always half the size of the one he placed in the *Banner*. The other, less important reason was that the service was atrocious. Mike and Shirley Hand, who owned the place, surely must have majored in surliness. They were the rudest pair I'd ever met. Mike had a real chip on his shoulder. Something I had written years ago was still stuck in his craw.

Shirley was in charge of the waitresses, and apparently she took them out back each morning and stuck pins and needles in them until they were bursting with rage. Then she unleashed them on her customers.

Except for the food, the Pines would have gone under years ago. But the food was pretty decent, if you could coerce someone to bring it to you.

I plopped down at the counter and was ignored. Ned Todd, a retired Bank of New England officer took the stool beside me. "If we get served before the weekend is out, we'll declare it a victory," he remarked.

"It's like we're intruding on them," said Harry Wintersteen, two seats away.

"That was a nice piece your guy did on tax bracket creep," said Ned. "You should send that down to the *Globe*."

"That was a good one, wasn't it?" I replied. Ned and maybe five others were probably the only ones to read it, I thought. Ninety-nine times out of one hundred, we got feedback about trivial stories. Anything which might educate or inform seemed to fall on blind eyes. That certainly wasn't always the case, but reader feedback from the more cerebral news stories wasn't abundant.

"That was some fish that guy had there in this week's paper, Ed," said Chris Noll, a local and excellent electrician, who was also sitting at the counter near the waitress station. "Where exactly did he catch it?" he inquired.

"Lake Carlisle," I said, knowing that Chris wanted a lot more information than that.

He caught the twinkle in my eye as I responded and said, "You ain't gonna tell, are ya, Ed? You're probably heading out there right now, ain'tcha?"

"Wrong, Chris," I said, "I was out there Thursday morning right after I read it. Caught two more, just like the one in the paper."

Chris knew I was pulling his leg, but that was exactly what Chris wanted me to do. You couldn't get into a serious conversation with Chris Noll if your life depended on it. He knew everyone in town, who was doing what, and he had a photographic memory. Chris could retrieve stories from decades ago and tell them like they just happened yesterday. Maybe Chris was always having the last laugh and making up ninety percent of his guff. A little of the guy went a long way, and we had just reached the "long way" point.

An unfamiliar couple walked in and took the one remaining booth by the door. Every eye on the place checked them out within ten seconds, but not a single person made eye contact with them. But it was a guaranteed fact that no one failed to notice someone new.

The woman was tall and slender, and wore a snug white knit top and jeans. He was a pretty plain-vanilla looking guy, and didn't seem to fit with her. He was also considerably older and looked like a disheveled Ronald Reagan. There was a strong physical chemistry between them. I always noticed things like that, it was part of my job. What were they doing here, I wondered?

This wasn't necessarily major news breaking here, but it was information that should be noted. So often, little pieces, filed away, come back into play and help to pull a news story into its real and proper context.

I watched Ronald Reagan get up and go to the cashier. Was he already complaining about the service? Hell, he just sat down two minutes ago, he's got another good eight minutes before his table even gets cleaned off. As I watched, the girl at the cash register walked over to the newspaper racks and picked up a *Banner* and brought it back to him. He paid her and sat down.

Why in hell did she give him a *Banner* instead of an *Eagle*? Maybe he didn't specify which paper he wanted and the waitress grabbed a *Banner*. That's even worse. Why the hell would she do that? Probably on orders from Mike.

This was the kind of twenty-four-hour love affair I had with the paper. I could never let go.

Damn! I'm suddenly not hungry.

Screw this place. I knew I shouldn't have come here. I'm getting out.

I was chugging down my coffee ready to leave when the waitress bayed, "What'll you have?"

I decided to lighten up and forget about the *Banner*. "Two eggs over easy, whole wheat, hash browns, sausage and a small glass of milk. Sausage patties, not links."

"Outta whole wheat, whaddaya want?" she blurted out without looking up.

"Whatever you got will be fine," I said. I noticed a wry smile on Harry's face.

Damn, why did she give him a *Banner*?

I finished my meal and went to the cash register to check out. Ronald Reagan was just getting up and was going to be in line behind me.

"Give me an *Eagle* too, please," I said to the cash register jockey.

"Here," I said to Ronald Reagan, "have a copy of the *Elgin Eagle*. It's the best paper in town." I smiled at him and told him why I felt qualified to make that statement.

"We agree," said his beautiful companion. "We read your paper at the motel this morning, and bought the other one to see if there was anything new."

"Was there?" I asked.

"No. We were looking at real-estate ads, and this paper hardly had any compared to yours," she said.

Ta-dah – all's well that ends well.

"Are you planning on moving to Elgin?" I inquired.

"Yes, I am, and I brought Dad along for support," she said. "Do you mail the paper?"

"We sure do. Would you like me to start a subscription for you?" I said.

"That would be lovely," she said. "Let me give you my name and address." I ripped off a corner of the *Boston Globe* I was carrying and handed it to her with a pen. She filled out the essential information while her father and I discussed who had the greasiest meal, him with bacon or me with sausage patties. She handed me the scrap of paper and my pen, and then said, "You will keep this subscription quiet, won't you?"

"Of course," I said, wondering what in hell she was talking about. I assumed she meant that she didn't want our mailing list sold.

I told her she would start receiving her paper effective with the next edition. I wished them happy house hunting and told them to call if we could be of any help to them.

"I just might do that," she said with a smile.

I hope so, I thought as I walked away. She was even better looking outside of the Pines. But then, so is everyone else once they slip out from under that dark cloud.

Now that's the way to start a weekend; have a five-dollar breakfast and sell a twenty-five-dollar subscription, and I hadn't even picked up the morning mail yet. The gods were smiling.

I walked down to the post office. There in the lobby, one of the local *grandes dames* was holding court, buzzing like a trapped bee. I sidestepped around her covey of listeners and began to extract the newspaper's mail from the PO box. The Saturday mail is usually large because it contains lots of checks. The small advertisers get a chance to play the float. They know that we can't deposit their checks until Monday, and they're betting that by then they'll be able to cover them. Of course, not everyone plays the float, but many, including myself, know how that is sometimes a necessity.

As I sorted through the mail, I tried to listen in on what was so exciting for the group congregated in the center of the lobby.

One of the ladies mentioned Ellen Rollins, and then I heard *Front of the Line*. They were talking about a hot Broadway show starring Ellen Rollins. Nothing important – I tune them out.

Gossip, gossip, gossip – I love it, but I don't have time to play right now. So I employ my no-eye-contact maneuver and slip out.

The fire department was holding its annual open house today and even though I had a reporter covering it, I decided to stop in and show my support. I drove out to the firehouse with the intent of staying just a few minutes and then slipping away. I'll never be missed due to the crowd.

But my plan was shattered when I arrived. There, in their dress blues, were twenty members of the volunteer fire department, and at this moment, only one couple and a newspaper publisher were in attendance. There was also a kid from the *Banner* taking pictures.

"Hi, I'm Ed Remington," I said to the kid. "You must be Stan McDonald."

"Oh, hi, Mr. Remington. It's nice to meet you," said the kid with a great show of sincerity and considerable surprise.

I always made it a point to get to know the *Banner* staffers, at least the ones who weren't local. Often, if they managed to hire a good one, we would try to lure him or her away. But it also really struck them that the publisher of the opposition paper would be kind and considerate and, God forbid, he even knew my name. I knew that they came from a situation where the very names *Eagle* and Remington were daily inveighed. That was one of the best things we had going for us. The *Banner* was so focused on us that they had lost sight of what it was that they were there to do.

"Did you see the new pumper, Stan?" I asked. I gestured toward the shiny new piece of fire-fighting apparatus that the department had added.

"No, is that it?" he said. "I guess I should get a picture of it," he said in a half laugh.

"Well, I think it's about the only news out here today," I said as he raised his camera and popped off a shot.

It was going to be a really terrible shot of a fire truck, typical of the *Banner*. I just couldn't let it happen.

"You know, Stan, I think you could get a much more interesting shot if you got some people in it. That would add some life and a sense of scale. I mean, that is one hell of a large truck and that isn't going to be evident to the reader unless you have something in that frame he can relate to," I said.

"Yeah, you're right," said Stan. He was totally befuddled by now as to why the so-called arch enemy was being so nice.

I had a cordial relationship with the *Banner* publisher and editor, both of whom had been shipped in by the absentee owners. Every now and then they would luck out and hire a nice kid. The kid would spend a year or two with them and would leave. He never had anything good to show for his time at the *Banner,* and would probably never work in journalism again. The name of the game at that age is to build a clip file, a collection of various stories and photos that can be used to demonstrate one's skills to prospective employers on down the line.

A stint with the *Banner* wasn't going to produce much bragging material. While at the *Banner*, the rungs were disappearing from Stan's career ladder. Hopefully he could generate a good story or two, cobble together an impressive array of photos, and find his way to another paper where his talent, if there was any, could be recognized. But for the moment, this was about as high on the ladder as Stan was going to climb. So why not teach him how to compose a good shot.

Besides, we already had our shot. Earlier in the week Chris had gotten a dynamite shot of the new tanker as it was reflected off of the polished chrome siren on the ladder truck. And standing next to the tanker was a little girl and her dog – unfortunately not a Dalmatian, but I'll bet Chris scoured the neighborhood looking for one.

"Do you always work on weekends, Mr. Remington?" inquired Stan.

"It's Ed, Stan," I said, "and the answer is, every weekend."

"I mean you, Ed – not the paper, but you."

"I mean me," I said.

"God, Arnold never works on the weekend, doesn't even come to the office," said Stan, making reference to Arnold Stripe, the *Banner*'s publisher.

I just couldn't pass up the opening, "I know, and it shows."

"He just doesn't seem to care," said Stan.

"I think you hit the nail on the head," I added. "It was nice to meet you. Feel free to stop in the *Eagle* any day and I'll show you around our shop."

"I'd like that," he said. "I'll probably have to sneak in."

"Absolutely," I said, knowing that if Arnold Stripe saw one of his people going into or coming out of the *Eagle*, he would go ballistic.

God, I would love to see that.

I headed back over to the office to sort the mail and see if I could catch up with Kurt, who had weekend duty. I also wanted to launch a system backup on our computer network. We had been negligent on that and it was only a matter of time before we were going to get royally stung as a result.

Kurt wasn't in the office but a note was on my desk. "Have headed to farm auction at Lakeville – back at one for the recital thing at the rec center. You asked to be reminded to BACK UP THE SYSTEM!!! Kurt. Coffee is on."

I went over to the coffee pot and took it into the john and dumped it. Kurt's coffee was about one part coffee to six parts water. It looked and tasted like weak tea.

I decided to launch the system backup. Sometimes the backup is difficult to start. Once it is going, the system is inaccessible for about six hours. So if I need any computer time, now is the moment. I decided to take a quick look at the inventory for the next edition. This manifest is merely a listing of what we are planning for the issue and where we stand with it as of that minute. Ideally one would like to see about one third of the stories completed by Saturday noon. That is rarely the case, but today we were at forty percent, and a closer look confirmed that it was a solid forty percent. Young reporters have a propensity for dumping a jumble of words into a file and calling it a story. It often isn't a story until it has been herded through considerable editing and follow-up. But this inventory looked pretty solid. That would make Monday infinitely more enjoyable.

Before launching the system backup I decided to enter the new subscription I had picked up that morning. I dug the piece of paper out of my pocket and opened up the computer application for entering subscriptions, scrolling down to the line for entering the name. I looked at the scrap of paper that Ronald Reagan's daughter had filled out two hours earlier.

Name, Ellen Rollins.

I sure had blown this one.

* * *

It was Labor Day and you could have shot a cannon down the main street of Elgin and hit absolutely nothing. I have never seen a deader town in my life. Tomorrow was Tuesday, September 3, the first day of school, the first day for our new reporter, Dennis Newell, and the day our new computer system was to arrive. I could think of better days for the new system to arrive. We were way behind schedule, we had no good, solid news, and the staff was in some sort of lethargic funk. And it was the lack of news that was causing that funk. We'd offloaded the new computer system and were going to install it late in the week. I was going to try to run both systems simultaneously until we got the feel for the new one. Quit complicating things, said another part of me. Install the new system and go with it.

Our mission is to chronicle the events of the towns in our readership area. We let the *Boston Globe* worry about New England, we let the *New York Times* worry about the world, and we let the *Washington Post* handle the zoo in Washington. We focus on our towns, and we will do a better job of covering those towns than the *Globe, Times* or *Post* put together. But our news is not always the hard-hitting, dynamic news that is splashed across the front of *USA Today*. Our menu consists mainly of reporting on the attempts by each of our towns to bring itself into the twenty-first century as best it can. And while that is happening, the residents of those towns are going about their daily lives, and we report that too. But it takes everything I can muster to convince a bright, young kid fresh out of a theoretical journalism school that a ham and bean supper in Carlisle is news.

We'd had more than our share of ham and bean suppers in the past couple of issues. The staff was getting restless. They are also not sure how this new reporter is going to fit into the grand scheme of things. The reason they were in a fog is because I hadn't told them. That is a weakness in management, but I haven't told them because I haven't fully figured it out myself. All I knew was that our advertising was growing by leaps and bounds. We had enough advertising to more than justify adding a third section to the paper, but that would open a larger news hole, and it would take another body to help us fill that hole.

"I think I got the whole damn parade in one shot," chirped Chris Bourbon as he bounded into the office. "I mean that was the shortest parade I've ever seen in my life. They had some sort of broken-down Shriner's band, a color guard, Boy Scouts, Girl Scouts, three or four Brownies and a lonely Cub Scout. Then came half a dozen kids with decorated bikes. Then some veterans – the guys with the funny hats, are those veterans or what?"

"They're from the VFW, Veterans of Foreign Wars. Go on," I said.

"They had a truck with either an Iwo Jima reenactment going on or else everyone was falling down, and then some guys in military uniforms, about ten or twelve, and then a few kids pulling a red wagon and one kid in the wagon with the only sign in the whole damn parade that said anything about labor. Hell, Ed, these folks were celebrating Memorial Day, not Labor Day," he said with a laugh. "And get this. The kids pulling the wagon with the other kid holding the sign, well, they're all brothers and sisters – ten of them. What kind of labor are they talking about anyway?" he said.

"Really hokey," said John Sedlak.

"But the crowd loved it, didn't they, Chris," I said. "Hokey and simple as it was, the people really enjoy that sense of community, and that's the bottom line. So we cover it, report it, and everyone is happy," I added in my grandfatherly tone.

"It's just so hokey, though," John said. "If they are going to put on a parade, why not do it right?"

"Because it is a total volunteer effort, John," said Kurt, "and they probably have a budget of a hundred and fifty bucks at most. And every year they talk about how much better this parade was than last year's. The fact is that I have been to three now and they are carbon copies of one another. But Ed's right, they love those parades." Kurt was the Carlisle reporter and maybe thought he should obliquely defend his town.

"They didn't know what to make of you lying in the middle of the street, Chris," he went on. "I thought Fred, the guy with the flag, was going to step right on you. Chris was lying smack dab in the middle of the street, looked like roadkill, and the color guard was marching right toward him. Chris didn't move except you could see that he was screwing with his camera. The color guard stepped around him and kept on going and then this guy went out to Chris. What did he want, Chris?"

"He told me that I was being disrespectful of the flag or something like that," snorted Chris. He'd obviously not let the reprimand bother him.

"Give me a break," intoned Sally from across the room. "Disrespectful of the flag!"

"How did that shot look, Chris?" asked Karen, yanking the words right out of my mouth. We were both looking for a Page One photo and this sounded pretty interesting.

"I used the seventeen," said Chris.

That meant that the shot had been made with a seventeen-millimeter lens, a fisheye lens. That could be a really interesting shot.

"I'm gonna be printing for a while," said Chris, disappearing into the darkroom.

"Chris, bring me the contact sheets for those parade shots as soon as you have them, even while they're wet," Karen hollered through the darkroom door. She wanted to get this Page One photo resolved early thus allowing her time to build the rest of the page around it. A contact sheet is just a printing of all of the negatives on a roll and each image is only the size of the 35mm film.

"Will do," said Chris as he emerged from the darkroom and headed over to the men's john. He always did that. I don't think I ever saw him go to the men's can first and then go to the darkroom. What a creature of habit.

I could hear the clickity-click of the tape recorder coming from Sally's area. I glanced over to see if she was also looking at notes and couldn't see any. I made a note to have a talk with Sally later in the week about this habit. Tape recording interviews was OK, but it must be a supplement to note taking. The reason was time, a reporter just doesn't have the time to relive the whole interview at one quarter speed.

The taped interview sometimes is a real blessing, as she found out with the Sir Thomas Robertson interview a few weeks ago, but those instances are rare and don't begin to compensate for the amount of time wasted in clicking the tape recorder on and off in order to write the story.

The Robertson fiasco had a cute ending. Sally listened to the tape and there was never any sort of mention about going off the record. She asked Karen to listen also and Karen concurred that Robertson had said nothing about off the record.

Sally made a duplicate of the tape and sent it to Robertson. She spent several days trying to decide what to put on the accompanying note. These ranged from "Up yours, you chauvinist bastard" to "I think you were mistaken in your belief that our interview was off the record."

She finally just sent him the tape with a little note that read, "Dear Mr. Robertson. Thank you for agreeing to the interview for the paper two weeks ago. I thought you might enjoy a copy of the complete interview for your records. Sincerely, Sally Herron."

She had effectively nailed him, but would he know it?

"I'm not going to hold my breath waiting for an apology," she had said as she popped the Robertson tape into an envelope.

"Good decision, Sally," I said. "We'd hate to lose you."

"What's the difference between flammable and inflammable?" hollered Susan Elliott, one of our ad sales reps.

"Nothing," said a half-dozen voices in unison.

"And if you don't like either of those, you can use imflammable," added Kurt.

"I knew it all the time," said Susie. She was way behind on her ads for the week. She'd done a fairly decent job of selling, but she had not turned the orders in on Friday. Now it was Monday and our production department was going to have to stay late in order to make up for Susie's negligence. I suspected that she had cut out early on Friday but couldn't prove it. But I knew she was going to catch holy hell from our typesetters and that would probably be sufficient punishment for such shenanigans. In addition to giving her a thorough tongue lashing, they won't even consider typesetting her ads until the last thing on Wednesday night. The hour or so pinched on Friday would cost Susie the better part of Wednesday evening. Since each ad rep was responsible for proofreading her own ads, this meant that Susie was going to get to come in at seven o'clock Wednesday night and spend about three hours going over her ads. She will do this, though, because a mistake in an ad means the advertiser probably won't pay for the ad and if he doesn't pay, that means no commission.

Judy Cerrrone, our production manager, was taking a week of vacation, and that allowed Susie to pull her stunt. On Friday, Judy would hound the sales reps to "get your goddam ads in here so we can do them right." Judy would also make certain that Susie paid a price. Super-organized would be an understatement for Judy. Susie would quickly understand that she had let down Judy, the production department, and the whole paper. Judy could effectively communicate the team spirit that was the *Eagle*, and that was a great asset.

The same traits made Karen effective as senior editor. She could respond to the individual wants, needs, and desires of her young staff and at the same time promote a phenomenal sense of team work.

And that is why the imminent arrival of Dennis Newell had the newsroom slightly on edge.

I asked Lana not to interrupt me for the next hour or so, and I sat down to define exactly what the new reporter's role was going to be. I buzzed Karen and asked her to drop in when she had a free minute or two.

"Now would be a perfect time," she said, and I nodded for her to come on over.

"I want to review this new reporter with you, Karen, one final time. We've pushed around quite a few options for the past year, but it is time to pour the concrete into the form. Do you have any additional thoughts, ideas, or suggestions?" I said. She handed me a memo which I'd written in July. I pulled out a copy to follow along. She continued, "I still think that memo is a good summation and Dennis is a perfect fit."

Great, I thought, we are over the first hurdle. Now how do we set Dennis into the flow of things without stepping on other toes? "Are we in agreement that his title will be general assignment reporter?" I asked.

"It tells it like it is," she said.

"As with all editorial staff, he reports directly to you," I said.

"I hate the word 'reports,' Ed. That's some of your old corporatespeak," she said.

"I agree, Karen, he doesn't report. He'll get his assignments from you."

Even though Dennis would be easing the load for everyone, people tend to get bent out of shape when something which they've been doing is suddenly assigned to someone else. "He can't do a thing without, in a sense, invading someone's current beat," I continued. "This is where we have to be most careful. If he is assigned a story in Carlisle for instance, he'll need to talk to Kurt for some background. We just want to make certain that Kurt doesn't try to offload some of the little Carlisle crap on him."

"I'm going to be very clear about that," said Karen with a sense of resoluteness that suggested that she had given this considerable thought. And knowing Karen, she had. In fact, following our standard pattern, she had already talked, individually, with the entire editorial staff and solicited input from all. Hopefully they would feel that this was a team effort.

"I think this is going to be very well received by the staff," I said, hoping to hell that she would concur.

She did. "This is a good move, Ed. The hire is a good hire and the timing is perfect and I think everyone is on board. And I also think we are going to find that Dennis will be more and more our go-to guy for stories that don't fit smoothly into our geographic beats."

"At the five o'clock meeting, you can outline the job and discuss how we perceive it." Karen framed staff meetings so that everyone felt they were taking something valuable away from it. We smiled at one another and she returned to her desk.

We had basically agreed to a new job that was going to be a work in progress. A perfect fit, because the *Eagle* itself was a newspaper in progress.

* * *

REMINDER: THERE WILL BE A SHORT 10–15
MINUTE STAFF MEETING THIS AFTERNOON
AT 5 PM IN ED'S CONFERENCE ROOM.

I shot the message into the computer network addressed to the entire editorial staff, plus Lana and Judy. Judy was not going to be there, but it was important that the editorial people see that even our ad manager is included in major discussions. So often, they were oblivious to the fact that without ads they have no news hole. And without a news hole they have no jobs.

"Network's frozen!" screamed Allison Zeller, our production manager.

These words were the most devastating two words we ever wanted to hear. And we were hearing them increasingly often. That was the prime reason for investing in the new computer system. The words "network's frozen" meant that everything that everyone was working on for the past half-hour or so had vanished into thin air. They were followed immediately by a barrage of expletives. "Shit!" "Dammit." "Holy shit." "Chrrrrrrrist!"

What made this one so painful was that I was the cause. Our system did not allow network email to be sent while production was up and running. It was one of the quirks of that early system. Because the system crashed, my email would never be seen by anyone and thus no one would know why the system crashed. But I had to come clean.

"I'm really sorry, folks," I said, "it was my fault. I was sending an email. Dumb mistake. I'm really sorry. The good news is that the new computer system arrives tomorrow and may be up and running by the end of the week. Sorry ..." I trailed off lamely. "Everyone take a five-minute break and go over to Day's and get something to drink on me. I'll get the thing rebooted and it will be up and running by the time you get back."

Everyone took me up on the offer and I handed Lana a ten dollar bill and told her to pay for everyone and to bring me a diet root beer.

I went over to the multiplexer and inserted the special boot disks. First I had to visit every computer in the building because they all had to be off. I made the rounds of the computers and then I popped in the first boot disk and the adjacent screen started coming alive with computer codes. It paused while I added a line of code and a dumb password, which everybody knew, and then the machine prompted me for the second disk. It went through its routine without a hitch and then I was prompted for the third disk. Whatever was on the third disk wasn't much because it usually just took ten to fifteen seconds to load and then the system sprang to life. And that is apparently what happened.

People started drifting back in. "Ed, did you fix the system?" said Sally.

"I did," I said.

"My computer isn't working," she said.

I flipped on my computer and also was staring at a blank screen.

"Guess it needs a reboot. Turn off your computer," I said, "and check all of the computers on that side of the room and make sure they're off too." I flipped off mine and returned to the multiplexer for reboot attempt number two. This had never happened before, but I wasn't reading it as a particularly bad omen.

"Don't turn your computer on," screamed Sally to Lana, who had just reentered the room. "Ed's having to start it up all over again."

"What's the problem?" said Lana. She walked over to the multiplexer as I was preparing to load disk one.

"Don't know. The first boot just didn't seem to take," I said.

"Are you sure all the machines are off?" she said.

"I think so," I said, "but why don't you check all of the ones over there," I gestured toward the production and advertising areas.

"All off over here, Ed," called Sally from the editorial area.

"Ditto here," said Lana.

"Here we go," I said, as I started to sequentially load the disks. Lana had a pretty good sense about how this computer system worked and I could feel her eyes lasering in over my shoulder.

Disk three shot up an error message with a number on it.

"What the hell is that all about?" said Lana.

I didn't respond, but went to my office and dug out the computer manual and turned to the error-message section. Naturally, the error message that was showing on the multiplexer's screen was not listed.

"OK," I said, trying to hide my growing uneasiness. "Let's start from the top. Go to every single machine and make sure it is off. Lana, please disconnect and reconnect every single plug on the back of the multiplexer. Sally, you trace every single cable from every computer in editorial and see if there is anything sitting on or squishing or cutting into any cable. John, give Sally a hand."

I wasn't the only one in the place who recognized that this was a potential crisis of major proportions. I could see the wheels churning in Karen's brain. She was thinking "contingency." But she had probably already arrived at the truth of the matter – there was no contingency plan for this scenario. It was one of the system's major flaws and the primary reason we were dumping it. I momentarily missed our earlier time with a room full of Underwood typewriters. The newer system had quite a few built-in redundancies, so that if one component failed the system could be temporarily reconfigured to get you through the crisis.

This was the price that one paid for being first. We were the first weekly newspaper in New England to go to computerized typesetting. We were now on our second generation and would take delivery of the third within the next twenty-four hours. What a hell of a time for this system to shoot craps – on its final issue!

After a thorough cable check, connection check, and any other kind of check we could manage, we tried again and this time received two error messages. Again, neither of them was in the manual.

There was one little island of safe retreat for us and although we had never used it, I knew it would work because I had tested it on my computer a couple of times. Using it we could, theoretically, get the newspaper out. But editorial was way behind schedule, (twenty-eight percent at Saturday noon), and almost forty percent of the ads for the issue had not been composed. We were about as plugged up as we could get. I wanted to point that out to everyone but decided that right now I should be showing everyone how we were going to end-run the system.

"Everyone come back here for a few minutes and I'll show you how we may have to proceed until we can smoke out this problem," I said, feigning confidence. If I lost it and got visibly angry, everyone in the room would follow. So I tried to act calm and confident that we could do this.

"Each of your computers has a –"

"Floppy drive," Kurt interrupted.

"Yeah, we can write on that," said Sally. "That's how we did it in college."

"No sweat," said John.

It turned out that almost everyone was way ahead of me on this one.

This was a little more of a problem for Judy and Allison and the production department. Every disk that was going to be written would have to be hand carried to the production department in order to be fed into the typesetting machine. All of the ads would have to be written on disks, so some means of keeping track of the gaggle of disks was going to have to be developed then and there.

"John, run down to Blanchard's and get a couple dozen floppy disks to match this one," I said. I handed him one out of my computer. "It has to match this description." I pointed out the relevant part of the disk label.

John looked at me as if to suggest that he knew enough to get the right disk.

"See if they have color-coded ones," I said. "I've seen them in catalogs, and that would be great for identifying where they came from."

John headed out the door as Chris joined the meeting, still blinking from a stint in the darkroom. "What's up?" he inquired.

"We've got a crisis," said Sally, "and we're trying to figure out how to keep going."

"Oh, OK," said Chris, "but when you get a moment Ed, or Lana, my computer isn't responding."

Everyone burst into laughter. "How long has your computer been on, Chris?" asked Lana.

"About a week," he responded.

Chris's computer was most likely causing the system not to boot up, I thought. Every computer must be off in order to restart the system.

Maybe.

Hopefully.

"Hold everything," I said.

Lana was right in step with me. "Everyone check and make sure your computer is off. O-F-F, off as in goddam *off*!" she shouted.

Everyone scrambled for their computers and Lana went into the darkroom in order to shut down Chris's computer personally.

I slipped in the first disk and all the proper prompts showed up as expected. I slipped in the second disk and the machine whirred and cranked in a way that seemed a little unfamiliar, but I assumed it was OK. Suddenly the screen illuminated with a message. This was not good, there were no messages due at this moment. Big trouble, I thought as my heart hit the floor. We really are in deep trouble. I leaned forward to see what the message was all about. But Sally had already read it.

"You put in the wrong disk Ed, it wants disk two," she said. The whole room erupted with cautious laughter punctuated with a few remarks about my family origins.

I put in disk two, as the screen was instructing me to do, and then, at the prompt, slid in disk three. This was where we had crashed earlier. There were at least eleven of us standing in a semicircle, eyes riveted to that system monitor. I closed the gate on disk three and the drive grunted and whirred for what seemed like an eternity. The drive light flicked on and off and about fifteen seconds later the screen flashed the words that everyone wanted to see. BOOT UP SUCCESSFUL – REMOVE DISK.

Cheers and hugs all around. Crisis averted.

I would love to know what went through John's mind as he walked in to find a room full of people celebrating. Lana calmly took the Blanchard's bag from him and, I presume, filled him in on the good news. John smiled, accepted Lana's hug, and as she was squeezing the life out of him looked over at me and said, "I even found colored ones."

I gave everyone a big thumbs up from across the room.

The scenario had a happy ending, but I was extremely bothered by the chain of events. The system wouldn't have crashed were it not for me sending an email at the wrong time. And the confusion in getting the system back on line was again the result of my not checking everything thoroughly. I had completely forgotten about the computer in the darkroom. I was really bothered by this and knew it was a signal that we needed something in addition to the way we were doing things. I didn't know what the fix was, but I knew that something had to change.

I also could see the gulf that was beginning to open between myself and a young staff fresh out of colleges and universities that lathered their students with computer experience.

Chapter Three

In early August, I had forced my meeting with Officer Sauer.
It was not a good decision. I suspected that Sauer felt that
regardless of what I promised about keeping him anonymous,
he was going to end up involved. I could tell by the way he
agreed to meet me on that August afternoon that he was re-
luctant to do so. And that was the way it turned out – the
meeting produced nothing. He didn't totally can the idea for
a follow-up meeting, he just mentioned that he wanted a little
more time to think about it.

But on this gorgeous late September afternoon, Sauer was
smarting from suddenly being thrust into the news by the police chief. It happened the night before, at the weekly selectmen's meeting. The agenda for the meeting was pretty routine, and Sally would be covering it. I told Sally that I'd be
attending for a part of the meeting because I was chairman of
a town street lighting committee and we were going to give our
preliminary report that night, and hopefully get a little more
money to hire some consultants to assist us with a subject that
none of us knew a damned thing about.

Standing in the lobby before the meeting, I saw Officer
Sauer entering dressed in civilian clothes. He said that he
was there as a part of the Recreation Committee, which was
giving a report on the delay in the new ball field.

The meeting moved along routinely. A few corrections
were made to the old minutes, some bids were acknowledged

and opened, and the selectmen progressed to Old Business. A woman stood to be recognized and identified herself and stated that she was not sure whether this was new business or old business but she wanted to know who would be liable if someone was bitten by the town's police dog.

My first thought was police dog? When the hell did we get a police dog? I don't think a single person in the room knew that there was a police dog.

The chief denied knowledge of any dogs and at the same time placed the responsibility for police dogs squarely on the shoulders of Officer Sauer. I found this odd and disturbing. I had been in the police station that afternoon, and watched as the chief gave a pooch a dog treat.

I glanced across the aisle to Sauer and could see the veins in his neck start to bulge. This was obviously something new to Officer Sauer and he was caught totally off guard.

He was called forward to explain. "We don't exactly have a police dog," said Sauer. "Officer Denaro's young German shepherd often rides in the cruiser with him and hangs around the station. He has never to my knowledge been used in police work, but I don't feel that his presence is causing any harm. It might actually be a small deterrent to someone thinking about stirring up some unrest or something."

"This is the first I have heard about this," said the chief, straightening up in his chair and trying to look as assertive and sincere as possible.

What arrogance, I thought. One of his own men has just acknowledged that the dog hung around the police shop, and this phony was pretending that he was hearing about a dog for the first time!

"Better look into this, Chief. We don't want any kids being bitten by dogs," said the select board chairman. The other two nodded in agreement.

What a trio of imbeciles, I thought. I doubted that anyone else in the room bought the chief's story. Maybe they hadn't bought it, but in my opinion they were swallowing the chief's story as they often did.

The meeting moved to New Business. I gave my streetlight report and asked for the money and was told that my request would be taken under advisement. That was code for "You got it, but we need to slow down the process so we look frugal."

Sauer was to present his report after me. I made certain to get up and leave the room in full view of everyone, including the chief. I thought about waiting for Sauer outside. If he was livid about the dog scene – maybe he was ready to vent.

No, I decided, let him come to me.

* * *

When my phone rang the following afternoon and Sauer was on the line, I felt that we were on a nonstop journey to whatever it was that had been gnawing away at him for the past several months. We agreed to meet that night at the same spot behind the Value Foods store at midnight, and I persuaded him to make it 10:30 p.m.

As I rolled around behind Value, I could see Sauer's cruiser was there. I pulled up alongside of him, and instantly, I could tell that this was a reformed person. He was ready to talk.

He didn't waste any time with pleasantries. "Ed, in early or mid March, you ran a story about us stopping a carload of pukes up on Dominion Street. Do you remember that story?" he said.

"I do," I said. "They were from Boston?"

"North of Boston, Revere," said Sauer. "And you remember that almost half a kilo of cocaine was found in the car?"

"Yep," I said. "The largest haul in the department's history, as I recall,"

65

"Right," he said. "Do you remember what happened after that?"

This game of twenty questions was for real, I sensed. The more details that I could recall on my own, the less "divulging" Sauer would have to do. And I also sensed that he had some sort of mental word meter going and when he had said X amount of words, the fountain would shut off. So I dug deep to dredge up as many facts about the bust as possible.

Dave Parr, our previous Elgin reporter, had handled the story. I had worked closely with Dave because the story involved quite a few issues about which we weren't real knowledgeable.

"The guys were let go, weren't they?" I said. "Copped some sort of plea bargain or something?"

"They were let go because —"

"Your guy had made an unlawful search of the vehicle," I interrupted. The whole incident was starting to come back. "You had made a traffic stop and —"

"Not me!" said Sauer, anxious to keep this detail correct.

"No, not you. Troxell, or whatever his name was, entered the car without permission and found the coke. Right?"

"Trainor, not Troxell," said Sauer. "Right."

"So Trainor is all excited, holding these four pukes at gun point. He calls for the state police backup and before they arrive, Trainor goes off on a fishing expedition inside the car," I said.

"Right," said Sauer. "And the next thing we know, they have some high-powered Boston mob lawyer up here who knows the law about illegal search and seizure inside out. And two days later these guys are released from jail and are on their way back to Revere."

What had been said up to that point was all included in our story last March. That meant that Sauer was holding his pièce de résistance, so I kept my mouth shut. Silence will almost always elicit a verbal response. And in this case it did.

"And what happened to the cocaine?" asked Sauer.

"The Elgin cops, of course, refused to return it," I said. "And there was no argument from the defendants, who were just happy to be getting out of here. It was in the paper."

"It was," said Bill. "What happened to the cocaine?"

"I don't know. What happens to cocaine after it is confiscated?"

"It's *supposed* to be turned over to the state in Concord," he answered.

"You mean it wasn't?"

"It's supposed to be turned over to the state," Sauer repeated with a checkmate smile on his face.

"So where did it go?" I asked. "Does the chief still have it?"

"Not anymore," said Sauer, "and this wasn't the first time that a drug haul didn't make it to Concord."

Holy Toledo, I thought, this is one hell of a story.

One hell of a story.

We were talking about $250,000 easily – crooked cops, major felony. We were also stepping up to a level where the stakes were much higher than our usual news presentation. Immediately, I thought of the libel aspect and how my newspaper could be gone overnight. I was also keenly aware that we are getting into an area where people might go to extremes to keep themselves out of such a story.

"What else can you tell me?" I asked.

"That's as far as I'm going to go," he said. "You can follow it from there."

"I appreciate the tip, and I promise you that you will never, in any way, shape, or form, be associated with this story. But I need more to go on."

"That's all I can say right now," said Sauer as he started his engine. "And you gotta keep my name out of this all the way, Ed."

"You have my word on that," I promised with all the sincerity I could muster. "But I've got to have information, Bill. We're just a little podunk paper out here in the boondocks. We don't have a large investigative staff, we don't have the dollars to pursue this. You have to give me more."

"I've said all I can say for now. If you dig, you'll begin to uncover more."

I went into full-scale pleading mode. "Tell me this, Bill. If the chief doesn't have it where would he get rid of it?"

"That's it for now, Ed," he said. He started his cruiser forward.

"Just give me a town," I begged. That information would at least tell us where to start looking.

"See you later," said Sauer. He disappeared down the roadway behind the mall.

* * *

The guy from the computer company called and said that he was going to be about two hours late. "You're a lot farther up there than I figured," he said.

"Did you ever hear of looking at a map?" I said. I was infuriated. This palooka had known he was coming to Elgin for six weeks, and in all that time he hadn't bothered to see where we are or how he was going to get here. Geeks may know computers, but they're clueless about everything else. Even my remark about not using a map hadn't registered with this chip with shoes.

It was Thursday and the first issue with stories by Dennis Newell was on the newsstands. Dennis had jumped right in, showing a surprising insight for someone so young and a willingness to work hard (but then, don't they all for the first several weeks). Above all, I could see that he really enjoyed doing the job.

I wanted him for the police chief story and was looking for a way to discuss it with Karen without divulging Sauer's involvement. I wasn't worried about Karen being able to keep her mouth shut. She's a true professional, but I wanted to protect her and Sauer in the event that she ever found herself sitting in the dock in some courtroom with a hostile attorney ripping at her.

The very fact that he was new to the territory made Dennis ideal for this story. He had about three years of newspaper experience and his apparently calm demeanor was a plus. But I had to find a way to turn him loose on the story without telling other reporters.

"Good morning, *Elgin Eagle*," said Lana on the telephone. "Just a minute, I'll see if he's in. May I tell him who's calling?"

My intercom rang. "Someone on line two wants to speak to Ed – he wouldn't give his name," said Lana.

I punched the flashing button for line two. "Hello?"

"Hi, Remington, I'd tell you who this is, but it isn't important to this discussion. I just wanted to say that I thought the story about the Baldwin Planning Board was really piss-poor journalism. It was terribly biased, rank amateur journalism," said this twit hiding behind anonymity.

Stuff like this really sets me off. "Listen, Mr. Whoever the hell you are. I'm more than happy to discuss this issue with you, but if you don't tell me who I am talking to, then this discussion is over."

"Who I am is unimportant," he continued, "but you should know that –"

I hung up. "If the phone rings again, Lana, let me answer," I hollered, hurling my phone book to the floor. Twits like this sometimes won't let it go, and if he called again, I wanted him.

The phone rang. I grabbed it and said calmly, "Good morning, *Eagle*. May I help you?"

"I'd like to speak with Mr. Remington," said a youngish female voice.

"This is he," I said.

"Mr. Remington, this is Pamela Korda, now Pamela Franklin. You ran a story about my wedding in last week's paper."

I detected a slight tremor in her voice and knew what was coming. I decided the best defense was a good offense. "Yes, Pamela. It was a lovely picture of you and your husband, but did we screw up the story?"

"Did you screw up the story!" she screamed, I mean *screamed*. "*Nothing* was correct. You left out half of the description of my wedding dress. You left out the fact that I wore my grandmother's wedding veil, you misspelled the names of the matron of honor and one of the attendants. And you left out the fact that my favorite cousin had come all the way up here from Texas for the wedding." All of that was said while *SCREAMING* into the phone.

Before I could respond she got going again. "I have waited twenty-eight years to get married. I have only done it once, and my one time is totally ruined by you and your paper — totally ruined. Your paper isn't worth a shit." She slammed down the receiver.

Well!

I jotted off a note to Judy, our production manager, and asked her to retrieve the raw copy for the announcement. It would answer most, if not all, of the questions. Were the misspellings our fault or did we receive it that way? It would also tell us who edited it and who typeset it. We did this often, not necessarily to assess blame, but rather to see if we could find our weak links and improve them.

The intercom rang and Lana announced that Jack Forrester, a local realtor, wanted to see me.

"Send him back," I said loud enough that Jack could hear it across the room. I met him at the doorway to my office. "What's new, Jack? How's the golf game?"

"Not bad, Ed," he said, "Shot an eighty-six yesterday."

He started to unroll a copy of the current issue and I knew that a complaint was coming. "You ran this picture of a house in today's paper," said Jack. "I sold that house five days ago."

"See how effective an ad in the *Eagle* is!" I said, realizing that Jack wanted some serious banter here for the next minute or so. But I just couldn't resist the commercial.

"How did that happen, Jack? Did you call in Monday or Tuesday and ask us to pull that house from the ad?" I asked, knowing that was the case.

"I gave Rosemary the ad on Friday, sold the house on Sunday, called her on Tuesday and told her not to run that portion of the ad – and here it is anyway," said Jack.

"Our mistake, Jack. Let's see the ad. OK, it has three houses in it. One of those is incorrect. I'll knock one third off the price of the ad, OK?"

"That's fair," said Jack. A hint of a smile started to return to his face.

"Good to see you any time, Jack. Thanks for stopping by. Sorry for the screw up, but when people call about the house you can proudly proclaim that you've already sold it. Maybe that will stampede them into buying something else a little faster."

"You never know, Ed. Good to see you too," said Jack as I walked him to the door.

The computer guy arrived right at lunchtime. He wasn't interested in eating lunch and neither was I. We had about one hour to talk before I had to get to our weekly editorial meeting. I asked him how he wanted to proceed and he said that first he wanted to walk through the whole system and see exactly how it was wired. Then new hardware would be installed and programmed. Finally he'd customize some of the software so that the repetitive items that we used in the paper could be handled with fewer key strokes.

All of this was good stuff, but I didn't want the guy doing it without either myself or Lana going to school on him. We wanted to know how to do it so that when he wasn't here and something needed to be configured, we would know how to do it.

I walked him around the room and showed him how we had things set up.

"What's that?" he said, pointing to one of our old computers. Of course he knew what it was but I think he was taking my pulse.

"That's part of our old system. Want to buy it?" I joked.

"Why are you getting rid of it?" he said.

"Because we have this new system. We don't need both," I said.

"Every one of your old computers is compatible with this new system," he said. "That old server or, what do you call it –?"

"Multiplexer," I said.

"That thing is useless, but the individual terminals will all work. They'll be slow, but they'll work as extra stations or even stand-alone units. We'll just develop a new boot disk for each and you can have a huge system here."

This threw open a whole new set of possibilities. All of a sudden we'd have nine extra computers to sprinkle around. Within a week, three of those terminals were sitting in the homes of three of our town correspondents and they turned in their weekly columns via a 5 1/4 inch floppy disk rather than hard copy that had to be retyped.

I turned him loose to install and tweak the system however he wanted, subject to Lana's OK.

I went into the editorial meeting and excused myself for being late. A heated discussion was brewing about the state's right-to-know law. This was an area in which the *Elgin Eagle* had gained considerable notoriety. I'd been interested in right-to-know laws since my corporate days. I'd even taken a course in it.

I'd served on the right-to-know committee for both the New Hampshire Press Association and the New England News and Press Association. I'd chaired the NE committee for the past three years and served as vice-chairman of the Newspaper Association of America's Freedom of Information Committee. Serving on these committees gave me access to some of the best legal minds in the country, and soon I found my phone ringing with right-to-know questions from fellow publishers.

About three years earlier, we'd locked horns with a district attorney over a right-to-know issue. We prevailed in that case. The *Boston Globe* heard about this feisty newspaper in New Hampshire taking on a powerful DA and pretty soon the skirmish was a Sunday *Globe* story. It snowballed from there. I loved the position of the *Eagle* being the paper that knows how to deal with these issues. But I also needed to make certain that my staff was up to speed on the subject, because a right-to-know issue can come up at any point and if you don't know how to react, you'll be shut out. It makes no difference who's right or wrong, because the news moves from "news" to "history" literally overnight. If you can't seize that news, you lose.

If you know what you are doing though, you can throw up enough legalities that the governing body will understand that to ignore your objections might cost the office holders their positions or lead to a costly lawsuit.

And right-to-know laws are kaleidoscopic, ever changing as various political special interests try to advance their agendas. Some are fervent believers in First Amendment rights.

Others, many others, support the First Amendment as long as it doesn't conflict with their particular agendas. Still others are clueless about any amendment and chime in just because it seems like the right thing to do.

I let the right-to-know discussion go on for a few minutes, and then reminded the reporters that we had an issue to plan. I asked each of them what he or she had for the following issue. We encouraged everyone to throw in ideas and suggestions, and discussed how every story would be illustrated. We inquired as to whether or not there was a need for additional artwork. We tried to get a feel for what was going to be on page one. We tried to smoke out potential bottlenecks that might require a given reporter to be in two places at once. It was a meeting with structure, but was allowed as much fluidity as we could muster because from such an atmosphere, true creativity flowed.

Karen took copious notes and fired out ideas. We wanted the meeting to be a weekly shot in the arm and tried to balance the look ahead with a positive look backward at the previous issues. We rigidly critiqued the most recent issue. We tried to do that first because egos were often bruised at that point and I wanted the meeting to finish on an up note.

Chapter Four

"The New Hampshire Primary," I announced. "How many of you want to get involved in that coverage?" Every hand went up.

"I don't do liberals," announced Chris.

"OK," I said, "I have been around this horn several times and, as you know, the *Eagle*'s New Hampshire Primary coverage was voted the top news story of the year two years ago by the New England News and Press Association. I intend to win that again."

Everyone applauded. It was real applause, they really wanted to win.

"Here's how we do it at the *Eagle*," I said. "We designate one person to be the point person for the whole primary, and that will be Dennis. Everyone else will participate in the interviews. There will be more than enough to go around, I assure you. Dennis, your job is to keep it all on track and keep it organized. There's a lot of grunt work involved." All of this information I had discussed previously with Dennis, but I wanted the whole team to know the game plan. This goal was a total effort with no ruffled feathers.

"We'll submit each story with byline or bylines from all who participate in the interview." My enthusiasm was bubbling over. God, I love this part of publishing.

The reason I was casting this now, I explained, was that we had a candidate coming through in a couple of weeks. His young and inexperienced campaign staff hadn't yet agreed to bring him by our office, but we had put in the request.

We told all candidates' staff, that the *Elgin Eagle* does not go to the candidates. The candidates come to the *Eagle*.

We wanted a clear shot at every candidate, unencumbered by the usual media scrum. I explained to the staff that sometimes we didn't always succeed, but most of the time, if we held firm, the candidates would acquiesce.

"And make certain to try to schedule our interview *before* the candidate heads off for whatever local event brought him to the area." Scheduling an interview after an event often resulted in an abbreviated interview because the main event ran over and the entourage was behind schedule. The pre-event interview also allowed us time to lengthen the process and prevent the guy from going down the street to the *Banner*.

It apparently never crossed the *Banner*'s mind to aggressively invite a candidate into their newsroom. Occasionally they would get one by default, but they usually interviewed surrogates, such as spouses or current or former lawmaker friends of the candidate. Spouses made for interesting personal glimpses, but other than digging out important nuggets such as the candidate's favorite food or movie, nothing ever came from a surrogate that added to a given candidate's issue knowledge.

A sad reality was that more people in Freda's Diner could tell you of candidate A's favorite movie, but had no idea of his stance on any issue.

Many small weekly newspapers, and an occasional daily, were content to go stand behind a rope line and listen to the stump speech and then play it back to their readers. The result was that their stories read exactly the same as the stories in most other papers, many of which were dailies and had reported the news days earlier. It also killed any opportunity for solid follow-up questions.

The *Eagle* had a polished routine that included a set of core questions at the end of the interview where each candidate was asked exactly the same questions as his competitors. We told them that at the beginning and we also told them that many of their answers preceding the core questions would be published in our next edition and a condensed version would be published again in the edition immediately prior to the primary. When we published that finale with the core questions, our readers could see every candidate responding to the same four or five questions. During the front of the interview we allowed each candidate to lay out his special spiel and vision, if he had one.

We treated them all exactly the same right down to counting the number of words allocated to each and making sure that all stories were within five percent of each other in length. We went out of our way not to editorialize about any candidate and we tried to show good photos of them and held the goofy photos until our April Fool's edition or our staff Christmas party.

Very few newspapers in New Hampshire would endorse candidates, because they felt that it would upset readers. I thought that was a cop out. The week before the election, we would write an editorial discussing our observations of each candidate and often recommend one from each party.

Many of our readers knew that we had gone a huge extra mile to interview candidates one-on-one, and we owed it to them to report our findings. We liked to think that we were reporting our research and impressions rather than advising people how to vote.

"Dennis, Senator John Dorn is coming through town two Saturdays from now. Plenty of time to gear up," I said at our weekly editorial meeting. "I've told his headquarters that we'd like a half hour or so with him. What you need to do is find if anyone wants to interview him with you."

"I'll do it," volunteered Sandra Garrett, our one and only editorial person who lived in Elgin. Sandra had been a reporter for a daily newspaper in Massachusetts and had moved to Elgin over a decade ago with her husband, a Delta 747 pilot. Shortly thereafter she arrived on our doorstep looking for part-time work, and that fit nicely into our scheme of things. "I interviewed him four years ago, or whenever the last primary was –"

"– and now you've thought of your follow-up questions?" interrupted Chris, always there with his double-edged wit.

The meeting erupted into laughter and Sandra laughed the loudest. "I'm still thinking of a couple," she giggled.

"We've got a couple of weeks to build our matrix of questions," I said. "That is exactly how it should work, Dennis. You can ask for volunteers for your co-interviewer. If no one wants to do it, that's a problem, but it has never happened; if you all want to do it, that is fine. In other words, we aren't shutting the door on any candidate to any one of you. I would just want Dennis and at least one other to get up to speed on whoever is being interviewed. So when Dorn shows up here in two weeks, at least two of you will be really savvy on him and his positions. Candidates are slippery. If you haven't done your homework, you're going to be left high and dry."

"What do you mean 'slippery, high and dry,' Ed?" asked Sally.

"During the last primary acid rain was a big issue," I told them. "The first candidate came in and sat down and Bob, our reporter, posed the acid-rain question."

"I support the Rosewell bill," said the candidate. "OK," said Bob, not having a clue what the Rosewell bill was all about.

Fortunately, Bob, knew he had been stiffed and he did some homework. The next candidate who tossed out the "Rosewell bill" answer was surprised when Bob reframed the question as follows, "Do you feel that the Rosewell bill is a satisfactory target for sulfur dioxide emissions?" The candidate, Governor Corbin of New Mexico, was stopped dead in his tracks.

"What did he say?" asked John, speaking for the entire young staff who wanted to know how this scenario ended.

"Corbin said something like, 'I think it is a good starting place,' to which Bob said, 'Many think we can do better than that, Governor Corbin.' Corbin was not going to escape this one easily. Being an astute politician, he threw it back to Bob: 'What would you suggest as an acceptable level?'"

"Forty percent," Bob replied promptly, "and cut the fifteen-year phase-in back to ten or twelve."

"Well, that's something we should look into," said Corbin. "We'll look into that and get back to you."

"That's a promise Governor?" said Bob. "We can count on that?"

"Absolutely," said Corbin.

"And he did look into it, and one of his people called Bob back to say that he was going to support the forty percent emission rate," I told them.

"And did he?" asked John.

"He sure as hell did," I answered. "And we made that happen. This little paper in New Hampshire made that happen. A huge shift in position for Corbin. Of course it was to no avail because Corbin dropped out right after California that year, but imagine if he had won. This paper had caused him to proclaim publicly a strong set of standards which would quickly reduce acid rain by twenty percent and accelerate the timetable in a big way." Grins were breaking out. My enthusiasm was becoming very contagious.

"A candidate campaigning in New Hampshire needs the *Elgin Eagle* and he needs us badly," I said. "In January and February, he doesn't, or shouldn't, give a damn about what the *San Francisco Examiner* thinks, because if he doesn't do well in New Hampshire, he'll never see the campaign trail in

California. So they are listening and they are taking notes. The *Eagle* has a tremendous amount of clout, and we aim to use it in the best way possible."

Everyone applauded again and the meeting ended on a high note. I had simultaneously lit five fuses and we were all looking forward to the arrival of Senator Jonathan Gregory Dorn of South Carolina.

The new computer system came on line without a hitch. Brad "no map" Nelson had been a great help and even hung around over the weekend to tutor anyone who was interested. We all were interested – that weekend was going to generate huge dividends for the paper. I slipped Brad a bonus of one hundred dollars for going the extra mile. He refused it. He was paid to do what he did, he said, and he had really enjoyed his stay in Elgin. I insisted that he take it, pointing out that his company paid him for working Monday through Friday. He had given us Saturday and Sunday. Reluctantly, Brad finally took the money and told us to call him direct any time we had a problem. That was a foregone conclusion.

"Did you go home Friday and Saturday nights?" I asked Brad.

"Naw, I slept in my van."

I retract any smarmy remarks I've ever made about computer geeks.

* * *

An office email greeted everyone when they arrived for work the following Tuesday.

```
DOES ANYONE WANT TO DRIVE THE PAPER TO
THE PRINTER TOMORROW NIGHT? $35 - SEE
ED  IF  INTERESTED.  FIRST  COME  FIRST
DRIVE.
```

Each week, after the paper had been completed, someone needed to drive the camera-ready pages to our printer, Patrick Press, located in western Massachusetts, about an hour away. We had used several printers over the years, but Patrick had the best price and far and away the best quality. The downside was the drive, although it was only twenty minutes farther away than the other press capable of printing our paper, those last twenty miles were tough – especially in winter.

For years we had employed a driver, but one day one of our reporters suggested that we might offer the job to someone on staff first. "Thirty-five bucks is thirty-five bucks," he said. Ever since, someone on staff had the first option of doing the run.

Picking up the finished newspaper was another story. Long gone were the days when we could haul it home in the back of my station wagon. We now owned a huge six-wheel truck that could back right up to the loading dock, allowing the printer to drive a forklift right onto the truck and send our driver on his or her way.

As I entered the office that morning, John was sitting at his desk reading the *Globe*.

"Morning, John," I said. "Hitting it early?"

"Never went home," said John. "Just got wound up and kept on going."

"So where do you stand?" I inquired.

"All stories are written and in the can," said John with a big grin across his face.

"Why don't you head home and get some sleep, John," I said.

"Can't," said John, "I got court today."

We rotated reporters for coverage of the local District Court each Tuesday. Lots of news often flowed from that session and it was important to be there. About two or three hours after the conclusion of the session, the court clerk would have a summary of the day's proceedings available for the press. That was when the *Banner* showed up.

"Go for it, John," I said as I picked up the phone.

Chapter Five

"Ed," said an excited voice on the phone, "get a copy of today's *Wall Street Journal* and look at the classified ads." The voice belonged to Ned Todd, the ex-Bank of New England guy. Ned was a great tipster for us.

"What's up, Ned?" I said.

"It appears that Sportstown is being sold!" said Ned.

"Sportstown!" I said, "Being sold?"

"Let me read you the ad," said Ned. "Its heading is 'Major Sporting Goods Mail Order,' and it reads as follows: 'A leading sporting goods mail-order firm seeks qualified buyer for entire business. Family owned, debt free, this company name reflects quality and service. Located in scenic New Hampshire, close to the Massachusetts state line, this profitable business is ready to go public and reaffirm its reputation as the leader in its field. Direct inquiries to' – and then it gives the name of a law firm in New York, no, in Boston," said Ned. "Hell, it's gotta be Sportstown, direct mail, family owned, near Mass."

"Jesus Christ," I said. "Sportstown for sale, what a story! Wow, thanks Ned, thanks a lot. I wonder why they're running an ad? Isn't this something that should go on behind the scenes?"

"Sometimes yes and sometimes no," Ned answered, "they're probably trying to make sure that every interested suitor has an opportunity to make an offer."

"This will page one in all the dailies tomorrow," I said.

"I'm not so sure," cautioned Ned. "This is not a part of the *Wall Street Journal* that most people read on a daily basis."

The blade on the guillotine was being raised, and if any alert daily saw the ad in the *Journal*, it would drop tomorrow morning. But if they missed it, we'd have a huge scoop the following morning, provided we could stitch together the thousand and one disparate pieces suddenly flying around in my head.

Holy Toledo, Sportstown was the largest employer in town. They employ eight or nine hundred people. What if they move? Why are the Howards selling? No kids, I'll bet. John and Sue Howard have no kids, so who is there to leave it to? But why run an ad? Surely they could find a buyer by just letting the word out. What a story!

I know a freelance writer who is excellent with business stories and this would be his cup of tea. But Peter freelances for the state's largest daily, too. I hesitated to give it to him because I didn't want him going to them with it. They pay a hell of a lot more than we do. No, Peter Langley had much too much integrity to betray a confidence.

The clock was ticking. This was just too big for our staff. I needed someone who really knew business reporting and knows the questions, the follow-ups and, particularly in this case, the players.

Maybe I could work a deal with Peter. I'd pay him the daily's rate, but he must do the story just for us.

I thumbed through my Rolodex and found Longlegs's card (Peter was six feet eight inches tall). There must be ten different numbers on the damn card. Every time I call this guy he's moved. I dial what appears to be the freshest number. The same thing happened this time. A groggy voice answered, "Hello."

"Peter?" I say.

"Yeah," the voice answers.

"Hi, Peter, Ed Remington," I reply.

"Who?"

"Ed Remington at the *Elgin Eagle*."

"I don't know no Ed Remington, pal, you want Peter Langley and this ain't him," growls the voice.

"I'm sorry, do you know his new number?" I say.

"Hey, what do I look like, freak'n information or something?" says the voice. And then he gives me a number.

"Thanks a lot, I really –" He's gone.

I scrawled the new number on a fresh Rolodex card and dialed.

"Hello?"

"Hi, Peter, Ed Remington."

"I was just thinking about you guys," said Peter.

Oh, crap, was he onto the story? That meant that others probably were too.

"Why's that, Peter?" I said.

"I read in some computer magazine about your new computer system. You're really plowing some new ground there, Ed. I think it would make a great regional story."

"It's quite a system, Peter," I said. I was thrilled that he wanted to do a story about us and even more elated that he didn't seem to know about Sportstown. "That would be a neat story, Peter, and we'd be happy to work with you on it." I drew in a breath. "Peter, exactly how do you work?" I said. "What I'm trying to figure out is if I assign you a story, does that buy your total and complete confidentiality or would you try to peddle it to someone else too?"

"Shame on you, Ed," said Peter. "When you hire me, you get me. No one else does."

"Well, Peter, I certainly believe you, but the stuff I've given you over the past few years probably wouldn't be of interest to anyone else anyway. But suppose I launched you on a blockbuster story. I mean *really* big. Am I correct in believing that the story remains between you and me?" I said, hoping that I hadn't touch a raw nerve.

"That's a valid question, Ed. And the answer is still an unequivocal yes, the story stays between you and me. If it's big enough, the dailies will pick it up and they always attribute it so we both win in the long run. Fair question, Ed. So what's the story?"

"Sportstown is for sale," I blurted out, knowing that I had just shot though the point of no return.

"Come again?" said Peter incredulously.

"According to an ad in this morning's *Wall Street Journal*, it appears that Sportstown is up for sale," I said.

"You're shitt'n me! Really?"

"Really," I said.

We went over the details and the short deadline. Peter knew the Howards very well and if anyone could get John Howard, founder and president of Sportstown, to open up, it would be Peter. I explained that I was going to put Sally Herron on the story too for some background and history of the company. Peter was concerned about the twenty-four-hour deadline but I had no choice. It was Tuesday morning and the paper went to the printer tomorrow night. I went ahead and gave Peter until tomorrow at 3:00 p.m. but told him that was positively as late as we could go. We also discussed the very real possibility that our scoop would be completely blown out of the water with the arrival of the metro dailies on Wednesday morning. But we were going to give it a shot, and Peter was champing at the bit to get on with it. As an added incentive, I told him that I would pay him the same rate as the daily for this one assignment only.

"You don't need to do that Ed," said Peter, much to my relief. "But I'll take it."

My intercom rang. "I'll take it," said Sally.

What was this, déja vu all over again? "What?"

"I'll take it," she repeated. "I'll take the paper to the printer tomorrow night."

"That will be great," I said. "Could you come in here for a second?"

"On my way," she said, and appeared at my door while I was still trying to park the phone in its cradle. "What's up?"

"Go over to Day's and get me a copy of today's *Wall Street Journal*. I'll explain when you get back." She was out the door before I could get my wallet.

I buzzed Lana and told her to be prepared for some big last-minute stuff.

"Ohhhh," she said, but knew enough not to inquire. She knew that I would fill her in when the time was right.

I did the same thing with Karen via interoffice mail. It was great to be able to send a note whenever I wanted to now.

Sally returned and handed me the paper. I opened it to classifieds and searched for the ad. God, it looked huge. We wouldn't have an exclusive on this, I was certain. The damn thing looked like a billboard. But on second glance, it was pretty well submerged in a sea of ink.

Oh, well, maybe we'll do better than the rest. Peter Langley will cover all the bases. He'd sure as hell better now that he was getting the dailies rate.

I showed Sally the ad and saw her make the Sportstown connection. She emitted a characteristic Sally "*Woooow*." I told her that I'd put Peter Langley on the story and I needed her to gather together some background information on the company. "Should I go out there and try to get some reaction?" she asked, demonstrating a great set of news instincts.

"Normally yes," I answered, "but at least for the time being let's forgo the reaction angle in favor of a slam-dunk scoop. If the story gets out, which I'm pretty sure is going to happen, then yes, you should get out there tomorrow and go for some reaction interviews."

"And the selectmen's reaction," said Sally, "and a few reactions from local merchants."

"Exactly," I said. "That's exactly how to approach it. In the interim, you should dig out the file on Sportstown – probably files, we have tons of stuff. Pick Sandra's brain, she might give you some other possible areas to pursue. And keep it well under wraps, Sally. We just could possibly hit a grand slam here."

"I hope so," she said. Her eyes gleamed with excitement.

Just then Karen came in the building, read her interoffice mail, and was on her way over to my office.

"What gives?" she said.

I showed her the *Journal* ad and outlined how I had assigned the story to Peter Langley and asked Sally to do the local angle.

"I'm so glad this tip came to you," said Karen. "You have that great connection with Peter Langley and you are also close friends with the Howards."

"We're co-drivers on this one, Karen, and it's going to take both of us to bring this home," I assured her.

"I wonder if we have a good file photo of Sportstown," said Karen. "One taken since they added the new front entrance."

"I'll take a look," I said.

"I'm on my way out there right now," said Karen. "Hal is doing some catalog work for them and I am dropping off some proofs for him. I'll grab a photo while I am there. I'll also snoop around and see if there are any strange suits hanging around."

We were on our way.

"Cool, cool, cool!" chortled Lana as the new computer and typesetting system flowed a story onto the page. "Beats the hell out of cut and paste." She walked across the room to the layout boards like a proud new mama.

"Ed, it's for you," hollered Sandra, waving her telephone at me. "It's John."

I grabbed the phone on Lana's desk.

John was at the District Court, and one of the cases was against a local doctor, believe it or not, Dr. Spark, who was a notorious wife beater. Everyone in town knew it was going on, but the thug in scrubs had never been charged. The black and blue wife never pressed charges against the creep. But the muggings were common knowledge and it was only a matter of time before the animal killed her.

Spark and I had tangled over a hospital issue a couple of years earlier. He was apparently one of those people who never had anyone say no to him. I was, in a sense, saying exactly that and the rage in his eyes was unforgettable. His face flushed, his skin seemed to grow taut, and were it not for a roomful of people at the reception, I think the guy would have taken a swing at me – never mind that I was almost a foot taller.

This time, it appeared the good doc had come close to killing his petite spouse, and she finally pressed charges and stuck to her guns. The case came up in court this morning. Right in the middle of the oral arguments, the two went at it again, screaming and lunging and calling each other every name they could think of.

John was going to hang around the court for a little while to see if anything more came of it.

"Write down everything that was said while you're waiting," I instructed him. When you're a witness to a scene like that, the adrenaline rush often pushes out the memory of what actually transpired. I wanted John to try to capture that while it was still relatively fresh in his mind – a mind that had been going steady for more than twenty-four hours.

"Who else was there?" I asked.

"Just the two of them. The housekeeper had gone home," said John.

"No, John." I laughed. "Were there any other newspapers covering the court proceedings this morning?"

"None," said John, "and Thelma's not telling any of them anything except for the official items."

"That's super. We'll see ya when we see ya," I said.

Tricky story, I thought, but definitely a story – wife-beating doctor, fits nicely along with gambling addicted minister, which we had reported several years ago. And let's not forget the molesting undertaker. Yup.

"Hubba, hubba," said Lana as another quarter-page of copy and photos emerged from the laser printer. "Sayonara waxer," she said as she popped the next section into place.

Things were humming in the newsroom. We also had a mini dilemma because we didn't know the status of the Sportstown story. Where the hell was Peter? Why hadn't he called with something? The guy had been given this assignment less than three hours ago, I reminded myself. He'd get back to us as soon as he had something to report.

Sally was busily poring through our newspaper morgue. We had files of old articles and bound copies of all of our issues for the current year and going back a dozen or more years. Keeping the files up to date was a real pain and went in spurts. One of the great advantages of the new computer system was that much of this information could now be dumped into a permanent database. When we wanted information on Sportstown, we'd just type "Sportstown" and violà, there it would be. At least, it is supposed to work something like that. We hadn't yet crawled along the learning curve to where we were exploring those possibilities, but they were going to be a great asset.

When John came in, I told him to pull together the Doc Spark wife beating story and send it to me as soon as possible. I called the newspaper libel hotline and roughly explained what the story was all about and what we intended to do with it.

"You're going to be OK with it," said the lawyer for the ser-vice, "but I want to thoroughly scrub it before you go with it."

"Don't worry about that!" I said. I knew that this was going to be a very volatile story. All hell could break loose.

Just then John called me on the intercom. "Spark story is in the system," said John. "It's in my subdirectory *HOLD* and it's called 'B and B.'"

"How did you enter B and B?" I said.

"B the letter, the word *and*, followed by B the letter again," John instructed.

"What's B and B all about anyway?" I said, unable to crack John's cryptographic title for the file.

"Black and blue," said John.

"Christ, John," I said, "go home and get some sleep. Good work."

John was up and out of the building before I could hang up the phone.

I called up John's story on my screen and first read it all the way through just to see where he was going. It seemed to flow OK – had a couple of typos and a run-on sentence or two. I then went through it again to see if there was anything potentially libelous in it. It seemed pretty clean. I decided to call Thelma at the District Court to verify the charges.

"Doc Spark's an animal, Ed," said Thelma. "You know she's made at least a half-dozen trips to the police station in the past two or three years, ready to press charges. And then, she decides not to."

"So what's going to happen?" I said.

"Well, as you know, he's out of the house, and has a restrain-ing order against him until the judge hands down a ruling."

"Which will be when?"

"Probably next week," she said.

"And what will that ruling be? I mean, what do you expect it will be?" She probably wouldn't try to venture a guess, I thought.

"Anyone's guess, Ed," she said, "but he was visibly upset."

"Of course he was upset," I said. "John said that he was ready to punch her out right there in the courtroom."

Thelma burst into laughter. "I'm talking about the judge, Ed," she said. "It was the judge who was upset!"

"This beating took place, allegedly took place, last Thursday night," she continued, "That was four or five days ago. This woman looked like she had been through a meat grinder. One eye was gone. Not popped out or anything, but swollen shut, and black and blue and yellow. It was horrible."

"John said her right arm was in a sling. Do you know who treated her and who prescribed a sling? Was it Spark?" I said.

"I dunno," she said. "He's an OB guy so I doubt he knows much about wrenched shoulders."

"Wrenched shoulder? Not a broken arm?" I asked. John had reported a broken arm.

"He damn near twisted her arm right off her body, the bastard," said Thelma. "Her shoulder area, you know, where the arm and shoulder meet, was all swollen up and looked like someone had strapped on a cantaloupe or something. This guy is a real, no-good shit," said Thelma, not leaving anything to my imagination.

"OK, thanks a lot, Thelma. Say hi to Art for me." I hung up.

Three things were rushing through my mind. First was a genuine fear that Spark had true homicidal capability. Second was the possibility that some other doc was a co-conspirator in this, which was a crime. And third was the incorrect fact about the broken arm that John had included in the story. It was a story with extraordinary legal ramifications and we couldn't afford for anything to be incorrect.

I pulled up Sandra's monthly school board story. This story always took lots of editing and normally Karen handled it. But this week I asked Karen to let me do it because I occasionally added a piece to the board story containing the information that I had received from my mole, and I had some information that would clarify some pending issues. It wasn't that cut and dried, but Sandra reported things in her story because that was how she saw them, but when the mole's facts came into play, much of what Sandra thought she saw was an illusion. It was a real challenge to blend Sandra's public version of the meeting with my behind-the-scenes version. Sandra's reporting was first rate and I didn't want to disrupt that. She knew I was thoroughly wired on this subject and we talked about it often. But Sandra, like most hometown reporters, didn't want to get into any controversy if she could help it. "I have to live here," she said. I bit back the words that rose to my lips: "I've been here for twenty years and will be here until I die." So, a lot of our school board stories had shared bylines.

I asked Sandra to come in for minute.

Sandra always took this meeting to be something much more than it was. To Sandy, this was some sort of monthly test, an audition, a performance review. To me it was merely a way to blend our two views of the school board into a scenario that worked for the reader. But Sandy wanted more out of it so I always tried to explain things in detail.

"Sandy, you say here that the board then recessed and went into executive session. What reason did they give for that executive session?" I said.

"They claimed that they had some personnel matters to discuss," said Sandy.

"And you mentioned here that they postponed a vote on the Conner Report, until the October meeting. What is the Conner Report?"

"You know, Ed, that report —"

"I know, Sandy," I said, "but does the reader know? You have to fold in a brief description about the Conner Report. I say brief because it has been discussed in great detail by this newspaper since last spring, and if someone doesn't have it by now, they never will, but you have to define it to some degree."

"You're right," she said. I could tell she was going to demonstrate that by the fact that elsewhere in the story she had done that but I beat her to the punch.

"You did a good job with the Sherman Proficiency Test report later in the story," I said and was met by a beaming Sandra Garrett. Things were OK, Sandy had passed her monthly exam. Now to find a way to turn her report of fantasyland into actuality. It was time once again to send a truth missile ripping through Morgan Mather's gut.

"Peter Langley's on the phone," said Lana. "What's he want?" she asked. Leave it to Lana to pick up on the fact that Peter Langley never calls to chat. He only calls when he is working on a story for us. I think this is Lana's way of saying, "I'm not going to push things, but I do want you to know that I know something is up. And because I'm not pushing, I expect to be brought up to speed within a reasonable amount of time. And for damn sure, before the rest of the staff." That, I suspect, was Lana's subtle message.

"What's up, Peter?" I was dying to hear his report.

"Got a problem. Howard's out of town, won't be back till Friday," said Peter. "They claim they don't know where he is. That's bullshit," he added.

"Boy, I doubt that anyone else there is going to comment on this," I said, thinking out loud. "If it was publicly held, we might get something from some financial officer or something, but this is John Howard's baby and no underling is going to say squat without John signing off."

"Exactly," said Peter. "I do possibly have a little more, though. You know they have a company plane?"

"The Aero Commander," I said. "I've made a couple of trips to Maine with the Howards in that plane."

"Well, I went out to the Elgin airport to see if it was there. It wasn't. I asked one of the kids on the line where the Sportstown plane was and he said it had gone to Florida today, so I suspect John Howard is in Florida. So I've already eliminated forty-nine other states," said Peter, with a laugh.

God, I wished I could laugh at a moment like this. Just loosen up and laugh with him for a second or two. But I was wound up tighter than a spring on this one. If the dailies didn't notice this story, we stood to have a huge, huge, scoop here.

"Let me work on this for a while, Peter, and I'll get back to you. Are you at home?"

"Yes."

"Will you be home tonight?"

"All night," Peter replied.

"I'll get back to you, Peter. Good job on eliminating those forty-nine states," I said, feeling that I had sort of joined in on Peter's levity.

Morgan Mather, it's your lucky day, I thought. I just don't have the ten or fifteen minutes that it would take me to do the school board sidebar, at least not right now. So Sandy's story may have to stand alone this week. Crap. I hate to let Mather get off that lightly.

I needed some time away from the phones, away from the noise. I had to sort out the John Howard thing. I got in my car and headed out onto the highway. It is the one place where I can go and no one can reach me.

Howard was in Florida. I seemed to recall that he had a place down there where they went for the winter, but where? I felt certain that John would talk with me if I could find him. Maybe I could call his house. I knew he had a house sitter who stayed there on those weekends when we'd gone to Maine. And maybe I could just call his office, and ask his secretary to give me his number. Both are good approaches and I decided to give them a shot.

I returned to the office and got no answer at the Howard house. The answering machine picked up and I could tell from the time it took for the tone to sound that not many messages had piled up. That was good news. First, it meant that probably no one else was chasing this story, and second, it might mean that there was a housekeeper there.

I called Sportstown and asked for John Howard. While the call was being transferred I snapped my Rolodex card off the holder and looked closely at the name I had penciled in the corner. Cynthia.

"Mr. Howard's office," said a voice.

"Cynthia?" I said.

"Yes," came the reply.

"Hi, Cynthia, Ed Remington at the *Eagle*. Is John there?"

"He's in Florida until Friday, Mr. Remington. Can I take a message and have him call you?" she said.

"Is there any way I can reach him? I have something important to discuss with him today."

"I'm sorry, Mr. Remington, but Mr. Howard was adamant about not being disturbed," she said. "I'm really sorry."

"How long has he been gone?"

"He just left this morning. He'll be back Friday night. So he won't be gone long, Mr. Remington," she said, trying to smooth over the fact that he and I weren't going to connect. "You could probably reach him then. He expects to be in by dinnertime Friday," she said, trying to be helpful.

"Very good, Cynthia, thanks so much," I said, trying not to sound disappointed. "If you do talk with him, please ask him to give me a call." I gave her my private number and my home number.

Well, I've confirmed that he was probably on that Aero Commander, because Cynthia said that he had flown to Florida that morning. Now where in the hell in Florida did he go?

I arrived at the airport at dinnertime. It was a small airport, and had a considerable amount of traffic thanks to its long, World War II vintage runways. It had been built during the war as an emergency strip. I had worked at an airport in my youth and loved being around the planes, the hangers, and the aero-ambiance.

The little terminal was also the headquarters for the base operator and the airport "cafeteria," which consisted of a half-dozen or so vending machines. It took about five minutes to dig out the destination of the Sportstown plane and to extract the Howard's Florida telephone number from the kid at the terminal. I called Langley from the airport pay phone, gave him the Florida phone number for Howard, and told him to go right at it in the morning.

I got home after midnight and rose with the sun at about 6:15 a.m.

As I drove past Blanchard's, Bill Blanchard was hauling bundles of newspapers inside his store. I stopped and rolled down my window and called, "Do you have curb service?"

"Only for you, Ed," grunted Blanchard as he slung another fifty-pound bundle of newspapers up the steps. "What'll you have?"

I knew that Bill would get the papers out of the bundles if I asked, but I climbed out of my car and helped him heft a couple of bundles. Bill was getting up there, and these babies do a number on one's back. I carefully slipped out a copy of each of the three metro dailies that had arrived, including the *Boston Globe*.

"Pop it on my account, Bill, OK?" I said as I climbed back into my car.

"No problem, Ed," puffed Bill, drawing the back of his hand across his brow.

I hurried into the office and tore into the *Globe*. No mention of the Sportstown story. I then, very deliberately, went back through the paper one page at a time, carefully perusing every column of every page. They had missed the Sportstown story!

Was it just a small potatoes story for them?

Did they know about it but not consider it important to their general readership?

I grabbed the largest New Hampshire statewide daily. No Sportstown story.

The second state daily, the same.

It was *our story*.

I tuned into the local radio station. Gathering news was not high on their agenda, but if a story came through the door, they'd air it.

The local news broadcast began and the lead story was about a missing cat.

I called Langley. "It's our story!" I bellowed into the phone.

"OK, I hear you, damn it," said Peter, obviously jolted from his slumber. "Really?" he added as my words began to etch through the membrane of sleep. "*No one* had it?"

"Not a damn one," I said gleefully.

"What a bunch of dorks," said Langley. "God, am I going to have some fun with this one!"

"Go at Howard at nine-fifteen, Peter," I said.

"I thought we agreed on nine-thirty," Langley answered.

"That was yesterday, Peter. We need to get things rolling, I have an open patient on the table," I said referring to my vacant page one.

"I'll get him, Ed. I'm sure he'll open up, he likes me."

"Go for it, Peter, talk to you in a couple of hours." I hung up.

Wow, what a coup! Now we had to gather as much information as possible without inadvertently grafting this story onto the Elgin community grapevine. We had to keep it under wraps as long as possible, even from our own staff. It was a true "need-to-know" story. Only those who "needed-to-know" would be told for the next few hours.

John waltzed in and I beckoned him into my office. The Dr. Spark story was going to be a big one with potential big repercussions, I told him. It had significant legal ramifications, and I wanted him to review every single fact in the story carefully. He assured me that the story was clean.

"Mrs. Spark's arm was in a sling, right?" I inquired. "What was wrong with her arm?"

"I think it was broken," blurted out John. He instantly knew that "think" was not the word I wanted to hear. "Good question, Ed," he said sheepishly. "I'm not sure exactly why she had her arm in a sling."

One wrong fact could be devastating, I pointed out. If Spark sued – and he is a ripe candidate for such action – a sharp defense attorney would take that one inaccurate fact and paint the whole story as pure fiction. I told John about my discussion with Thelma, the court clerk, and her belief that the arm was twisted. John understood the seriousness of what I was saying, but I could see that he was also upset, if not mad.

"John," I said, "you came upon this story when you'd been up for more than twenty-four hours. Mistakes are certainly understandable. Now that you're rested it's time to thoroughly scrub that story. Make absolutely certain that everything we say is factual." We were playing with live grenades here, and John needed to get it.

He laid a wounded-puppy look on me and headed for the door.

"And John," I injected as sort of an afterthought, "if you don't want to add your byline to this story, that would be perfectly understandable."

"Why would I want to do that?" inquired John.

"Because the repercussions from this story are going to be big. Some people will call John Sedlak some sort of sensationalist reporter, others will lean on the *Eagle* like nothing you have ever seen. It's going to be real ugly for a while." I rose from my desk.

John's eyes confirmed that he'd gotten it.

Sometimes to get someone's attention you just need to use a bigger two by four.

As 9:15 a.m. approached I felt my stomach knotting. Kurt brought in a bag of donuts and everyone descended on him like moths drawn to a light. I knew I couldn't eat until we had the Sportstown story rolling. I called Bill Blanchard to ask if he'd charged to our account the three newspapers that I'd picked up earlier that morning. He hadn't. "Haven't gotten around to it yet, but thanks for calling." That was Blanchardspeak for "I completely forgot about it."

"Peter Langley's on three," said Lana. She looked at me from across the room with a profound grin. She'd smoked out the fact that something big was brewing. And she knew I wasn't going to broadcast that story until I absolutely had to.

"Yeah, Peter." I plopped down in my chair and grabbed a tablet to make notes.

"No answer at Howard's," he said bluntly. The ominous way he said it added another veil of black to my darkening hopes for a mega story. "No answer, no answering machine, no nothing."

"Stay on it, Peter," I said. "He'll show up," I added, trying to keep Langley enthused about the story. "Try every thirty minutes."

"OK, Ed," he said, trying to keep me enthused, I thought. "I'm going to be here all day if you need me."

"I need you, Peter, I need you to make contact with Howard. Stay on it." I hung up.

That was the pattern for the next eight hours.

I briefed Karen and Lana on the Sportstown story. I didn't need to go into a lot of detail as to why all the secrecy, but keeping a story of that magnitude out of sight, until perhaps the last minute was going to have a major impact on how page one was going to come together.

Howard had disappeared from the face of the earth.

We extended Langley's deadline from three to four to five to six.

Six-thirty, it was time to bite the bullet. Page one was sitting there empty. My staff knew that something big was brewing, but only one had been brave enough to ask, and then in a circuitous way.

"Got something good for page one, Ed?" asked Kurt.

"Working on it, Kurt," I replied. Kurt knew to drop it right there.

At six-thirty I turned Karen loose on page one. Fortunately, she had been tinkering with it most of the day and had a fallback plan ready. The issue was pulling together and we decided to put the Doc Spark story on page seven. A wife beating wasn't an uncommon event, and although a doctor administering the blows was a newsworthy twist, it wasn't a Page One story. Chris came up with a picture he had shot at the hospital benefit baseball game a year ago. It showed Spark with a bat in his hand. Chris knew where the jugular was, for certain. We told Chris to hold the photo for a sports story.

The paper had to go out the door at 9:00 p.m. The printer prints two weekly papers each Wednesday night and a throwaway shopper. The *Eagle* is their largest print run and they like to have the press rolling at 1:00 a.m. It takes them about three hours to prepare our paper for the press from the moment our driver walks through their door.

Karen and Lana had a preliminary page one done by 8:00 p.m. and we were waiting for some last-minute photos before piecing together the jump page. Most Page One stories jump from that page to conclude elsewhere in the paper. We tried, if possible, to send all jumps to the same page. This made it easier for the reader. It was like putting together a jigsaw puzzle and Karen was the most skillful person at doing it I've even seen. She sketched it out, called dummying, and it always fit. When I dummied a page, it was a hit-or-miss proposition. So I always followed my dummy with a hands-on session in order to make it all fit. Karen could sit back and watch others implement her carefully drawn plan.

"So what was holding up page one?" asked Kurt, feeling that it was now safe to inquire.

It was as though a flash freeze had gripped the room. No one moved and no one spoke. I hadn't seen the question coming and I was caught completely off guard. Should I let it out now? Was there a possibility that the story might be valid a week from now? No chance. Tell them.

"Anyone want to guess?" I said.

Silence.

"There is an unconfirmed rumor that Sportstown is for sale," I said. I heard gasps around the room. "There was an ad in yesterday's *Wall Street Journal* that we're certain was about Sportstown, but we can't find the Sportstown owner to confirm it. The law firm mentioned in the ad won't return our calls. Every damn one of the daily newspapers missed the story, so we have the potential for a huge scoop, but we can't go without confirmation from John Howard."

Several people suggested avoiding a direct confirmation but I wasn't about to go ahead and throw it out there without speaking to John Howard in Florida, or wherever the hell he was. Sally was upbeat that the story might hang around and remain undiscovered for another week. Chris volunteered to go to Florida to root out Howard, and Lana told everyone to get the hell out of her way so she could box up the paper and push Sally out the door with it.

Sally left at 9:00 p.m. sharp. We opened the office refrigerator and broke out two six-packs of beer, a tradition each week after the paper had been put to bed.

"*Eagle*," said Chris, grabbing a phone. "Yeah, right here." He thrust the phone at me.

"Hello," I said, as I swigged a sip of beer.

"Ed, it's true, Sportstown is going down! I just talked to Howard," shouted Langley.

"Holy shit, Peter! Hang on!" I exclaimed. "Lana, call what's-her-name at the Blue Bird Mini-Mart and ask her to try to flag down Sally. She's in a red VW bug. The Sportstown story is a go. Allison, call Patrick Press and get the lead pressman, Tom, on the line. What's the story, Peter?"

Langley had reached Howard at 8:45 p.m. They'd been deep-sea fishing all day. Howard was very forthcoming and Peter got the whole story. The company was indeed up for sale and they already had an inquiry. Howard confirmed that we were the only ones to reach him. He wanted to know how we did it and Peter told him to talk to me when he got back.

We had it – now what do we do with it? Our paper was rolling through the dark New Hampshire night in the back seat of a red VW.

Somehow Sally eluded the Blue Bird Mini-Mart dragnet. Marie, the night manager had actually locked the door and stood by the highway for about five minutes looking for Sally's unmistakable red Volkswagen, but to no avail.

I got Tom the pressman on the phone and we agreed to swap positions with the other weekly paper. This meant that our paper would not be ready for pick-up at 4:00 a.m. but closer to 5:30 a.m. That would delay our arrival on the newsstands by about twenty or twenty-five minutes. It would cost us the ability to make the mail in a couple of the smaller outlying towns, but all in all it wasn't a major blow.

We asked for Patrick Press to bring in a typesetter and we would fax down our story as soon as it was ready. Karen had carefully measured the entire front page and the jump page and we knew what we had to work with. Langley headed down to our office to compose his story on our system.

The beer was put away and no one left the office. We had a huge story here, and everybody wanted in on the action.

Things didn't progress exactly as we wished. Patrick Press had a hell of a time getting a typesetter to come in and do the story. Langley had a lot of information from Howard, but had to get it all into fifty-four column inches of space. We had forgotten about Sally's sidebar concerning the Sportstown history, and when it was added into the mix we suddenly found ourselves without nearly enough space. Fortunately, Karen had dumped in an ad promoting the *Eagle* on the jump page so we were able to yank that and instantly pick up an additional twenty-four inches of space. We pulled another jump off of the jump page and moved it further inside the paper. All of this was done over the telephone with an assistant pressman at Patrick trying to follow Karen's dictated instructions. We missed the press deadline by thirty minutes, but fortunately there were no jobs after us and the delay only cost us some overtime pay.

We wrapped things up at a little after midnight. Everyone was so tired, and so elated, that no one had the energy to go home. One by one they trundled out. I was the last to leave. I grabbed a beer and headed to my car, and as I glanced back at the building I noticed something amiss. Someone had left a desk lamp on inside.

To hell with it. I tossed the half-empty beer into the bushes behind our building. God, I love this business.

I was so wound up by the time I got home that I couldn't sleep. I called my daughter, Missy, in California in response to a message left on my answering machine. Nothing urgent, just time to touch base. She was stunned by the Sportstown story. She had worked there while in high school and worked with Sue Howard at the local hospital as a volunteer. Missy was an assistant DA and I ran the Doc Spark story by her for an opinion. "It's about time she nailed the creep," she remarked. "But Dad, this could get sticky."

I didn't need to hear that. She modified it a bit by adding, "I think you're on solid ground, but he could really muddy the waters for a while. I don't think he will, for fear of all of the earlier batterings coming out." She then added, "I'll come home and personally defend you if you need that. He's such a creep."

She is a tough kid, and she can hold her own against a whole courtroom full of Sparks and/or sharks. She also has one of the most compassionate hearts in the world.

Chapter Six

It had been almost fifteen years to the day since my wife Nicole died when her flight exploded in the night above the Rocky Mountains. My son and daughter and I were going to meet her and we were all heading for a much-needed vacation in the San Francisco area. It was the longest and most critical day of my life and in the lives of both kids.

But we pulled together and formed a bond that was as solid as any bond between three people could ever be. My son, Phil, had just started medical school in Ohio, and was certain he was going to remain there for a while because they were doing some leading edge work in limb reattachment, which he had decided was for him.

Missy was at Yale Law School and was already swatting away job offers, even with one more year to go. Nicole's death could have been a catastrophe for Missy, but she pushed through it.

The house was torture without the kids and Nicole. It was time for a midcourse correction, said my inner soul. I had spent over two decades in the world of advertising in New York. When I graduated from Columbia, I was offered a full-time position with one of the top ad agencies in the United States. I had worked for them part time while going to school and that job offer was the biggest break of my life. I eventually became the account executive for one of their big three accounts, a major soft drink company, and I was allowed to build my own creative team. Things were going along great and then the company was going to be sold to another top firm. It was a perfect blending of advertising accounts except for our soft drink account, which was going to conflict with another soft drink account in the acquiring agency. In the end, I started my own firm and took my creative team with me and the soft drink account, which I had initially landed more than a decade earlier.

I loved the ad business. We grew to fifty-six people, but when Nicole died, I knew I had to get off that train. One dinner at the Cattleman Restaurant and the agency was sold. And fourteen years ago, I found the *Elgin Eagle* for sale in the classified pages of *Editor and Publisher*. Ninety days later I owned the *Eagle* and was moving into my New Hampshire home.

In New York, I had become a workaholic. My doctor admonished me to slow down and I was working on that aspect of my life. Being a country editor in New England was the best possible therapy, I was sure – sitting around the ol' wood stove a-spittn' and a whittlin'.

Hah!

The clock struck two, then three, and four before I finally got to sleep. As if on cue, the phone jolted me awake two hours later.

"Ed, is there a problem with the paper?" It was Bill Blanchard. He was opening his store and couldn't find the bundles of *Eagle*s. "I only had to load in two puny bundles of *Banners* this morning but no bundles of your rag. People get mad at me when they aren't here."

"They should be there in just a few minutes," I proclaimed, squinting at the clock. "And Bill, I promise you, it is worth the wait. Big Page One story."

"What's that?" said Blanchard. "Who screwed who?"

"It's not that juicy, Bill," I said. "But trust me, it's worth the wait." I hung up before he could reply.

Rather rude, I thought, and I made a point to drop by later in the day and make sure he wasn't upset.

By the time I got to Freda's the paper was there. Everyone in the place had an *Eagle* wide open on the counter or table. Others had it folded, the way subway commuters do. And several were poaching on a copy held by someone sitting next to them. The Sportstown story was far and away the most significant story we had ever published as far as impact on the town was concerned. When the largest employer in town may be leaving, it's news, and we had it – right there! No one had it, not even the *Globe*. The *Eagle's* biggest exclusive ever.

But then I noticed something that previous experience had taught me. The human story, the personal story, will get first attention. It appeared that no one was reading about Sportstown. Doc Spark had commandeered the attention of the morning crowd at Freda's.

As I passed Bert Tozer, who owned a local travel agency, he put his finger on the Spark story and made a clinched-fist gesture that translated, "Good job."

"Whoooa," said Peter Richards, "the shit's gonna hit the fan over this one, Ed." Several others nodded concurrence, as John Griffey and Bob Hamilton, two locals doctors made a hasty exit to keep from having to comment, I suppose.

I grabbed a cup from under the counter and filled it with Freda coffee, which looked like it had been imported from the Charles river.

About five minutes later, while people were digesting Doc Spark and now Sportstown, Harold Williams, owner of Williams Department Store, tapped me on the shoulder. "This is yellow journalism, Ed," he said, a slight tremble in his voice. "There's no place in Elgin for reporting like this," he added. The room fell silent. "I don't quite know what to make of it, but my instinct is to not run any more ads with your paper until further notice."

Harold's reaction was something that went with the territory. "Publish nothing and offend no one," Benjamin Franklin had supposedly said. Many stories are upsetting to one segment or another of the population. I had learned that we didn't have the luxury of choosing or creating the news. We are there to report it, all of it, the good along with the bad.

What bothered me about Harold's pronouncement was that it was so public. This was grapevine fodder at its finest. Even though we were right, a lot of damage control could be needed as his statement metastasized and roared down the town gossip gulch. I could see that Harold was not about to listen to anything, so I decided to wait until he left. I'd see then if I could frame the situation in more favorable terms.

Harold paid his bill and spoke to no one as he left. I had a sense that Harold wasn't exactly sure that his instant reaction was the correct one.

As he left, everyone in the place turned as one and looked directly at me. Not only did I need to execute some damage control, it was expected by this audience.

I turned my palms heavenward and said, "We didn't make up that story. The *Eagle* reports what happens in court."

"It is guts journalism, Ed," said Peter. "Your spineless competition didn't do a story on it – in fact, they even left it completely out of the court log."

"Let me see that!" I exclaimed. I practically grabbed the crumpled *Banner* out of Pete's hand.

I again felt every eye in the joint on me as I combed the *Banner*'s court log. Jesus Christ, they *did* leave it out. What a bunch of wimps! And what a marvelous show-and-tell for anyone wanting to know the difference between the two papers.

"When your job is to report the news," I said, "you have to report all of it. You can't be selective." Was I being too preachy? I just wanted to get out of there.

"Could I get this to go?" I said to the surly little waitress who had just thrown down my plate in front of me. "I forgot I have a meeting this morning." I watched the eggs, sausage, and toast slide into a grease-coated heap on a paper plate.

Walking back over to the newspaper office, I pitched my oozing breakfast into a dumpster. I thought of the incongruity of people riveted to the Spark story and practically ignoring Sportstown. Both were big stories, and both were going to be a part of my life and Elgin's for quite some time.

For the next two days, the calls were pretty evenly divided between pro-Spark and anti-Spark. Harold Williams made good on his threat and told Rosemary that he would have no ads this week. However, he did call me over the weekend and confided that perhaps he had overreacted. He explained that he and his wife had been friends of the Sparks for years. But he also acknowledged that he understood that we were reporting only what had gone on in the court. And he had certainly picked up on the omission of the incident in the *Banner*. "We're wondering what else they haven't reported over the years," he declared, sounding very distrustful.

The *Banner*'s omission of the Spark incident was a sort of "omission grenade." It took people a few days before that grenade exploded as people began to ask the same question that Hal Williams had asked, namely, "What else is the *Banner* holding back?" It was a huge breach of trust and was going to have equally large long-term consequences, I'd make sure of that.

To me, this was the true personification of the *Banner*'s entire approach to the news business. They were news manipulators. Their paper was a house organ for the town. It slanted, distorted, and even omitted news in order to shape things into a predefined concept of what should be. Not only were the publishers an embarrassment to the profession, but they were unethical competitors to boot. And the sooner I could write their epitaph, the better.

Doc Spark called about five hours after the paper came out. He lit into Lana, and he lit into me. He vowed to "sue our ass" and he declared that "John Sedlak has written his last story."

I never said a word, just listened to him rant and rave. My silence was deafening and only provoked him more. When he had ended, I thanked him for calling and hung up.

Lana was pretty shaken up by his call. I explained that it was certainly not unexpected, but I thought he had a little more class than that.

"Wife beaters ain't got no class," she hissed, emphasizing the "ain't" in order to paint the fact that they were low class, if any class at all.

Tuesday's mail contained a letter from an attorney Spark had retained. It was a firm out of Worcester, Massachusetts with about fifteen names on the letterhead. It declared that they had been retained by Spark and asked us to send them everything we had concerning the story. I knew it was a bogus threat, I owed them nothing. I wrote a brief decline, then decided not even to glorify their letter with a response.

There was no doubt that we were on totally solid ground, but if Spark sued, the legal bills could go as high as $10,000 before my deductible kicked in from my libel policy. We could countersue for legal fees, but the good ol' boys of lawyerdom rarely paid much attention to reimbursement for legal fees, because winning lawyers would pump up their cost, fees, and expenses to ridiculous levels.

A $10,000 expense was not something I needed in the wake of a new computer system and a new addition to the staff. But Spark was an obstinate jerk and I was prepared for the worst.

Karen and I were on the same page as to assigning Dennis to the police chief story, but I still hadn't told her what it was about. She needed to be brought into the loop right away because she was going to have to help provide some cover for Dennis, who was supposed to be lifting some of the load off other reporters.

I called them both into my office and explained the story without mentioning Sauer's name. When Dennis asked for my source, I told him that it couldn't be revealed.

"Where do we start looking?" asked Karen.

"Beats the hell out of me," I said. "Where does one go to unload a quarter of a million dollars' worth of coke?"

"Boston, maybe Lowell," said Dennis. "If it's Boston, I can get some help from a friend of mine who works for the *Globe*. If it's Lowell, I'm clueless."

"What's your friend do at the *Globe*?" I asked.

"Grunt stuff mainly," said Dennis, "but he's done a lot of police stuff and he knows a lot of people."

"That would be a great help," I sighed, "but it would be nice to know where to look. I'll get in touch with my contact and see if I can get some more direction."

I ran down Sauer the next morning at the soccer field, where he'd coached a youth team for the past two or three years. Not enough of his players had turned up yet to field any sort of pre-game drill, so this would be a good time to talk to him. As I approached him Sauer started to walk down the sideline, cutting himself out of the pack. When I caught up with him he said, "Make it look like we're talking about soccer. What do you need?"

I gave him a big smile and made a wide, sweeping gesture toward the field. "Where were these goods sold?" I asked quietly.

He stopped, pulled his arms up to shoulder level, and brought them together in front of him. "Boston, right off of

Kneeland Street," he replied. He threw his head back and laughed.

I imitated his hand gesture and asked, "Any names? I need a name."

Sauer turned to start back up the sideline toward his team. "Donal." He took a few steps and repeated, "Donal."

"Got it," I said, giving another broad, sweeping gesture towards the field.

Dynamite, just what we needed – a clue about which I didn't have a clue.

Dennis wanted to work on the story over the weekend. "On my own time – my decision," he added. Neither Karen nor I had any objection to that. He went to Boston and talked with his friend. "Donal" didn't ring a bell, but the friend told Dennis that it was probably still a good lead. There are in-town drug deals, he explained, and a whole separate part of the street culture deals with the out-of-towners. They are leery about out-of-towners because no one knows who they are. Donal was probably the gatekeeper for the out-of-town buys and sells. There was certainly one more layer after Donal and probably two.

He told Dennis that he would discreetly ask some questions and get back to him. He also leaned on Dennis for access to the story. Nothing doing, Dennis told him. The guy said he understood but would like to be a part – when it broke.

Dennis's sensitivity to my concern about protecting my source was refreshing. I wasn't going to let anyone else into this. I had made a promise to Sauer, and I was afraid that letting in the *Globe* could create a situation that would be hard to control. I was also concerned that when Dennis's friend understood that we weren't going to immediately cut in the *Globe*, his assistance might taper off, so it was important that we stay right on this while we were getting help.

Chapter Seven

"Hello, Mr. Remington," said a tentative voice on the phone. "This is Ellen Rollins. My father and I met you few weeks ago at the restaurant. I bought a subscription to your paper. Do you remember?"

"Of course," I said. "What can I do for you?"

"Well, first of all, thank you for starting my subscription to the *Elgin Eagle* so promptly. It arrived the next week and I so look forward to Saturday mornings, which is when it arrives in New York," she said.

New York? Oh, hell yes, Ellen Rollins, Broadway star, missed story. "We're here to please, Ellen," I said. "How have you been?"

"Just fine, Mr. Remington."

"Let's make that, Ed, Ellen."

"Fine, Ed. I also wanted to thank you for respecting my privacy when we met in Elgin. That meant a lot. Dad and I commented on how polite you were and how you treated us just like – well, real people, I guess," she said, stumbling for the exact words.

I didn't want to admit that I hadn't known who she was when we had met. If I had, though, I believe I would have treated them exactly as I had. People need self time, even celebrities. No one should be interrupted during Saturday morning breakfast – no one except a newspaper publisher, and he is fair game.

Ellen had recently finished a three-year run with the hit show *Front of the Line*. She had never missed a performance, and now she wanted some time away from the lights. She'd read about Elgin in a magazine article and she and her father had visited the area a few years earlier.

"I've been talking with a local real estate person, and I'm very interested in a house on Lawford Lake," she told me. "Are you familiar with that?"

"Sort of, Ellen – I live on Lawford Lake. Who has the listing, Evergreen Real Estate?" I said, knowing that I was right.

"Exactly. Gee, everyone knows everything up there, don't they?" She laughed.

"They do, Ellen, but not many know of this listing. I do, because you would be my next-door neighbor, although we'd be almost half a mile apart," I said.

I wondered what Ellen's husband would do up here. He might be connected to Broadway in some form or another, or perhaps he was living off of her.

"Well, Ellen, if you want to know about the house, it's a gem," I said. "The elderly couple who used to live there, the O'Conners, have moved to Florida. He was some sort of hotshot at MIT before he retired. It was their getaway. They moved up here, winterized the place, poured tons of bucks into it. Can't say much for the neighborhood, though," I added.

"I was hoping to come up this weekend and see it," said Ellen. "I would take the train to Brattleston, Barrettboro, what … –"

"Brattleboro," I said, cutting her off. "Two trains each direction every day. I ride it all the time."

"Brattleboro, of course," she said. "How do I get from Brattleboro to Elgin? I'll rent a car, but do I do that in Brattleboro or Elgin? And if in Elgin, how do I get there from Brattleboro?"

"You can't get from Brattleboro to Elgin. You're talking about the sticks here, and public transportation doesn't exist. But I'd be happy to pick you up."

"Oh, no, you don't have to do that," she replied.

"It's no problem, I do it all the time. It's a service we provide to all of our new readers," I said.

Thus began my relationship with Ellen Rollins.

I met her in Brattleboro and took her to Elgin's one and only motel. She had never married. Her whole life had been consumed by New York theater. But Ellen was a savvy woman. She knew that there was much more to life than crowds, applause and notoriety. She yearned for space and solitude, and she was ready for something new in her life.

On her second trip to Elgin she stayed at my house, in Missy's room. We talked a lot about whether she should buy the O'Conner place next door, but it sold before she could even make an offer.

Within two or three months, Ellen's life had undergone a dramatic change. She now made frequent trips to New Hampshire from New York. I invited her to stay with me as long as she wished, and we became very fond of one another. She had eluded the New York media, and I kept her under wraps at my end. One day Ellen suggested that we go into Elgin for dinner. This would be our first public appearance in the almost three months that we had been together. We discussed the ramifications of what would happen when she was spotted in Elgin. We agreed we'd deal with that if and when it happened.

Surprisingly, we weren't spotted until our sixth or seventh outing. Well, certainly we were spotted the first time she visited New Hampshire, but no one interrupted us for a long time, and that spoke volumes about the civility of this wonderful town. By this time we'd known each other for almost eight months, and the possibility of marriage had cropped up. We'd been to Cleveland to visit Phil, who had gone into private practice. And Missy had been to Elgin twice. She and Ellen really connected.

Ellen was no longer in the spotlight and she was loving it. I thought at first that a few months away from the adoration of the masses and she'd want to get back into the limelight. But she reveled in the solitude and tranquility of living on our lake. She could shop in Elgin, and no one would bother her. She could go to the local movie house, and no one would bother her. People approached her for an autograph only rarely and she always obliged. The autograph was truly given in appreciation and not as a duty.

Ellen's father spent the holidays with us, as did both kids. It was a glorious time. We were engaged on Christmas Eve, and planned for a May 2nd wedding. Ellen wanted to be married at the house. It wasn't going to be a tiny wedding. "I am only doing this once," she declared, "and I want to do it right."

She turned out to be very proficient with a camera and she was soon taking pictures for the paper. She loved joining in the editorial meetings and getting photo assignments. How she put up with Chris Bourbon's shenanigans is beyond me, but he taught her how to process film, how to use multiple lenses, filters, and film, and how to compose a shot.

Our relationship could not have been scripted better. She had the softest blonde hair I had ever touched and an equally soft heart. Ellen was connected with the world. That connection had been on sabbatical while she did her New York bit, but she wanted it back and she was going to get it. We connected on so many planes. Our differences were minor. I loved professional sports, she couldn't have cared less. She loved museums, I could live without them. We both loved music, theater and reading. We enjoyed outdoor sports such as cross-country skiing, hiking, canoeing and backpacking. We both loved dogs. And as the months wore on, we learned how much we both loved each other.

Ellen thought I worked too long and too hard and I promised to pull back. I loved my work, but now it was time to love my new wife.

* * *

Bill Blanchard called the day the Sportstown story broke. "Want a poll, Ed?" he said.

Several years earlier I had asked Bill if he would poll the clientele at his little store about a proposal that was before the town planning board. When the results of Bill's unscientific poll came in, they were very similar to the final vote at Town Meeting. I'd asked Bill for a poll several times since, and it's turned out that his clientele were a very accurate bellwether group for getting the sense of the community. Bill agreed to give the results of his poll only to the *Eagle* and we were free to use them however wanted.

This time Bill was initiating a poll.

"Sure, Bill, that would be interesting," I said.

"I can give you an unofficial poll right now," said Bill, "based on what little I have heard so far today."

"What's that, Bill?" I inquired.

"It's about time that Joleen Spark stood up for herself, but you guys sensationalized the story just to sell papers," Bill said.

It was amazing. Everyone in town knew this creep was pummeling his wife, yet when they saw it in print, they blamed us. It was as if we were responsible for making this hitherto rumor become true.

Bill was trying to let me know that a lot of people were behind us on the story, but weren't prepared to hand us any freedom-of-the press award. "Let's poll Sportstown, Bill, and we'll let the Spark thing work its own course," I said.

119

We faxed a copy of the Sportstown story to John Howard in Florida. John didn't have a fax in Florida and he asked us to send it to a local Merrill Lynch office down there and he'd pick it up. He called that afternoon to say how pleased he was with the story. He wished he had been a little more positive about the company remaining in Elgin, but acknowledged that the decision might not be his to make. Sally's sidebar also received praise from Howard. He volunteered that the *Globe* and four or five other papers had been trying to reach him all day, but the Elgin office was not giving out his Florida number. "If they want it, Ed, they can find it just like your guy did," said John. "How did he get it, anyway?"

"That's a trade secret, John." I laughed, damned certain that I wasn't going to tell him that the kid at the airstrip had been our "Deep Throat."

That was good news, because if anyone wanted to carry a story about the Sportstown sale, their only source of information, right now, was the *Elgin Eagle*, and any respectable newspaper would attribute the *Eagle* as its source. It wasn't a big deal, and the public didn't give a damn one way or the other, but to our staff it *was* a big deal. They looked at attribution as having another paper eating out of our hand. It didn't happen often, but when it did, it was a real morale booster. There was a downside to such recognition, too. Every time one of our reporters was mentioned in a major metro daily, another silver bullet was slipped into his or her resume cartridge belt, and those bullets would be expended during some future job search.

Four or five people called and said they were canceling their subscriptions over the Doc Spark piece. They never do cancel, but it makes them feel good to make the threat. It's a good barometer as to how a story touches nerves. Four or five irate calls is a very high number for us. There probably is some sort of formula we could apply to extrapolate the degree of disapproval. But one thing was certain, the story had touched nerves.

The following month, the Spark case was going to be heard in a court in Nashua, because the local judge was a friend of Spark and had to recuse herself. The week after that, the politically appointed judge in Nashua basically slapped Spark's wrists and told him not to do it again. When John called, the judge tried like hell to avoid the call, but John got him late one afternoon and he said something to the effect that *"this guy has patients*, and jail time would be detrimental to Spark's patients."

This became fodder for an editorial about meting out justice according to profession. The Nashua paper picked up the editorial and reprinted it. This, in turn, elicited a snippy letter from the judge. That letter launched a second editorial, which again, was picked up by the Nashua paper. No second letter arrived from the hack judge.

About two weeks later, a huge document arrived from Spark's legal gurus in Worcester. It was a scary-looking document. Page after page outlined what a terrible newspaper we were and showed how we had a "pattern of persecution." I couldn't believe that I owned a newspaper that was capable of such heinous things.

Our attorney dismissed it as nothing more than an attempt to get a quick settlement – an effort to slam us financially. They still hadn't sued, he pointed out, this was just making some noise. I deemed it marking the territory. The libel-hotline attorney said basically the same thing – they have nothing. But I was bothered by our attorney's apparent willingness to look at a settlement. The argument was that though we would likely prevail, a settlement would be paid from my insurance, less deductible. If we fought, we might win, but we'd still have to pay that deductible.

What a sorry state of affairs is the legal system in this country.

I wasn't settling with anyone. If Spark wanted a fight, he had one. I just hoped that Joleen Spark lived to see the outcome.

We sent back the bundle of legal documents wrapped in a trash bag. It was probably a little too subtle for Spark's sharks to pick up, but I felt damn good doing it.

About four weeks later was the annual hospital ball. I was on the hospital board and couldn't get out of going. Ellen was going to go with me and make her first big public appearance in Elgin, but her father had a mild stroke the day before the meeting and she rushed back to Connecticut to be with him.

Missy was in town for a few days and volunteered to be my date. I couldn't have been more pleased, never mind that Missy had to dash down to Boston to get something to wear. And of course I would foot the bill.

Holy cow, what a bill! But what a delightful outfit she picked out. When we left the house that night I couldn't have been more proud of my daughter.

The Hospital Ball Committee had done a marvelous job decorating the Town House with an autumn theme. The weather cooperated, a cool, crisp fall evening with a full harvest moon. They even had valet parking although the valets didn't seem to be old enough to drive. Nonetheless, I wanted Missy to have an opportunity to make an entrance, so I drove up and turned my Wagoneer over to a kid who hadn't reached puberty. Missy stepped out of the car, adjusted her full-length cape, and sauntered elegantly up the stairs of the Town House.

I spent much of the night introducing Missy around. I was amazed at how many people she knew. Her years of volunteering at the hospital had acquainted her well with this crowd, and she knew as many people as I did.

The music was great, Missy was lovely, and when she and Dr. Todd Fenton took the floor to do a fast dance, they had the floor to themselves. It wasn't that others were unwilling to dance fast, it was just that Missy cut such a stunning profile that all anyone could do was sit there and watch. She had such a great time that we stayed longer than I normally would.

On the way home we discussed people we had met, who looked good and who looked ridiculous. Missy asked me if I had bought Doc Spark a drink. We laughed. "Dad, I'd be willing to bet that the Spark lawsuit will be dropped," she remarked.

I told her that I didn't think it would. "The guy has revenge on his mind, Missy."

"He also has a series of other batterings in his past. I had a brief chat with him tonight *at the bar* and I reminded him that every one of them will be brought out if there was a trial. And I told him that those batterings would include those of Joleen, and perhaps others."

"What others?" he had snapped.

"Dr. Spark, we're learning more about you every day," she retorted.

She was good at reading expressions and eyes, she said, and when she mentioned 'others,' his face told it all. There definitely had been others, she was certain. The guy wasn't married until he was thirty-three years old, so she concluded there must have been many women in his life before Joleen. Now he was wondering if I'd made contact with them.

"How do you know he wasn't married until he was thirty-three?" I said.

"I looked it up. I told you the day this story broke that I would personally come back and prosecute the creep if you wanted." She smiled, then added, "But this case will never come to trial because Spark doesn't want those 'others.' He's toast, Dad." She snapped her fingers.

In early December, the Spark stooges made one last feeble attempt to extort a settlement, but we refused. I would have sent that reply back in a trash bag too, but instead I sent it back in a plain manila envelope with a return address that read M. Remington.

Missy, you're a tiger.

Chapter Eight

Things were humming at the *Eagle*. The employee mix was excellent, the work ethic was exceptional, and everyone was committed to producing a top-quality product. But I still sensed that something was missing, and that was troubling. We had basically dismissed the *Banner* as a competitor, and now had our sights set on the *Arnett Messenger*, a daily newspaper in the thriving metropolis of Arnett, some twenty miles due north of Elgin. The *Messenger* was probably our most significant competition, not so much for the news product, but for advertising dollars.

The Arnett paper was in a perfect business position. It had no print competition other than a couple of local throwaways. It was picked at by several local radio stations, but any newspaper worth its salt can overcome market-share pressure from broadcast media. But the *Messenger* wasn't worth its salt. It was a rather wimpy paper, given to responding to its readers' whims. It was usually the first to embrace the latest political fad, trend, or avenue of opportunity. Politically, the publishers were consistently for whoever looked like the winner. They heavily favored opinion from the right, but often stumbled over themselves in the rush to embrace an apparent winner, regardless of political slant. If ever there was a demonstrative case of complacency brought on by lack of competition, the *Messenger* was it.

Six of the twenty-two towns claimed as its circulation area were also covered by us. The *Messenger* coverage was lazy and listless, however. Its idea of reporting on a selectmen's meeting was to call the chairman and publish whatever he or she said. This, naturally, produced nothing more than black-and-white spin control. No controversy, no conflict, everything happy in Happyville. So when our reporter actually attended a meeting and reported what happened, our story often bore no resemblance to the *Messenger's*. And the material the *Messenger* was omitting was the material that selectmen, boards or committees considered controversial. Thus, when the *Eagle* did report it, we were branded as a sensationalist yellow rag. That label didn't bother me much. What I did find disconcerting was the fact that many people bought into that argument even though they had no interest or even desire to know what was going on in their local governmental bodies.

One such incident involved an official in Rutner, a tiny community located midway between Elgin and Arnett. Although its population was small, Rutner had an abundant share of heavy hitters. With its plentiful natural resources and scenic vistas, Rutner real estate was among the most sought-after in the state. Almost half of the population were summer people. The rest were captains of industry past and present. Through snob zoning it shed undesirables like raindrops from a freshly waxed car. The town government's rules and regulations meant nothing until the pedigree was perused.

Kurt Strongman covered the happenings in Rutner. He didn't attend every town meeting but his persistence outnumbered all other media probably ten to one. Kurt had the lay of the land.

Shad Irolo, a descendant of an old-line Rutner family, was ready to subdivide the family estate. The Irolos had made it big during the textile era, but a couple of generations of drunks had pretty much consumed the family fortune. Shad and his brothers finally broke the mold of Irolo worthlessness, but the damage had been done. Despite Shad's valiant and notable management of a large lumberyard in Arnett, the taxes on the family homestead finally outstripped his ability to pay.

The Irolo brothers had over twelve hundred acres to dissect. Their plan was to slice off two hundred acres for development into ten and twenty-acre lots. In short, it would have virtually no negative impact on Rutner. In fact, it would add twenty new tax-paying units to the town coffers. But Shad made a major error right out of the chute. He retained his Dartmouth classmate, Ben Gerrard, as his attorney. Gerrard lived in Greenland, a small village north of Arnett. He practiced in Arnett, basically doing family and corporate law work.

In Rutner, however, everyone dealt with Peterman, O'Keefe and Williams, an old-line Concord law firm. All the firm principals had Rutner attachments and all were members of the esteemed Rutner Country Club, a true good-old-boys club. If things didn't pass muster in the men's locker room of the Rutner Country Club, they simply weren't going to fly.

Such was the case with the Irolo application. Within weeks of submission, it was starting to become ensnared in a web of bureaucratic bullshit. Kurt spotted it; even predicted it, in fact. As soon as the Irolos hit their first wall, Kurt was quoting chapter and verse from the Rutner master plan which indicated that the Irolos were indeed playing by the rules of the town. Such alert reporting, however, stood alone, because it was never echoed by the *Arnett Messenger* which, being a daily newspaper, naturally had more credibility than our little podunk weekly.

"They are clearly in violation of their own laws," Kurt noted, "so watch now, they will concoct a whole new interpretation of the law."

"What's Ben Gerrard's take on this?" I asked. "He's representing Irolo, why isn't he squawking?"

"He will," said Kurt. "Ben is never afraid to speak up. He's just waiting for the best time."

The problem with waiting until the best time in Rutner is that it may never materialize. The rules were written by the town counsel, they were interpreted by the town counsel, and they were enforced by the town counsel. And the rules had no shelf life. They were changed, amended, reinterpreted, and ignored purely at the whim of the Rutner inner circle. It had been that way for decades.

Through the *Eagle* reporting, though, some Rutner residents were beginning to show their discontent. Six months ago, the selectmen had refused to produce minutes of one of their meetings. Kurt leaned on them. They refused to return calls and failed to respond to a written request. We went public with their stonewalling and lo and behold, a couple of letters to the editor in support of our position arrived. This was a very strong indicator that there was unrest in Rutner. I didn't recall ever receiving a letter to the editor from anyone in Rutner about anything. Suddenly two showed up inside of ten days. So we felt we were plowing some new, quite possibly favorable turf.

About four weeks after the Irolos' initial request for a zoning ruling, the planning board convened and immediately went into an executive session. This was a procedure whereby committees and boards could discuss sensitive matters such as personnel, salaries or legal concerns. It is an okay law on the surface but more often than not, it is used to circumvent public accountability. Executive sessions, which we always referred to as "secret sessions," were more and more becoming the rule rather than the exception. We were spending an inordinate amount of time trying to get public officials to tell us what the hell was going on in their town or within their specific areas of jurisdiction.

There was no reason in hell why the Rutner planning board needed an executive session to discuss the Irolo application. Kurt put forth a vocal protest the minute it was called. He stayed around for two and a half hours until the session ended. By law, the board must then reveal what transpired. Their response was exactly twenty-six words long. "The board discussed the application by Irolo, et al. to subdivide their property. No decision was reached and the item was tabled until next month's meeting."

Kurt raised holy hell. Their meeting was illegal, he informed them, and so was the report. They ignored him.

The following morning Kurt and I decided that we needed to demonstrate to Rutner that we meant business. I called the publisher of the *Arnett Messenger,* Tim Devine, and asked him if he knew what had happened at the planning board meeting. He didn't, so I gave him a blow-by-blow account and invited him to join us in a dual "Freedom of Information Request" directed both to the attorney general of the State of New Hampshire, and to the county attorney. If we could get the county guy involved, we could get things rolling within a day or two. Dilly-dallying with the state AG might go on for months. I'd go at the County Attorney first and if he clutched – which he probably would – then we'd jerk the AG's chain.

Devine said he'd talk to his legal counsel and get back to me. This was a typical *Arnett Messenger* response. They never made any sort of decision without studying or analyzing it to death.

I hung up the phone to Devine and told Kurt to pump out a Freedom of Information request to the Haskell County attorney.

"It's a waste of time," said Kurt, "but maybe he'll come through on this one."

"I'm afraid you're right, but it would sure be a time saver if he'd rule for us."

"He won't."

"Let's try."

We got a half win from the Haskell County DA. He ruled that the report was illegal, but declined to rule the meeting itself illegal. We had, however, demonstrated to Rutner that the *Elgin Eagle* was on their case.

The day the ruling came down, Tim Devine at the *Messenger* called and said that his people had decided that it wasn't worth the expense to file the request. This super-cautious approach was putting the *Messenger* into a stall. It was just a matter of time before it came crashing down to earth.

Expense? It cost us one fax and we had it wrapped up in seventy-two hours.

* * *

It was April Fool's Day, and by the end of the day, I didn't need a calendar to know that. I was turning the key in the lock of the office when I heard the phone ringing. I knew it was going to be another early morning classified ad placement because most classified ads are conveniently called in when our classified department (Lana) isn't at work. If this call had been five minutes later, Lana would have handled it, but it was my call to answer so I rushed over to nearest phone, grabbed a classified input form and answered the phone. "Eagle Classifieds, how may I help you?"

"Is that you, Ed?" said a voice.

"Who's this?" I asked.

"It's Deb, Debora Kennedy. How are you, Ed?"

"Hey, Ducky," I said. Her full name was Debora Underwood Kennedy, and we'd made her initials into a nickname. "Where are you? What are you doing? Are you ready to come back?"

Ducky was one of my best reporters ever, straight out of Syracuse with more worldly common sense than anyone I have ever known at her age. All through college she had volunteered for various organizations in and around Syracuse. In the summer, she found career-enhancing, financially lucrative employment. She had been a waitress, file clerk in a law office, an assistant librarian, a production assistant for ESPN, and an honor student at Syracuse. A journalism major, she shot out some resumes and we hired her ten minutes into our first and only interview. Eighteen months later, when she left to join the *Lowell Sun*, it was like someone pulling out one of your good teeth. The very fact that they are extraordinary employees cements the next step – they will be grabbed up by newspapers that can pay more and offer a better path for advancement.

"I only have a minute, Ed. Yesterday at a hearing here in Boston, a woman involved on a drug charge suddenly started chirping like a songbird to the media as the gendarmes as she exited the courthouse. I was part of the press scrum that was tagging along so I didn't hear everything. But one thing did catch my ear. The woman started complaining about how unfair it was that law enforcement was picking on innocent people like her and ignoring what was going on right under their noses. Then she blurted out something about doing deals with cops in such and such and such and such, and in Elgin, New Hampshire. I don't know if there's anything to it, Ed, but the Elgin mention certainly got my attention."

"Mine too, Duck. What's her name?"

"Hang on, Ed, I've got it in my notes here. OK, here it is, Linda Parlagen ... Crap, it's one of those long Italian names, Parlenge ... no, no, scratch that, different hearing. The name is Donna Lemoine, and she's from Lowell."

"Thanks so much, Duck. Keep your ears open and we'll do the same."

"Law enforcement is all over this," she added. "I think she has a lot of information to share, and they'll tease it out of her."

"Thanks again, Duck. Come on up and see us sometime, the sooner the better. Are you sure I can't sell you a classified ad?"

My notes from the phone call were virtually illegible. I transcribed them into a separate computer file as best I could. To camouflage the file from any surfing eyes within our news room, I gave it the innocuous name, "Donna L," for Donna Lemoine or Donna from Lowell. I often used code file names, but often the code was so esoteric that I couldn't find it again. So I added the file name in a couple of different directories in the hope that I might be able to retrieve it. "Donna L – Donna L – Donna L," I murmured as I typed it over and over.

Holy crap, could this be Officer Sauer's "Donal?"

* * *

There was an orderly flow to the routine at the *Eagle* on Wednesdays, the day before the paper hit the newsstands. Because we meticulously tracked our progress throughout the week, on Wednesday morning we had a pretty good understanding as to where things stood. But the news doesn't know, or care, about deadlines. It happens when it happens, an explosive in the middle of the Wednesday countdown. Tensions on the part of some staffers were much higher than others because when it all came roaring toward the final funnel, there had to be a sense of orderliness in order to get it through. Humor was the shield to deflect anxiety, but even that had to be somewhat nuanced. Roars of laughter in one corner didn't go down well with others who were doing their best to control the process and move it forward.

One of the downsides of a weekly paper is that the reporters are often raw and untested, and their ability to deal with deadline discipline is shaky. Their life experiences often prevent them from seeing potential roadblocks in the path of taking their story from beginning to end. A good editor can quickly take the pulse of a new reporter and apply the needed pushes and shoves in order to accomplish the goal for a given week, at the same time improving the newcomer's skill set.

The weekly editorial meeting was much more than just assigning stories. It was an opportunity for reporters to ask questions about approach, history, or potential roadblocks. Karen and I had a perfect double-pronged approach that allowed us to inject possible takes on an assignment without the reporter feeling directed from on high. Karen in particular put forth ideas in such a way that a reporter felt it was his or hers. We often sent reporters out of the editorial meeting with multiple mental sticky notes that saved reporters a lot of wasted energy developing a story.

Much of our success came in a long string of great hires. This was Karen's strong suit. She only misfired a couple of times in her hiring of new reporters. She read body language like a seasoned trial lawyer, and her ability to read between the lines of a resume was uncanny. Anyone Karen interviewed was probably good *Eagle* material – she didn't waste time with unqualified applicants. My faith in Karen usually led me to interview only applicants whom Karen thought were valid prospects.

Out of respect to the applicant, and to facilitate our time, we agreed that if Karen wanted me to talk with someone it would be on the same day as she conducted the initial interview. This kept applicants from having to schlep into Elgin twice. It also meant that on the day of the interview, I had to set my schedule up in such a way that I could continue the interview process if we had a live one.

In the days before our computerized typesetting and page layout were on site, Wednesday afternoon was like a powder keg. The tensions climbed as late afternoon approached. Our phalanx of proofreaders were all now in the room and every strip of copy was being read and reread. We prided ourselves on the accuracy of our newspaper and much of that was because of this dedicated group of "comma cops," women who descended on the building each Wednesday. Any mistake was labeled with a sliver of dayglow tape, the correct line was written out on a sheet of paper, and after ten or fifteen lines were on the page the typesetters would churn out the corrected goods and run the whole sheet through the waxer. Then the production people would trim out each line and carefully paste it over the line that contained the mistake. There were hundreds of such fixes each week, and the system worked great as long as calm prevailed.

At 6:00 p.m., we felt that we had rounded the final turn, and down the stretch we came. Everyone knew his job and if someone wasn't involved in this final run he got the hell out of the room. There were lots of moving pieces in play and everything had to work. A typesetting machine that suddenly died was a major crisis, but we could and did work around it. An addition to a story or a late ad royally screwed things up because the jigsaw puzzle of laying out the whole paper was suddenly out the window. But through years of experience we had learned how to build various elements into the design so that such changes could be accommodated.

I loved that tension. It was the battle of the deadline and it happened fifty-two times a year. Each week was a small war, and the resources and troops had to be deployed in such a way that they all came together at a precise point in time. Watching our people operating as a cohesive team was a thrill that never got old.

At 9:00 p.m. the completed pages – the boards – had been pasted up and counted and were secured in a large box. It was time to deliver them to our printer. Two separate teams carefully counted the pages (now labeled the *boards*) in the box, because if one page is missing, the paper can't be printed. We actually did that once and the result was the *Elgin Eagle* had two drivers traveling down the highway about three miles apart. One was carrying twenty-seven pages to the printing plant, the other was carrying one. The plant was forty-four miles away.

Sally, who had volunteered to do that night's run, asked if someone else could do it. She felt lousy, and looked it too.

"I'll find someone, Sally," I said. "Go home and recharge those batteries."

I often did the run to the printer myself because I loved the printing end of the weekly war. I drove our large three-axle box truck to the printer and waited until the paper was printed and then brought the whole load home. If someone else delivered the boards, he or she just dropped them off. At 3:30 a.m., another driver from Elgin would crank up our truck and head out to pick up the finished press run.

At nine o'clock I headed out the door and at 9:55 p.m. I walked into the printing facility, five minutes early. The lead pressman, Mojo, met me halfway between the door and the press. "You're early, but it don't mean yer gonna get the finished product any earlier," he said, pleased to spar with a customer.

"I would hate for that to happen, Mojo. It would totally screw up my routine."

I wandered around the press room for a few minutes and then headed back to the truck for a few minutes of sleep. It would be several hours before the presses started to roll for this edition, and that was the moment I loved. The work of all our people, acting together for the past seven days, was locked into the gigantic six-unit press. Web printing basically involves threading the paper through all the units, then turning on the presses and *laissez les bons temps rouler*. Let the good times roll.

The most pleasant sound of the week was the warning bell that rang seconds before the presses started to roll, making sure that no one had an arm or shirttail near the huge revolving drums because that really screws things up.

Slowly, like a giant locomotive pulling out of the station, the presses begin to turn. Gradually, they go from a grind to a hum and eventually everything is rolling at the proper speed and white paper is shooting out the end of the press line. Then a switch is thrown and the paper makes contact with the printing rollers. The ribbon of white paper springs to life as images are transferred, offset, to the paper. It's like watching a birth and I never tire of it. To see the first copies of our paper come rolling off the end of the press is priceless. And those first few copies, in fact many early copies, are pitched into the recycle bin while all the press units are again calibrated to ensure that the printing is perfect. It is always triumphant. It is approaching the close of another weekly chapter of the *Eagle*, and at that point we are already about eight hours into the next chapter.

Dennis was ready to roll with the Donna L. link. Based on Duck's call, we believed that Donna L. led back to our chief. But this was probably going to involve the layers of lawyers and courts, and then it would most likely be lateraled to whatever law-enforcement agency wanted to deal with a scumbag police chief in Elgin, New Hampshire. Given the amount of money involved and the fact that the drugs and money crossed state lines, the information might rise to an even higher level. Sorting all that out was the court's problem; we'd just follow the lead that had first been given to me behind the Value Foods store.

We knew that Donna L. had not been incarcerated, yet. But was she accessible? A quick call, (well, relatively quick), to the Boston court revealed that her court date was several weeks away.

"I wonder if your former reporter could contact her before that and see what she has to say," said Dennis. That pleased me to no end. It told me that Dennis had this in proper perspective as far as time was concerned, and it also was a good use of potential resources.

In the grand scale of things, we were just a tiny little sliver in the vast media universe, and our pool of investigative reporters consisted of none. Yes, we had people capable of asking the right questions and doing excellent follow-up, but we didn't have the luxury of assigning someone to a story and ignoring everything else. An auto accident in Elgin and a new auto-body shop in Rutner could be back to back in the weekly news queue of any of our reporters.

Dennis disappeared to see if he could contact Duck in Lowell in the hope that she might be able to open some communication with Donna L. If we could get a head start without having to wade through the court process, we'd move much faster and retain what we were sure was our exclusive position.

It was a rainy, foggy, cold March day and I was determined to make the next series of meetings as brief as possible. Every Thursday afternoon we held three separate staff meetings. The first, at 2:00 p.m., was with the editorial staff and consisted of a review of the current issue and a discussion about what was coming up for the next issue. There were ongoing stories such as new housing developments, civic improvements, etc., and there was the usual group of meetings of various boards and committees among the fourteen towns we covered. There were always requests to cover various art stories, and "art" was often loosely defined. Finally, we had feature stories, items that had come to our attention that propelled them beyond the usual. Overlying all of that was the usual content of sports, obituaries, police logs, real estate transfers, schedules of community events, and opinion.

Some thirty-six percent of our readers immediately turned to the sports section, the most highly read section of the paper. Second was the obituaries, followed by the police log. But we didn't pay a lot of attention to those statistics. Feedback from our readers demonstrated that our weekly newspaper was thoroughly consumed. And that was our mission – to provide a weekly supply of information, much of which they wouldn't find anywhere else.

Each reporter was responsible for X number of our readership towns, plus helping with other sections of the paper. Everyone carried a camera at all times and was supplied with a portable police/fire scanner. We didn't want totally vertical job assignments *because* there were so few of us covering a huge amount of territory. The management task was to keep it all running harmoniously.

Following the editorial staff meeting, I convened the advertising staff meeting. We always scheduled it for late in the day because Thursday afternoon was a prime time for selling ads for next week's edition. It was also the time when our ad reps would burst through the doors of local businesses and proudly show them how great their ads looked in the print. The routine at the ad staff meeting was to evaluate the ads in the current edition and discuss various accounts that were divided among our three sales people. Each has a territory to cover and his or her own approach as to how to sell the *Elgin Eagle*. The ad staff was my hyper group of employees and the meeting usually resembled a carnival run amok. It was generally a short meeting, but it served a very important function in that it allowed the sharing of approaches among the ad staff. And because there were three of them visiting businesses throughout the region, they were often the people to snare the first lead of a potential news story.

"This is a great ad," said Rosemary, my senior ad representative pointing to an ad for a local hardware store. "The placement is even better. What the hell is the Campbell Soup position, Ed? He was pleased he got it, whatever 'it' is."

"You're all too young to remember the *Saturday Evening Post*," I said, "but Campbell Soup had negotiated a permanent placement on page three for their ad. I think it was to be placed right after the first blast of editorial matter, and that was usually page three." I added quickly, "No, I wasn't active in the ad business back then, but when I was, people still referred to the 'Campbell Soup position.'"

The ad staff always had customers requesting special positions, such as page three, opposite the obituaries, next to the police log, etc. But I always advocated that if a newspaper is properly laid out, the reader will find those ads of interest to them. That had been proven over and over again, but it was a tough sell with most advertisers. To counter requests from all advertisers to be in a specific position, we charged an additional fifteen percent of the cost of the ad and only ads of a certain size could request position.

We paid lots of attention to the art and science of newspaper design and layout. Buying a special position in the *Eagle* was not necessary for an ad to be effective. Again, the research had shown that readers would find the ads of interest to them. But they'd only find them if the newspaper was properly laid out and led the readers to those ads. There's nothing a paper can do to make anyone act on that ad, but we did deliver readers to ads throughout the *Eagle*.

"Can we get some better illustrations to use in ads?" said Anita, our newest ad rep. "This stuff is kind of hokey."

Rosemary pointed Anita toward the shelves of books of illustrations behind her and told her that surely she could find something in there, rather than in the generic books that were supplied each month from the Newspaper Art Service (NAS).

"But it takes forever to dig something out of those books. At least the NAS books are indexed."

"What kind of illustration are you looking for?" asked Rosemary.

"Something to do with gardening, planting seeds, and stuff like that," said Anita.

Rosemary turned around and grabbed two books off the shelves. She opened one and flipped through the pages for about five seconds, then did the same with the other book. Like a third-grade teacher she opened each book to drawings of happy gardeners doing their thing.

"You win," said Anita, and a group hug ensued.

They all understood that as each succeeded in selling ads, the paper grew in size, begetting more ads, and larger ones too.

The third meeting of the day involved the entire staff. We scheduled it for 5:00 p.m. because the ad staff was hard at work on Thursday afternoon. At this point everyone was pretty well wrung out and building the old esprit de corps was an uphill slog. But it was important that everyone realize that he was a part of a larger whole. Even our administration and production (typesetting) staff were invited, although they rarely came. I tried to keep this meeting short and found that a plate of crackers and cheese along with a couple of six-packs of beer was an enticement to come.

Chapter Nine

Suddenly the police scanner came to life as a call went out to all Elgin rescue personnel to respond to a reported missing aircraft perhaps near the western summit of Mt. Ralston, a twenty-nine-hundred-foot mountain that abutted Elgin. Normally, all our reporters, at least those with their emergency scanners turned on, would respond from wherever they were when the call came in. This Thursday however, almost the entire editorial staff was in our newsroom, giving us a unique opportunity to quickly establish an attack scheme that might get one or two of them through to the scene before the local gendarmes cordoned off access roads to the mountain. While they were sorting out their logistics, the scanner amped up the response to fire and rescue personnel from four additional towns. This was going to make getting access to the scene even tougher.

Chris, who was listening to the scanner speaker we had mounted in the darkroom, came flying out of the darkroom with his camera bag in tow. He dumped a couple dozen rolls of film on the table for everyone to share. "Get'em while they're hot!" he screamed, and headed for the door.

"Hold on, Chris," shouted Karen. "We have to figure out how we should approach the mountain. How many trails go to the summit on the west side?"

"Three known trails and one abandoned one," said Ken Hipp, our Carlisle reporter. He was one of our home-grown reporters, and he knew lots about Mt. Ralston. "I think we should go to the trailheads of the three known trails. Your trip up will be much faster if you can get in before they're blocked off. Once they are roped off, you will have to try to bushwhack your way up the mountain – not recommended. But there is an abandoned trail, the Meadow Trail, that starts quite a way south and goes almost straight up. About halfway up, it comes within a few hundred feet of the Lone Oak Trail, and that intersection would be well out of sight of the gate blockers at the trailhead."

"I want to help," said Sally, "but I don't know where any of those trails begin."

"I'll take you to the beginning of the Shetland Ridge trail," said Chris.

With Ken's help, Karen assigned each reporter to a different starting point. "Stay out of the way of any rescue efforts, and come back here when you're finished so we can figure out the next step. I'll be here until I hear from each of you." The scrum bolted out the door. "Get back here when you know something!" she screamed in a last desperate effort to keep control over this effort.

"As for you," said Karen, lightly cuffing me alongside my head, "go home and get some sleep and I promise to call you the minute we know something definite." That's how Karen and I worked; she was my senior editor and I wanted her to take the lead.

A plane crash was a high-stakes story, not something that registered on our experience monitor. It could very well be breaking news only for the news organization that got there first. It was going to be replete with lots of confusion on the part of law enforcement as to who had jurisdiction. Mt. Ralston was firmly within the boundaries of Carlisle but the access roads on that side of the mountain began in Ripley, Carlisle, and Tucker, and each cop shop would be anxious to defend its access point. So like many previous intertown occurrences, this had all the potential of being a real small-town showdown.

No sooner had our herd of news hounds scampered out the door than Harriet Leistner waltzed into the office with a classified ad for a free cat. A wealthy family in New York had transplanted Harriet to Elgin twenty-five or thirty years earlier – she just wasn't what they wanted NY society to see. She had a happy view of the world, and always looked as though she'd just gotten up from a long night on a park bench. Her wardrobe consisted of layers upon layers of shirts, sweaters, and skirts, rarely changed, and her smile was infectious. Her flaming red hair had pretty much left the scalp, but when remaining tufts caught the sunlight her head looked as though it was on fire. We always had a great time with Harriet. The town had basically adopted her. Few people knew that, if she wanted, her trust fund would allow her to purchase the whole town.

Harriet was the Elgin "animal lady." Rumor had it that she had at least a dozen cats, a half-dozen dogs, and numerous flying critters in her house. Periodically she came in to take advantage of our policy of running free classified ads for lost and found animals as well as for animals that people wanted to give away. The incongruity of the millionaire heiress taking advantage of a free $3.50 ad was never lost on me, and made me love her a little bit more. She always brought in the animal in question, to verify, I assume, that the critter actually existed.

Seeing Harriet standing there cradling a little black kitten, I was struck by the magnificence of the news business. Within five minutes we'd shifted gears from an ad placement to a potentially disastrous plane crash to a classified ad for an adoptable cat.

"I hate to get rid of her," said Harriet, "but I just don't have room right now. They just keep coming and coming."

"Have you ever thought about having them fixed?" injected Lana. "That way you could avoid the problem of overcrowding."

"I don't believe in contraception," said Harriet.

Lana decided to push this a little further. "Well, it's not really contraception," she said. "It's merely having them fixed with a tiny cut of the knife."

"The Bible is against contraception, and so am I," huffed Harriet. Lana knew it was time to terminate that discussion.

"We'll have the ad in next week's edition, Harriet. You be sure to let us know when the kitty is adopted. What's the kitten's name?"

"Snipper," said Harriet as she turned and left.

Lana buried her face in her sweater, but her chuckles seeped out around the edges.

That layer of levity was needed right then, but I couldn't help thinking that Harriet had just availed herself of our free-ad policy, and now she was heading over to the *Banner* office to place the same ad and hand them four dollars for the privilege.

I got home at 6:30, thirty-six hours without sleep, and a glance at my watch underscored that fact. The adrenaline was fading fast though, and all I wanted was to throw a frozen pizza into the oven, pop open a Heineken's, and hit the hay. Ellen was still in Connecticut with her father. The pop of the cap coming off the beer coincided with ring of the phone.

"Hello?" I growled.

"Is this Ed Remington?" inquired the caller.

"Yes, it is. Who's calling?" I said. All hell was going to break loose if this was a telemarketer.

"John Dempsey, AP New York. I can't reach anyone in our New Hampshire bureau and I was wondering if you can share any information on a reported plane crash in your area this afternoon," said Dempsey. His voice indicated a deadline pressure.

We were all over it, I told him, but had no reports so far. He was hoping for something to feed to the late-evening news programs and I promised to call him the minute I heard something.

Working with major media outlets was always a big deal. It said that people valued our work and it burnished our image as a creditable and professional news organization.

Dempsey's call added to the urgency of what was about to go down, and that meant that I was not about to go down. I wolfed down the pizza, staring at the phone waiting for something to happen. At 8:00 p.m. the phone rang. Chris, our photographer was back in the office as were Sally and David.

"A definite crash," he said. "Rescue crews were just arriving at the scene when I left. No details as to how many were on the plane, et cetera. And access to trails has been cut off."

"How can they be so sure there was a crash?" I said.

"Because a hiker saw the plane fly right over him," said Chris. "And get this, he, the hiker, was lost and had no idea where he was. He was just heading down knowing that eventually he would find a road or house or something. So he wasn't a lot of help in pinpointing the wreck, but he had heard it hit."

"He was probably the only person on the mountain in that weather," I said.

"Who's in charge of the rescue effort?"

"Everyone and their fucking dog," huffed Chris.

"Thanks, Chris. Let me talk to Karen."

"She's across the street grabbing some takeout. I'll have her call you as soon as she returns."

"Tell her I'm on my way back down. Did you get any photos?"

"Yeah, lots of rescue types looking for something to do — nothing great, and all the other rags eventually got there too, but no one got on to the mountain as far as I know," he said.

Bit by bit our story materialized. Ken had used the abandoned trail and found the crash site about six hundred feet from the summit. No rescue personnel were there and two of the three occupants of the plane were still alive, one in the plane and one underneath it. The pilot was dead. Ken was ready to cut across to the Lone Oak trail when he heard the rescue crews coming up. He hollered at them and when they were within range of understanding him, he told them there were three people who were going to have to be carried out and two of them were alive.

Within the next forty-five minutes Ken shot about seventy-five photos, many of which were requested by rescue personnel. No one worried about what Ken was shooting. Most knew that we weren't the *National Enquirer* and that we would exercise good judgment in selecting our photos.

Ken's photo flash gave out about halfway down the mountain. With no more possible shots on his palette, he worked his way to the front of the descending procession and sprinted the rest of the way down.

He burst into the newsroom and in two sentences explained what he had seen. Chris started to drag him to the darkroom to process his shots.

Chris could process the film alone, and I needed Ken to replay what had happened for me. The photos could wait but the AP was champing at the bit for info and, as of that moment, only Ken Hipp had the facts.

I called the AP office.

"John Dempsey, please."

"Who's calling?" said a rude voice.

"The White House," I said, knowing that would cut through the ice quickly.

"Hi, Ed. What's up?" said Dempsey, who was a beat ahead of the switchboard.

I gave John everything we had. I knew he would credit the *Elgin Eagle*, but I asked him if he could insert some language that mentioned Ken Hipp. "I'll give it my best shot, Ed, but the fuse is short here. We only have ninety minutes until air time."

"I fully understand, John. I know you will do what you can."

"I owe you a big one, Ed," he replied and hung up.

I could have negotiated a financial payment from them, but holding a news bargaining chip could be more valuable down the line.

Breaking news from New Hampshire this evening.

A small plane slammed into the side of a mountain.

Miraculously two of the three passengers survived.

The story ran on all three of the major network newscasts. All of them credited the *Elgin Eagle*, and one mentioned Ken by name as being the first on the scene. All of them credited him with being instrumental in leading rescuers to the scene.

When I got home, at midnight, there was Ellen. That was the perfect way to end forty-two sleepless hours. She had seen the evening news and was ecstatic over the attribution to the *Eagle* at the beginning of the newscast.

But I wasn't through yet.

AP New Hampshire also called and asked if they could buy some of our photos. Ken and Chris had already made some prints of their shots and some others for just such purposes. AP said they would have a courier there by 1:30 a.m. When they asked about the cost, I told them there would be no charge but I wanted an attribution that said, "Photo(s) by the staff of the Elgin Eagle."

"The photos will be inside the screen door of the office," I said. "We're going home to bed!"

What a day. I love this business!

* * *

Over the weekend I had some time to think about the massive staff response to the plane crash. We really had seen a great team effort and some sort of recognition was due. Ellen volunteered to become the Minister of Recognition. We decided that we would really amp up the forthcoming Christmas party.

I really liked being a mentor for our young staff. Most of them were fresh out of college, usually journalism majors, very intelligent, and about as worldly as your average puppy. And while they had impressive grey matter, there was still a reckless flame that was difficult to snuff.

When we hired Dave Harrison, he was straight out of the journalism program at Syracuse and was confident that the doors into professional journalism would swing wide open for him. Six months after graduation Dave was still looking for those doors. He had rewritten his resume a dozen times and had a different version, we later found out, tailored for whatever job he was going after.

Under "other interests" the version we got listed leatherwork and reading. I later asked him about the "leatherwork" and he confessed that he made it up because it sounded nonthreatening, but also creative and somewhat industrious.

"What if the interviewer was into leatherwork and started to debrief you on the subject?" I asked.

"I'd have been screwed. I'm not even sure what leatherwork means!"

I assured him that the mention of leatherwork was not key to our hiring him.

About three months after he started to work for us he called me at home one Sunday morning and asked if we could talk. That was usually code for, "I've found a better job."

I told him to meet me at the office at 1:00 p.m.

Dave's reason for talking wasn't about leaving us, it was about hoping that he wouldn't be fired.

"Last night I was driving home from a party and was smoking a joint when I saw the flashing blue lights in my mirror," he said. "I rolled down the window and tried to drive a little farther to allow the smell to exit the car."

When the cop pulled up behind him and Dave suddenly realized that he still had the joint in his hand, "It was too late to toss it out the window, so I ate it," he said.

I burst out laughing. "No salt, no pepper, just a plain joint?"

Dave finished the story. "The cop has to have smelled the weed, but there really was nothing he could do. He shone his flashlight around the interior, but legally he was helpless." He had pulled him over because he had a tail light missing. He also mentioned that his son played for the local Little League team and he knew Dave was the guy who sometimes covered those games.

"Then he let me go."

Dave's concern was that the incident would be conveyed to the police chief, who would pass it along to me. That was not how he wanted the story to unfold.

What's done is done, I told him. He was a jerk for doing what he did, but there was no penalty to pay for the error in judgment. He now could be a target for a future traffic stop, I warned him, and next time they could be armed with a search warrant. Chief Harley would like nothing more than to be able to produce a scalp from an *Elgin Eagle* employee.

"Get the pot out of the Pinto, fumigate the thing, and get that tail light fixed," I told him as I tried to project professionalism over parenting. "I also wouldn't share this story with anyone." The image of a guy chowing down on a lit joint was hilarious.

Much of small-town New England is governed by a board of selectmen or a city council. And the annual town meeting is an institution that will be around for many years. This also holds for many school districts, which are theoretically governed by annual school-district meetings. Usually these meetings grant the school board the budget it requests, but no meeting escapes a hot debate over some miniscule piece of the budget that has lodged in the craw of a vocal attendee.

Such was the case at the preceding night's school meeting. Attendance was impressive, more than four hundred. Add to that another forty or fifty people, mostly students, and we had a crowded high school gym.

In the front row, as usual, sat the four Wise Ones. These were the local self-appointed overseers of the school budget, two men and two women. As a general rule, if there was money about to be spent on anything related to schools, they were against it. That's a pretty broad brush and they did from time to time vote in favor of some expenditure. But as a general rule, these curmudgeons were basically out to kill any increased expenditures for education. None of them had kids in the system – now – and all of them were certain that they knew much more about the ins and outs of education than any professional school administrator.

The school budget was the first item on the agenda. As it was actually below the budget for the preceding year, the four Wise Ones were content, and twenty-two minutes after the meeting was called to order, the $8.9-million dollar budget had been approved.

Next up were additional articles that were to be added to the budget. Some of these were pro forma exercises, such as formally accepting bequests and grants. Some had to do with school-district policy and that would occasionally generate some squirming in certain smaller towns that felt sure they were shouldering more than their fair share.

But the item that created the most interest was a proposal to install an additional fan in the woodworking shop at the high school vocational-education center. It wasn't part of the budget because it had been proposed after the deadline, so it appeared as a separate article to be voted on by those in attendance.

Sally was our lead reporter at the meeting. While the routine articles were being voted on, she was in a remote corner of the bleachers composing her story on our new TRS-80 laptop computer. People kept interrupting her in order to get a look at the tiny computer and, being Sally, she did a complete show-and-tell.

Then the woodworking shop fan issue came up: Article 16 out of a list of 23.

I make a habit of writing times on my agenda for the meeting, and I jotted down 8:32 p.m. as the start of the discussion.

"This is an issue of health and safety for the students," said the Ripley member of the school board. "And I think all will agree that health and safety come first and foremost where our children are concerned." I heard echoes of "God Bless America" coursing through my brain.

"There ain't noth'n unhealthy about a little sawdust," hollered Arlie Wolf, a crusty old Yankee who sold cordwood and goat cheese.

"Would the speaker please approach the microphone and identify yourself and your town?" said the meeting moderator.

"Arlie Wolf, everybody knows me," he hollered in reply.

The moderator repeated his request and, with the encouragement of some of those sitting around him, Wolf reluctantly made his way to the microphone. He flipped the switch on the barrel of the mic and gave his name and town. He'd inadvertently turned the mic off rather than on, so people began shouting at him to turn it on. The advice was coming from all over and Arlie, who didn't hear well, was totally flummoxed as to why people were suddenly yelling at him. A benevolent soul across the aisle, Joe Day, got up and turned on the mic that Arlie clutched like a death grip on a crappie.

"Is this goddam thing on?" he shouted. The sound system gave a screeching feedback which was drowned out by the laughter.

He was told to give his name and town but by now his finger had again turned the mic off. He gave his name and again the crowd began to yell at him. These were intended to be supporting yells with helpful information like, "Turn the mic on!" Arlie was beginning to feel like the lonely gladiator in the ring looking up at a sea of downward-pointing thumbs.

Again the helpful soul reached up and flipped the switch to ON just as Arlie yelled, "What a bunch of shit."

The whole gymnasium was in a state of joyous uproar. Even the moderator had to take a few breaths before he could call the meeting back to order.

When debate on the fan finally began, it lasted for just over an hour. Many people enlightened the crowd with their experiences in their woodshops while others injected everything they could think of that might ring a safety chord. The article finally passed via a voice vote and we could move on to the final six articles.

The Arlie show worked to our benefit because even though Sally was on deadline, we knew the *Banner* reporter was through for the night, because their press time was even earlier than ours. They had left before the woodshop article came up. But the debate pushed us to our deadline precipice. We had to get this issue to bed within the next hour so it could be on the newsstand in the morning. Once the fan issue was voted on, eighty-five percent of the crowd left. Everyone had had enough, and the final six articles were dispatched within thirty minutes.

Sally dashed out with the eighty-five percent after she asked John to hang around to the end and grab a few reactions. Having the new little computer was a huge boost for productivity, and Sally's story was filed minutes after she arrived back in our office.

Ellen and I chatted with a few folks after the meeting and then headed outside. There in the parking lot standing beside his pick-up truck Arlie was holding court with about twenty people, still railing about the stupid mic. He'd obviously had several pops in the previous half-hour or so and the parking lot suddenly turned into Hyde Park Corner America.

Ellen dashed over to our car and grabbed our vintage Speed Graphic camera. This was an ancient camera with the bellows that cranked out, and was rarely used nowadays except in studio portrait settings. But we had ours outfitted with a Polaroid adapter that enabled us to shoot four-by-five black and white photos and bypass the darkroom. The quality suffered a little, but the ability to grab a late photo was more than offset by the slight reduction of quality. The camera, with its cumbersome flash attachment, was a significant piece of hardware and we rarely used it. When there was a need for a last-minute photo, this was the only way to go.

Ellen grabbed one perfectly focused shot. It ended up on page one below the fold. It showed Arlie with one hand outstretched toward heaven, an intense look in his eyes, and a chain with about five thousand keys hanging from his belt. On the back bumper of Arlie's truck was a bumper sticker announcing, "Red Sox Fan." But Arlie's canvas jumpsuit blocked out most of the sticker so all you could see was the word "fan."

On the way home I remarked on how lucky we were that Ellen had the Speed Graphic camera in the car. "I knew we were up against the deadline, that the dark room was not going to be in play, and that something with hundreds of people in attendance might just produce a photo or two."

"Well played," I said.

"Actually, it was in the car because I took it home today to clean the rollers on the adapter. We just lucked out tonight," she said with a laugh.

"I lucked out the day you came into my life," I replied as we raced toward the office.

Elgin has a community cable channel and the guy who owned it had little interest in it other than to supply some tax shelter. However, he did broadcast meetings of the Elgin Board of Selectmen and some meetings of zoning or planning boards. The broadcast was actually on about a thirty-minute delay because it was all shot on VHS tape and when the cartridge was full it was driven out to the building that housed the cable TV equipment. That also meant that every meeting would have unscheduled gaps while the tape was being changed on the stationary camera.

Nothing is quite so boring as watching a fixed camera focused on a meeting, any meeting, anywhere. Covering a meeting is much more than just listening; it is also watching, noticing body language, noting who is there, who leaves, who arrives. All of these tangential factors reflect the totality of the meeting. And that was the gulf that separated the *Elgin Eagle* from the *Banner*. We almost always had one of our reporters or a paid correspondent at select board meetings. We also had live bodies covering various controversial meetings from other governmental entities in the area. That was our mission – to tell our readers what was going on. Sometimes we used our editorial page to put in our two cents worth. But when it came to straight news reporting, I was adamant that we would play it right down the middle. While the *Banner* came across as the house organ for Elgin, we wanted to be known as the *NEWSpaper of Elgin*.

Often, that devotion to reporting *what actually happened* caused mega strife for the paper and our staff. Just as occurred when we reported the Dr. Spark wife-beating incident, we occasionally would get chewed out by local officials or townspeople.

"You're turning into a sensationalist rag," sneered Ed Smith one morning at Freda's. "John Garneau ought to sue your ass."

"Over what, Ed?" I said.

"Portraying him as a bumbling fool, as you do right here," he said, pointing to our story on last night's select board meeting. "That's disgusting."

Garneau, a member of the select board, often let his political beliefs interfere with his town obligations. Usually the other two selectmen let him bloviate and then got on with the business at hand. But last night the issue concerned a significant opportunity for the town to access some substantial matching funds from both state and federal sources.

As the debate unfolded, Garneau went farther and farther out on his political limb. With each advance the other two selectmen gently took him apart. It wasn't hostile or abusive, just an easy demonstration of the fact that Garneau was clueless about the issue. Slowly the limb started to bend and eventually crack.

Prior to the discussion, Garneau voluntarily, and heroically, removed himself from the selectmen's table, saying that he would prefer to address the issue as a citizen. That seemed to suggest that the other two selectmen weren't citizens, but we let that one go.

However, by addressing the panel as a citizen, Garneau was not in the view of the fixed cable TV camera. Viewers could hear him but could only see his profile from behind. Had they been able to see him they would have seen that he was getting lots of on-the-spot coaching from several acquaintances. He had a stack of notes that apparently he hadn't bothered to read. He repeatedly fumbled through the pages, looking for anything to bolster his case. While all of this was out of sight by cable viewers, it was in plain view of the few people in the audience and the only member of the media in attendance – Dave Harrison of the *Elgin Eagle.*

And we reported it all. The *Banner* story, a recapitulation of the cable TV coverage, totally omitted the constant prompting that Garneau needed and was silent on the confusion with his notes. It was written from the point of view of a cable TV viewer. Dave's story gave a blow-by-blow of the meeting without a hint of editorial comment. It discussed the issue and how Garneau's opposition unfolded as it simultaneously imploded.

So, in response to Ed Smith's loud complaint that our coverage was "disgusting," I said, "Were you there, Ed?"

"Nope."

"Well, we were, and we're just reporting what we saw and heard."

No one in the restaurant acknowledged that they heard the exchange, but a quick look around showed everyone fussing with their coffee mug and silverware as they took it all in.

There have been instances over the years where a reporter "rounded out" a story, reporting something that *probably* occurred. But such lapses are the rare exception. There have been some descriptions of after-game celebrations that were fabricated because the reporter had left the game when the local team was ahead twelve to zip and the assumption was that after the victory a good time was being had by all.

We don't tolerate rounding out stories and we don't tolerate reporting, as a fact, something that isn't ironclad: but young reporters, and even a veteran, will occasionally cut that corner.

* * *

Three bears, three stooges, three blind mice – three is a symbolic number in our culture. Ellen was attending her third local kids' baseball game of the week. She was with a friend of hers who had a daughter playing on one of the teams. Ellen always had her camera by her side. There weren't enough kids in Elgin for separate boys' or girls' teams, so whoever showed up was going to be assigned to a team. It made for some fun baseball. Missy had played on one of those teams and at her first time up at the first game of the season, she smacked a triple into left field. She got to third solely due to the hit and not to the usual overthrows from one defender to another. As she pulled up at third, one of her male teammates said, "Wow, she's pretty good – for a girl." Missy heard the remark and I'm certain that if she had still had the bat in her hand that it would have been brought into play.

Ellen decided to grab a few shots in case John could use one in next week's edition. She had covered enough games to know that standing just alongside third base gave a good overview of most of the field as well as being able to see crowds and dugouts (actually benches – Elgin didn't have dugouts or even shelters on these fields).

The sun was setting, which was narrowing the effective range of her camera. She took her final photo and was returning to the bleachers to join our friend when she noticed a shot that "I just had to get."

What Ellen noticed was a ten-year-old boy leaning up against the backstop. In front of him he had both hands on a bat that was resting, barrel down, on the ground. His hat was askew and the uniform showed that he had already seen some action, as evidenced by the dirt on his chest and pants, and emphasized by fact that his left knee was protruding out of a tear in the uniform. Add to that was the dirt smudge on his face and Ellen knew that she was looking at a living, breathing Norman Rockwell painting.

She also knew that if he saw her setting up the shot the spontaneity of the moment would probably poof and vanish.

As she looked through the viewfinder it was evident that the absence of light was going to mask all of the good things that she wanted to show. So she made a decision to push the film. This meant that when the film was developed, Chris would process the film for more time and also increase the temperature of the developing chemicals. This overdeveloping would offset the underexposure of the image. It also meant that everything Ellen had shot earlier on that roll of film was going to be subjected to the same tinkering of the chemicals and would most likely be lost. No problem – this was the shot she wanted.

Her description of getting the shot sounded like something out of the playbook of a great white hunter. "I knew if he saw me taking the shot that he would do something," said Ellen, "and anything other than what he was doing at that moment was going to result in an opportunity lost." So she decided to work her way quickly but casually down the baseline from third towards home.

"Along the way, I pretended that I was taking pictures of the crowd of parents in the third-baseline bleachers. Ever so slightly I worked the camera over to where I had the kid in frame," said the Broadway star turned sports photographer.

But she was still worried that the kid was too far away and that getting him into a decent print was going to involve significant degradation of detail. "So I crept closer and began to worry that I was getting very close to the baseline and I was either going to disrupt the game or get hit by a baseball. I also had no idea what was going on with the game and whether my target would suddenly be bolting onto the field," she said.

There was only one out, so her plan was to wait for the next out and then walk between home plate and the backstop and get a shot of the kid head on. "I couldn't just stop, point, and shoot," she said, "so I switched to my twenty-eight millimeter lens, which would give me a much broader field, and if I had him relatively close to the center of the frame there would be minimum distortion when we cropped and extracted his image from the rest of the print."

She could have lost everything if there had been a double play, but double plays are not routine at this level of the game. As the batter struck out, Ellen launched her journey. Shooting from the hip, she repeatedly fired at the backstop kid. She knocked off seven shots with the subject pretty much centered in the frame in five of them.

The contact sheet of Ellen's shots came up from the darkroom Monday morning. Chris had pushed the hell out of the film and the images appeared to be crisp and clear. When Ellen showed up the buzz started. She had nailed it and immediately I asked Chris how much we could enlarge it. "How much to do want?" he said.

"Full column height," I said, "from the bottom to the top of the page, all twenty-one inches."

"It will make it," said Chris, and he disappeared into his dark hole.

We ran that picture in a full-page house ad, an ad about us. The "Rockwell picture," as we later dubbed it, took up three of the six columns on the page. We cropped the photo so that the only thing the viewer saw was the kid. The remaining three columns were all white space with a little copy block centered in that sea of white. The words said: "If the *Elgin Eagle* doesn't report Johnny Davis's home run – who will?"

That ad was voted the top self-promotion ad in the country that year for all weekly newspapers. In addition to the national recognition, a major film company pledged to supply us free film for the coming year, and the camera maker sent us three cameras that were delivered by a factory representative. He spent four hours showing us the ins and outs of the camera. He took a happy team photo for the company magazine and left. Two minutes later he reappeared with six camera bags. "I had these in the trunk and thought you could use them," he said. "Thanks for the hospitality, you have a great group here." I like to think that the "sense of family" that had developed in our operation had reached out and grabbed the camera tech. The bags were an unexpected surprise and a great way to conclude the day. I sprung for a couple of six-packs and everyone sat around and replayed the camera instructions they had heard that day. The ad and administrative staff had not participated in the camera talk, but they were glad to be included in the impromptu afterglow.

The story didn't end there. I sent the print to a professional film-printing outfit in Dallas and asked them if they could enlarge it to something in the area of eight feet tall. They said they could easily get six feet and I turned them loose. A month later the rolled-up image arrived. It was given to a local painter who laminated it to a piece of plywood, and then put three coats of varnish over the whole thing in addition to a stand to hold it upright.

That "sign" stood in the middle of our newsroom for years. It conveyed our mission to my den of eager young reporters much better than I could. There is a world going on in the fourteen towns we covered and our mission was to report that world, try to explain that world, and in some cases interpret that world. That sounds simple and direct, but establishing that approach was a huge assignment. Affixed to the top of the picture were the ribbon and medal that Ellen was awarded, which echoed the thought that you can be recognized for reporting on life in rural America.

We were in Kansas City the night Ellen won the award. When she returned from the dais with her award in her hand she said, "This is far better than any opening night." The beaming look on her face confirmed that she really felt that way. The MC at the event took his moment at the microphone to enlighten the audience as to the previous Broadway identity of Ellen Remington. Normally this would have bothered me, but it seemed to graft itself nicely onto the camaraderie of the four to five hundred journalists in attendance. The sustained applause confirmed that.

There are hundreds of moments that stand out as memorable, and when they have a poignant component that makes them personal jewels that are carefully packed away in the special places in the memory that are reserved for such instances. Another such moment involved "Mr. Fritz." For a dozen or so years, Walter Fritz had been one of our drivers, who faithfully showed up at 6:00 a.m. every Thursday to drive a seventy-five-mile route to deliver newspapers to thirty-five separate establishments. Not only did he deliver the new edition but he also picked up any unsold copies from the previous week. He would write up a ticket for the papers sold and collect the money before heading out. He never said much and he never missed a Thursday. He even showed up one week with a broken arm and insisted that he could handle the job. Snow or ice on the roads only meant that he would leave home earlier so he'd be waiting at the *Eagle* office when our delivery truck pulled up from the printer. His work ethic was a hundred on a scale of a hundred.

Walt's wife, Emma, accompanied him sometimes, and while they were a really cute couple, I always sort of sensed that Walt would prefer to do his route alone.

We ran a nice obituary when Walt died and the family had a private service. Two days later, Emma came down to the office to ask if she could have some of the return issues of the newspaper that contained the obituary.

"Absolutely, Emma. How many shall I save for you?" I said.

"Well, we have forty-six children, grandchildren, and great-grandchildren. Would forty-six be too many?" she asked with a hint of doubt in her voice.

"Why don't we make it an even sixty, Emma. I don't think your clan is through yet."

Emma giggled, and then broke down. Walt so looked forward to Thursdays delivering the *Eagle,* she told me. He loved getting out and seeing some of the area every week. "Most important," she said, "it gave him a weekly destination, a feeling that he still had something to contribute. And the fact that you always included us in all your *Eagle* get-togethers, like going-away parties and your beautiful Christmas party, made both of us feel that we truly belonged. You've always been nice to us little people."

"You certainly *did* belong, Emma. Walt was family and so are you. Everyone had a job to do and Walt couldn't have done the job any better. And the only little people I know are from *The Wizard of Oz.*"

Emma's "little people" remark stopped me dead in my tracks. It was one of those things that sticks with you forever. Over the years I have relived that moment, and it still saddens me that anyone would feel as if his or her place was beneath any other's. Yes, people can have more money, more things, more stuff, but those are just the ornaments on the tree. The trunk, the core of the tree, is what is important. And I hope, I think, that over the years I have acquired an ability to see that core quickly and clearly.

I made a note to make certain that we gathered up sixty returns the following Thursday. Generally we would bring in the returns, take the best ten, and wrap them up and put them in our archives. We always kept ten or fifteen in a rack in the office for people who had missed the issue. The rest would be pitched into the dumpster. Thursday night when I got home I remembered my promise to Emma, and at 8:30 that night the publisher of the *Elgin Eagle* was dumpster-diving retrieving newspapers. No one saw me but a passing raccoon, which doubtless wondered, "Who's this new guy in the neighborhood?"

As a board member of a national press association and regional press associations, ten to twelve times a year I was either huddling with fellow publishers in and around Boston or,
in the case of the national association, somewhere else. There
were lots of issues to be discussed as they related to the association or perhaps to the entire newspaper business, and at the
end of the day multiple gaggles of publishers always crowded
the local watering holes. One issue that always came up was
obituaries.

Some papers, ours included, ran obituaries for free. The
content came from the funeral director or directly from the
family. The *Banner* had started charging for obituaries,
a practice that soon became standard operating procedure
across most of the newspaper community. I wrestled with
whether or not to charge. The revenue from obituaries would
be an endless stream and a nice addition to the bottom line.
But something was in my craw and it had to do with reading
the obituaries in the *New York Times, Boston Globe*, and other
major metro dailies. The obituaries featured people who had
either led a life of accomplishment or a life of privilege. And
while I fully grasp the fact that the *Times* can't print a full
obituary for the four to five hundred people who die each day
in New York City, I still have an inner voice that asks, "Is the
death of John Smith, the Brooklyn sanitation worker, something that is ignored in exchange for printing a frothy obituary
about some privileged polo player whose sole accomplishment
in life was to spend his trust fund?"

All obituaries are news, and not all news makes it into the
paper. All obituaries are also a public record of a life and in
many cases are the only record that most families will ever
have. Yes, the obituary for Yul Brenner, Simone Signoret, or
Ricky Nelson is going to be of interest to a lot more readers

than the write-up about a local sanitation worker. However, I felt we had a community obligation to chronicle the births and deaths in our area, and we worked closely with the local funeral homes to make that final story an accurate reflection of the person.

Some national funeral directors group put out a form for the bereaved family to fill out. Good funeral directors worked with the family to make sure it was complete and accurate. We always wanted a good picture. This sometimes took some doing, as when we were handed a family reunion photo and told that the deceased was third from the left in the back row! If a funeral director gave us incorrect information it made no difference, we took the hit. Most information coming from the local funeral homes was accurate, but often with noticeable omissions because a part of the deceased's life was something that the family was trying to forget.

If the obituary was about an accountant or engineer, the family would often show up with an eight-page blow-by-blow account of the deceased's life that had been written years ago by the now-deceased. We would squeeze lots of that information into the finished piece, condensing it into phrases such as "Stints with several engineering firms eventually led to XYZ Corporation, where Sam became senior vice-president."

For several years, we would send the family half a dozen laminated copies of the obituary and eventually the local funeral homes took that upon themselves along with a convenient ad suggesting that if you like the way we treated Sam, please use us again.

One day, Riley, one of our typesetters, jumped up from her machine and rushed over to the paste-up boards where the actual pages were being configured. A quick review of the boards elicited a "Jesus Christ, look at this!" She was looking at a story about an elderly couple who had both died on the same day, the wife in a nursing home and the husband at home. She expired in the morning and he in the late afternoon.

But this was only half of the story. And that's what had suddenly resonated with Riley, who had typeset most everything thus far for that issue.

"Jesus!" Riley bellowed again. "This can't be right."

Pasted up on the boards was a pair of obituaries about a couple who had died on the same day. Hanging above the boards, waiting to be pasted up, was another pair of obituaries with the same story line, an elderly couple who expired within hours of one another. The four obituaries came from two different funeral homes, so no one had stitched together the extraordinary coincidence that had just occurred in and around Elgin, NH.

This presented us with a dilemma. Did we bother the grieving families with the fact that the passing of their loved ones was also a statistical anomaly, or did we wait a week, let the funerals play out, and then pursue the story? We debated that for about ten seconds and then Karen got on the phone. Both families were very cooperative and both felt that their loved ones had gone out in a blaze of statistical sizzle. There was a slight downside in that once our story broke, the regional and then the national media descended on the families, delaying the needed closure for a week or so.

Two national television networks asked to send up crews to interview Karen, but she turned them all down. "Everything we know about this is in the story," she told them, and it was. In a brief period of less than forty-eight hours she pulled together all the loose strings and blended it into a touching story about true love and broken hearts.

Chapter Ten

My advertising background was both a pro and a con in this smaller world of retail advertising. The basic ad principles are the same as with the big accounts, but explaining that to a local lumber dealer or pharmacist is a whole different kettle of fish. When our NY agency was talking advertising with one of our major clients, the CEO might be sitting in on the presentation, but most clients relied on their in-house advertising and marketing experts to craft and shape the message. When the CEO or other corporate brass hats were in the room, in fact, the creativity rocket was never launched. I think the reason was that the true creative process often starts in the stratosphere and is then brought back to earth. An off-the-wall suggestion is a great way to get the conversation going. But that outside-the-box approach generally doesn't resonate with corporate captains.

With the small retailers in Elgin, the CEO and advertising expert are often one in the same. Sometimes they are also the chief financial officer and janitor. So the "science" and the "art" of advertising is a message that is best subordinated when talking about their weekly ad. As one local merchant put it, "I don't care about all that crap. All I want to know is, how much is it going to cost?"

Whether it be an ad for General Motors or for Attic Treasures antique shop, the basics of advertising are identical. And that is the message that I try to instill in my advertising representatives. I didn't want ad "order takers," I want people who understand advertising basics, goals, measurements and timing and can communicate with their clients quickly. Retailers in our area are being bombarded with ad sales people from at least a half-dozen print sources and a couple of radio stations as well. Each sales call represents an intrusion into the time of the retailer, who may also be the only employee. After a while, many of them don't know who they even talked to, what they agreed to, and what the cost would be.

And that's why we formed "Au, Advertising University, to Make Your Gold Go Farther." It took a little explaining for people to get the connection between "Au," the chemical symbol for gold, and "university," but the concept was unique and it paid off.

Rather than have my ad team go out and repeat the basics hundreds of times, we held seminars in our office and invited advertisers to come to our presentation.

"Here are my five names for next month's seminar," said Vickie. "All of them can make it on the thirteenth." Each seminar was put together with one ad representative nailing down five advertisers, and then the other two representatives would recruit five more apiece. Lots of conversation took place to prevent having competing retailers in the same seminar. We ran four seminars of up to fifteen retailers each, with a minimum attendance of five.

I would introduce everyone and give the attendees a trip around the *Eagle* office. Without fail, the highlight of the mini-tour was time with the *Eagle*'s dog, Typo. Maria Hardin, the Boston owner of the mother dog, visited Elgin every summer and one summer told us that she had an unplanned litter of four pups, only two of which lived. "Would you be interested in adopting one?" she asked.

"Nope, I don't think it's fair for a dog to sit at home all day alone," I said. That was supposed to be the end of the conversation. Five minutes later she was back, this time with the eight-week-old puppy in tow.

Suffice it to say, Typo fit right in at the *Eagle*. Missy gave him his name, and he came to the office every day and greeted everyone who came through the door. He could sense when people had chips on their shoulders and would let loose a low growl.

Everyone in Elgin knew Typo, who accompanied me on lots of strolls, assignments and trips. He was a local celebrity and it never went to his head. When the newspaper staff marched in the annual Elgin Days parade, Typo led the *Eagle* procession and people by the hundreds hollered, "Hey, Typo!" He loved everyone and was particularly affectionate to kids and residents from the local rehabilitation center. He seemed to sense that they needed some quiet, soft affection, and that was his specialty.

Typo was our goodwill ambassador and he set the informal and relaxed tone for the ad seminar. I introduced everyone and then turned the meeting over to the ad staff. This presented the ad reps as experts, which they were. I spent months working with our team and getting their feedback. After our first seminar we fine-tuned the seminar template to lock in on a professional presentation, complete with slides and critiques of the previous ads of those in attendance.

We wanted every ad to work. In the *Banner*, once the retailer agreed to run an ad, that was obviously the end of their concern. Ads were not only poorly created but also poorly placed in the paper. And because their paper presented such a weak news product, most readers never got beyond a skimming of page one, so ads placed inside never saw a reader.

"How many advertising messages would you guess the average American is exposed to each day?" Vickie would ask.

Attendees would throw out all sorts of numbers before Vickie switched to a slide saying seventeen hundred.

"So your ad is competing with one thousand, six hundred ninety-nine other impressions, and it is *your* job and *our* job to do everything we can to get readers to your ad, to get them to read it and get them to act on it," added Vickie with the confidence that underscored that she knew this issue.

"If your ad is not of interest to a given reader, the odds of him stopping to read it are near zero," said Vickie, "but between us" – gesturing back and forth to the audience and our ad reps – "we want to do everything we can to get someone to your ad and then, if they are interested, consume it."

She would then show a slide of a cartoon character with a mouthful of newsprint.

Anita, a former teacher, knew instinctively how to organize her piece of the presentation that basically waltzed the attendees around and around until they finally arrived at the desired location.

We concluded each seminar with a short session of critiquing ads from those in attendance.

"These are going to be very bare-bones critiques, but we'd be happy to sit down with any of you if you'd like a more in-depth analysis," said Rosemary. "Just make sure you make an appointment first." We would then critique ads from the *Eagle* and the *Banner*.

Most of the *Banner* ads were pretty pathetic – no eye appeal, no hard information, and stressing no benefit. We didn't say which paper a given ad was from. Most of the ads that ran in the *Eagle* were better constructed than those from other papers. That wasn't a blanket rule, because often the ad we ran in our paper was exactly what the retailer wanted. Some of those were OK and some were terrible. One of the stealth benefits of the seminar was an opportunity to twist some advertisers out of some bad habits.

One retailer, who had gone out of business, always wanted the name of his store presented vertically so the reader had to read down to see "Bart's Paint Palace." That might work in China, but with sixteen hundred ninety-nine other impressions to go, the reader wasn't going to waste time deciphering Bart's great idea. What caused this kind of stubbornness on the part of retailers to ignore ways to improve their ads? Usually it was because one person came into their store after a whacko ad ran and said, "I saw your ad in the *Eagle*, Bart, jumped right out at me." Unfortunately, Bart never followed that by asking "What did the ad say?"

The answer, most likely, would have been, "I dunno, but I saw it."

Rosemary came up with a great conclusion to end the three-hour seminar. Our newsroom had a small, windowless balcony and as the end neared she would build up the suspense and then sliding down a wire from the balcony would come fifteen furry little *Eagle* toys, each with a personalized diploma for the attendees, announcing the successful completion of the *Elgin Eagle* Advertising University. Yes, they were golden eagles.

* * *

"Deb and I need a couple of minutes with you. Is this a good time?" said Karen on the intercom.

"Come on in," I said, although it was going to make me late for a local Chamber of Commerce board meeting.

Karen came in and Deborah followed. Neither was carrying a notepad, so I assumed this wasn't going to be a pitch for a story idea.

Deborah Bell was a great hire that almost fell into our lap a little over a year ago. A cum laude graduate from the Medill School of Journalism at Northwestern, Deborah was one of those hires who would be on her way to a daily within eighteen to twenty-four months. While she was with us I knew we were going to get a dynamo work ethic and a high level of pro-

171

fessionalism that many smaller papers lack. Multiple visits to her grandmother in Ralston had introduced Deb to the *Eagle*. She was over six feet tall with long dark hair, and when she walked into a room, people took notice. In addition to being a natural journalist, she was also just what we needed on the company volleyball team, a tall, athletic woman who could spike a ball at the net with such force that opponents didn't even try to defend it. Her father, who was a *Washington Post* bureau chief, loved visiting his daughter and hanging around our newsroom.

"Go ahead, Deb, tell Ed what you just told me," said Karen.

Deb began to unfold a story that was potentially one of the most explosive we would ever confront. It could lead nowhere as far as news content was concerned, but it raised an issue that would require some careful thought.

"Two weeks ago, when I was heading home on Wednesday night, I was pulled over by a cop at the intersection of Williams and the highway. Last week, the same thing, but this time farther down Williams and Carol, my neighbor thought I was getting a ticket. And last night he was parked at the end of my driveway in his cruiser. Same cop, no tickets, no charges. All the neighbors see him and I'm sure they all think I'm doing drug deals or something. In short, I'm being stalked," said Deb, "and it's scary as hell."

"Who's the cop?" I asked, "Local or state?"

"It's Thomas, the Elgin guy," said Deb.

Thomas was not a credit to the force. He was an anger-management dropout who had come out of the police academy a couple of years earlier with an overblown sense of entitlement and importance. During his two-year tenure on the Elgin force he had instituted numerous dustups with teenagers around the region. He was all show and no go, and on one occasion had actually pulled his weapon at a routine traffic stop. If there was a crowd anywhere in town you could count on Thomas showing up complete with his service revolver, baton and mace attached to his belt. He loved the "authority" that the uniform granted him, but his people skills were minimal and whatever ones he showed were transparent as hell. In short, he was far from what you want in a local cop, but Chief Harley liked him. And if the chief liked him, that was good enough for the selectmen.

"So here we have this cop stalking a young lady and the question is, who do we tell?" I said. "There must be some sort of professional-conduct commission or board in the state that can deal with things like this," said Karen. "But they're probably all in bed together."

"That would be my first thought," I said. "And any complaint is probably going to be strained through the chief first."

"And Thomas was the chief's hire, I was told. In fact he made a big deal when he hired him," said Deb. Given the severity of the situation, she exhibited a remarkable sense of control.

"Had you done something to warrant the stops?" I asked. "Have you received any tickets or warnings?"

"Nothing," she said.

"How did he stop you, blue lights and all that?"

"Yes, a quick flash of the lights," Deb recounted, "and then he would approach my car and start in with 'Hi.' 'Where are you going?' 'What's in the paper tomorrow?' All chit chat. I asked him last night how he knew where I lived and he said with a grin, 'car registrations say a lot.'"

Thomas obviously knew that our entire staff left the building every Wednesday night about twenty or thirty minutes after the paper left at nine. We usually shared a beer and then dragged ourselves home.

"You have a beer with us every Wednesday, Deb. Has he ever mentioned alcohol?" I queried.

"Never, just meaningless chatter. Last week he said that we should get together sometime."

"And, of course, he's married," said Karen.

I assured Deb that this was going to be at the top of my to-do list. We would get it resolved.

I left the office, grabbed a cup of coffee from Freda's, and headed down Spaulding Farm Road, where I could enjoy some quiet time to sort this out. I felt I was in check. A rotten cop, a rotten chief who, we were certain would not intervene, and a do-nothing bunch of selectmen. Due to the regularity – three weeks in a row – of Thomas's hits on Deb, I concluded that we could probably get evidence visually and orally the following week. But that was going to subject Deb to driving into the situation once again and I didn't want to do that. If we just filed charges, it was going to be our word vs. theirs and it would end up being a gaming table for attorneys on both sides. A temporary fix would be for Deb to find a new route home on Wednesday nights, but that wouldn't guarantee her safety now that Thomas had found her address.

Surely we weren't the first newspaper to face this kind of dilemma. I decided to call some fellow board members at the national newspaper group. My first call was to Callie Blythe, the vice president, whom I'd had known for almost a decade. Callie published a tremendous weekly in Colorado and was a solid board member notable for getting things done.

What a great first call. Callie, it turned out, was also the chair of the Publishers' Legal Committee, which she informed me had the wherewithal and the funds to join in on situations like this one. She would talk to the attorneys who handled this and either she or one of them would get back to me. I explained the urgency of the situation, that I didn't want my employee at risk. Callie understood fully. She told me not to worry, someone would be on this as quickly as possible.

An hour later, I received a call from Curtis Woodard, a Boston attorney who specialized in media issues. First, he commented on how much he enjoyed Elgin and volunteered that he was often up here with his family to enjoy "the bounty that Mother Nature has laid at your feet."

I walked him through everything Deb had told me and when I mentioned the remark about Thomas finding Deb's address via her car registration, Woodard said something to the effect that Thomas had committed a fatal error. The alert neighbors were also key he explained. He asked if I could type it all up and fax it to him so he could review it. I had already typed it up and while we were talking, Lana faxed it to him. He also wanted copies of the last three town budgets. I didn't ask why, but we tore those pages out of the printed town reports and faxed them too.

An hour later, Curtis called back and confidently outlined the procedure.

"There's a little head fake here," he said, "but I'm confident it will work and end this very quickly. We probably got him with the illegal use of auto registration data, however that might create an opening allowing him to weasel out. But the others who can corroborate her story concerning the interactions should seal it."

At the Elgin selectmen's meeting that night Dave Harrison, our Elgin reporter, showed up with his mini-tape recorder. I met with him in the afternoon and casually asked him how the recorder worked in such a large room.

"It works great," he said, "but you have to put it right on the table and it needs to be close to Clackers," (a nickname one of our reporters had given to Jarvis Jackson, a selectman whose false teeth made him mumble and occasionally whistle while he talked). "If the recorder is anywhere except in front of Clackers, you'll never hear him. Even when you do hear him, half the time you can't understand what he says."

"Who else records the meetings?" I asked.

"No one."

That bit of information was going to be crucial to Curtis's head fake.

The following Monday, John Garneau, the chairman of the selectmen, received a certified letter from Curtis Woodard, Esq. It was written on letterhead with no fewer than fifty other attorney's names on it, all part of one of the top law firms in Boston. The letter stated that Officer Thomas of the Elgin Police Force was harassing one of the female employees of the *Elgin Eagle*. It explained that this employee feared being alone in her car. It listed three incidents, all within the previous month, and concluded that recorded and visual evidence were potentially a part of the case. It demanded that Officer Thomas be removed from the force within the next ten days or an official public complaint would be filed. The letter included some examples of similar cases that the firm had prosecuted and listed the cost to each municipality that chose to get involved in such skirmishes. That explained why Curtis wanted those town budget figures. The town budget line for legal expenses was far less than the town could anticipate incurring should it decide to fight the Thomas case. The timing of the letter allowed the selectmen to handle this at the next meeting in an executive (non-public) session. And at that meeting they couldn't help but notice the *Eagle's* tape recorder capturing everything they said. Of course the deliberations on Thomas were not going to be public, but the process of getting into and out of those executive sessions *is* public and was a virtual timestamp as to when the process began. The deadline set by Curtis allowed time for the chief to interview Thomas before making a decision. Their escape was to jettison Thomas for "budgetary reasons," hand him a couple of thousand dollars for separation pay, and toss him over the side.

The potential municipal financial tsunami made us confident that the board was not going to give the chief the option of retaining or discharging Thomas. By allowing a few days for the selectmen's decision and the chief handing Thomas his walking papers, the town, the chief and Thomas could all arrive at the "budget" cover story. In exchange, the *Eagle* would be mute and only report the cover story. And sadly, Thomas's behavior would be buried. Within a few months he would probably sign on with another police department with a glowing recommendation from Chief Harley.

Should the town opt to side with the chief and Thomas, on the other hand, this case was now on Curtis Woodard's docket, and Curtis knew the drill. He also still had the illegal auto registration search in reserve. And the cost would be handled by the Publishers' Legal Committee.

We were still concerned that before the Thomas matter could be resolved, we had one more Wednesday night trip home for Deb. I asked her to let me have someone drive her home that night and she said she would take a circuitous route. I told her I didn't want her to do that and I volunteered Chris Bourbon to be her designated driver. Deb and Chris agreed and at 9:35 the following night, Chris and Deb, in Chris's car, crossed the intersection of Williams and the highway. Neither of them gave what would have been a final wave to the officer in the cruiser parked on the side.

* * *

My favorite moment of each week was Sunday morning when I had the whole newspaper office to myself. If the phone rang I had to answer it, but that was rare. The quiet and solitude of the empty office were my recharge. Our newsroom had a central wood-burning stove and there were smaller stoves in my office and in the production area, all backed up by oil heating. But once we got ample insulation and double-pane windows

177

installed, the woodstoves could handle about seventy percent of the load. We also had a Trombe wall, one of the largest passive solar panels in New England, attached to the back wall of our building. A Trombe wall is basically a gigantic airtight glass box that quickly captures the heat from the sun and with the assist of a tiny little blower, sends that heat into the building.

On Sunday mornings, I stoked up the small stove in my office, brewed a pot of coffee, perused the *Boston Globe* and *NY Times* and then turned on Robert J. Lurtsema's Morning Pro Musica on Boston's *WGBH* radio. The program started with chirping birds and some Respighi or Gabrieli, then rolled through hours of wonderful music that drilled down to my innermost core.

The result was a temporary suspension of the usual multitude of issues that were constantly on the palette, and instead a clean canvas asking for a creative brush.

This was about as good an environment as I was ever going to get in which to craft an editorial for the coming edition. As Bach, Beethoven, and Brahms played in the background the words would materialize. None of this was world-class writing, but creating in this musical environment really worked for me. Sometimes, as the music hit a crescendo, my writing did the same, and it was time to pause and perhaps start again.

I think it is the orderliness of classical music that also aligns the thought process. Maybe it was just the absence of the usual day-to-day noise that allowed something different to bubble to the surface of my grey matter. But Sunday mornings with Robert J. were a weekly must in my biorhythms.

* * *

Dennis and Sandra did a great job with the visit of Senator Jonathan Gregory Dorn of South Carolina. About eight inches of snow fell the night before and his appearance was in doubt, but his entourage, two cars and a press station wagon showed up five minutes early.

We saw them drive up to the building but waited for them to come to the door – you don't want to appear too anxious. First we'd show them the restroom and offer them a cup of coffee. We'd also show members of the entourage which phones were available. Before their arrival we had thoroughly policed the area around the phone before letting anyone appropriate it. After everyone was introduced, Dennis took the lead. Chris, our photographer, occasionally popped in to grab a few quick shots, but the photos were usually shot by the reporters conducting the interview. I often sat in on these sessions, but liked our staff to run the show. If I had a question, I might inject it near the end of the interview; but our people took this part of their job very, very seriously. If there was a question that should be asked, they usually asked it.

We saw our role as surrogates for our readers. To talk with candidates one-on-one for an extended period of time afforded us the opportunity to explore issues more deeply than anyone could do at a public gathering. We also tried to have more than one way to ask the same question in case the candidate wanted to play issue dodgeball with us. We took an advocacy rather than adversarial stance, aiming to deliver meaningful information so that readers could make up their minds as to what a candidate really believed. This required good home-work. Once we threw out some relevant facts and figures, the candidate usually honed his answer with regard to the reality that the interviewer wasn't going to swallow the usual politi-cal pabulum. The drive for clear answers demanded that the reporter maintain focus – easier said than done, but a unique skill that Dennis possessed!

The senator asked if Sandra hadn't interviewed him during the previous primary. She had, and I gave the Dorn an A+ for either good data files or a super memory.

Dennis began by tossing out a couple of "ambiance questions," like the vagaries of traveling through New England weather, things going on in Dorn's home state, often a sports question. Next Dennis reviewed how we were going to proceed and told him about the core questions that would be asked of all candidates during the final phase of the interview. We rarely would let anyone into the interview except for our people, the candidate, and perhaps an aide. This was designed to keep future interviewees from knowing the core questions in advance – keeping the playing field level. The traveling press could take photos before and after and time permitting, we would also invite them in for a few final few questions.

About five minutes into the Dorn interview, the town's fire whistle started to blow and the scanners in our office came to life. "Reported fire, Tom Thumb Market, Main Street, Elgin," came the call.

Tom Thumb Market is right across the street from our office. No responders had yet arrived on the scene, but because it was in the downtown area, the standing protocol was to call in the entire department. Once firemen were on the scene, they could adjust the response accordingly.

Within a few seconds of the first call, sirens were already screaming as volunteer firemen scrambled to get to the station, suit up, and head out. While the senator was still going on about whatever, Dennis, Sandra, and I were craning our necks to see this fire on our doorstep. Chris scooted out of the darkroom – we didn't even know he was in there – grabbed a quick shot of the senator and headed out the door. Dorn was still going a mile a minute, oblivious to this Charlie Chaplin runaway that was building right before his eyes. As he glanced around the table, he saw no one with whom to make eye contact. Everyone was straining to look out the window.

When multiple emergency apparatus arrived outside, their sirens piercing every corner of our office, Dennis called a time out. Even the senator was soon standing at our open window watching the excitement. Sandra's shot of Dorn in the window with half the Elgin Fire Department trucks in the street and the smoking building in the background became our Page One photo that week. The traveling press who were armed with cameras got similar pictures. And for several days, the Tom Thumb dumpster fire photos with the senator looking on, made it into several leading newspapers across the country.

The fire was confined to a dumpster, but something inside the dumpster, probably engine oil, created volumes of dark smoke that made things look worse than they were. The whole thing was under control in about two minutes, and the interview with the senator resumed. The senator told us about a huge fire in Charleston in the 1800s, and Sandra actually worked that factoid into her story.

* * *

The little Catholic parish in Harlow had been looking for a new priest for over a year. They tried to make it appear that the delay was due to the fact that they were conducting a diligent search in order to find just the right shepherd for their flock. But according to some disgruntled parishioners, the true reason was that they had very little money to offer any candidate.

We kept in constant touch with Jim McCormick, the head of their search committee. Periodically Sandra, our staff Catholic, would inquire as to the status of the "nationwide search" that was being conducted.

One morning, Sandra ran into McCormick as both were arriving for their share of Ash Wednesday ashes at St. Timothy's Parish. McCormick pulled her aside and told her they had just concluded a deal for a new priest and they were preparing a press release to announce it. Sandra quizzed McCormick and found out that the new priest was semi-retired from a rural Louisiana parish. She sensed that McCormick wasn't going to divulge any more information until the search committee had prepared a press release, but he never said as much. Waiting for a press release was going to kill our "first with the news" effort. But Sandra got the name of the new priest's former town and that was all we needed.

A couple, actually quite a few, phone calls in and around Lorient, Louisiana and Sandy soon had enough information to identify the new priest and fill in a little background about his past. When she finally reached him, he was most cooperative and withheld nothing.

Sandy then called Jim McCormick to check on the accuracy of the information she had gathered. He complimented her on her diligence and confirmed that the info was accurate. She asked him if there was any real problem with our going with the story and he said something to the effect that what we had put together was probably much better than anything they could crank out. But he didn't have a photo of the new priest, which we really wanted, and he implied that trying to get the photo out of the clutches of the search committee could result in an effort to try to hold the story. We decided to go with the story sans photo. The headline read:

Harlow Calls
Louisiana Priest

So far, so good. Because this was a last-minute story, we had a space problem. So we yanked out a house ad, a self promotion about subscribing to the paper, and that got the story some decent space near the top of the page. In fact, there was abundant space. In an attempt to fill in that little sea of white, someone decided that the headline could use a "kicker," an extra line of type just above the headline.

And thus, the story went out with this combination of headline and kicker:

Hominy and Homilies

Harlow Calls
Louisiana Priest

The next morning, many commented favorably on the "Hominy" headline. A few thought the kicker was disrespectful, but it generated a lot of favorable buzz.

There is a silent rule among New England news organizations that you need to tread very lightly when discussing the Catholic Church, which is one of the major religions in the area and has a lot of clout. We never intentionally poked fun at any religion, but occasionally someone would read something into our choice of words that would get a phone call from me to talk it through.

One year an evangelical preacher was caught with his hand in the till and in the company of an occasional non-wife companion at various out-of-town hideaways. Many revered the guy, and he was the beneficiary of many extras in addition to his over-the-top salary – free cars, vacations, plumbers, electricians, theater tickets, gift certificates. Even when rumors started to escalate, the hero worship didn't abate. Finally, the congregation threw him over the side. We hadn't pursued the rumors, and we had neither the time nor the inclination to chase the story after the fact. The congregation was embarrassed and mortified. When he was finally canned, the congregation mounted a full court press for us not to reveal any of it.

Once they turned up the pressure, I asked for a meeting with their governing board. I didn't want to get into a discussion with them, I simply wanted them to know that this was not the kind of story that our paper was going to report. The reason I called the meeting was to keep any of them from thinking that a little pressure would make the *Eagle* back down. Quite to the contrary; whenever pressure mounted for us to spike a story, we instinctively asked ourselves, why? We reported that he had been dismissed for personal reasons. The local community could fill in the blanks. Readers of the *Banner* were never told anything.

Our job was to report the news, all of it. There is a huge responsibility that goes with that and we always tried to keep that front and center. There certainly are moments when someone or some group really doesn't want their news in the paper, but once exceptions start to be made, there is going to be mega trouble ahead.

Our "Hominy and Homilies" kicker was fun, but others backfired. Headlines are often written by someone other than the author of the story. The reason is that when the story is written, no one knows whether it will be displayed in a single column or spread across two or three. A one-column story is going to require a short, succinct headline, while a multiple-column display allows for additional verbiage. Once the layout is determined, a headline must be composed to fit the layout. Time permitting, our proofreaders summon the writer to add the headline, but as the clock ticks down to that moment when the paper must go out the door, many people are conscripted to assist with headline writing. That is when the genie often scampers out of the bottle.

The most important rule for any headline is accuracy. The headline writer has to boil down a five-hundred word story to seven or eight words. Layout permitting, he can add a little more explanation via a kicker or a subhead, which is an additional headline below the main head.

The *Eagle* had numerous headline train wrecks, but the La Leche story always commanded the top spot of headline misfires.

The La Leche League of New Hampshire, an organization that promotes breast feeding, sent in a long news release announcing an informational gathering scheduled to occur in Elgin and promising that attendees to the morning meeting were welcome to stay for lunch, compliments of the organization. The release was cut down to something that still conveyed all the pertinent details and also informed the reader as to the purpose of the organization. Time was short, and in the rush to get a headline for the story, a well-meaning staffer hammered out:

Breast Feeders
Plan Free Lunch

Chapter Eleven

Elgin, with its population of 7,500, was the urban center in our readership area. Roughly, our range for readers was twenty miles each direction, or a little over 5,000 square miles. None of the thirteen other towns we considered in our readership had a population of over 4,000 and most were in the 2,000-4,000 range. The total population inside our readership was estimated to be about 50,000. But Elgin, joined with its contiguous towns, was the hub for lots of goods and services. Three grocery stores battled for customers and getting that weekly ad from each store was a goal for all newspapers and throwaways. One of the three stores, Len's, was located in Wells, just five miles from Elgin. It ran a piecemeal ad with us each week. We were the only paper it used, but their ad required a tremendous amount of work because we had to build it from scratch.

Vickie, our ad rep who handled the account visited Len every Thursday morning to deliver the current edition of the *Eagle* and pick up Len's list of forty or fifty items to be featured in the next week's ad. The cornerstone of the ad always featured a cut of meat. Len was as reliable as they come, and he was always ready for Vickie. Their meeting never lasted more than fifteen minutes, which was good for both of them. Vickie dashed back to the office and began to exhume pictures of lettuce, orange juice, dog food and paper plates from our clip-art volumes. The task required the patience of Job, but Vickie did it fifty-two times a year and knew exactly what clip-art book had the best looking pork chop or the perfect bunch of bananas. She assembled the components, made a rough drawing of how it should all go together, and handed it over to our production crew for typesetting and pasting.

This week Vickie had an added a new ingredient to the weekly grocery gavotte. Kathryn Wagner stopped in to pay for her subscription. She was accompanied by her son Robert, who suffered from severe cerebral palsy. Robert was curious about everything in this new surrounding, and his loud voice reflected that excitement. It was a disruption, but it wasn't going to last and I could see by the way Robert explored various items around the room that there was a genuine curiosity and not just some sort of temporary stimulus. Lana sensed that too, and took time to show him around to various locations in the room from editorial to production. When she brought him to my office and introduced him to me he grinned and said something that was incomprehensible to me, but Lana and Kathryn got it. "He's saying 'boss.' He knows you're the boss."

Vickie, who was observing all of this, soon she joined the tour.

I had served on the board for a cerebral palsy organization in New York and we had many occasions to interact with that constituency. I quickly learned that an inability to walk or speak did not inhibit an ability to learn and think. We donated our ad services to the organization and our campaign featured those afflicted with cerebral palsy who had done some amazing things. So it was satisfying to see Vickie and Lana join in Robert's exploration of this new world rather than shy away.

The following Thursday morning, Vickie had Kathryn bring Robert back to the *Eagle* to watch her create the grocery ad for Len's. Vickie's patience was not severely tested because Robert was a quick study. About a month later, the Thursday morning grocery ad composition was totally handled by

Robert. He went through multiple clip-art books looking for the right picture of a box of Tide or a cluster of grapes. Vickie was very astute at anticipating those items on Len's weekly list that might be foreign to Robert, or any male. She had total control of the process, but only she was aware of that. Watching Robert get to work on the ad was a wonderful sight. It brought a focus for him, it was entertaining, it was challenging, and it gave him a purpose and a weekly opportunity for accomplishment. His arrival with his mother was always sort of a mini-hootenanny, but once the meet-and-greet was over, Robert instantly started to pull tight focus. He looked at Vickie and his eyes asked, "What's on the agenda today?"

Kathryn soon felt comfortable leaving Robert while she ran some downtown errands, and after a few corrections Robert quickly understood that everyone in the room was carrying out an assignment the same as him, and kept out of their way.

He was a brilliant young man. This weekly interaction gave us a wonderful opportunity to see a Robert that most never saw. My favorite moment was one morning when he came over to my office with a question. He was following Vickie's layout and came to a loaf of Wonder Bread that Vickie had priced at $55. Robert wanted to verify the correct price, but wasn't going to change anything that Vickie had given him. I looked at Vickie's layout and it was obvious that she had inadvertently used a dollar sign instead of the cents sign. "You're absolutely right, Robert!" I said. "Great catch."

He smiled and said something like, "I thought it was wrong," then went back to his desk.

Kathryn and Warren Wagner spent a fortune on private tutors for Robert and it paid off. Robert was just as intelligent as the average fifteen-year-old, if not more so, but that knowledge was locked up and hidden. To see it break through into the light was a meaningful moment for me, but was well within the self-awareness of Robert. This fast-paced world often won't take the time, or lacks the desire, to slow down and see beyond the surface.

Thank you, Vickie, for making that Wonder Bread mistake. Without it I would have never experienced that wonderful moment.

One of the other big, local grocery stores opted to have a weekly flyer inserted in the paper instead of running an ad. Flyers can be less expensive than ads, but they're often not read. One month we sent our photographer to the post office on the day one of the local throwaways arrived. The trash cans were overflowing with throwaways that made it all the way from the PO box to the garbage. Why? Because the freebies have little news value and the recipient has no financial investment in the item that was stuffed into his mailbox.

When someone plunks down thirty-five cents for a copy of the *Eagle*, he's not going to throw it away until he's gotten his money's worth. A freebie shopper that comes unsolicited through the mail has not attained a position of importance in the grand financial scheme of things. Even those who occasionally read a shopper are usually only getting puff pieces concerning the shopper advertisers. Even nonprofits, who have no ad budget whatsoever, get little mention in a shopper.

Most copies of the *Eagle* will, at least, be picked up and opened, and the mission of the ad is now significantly under way. And using the proven fact that readers will notice ads of interest to them, it makes sense to have an ad in a paper that is going to escort readers from page one to page twenty-four or twenty-eight, delivering information they can't get anywhere else. And along that visual journey our paper exposes readers to dozens of ads. If an ad is not of interest to them there is little we or the advertiser can do to turn up the heat. We deliver readers to the advertiser's doorstep. Whether or not they are ready to enter is beyond our control.

Our picture-taking session was to demonstrate how many of those printed throwaways died right there in the post office. But we noticed that the trash bins were also packed with pre-printed inserts from a variety of newspapers, throwaways and magazines. People would extract their newspaper from the PO box and on the way out the door, shake out any and all flyers and inserts – anything loose.

But we inserted a flyer for Global Grocery every week. And our attempts to change that to an ad fell on deaf ears because the decision was being made at a corporate headquarters that was responsible for dozens of stores. And the flaw in that practice was that many items shown in the flyer were never even stocked in the Elgin store. After a few misfires, grocery shoppers ignored the Global flyer. In fact, it was the butt of local jokes suggesting you are about as accurate as "a Global Grocery flyer."

The third grocery store, Value Foods, was a challenge for us principally for the same reason; decisions were made in a corporate tower three states away. Try as we might we couldn't break through and convince them that using the rival *Banner* might have been a good ad decision a decade ago, but today the *Banner* was an afterthought for most area newspaper readers. But a newspaper battle in Elgin, NH has a tough time getting on the radar of corporate ad executives who are trying to negotiate and direct gargantuan media buys in Boston or Providence or Hartford. Playing my NY agency experience as a possible entree, dwindled each year as a younger tribe of ad execs in the grocery corporate suites had never heard of my old agency whose name disappeared on the day it was sold.

I finally connected with Mark Ingelstrom, a senior ad advisor for the chain. I drove to their headquarters outside of New York and had a great lunch with Mark reminiscing about Madison Avenue days. I pitched the reasons why an ad in the *Elgin Eagle* was infinitely superior to an ad in the *Banner* and

Mark got it immediately. He cautioned me that he was merely an "advisor" but my reasons for them making a switch were pretty much black and white. "I still have to make them think it was their idea," he said, "but this should happen."

And it did, completely out of the blue. About a month later, a two-foot-long cardboard tube came in the Friday mail. That meant there was some camera-ready copy inside. It didn't necessarily mean it contained a paid ad, we also ran lots of pro bono ads for the Ad Council on subjects such as smoking, safe driving and so forth. Lana pulled the sheet out of the tube and let out a yell that could be heard in Boston.

We had done it. A new three-quarter page, camera-ready ad from Value Foods was going to begin running in the *Eagle* the following week. The financial implications were extensive, the potential to parley this acknowledgment from a major grocery chain into local non-advertisers joining the group was huge, and our current advertisers would receive reinforcement that their decision to advertise with us was sound. It also threw open the doors for wider circulation, because the only grocery ads that would now be available in the area were in the *Elgin Eagle*.

The battle to round up all three grocery ads had been going on for years. Often we had given up and settled for focusing on other things. This was a major victory and I wanted to share the moment with our entire staff; but I also needed to get out of the office and head down Spaulding Orchard Road to clear my head. I called Ellen and told her we needed to talk. She immediately was worried and I assured her it was good news.

I gave her the good news in the car. She let out a yell and we embraced at fifty mph. We had discussed this task for years and she was very much up to speed as to the ramifications and she added a new one. "Now I can shop there!" she exclaimed happily. All of our entire staff were very loyal to our advertisers. Perhaps it was more as though we simply tried not to patronize non-advertisers lest they think their misplaced ad in some paper other than the *Eagle* was working.

"I want to really celebrate this with the staff," I said. "Any suggestions?"

"Pay everyone's grocery bill," said Ellen with no hesitation. "Or at least, part of it."

I returned to the office and posted a notice of an urgent staff meeting at five p.m. At the meeting we revealed the Value Foods success and said that to celebrate, all full-time staffers should shop at Value next week and bring their grocery receipt to Lana and she'd reimburse them for the first twenty-five dollars. For part-timers we offered fifteen dollars. "And for Christ's sake, don't shop until Thursday or later – after the paper comes out!" warned Lana.

The idea struck a chord on many fronts and welded us together even more solidly.

So all three grocery ads were now going to be in the *Eagle*. Len's weekly ad, which we composed in our shop was always placed in the Wells section of the paper, the weekly insert from Global Grocery was tucked into the fold of the paper, and now an ad from Value Foods. As the paper was laid out the following week, the Value ad was initially positioned on the back page, which many consider a premium spot. After some discussion we decided to place it elsewhere lest Value lay claim to that position thenceforth.

The following Thursday I rushed down to the office and sat there like a park statue staring at the Value Foods ad. It was at that moment that it all finally hit me. We had just won the trifecta and this ad was a keystone to advancement on many other fronts.

I headed down to Value Foods to touch base with Leo Levesque, the store manager. Leo was a dictatorial manager, it was rumored. One day I had watched him berate a stock boy in front of customers to the point where the kid tore off

his apron and ran out of the store. I remarked to Leo that
he might have been a little tough on the kid. "The kid was
a loser," he rejoined.

Nevertheless, I did occasionally stroll through Value Foods
and pick up a few items, just to let Leo know we were still
there. The incident with the stock boy was pushed into the
background. I entered the store and circled around to where
all the news racks were, one at the head of each checkout line.
Research showed that racks placed in that position resulted
in the most newspapers being sold – almost as an impulse
item, I guess. We supplied the racks and stocked them every
week when we delivered the paper. As I rounded the corner to
look, there was Leo on his hands and knees with newspaper
all around him, pulling out the Global Grocery inserts.

"What are you doing, Leo?" I asked.

He glanced up, then returned to his task. "I'm not carrying
any ads for my competitor in my store," he snapped.

"You can't do that, Leo," I protested. "You don't own those
papers and your customers are entitled to everything that is
in them."

"Not in my store," he said, and moved to another rack.

I followed him. "Leo, if you want to basically disfigure a copy
of the *Eagle*, you have to buy it first. Then if you want to sell
your customers damaged goods, that's your decision."

"This is my store and those are my rules." And another
stack of newspapers was denuded from their Global Grocery
inserts.

Several store employees were tuning in on the exchange.
One was picking up the discarded inserts while another directed customers to an aisle not blocked by a store manager
acting like a dog digging a hole.

I was heading out of the store when one of the cashiers, who
I knew from youth soccer days, said quietly, "He does it every
week, Ed."

When I got back to the office my whole body was shaking. I knew I couldn't stop Leo, but I was certain that higher-ups in the Value Foods organization would frown on such activity. But what would be the outcome? I'd worked for years to land this account and now, right out of the chute, was I going to lose it because I reported on the asinine behavior of the local manager? I had no hesitation about making the call, but to whom? I had landed the account thanks to the support of Value Food's advertising advisor. Should I call Mark and ask him to run interference, or should I go at the corporate ad manager?

I decided to call the head ad guy, Daniel Sirois. I called him, and amazingly got through. "This is our first day in the *Elgin Eagle*, isn't it Ed?" he said.

I was stunned that he was aware of this seemingly small singular event in his broader landscape of ad management. "You bet, Daniel, and we're delighted to have you as a part of our growing family," I answered, knowing that I was about to move this chatty conversation from A to Z.

I then laid out for Daniel what I had just witnessed at his Elgin store.

What seemed like hours of silence followed. Had I just dug a bottomless pit and kicked myself into it? But then Daniel said, "I don't believe what I just heard. Did others see it happening?"

"Every cashier on the line saw it, Daniel. So did a customer or two, although they may not have known what was happening," I replied. Was I building a case or constructing my own guillotine?

"I don't believe what I just heard," Dan repeated. "Thanks so much for calling, Ed. I know this was a tough call to make, but frankly, this is embarrassing."

I never learned specifically what actions the Value Foods corporate gurus took in regard to the incident, but chatter around the store's meat counter revealed that at the time of the incident Levesque was about two years short of retirement. Rather than can him, Value moved him to a new position of assistant store manager, ostensibly to help train his successor. Not being the big Kahuna apparently didn't go down well with Leo, and he bailed out about six months later.

Every town and city has its own rhythm or cadence that is very personal to the observer. Some people find New York City loud, noisy, and totally overwhelming. Others feast off the city's energy, sound and intensity. How is Elgin perceived? If you want twenty different answers, ask twenty different people. Each of us has his own individual lens and that reality makes up the substrata for the weekly packaging of the *Elgin Eagle*. We're not a monolithic town or region. All opinions must be respected and in play.

The prime testing ground for that approach is the NH Primary. This quadrennial theater is played out on the NH stage and is delivered to us by default. Any news organization can participate. This was my thing, and my personal obsession easily transferred to a bright and energetic staff when they grasped the magnitude of what they had spread out before them. There is, of course, nothing esoteric about the NH Primary, but when one takes a step back and analyzes what's going on in our backyard, the responsibility and the excitement are immense.

This political duel, involving combatants from both parties was taking place in our forest. Many candidates are severely untested at this stage in their quest for the highest office in the land. The *Eagle* didn't deal in dirt and it didn't deal in rumor. Dirt and rumor are certainly a part of the vetting process, but any news organization that goes there must have the investigative muscle to see it through. Many candidates are dressed in a coat of armor designed to withstand intensive scrutiny. Our job was to get inside that protective wrapping and deliver some news that our readers hadn't seen before.

Many hired political operatives knew that we approached the contest from that point of view, and some wanted to steer their candidate around us to a safe haven where he or she can deliver the stump speech with no serious questions or demands for clarity. Over the years we developed a reputation for being fair to the candidates and didn't assail the interviewee, but we knew the drill. The *Washington Post* called the *Elgin Eagle* "The Primary weekly newspaper in NH," and that brand was burned on our forehead and demanded excellence. After the *WaPo* feature, a visit to the editorial offices of the *Elgin Eagle* in Elgin, NH became almost mandatory for serious presidential aspirants.

"That was the most intelligent interview I have ever had," said Senator Jim Gardner (D-VA). "But please don't repeat that until after the election!"

Governor Ed Downey (R-WA) gave us a similar accolade. "You were prepared, patient, and extremely fair today," he said via telephone from a hotel room in Manchester. He too asked that his compliment be kept quiet, but he wanted to express his pleasure with being "taken seriously, as demonstrated by the caliber of the interview." Publishing that statement was hard to resist, but it was important not to create hard feelings between the governor and other papers.

Sadly, our excitement in reporting the primary from the inside out was not something that a majority of our readers cared about. About sixty days before that last primary, one of Bill Blanchard's Convenience Mart polls showed that slightly less than half of *Eagle* readers read our political stories. We also were using a national syndicate that sent us a weekly crossword puzzle, and part of their package was an offer to run a one-time poll of one hundred and fifty *Eagle* readers to see what parts of the paper were most read. Of course, the crossword puzzle was one of the features mentioned and we were allowed to suggest another four features or sections. To make the poll a little more accurate, seventy-five of the calls consisted of the pollster listing the features, putting political stories into the mix. The remaining seventy-five calls were dubbed "unaided recall," with the respondents asked to name the five things they liked most about the paper.

In neither instance was political reporting near the top, but it had enough heft. The syndicate poll showed that those who liked our political reporting felt very strongly about it. And after the *Washington Post* cited us, how could we not continue?

The radio stations in the larger cities in our part of the state sometimes interviewed a presidential candidate, primarily when the candidate wandered through the door looking for some free air time. Most radio guys were on the music model and not news. Occasionally a station would distinguish itself with a knowledgeable candidate interview, but it generally wasn't something within their comfort zone. They were more interested in spinning the top forty than picking the brains of possible future presidents, but with the candidate standing there in the lobby looking like a forlorn puppy, the morning platter countdown was probably going to be interrupted.

Whenever a candidate did suddenly show up on the airwaves it was comedic to say the least. First, you usually had a candidate who was scratching for recognition and probably under-scheduled. Couple that with a DJ who might never have heard of the candidate, and listeners were treated to ten to twelve minutes of heavy, penetrating, take-no-prisoners chatter about NH weather, favorite recipes, and a blast or two of campaign talking points.

The Oscar-winning radio event involved a disc jockey called Johnny Record. JR was getting ready to cue up "Sweet Dreams Are Made of This," by the Eurythimics when a candidate showed up hat in hand. JR, who was a Marine veteran, tried to open a conversation about the candidate's war record, hoping that he could kill some time by creating an *ooh-rah* moment. The candidate revealed nothing about his glorious war record, because there was none. He had spent the war in Canada, to "continue his education." However JR wasn't aware of that and kept going on and on about the military, troops here and abroad, and weaponry. It wasn't an interview at all, but eight to ten minutes of JR's military views.

At the end of the interview, the candidate said that he had never served in the military but had "great respect for all who did." To which JR remarked, "Oh, you were never in the military, I didn't know that." Listeners had already figured that out, JR!

Accuracy and fairness were the two pillars that supported our reporting, and somewhere along the line I think I incorporated "helpfulness." The helpfulness piece probably surfaced most when doing any kind of political story, be it local, state, or national politics – explaining to our readers why an elected official, because of parliamentary rules, might need to vote for something before voting against it, for instance. But even as we made every attempt to stitch ethical and helpful guidelines into our reporting, one certainty was guaranteed to bubble up when writing about candidates – some readers are going to take issue with what you write. We didn't get a lot of vitriolic feedback or hate mail, but people weren't shy about sharing their take on a story even though the letter writer wasn't there when we conducted the interview. The complaints usually centered around something that the reader thought we had omitted from the story. This pattern became more evident when we were reporting on a gathering or rally that some presidential wannabe held in our area.

It was difficult to get a good sense of the crowd at a rally because most in attendance were already for the candidate before the rally and were just there to validate their belief. Reporting on political rallies is a challenge, because very little "new" comes out of such gatherings. The only hard news is that a rally was held, X number of people attended, and what entertainment was provided. Questions of the candidate were certainly news, but very few candidates were comfortable opening up the floor to unscripted questions. The more experienced campaigns often spiked the audience with operatives who asked questions to which the candidate conveniently had a snappy answer. Every now and then, a local would outshout, or outmuscle one of these planted questioners and the candidate suddenly got a question that wasn't part of the script. When one of these spontaneous missiles was launched at a candidate, the body language was priceless. First the microphone changed hands or was adjusted in order to buy some time. Then the candidate would shift from one location on the platform to another, trying to formulate a response. These non-scripted questions were where some real news nuggets might lie, but they came up so quickly that few, including us, were prepared for the response.

We did, however, once dig out a response that suddenly had national implications. We were interviewing Senator James Sparkell (R-TX). Sparkell had been in the Senate for three terms and had served on the budget committee from the beginning. He had all sorts of advanced degrees in business and economics and a set of life experiences that made him the one person on the committee that practically everyone admired.

When his campaign agreed to have him visit our newsroom, we quickly recognized that we were ill prepared to take any sort of budget discussion much beyond conventional chatter. So Dennis arranged an evening gathering with a couple of college professors from area business schools. We lured them in with the promise of free pizza and beer, signaling that the get-together was going to be totally informal.

What we didn't know at the time was that meeting was where we packed together a little snowball and pushed it over the side of the hill. As it progressed it grew larger and larger.

As the group consumed pizza and swigged beer, Dennis and his professors dissected Sparkell's record and reached a conclusion as to where they thought he was heading. Karen was part of the group, and John Sedlak, our sports reporter, asked to sit in on the meeting. "I was an economics major in college," he said. "Maybe I can put it to use." By the end of the night, the group had pretty well formulated a line of questioning for Senator Sparkell that could possibly lead to something with real news value. No trick questions were involved, just a process of building on past and current responses. They agreed to reconvene the meeting two days before the arrival of the senator to clean up any loose ends and plug in any new information.

One of Sparkell's local supporters was Bradley Charles, a former U.S. representative and a good friend of the paper. A week before the interview, Brad called and asked if he could attend our interview with Sparkell. I told him that it was all right with us if the senator agreed. "Actually, Ed, he asked me to call you to see if it would be OK for me to sit in," said Brad. "Your reputation precedes you. And I mean that in the most complimentary way."

The scheduled tune-up meeting was canceled because nothing significantly new had emerged since the original meeting with the college professors. Dennis, John, Karen, and I had met twice and were ready with about three separate approaches to tease out some news from the senator. Even though I had attended those meetings, I knew that the details surrounding these meetings were topics beyond my understanding. I could ask a good question, but getting the question launched is easy. What one does with the response via the follow-up question can lead to the fertile ground where the tall corn grows.

Sparkell's interview was scheduled for the weekend. Usually candidates were in Elgin en route between city A and city B. This was a 10:00 a.m. interview and we had a one-hour slot. It was a tremendous interview, with lots of back and forth exploring and clarifying of issues. At one point Senator Sparkell grabbed a notepad and drew a detailed diagram on how something would work. John took the diagram and made some changes, opening up another channel of thought as opposed to a dismissal or argument. I knew where Dennis was trying to go but the senator would stop short of where we sensed his ultimate quest was going to take him. At one point he asked if we could go off the record. We always honor that request, but so many public figures had been burned, even after assurances that they were off the record, that most never even bothered to discuss it. When Sparkell asked to go off the record here, Duncan Burns, one of his aides said, "Senator, I don't think we want to go there. No offense meant, Dennis."

Former representative Brad Charles chimed in. If the *Eagle* said it was off the record, he said, that meant it was off the record. So we turned off the tape recorder, put down our pencils, and waited for the senator to finally get to where we hoped he would go. He didn't. His "off-the-record" remark revolved around a personal story that could have caused some embarrassment, but in his mind it clarified an earlier statement he had made. It did, but it didn't add a single new thread to the tapestry we were trying to weave.

After the interview, Sparkell remarked that he had rarely been through an interview like that and he congratulated Dennis, John, and Karen for their diligence. Much as we enjoyed the praise though, the news we wanted hadn't materialized.

The senator left our office a little after eleven and his entourage swung by the office of the *Banner* to pick up Mrs. Sparkell, who had spent the last hour sharing cookie recipes with a reporter. According to John, who was headed toward Freda's, the *Banner* interview with the senator took place on the sidewalk and lasted approximately two minutes. Their story dished up that "Senator Sparkell commented on how his campaign is gaining considerable momentum thanks to people such as Rep. Bradley Charles." They then quoted, practically verbatim, the talking points in the campaign's news release about the rally that was held later that day. Plus, of course, *Banner* readers got some yummy recipes from the interview with Mrs. Sparkell, something that *Eagle* readers were going to miss. But the thing that sent my staff into a frenzy was the picture of the senator and his wife standing in front of the *Banner* office with a thirty-six point headline reading:

Sen. James Sparkell
Visits the *Banner*

Our Sparkell interview still had some fire left in it. And that smolder started to glow Tuesday night when I received a call from Duncan Burns asking when we put the paper to bed. I told him nine Wednesday night. "I'll get back to you," he said. "Keep a hole open on page one."

"Oh, for Christ's sake, Dunc, don't leave me hanging," I said. He knew that I wasn't so much angry as I was a hungry newshound on a short leash who just had some red meat dragged across in front of him.

"That interview with your team on Saturday got some wheels turning here, not only about the damn New Hampshire Primary, but on the Hill as well. We had a conference call on Sunday, another yesterday, and all of us are back in DC today and the topic is still front and center," said Duncan. "There are still a couple of things that need signoffs, but we may have a blockbuster story for you tomorrow."

He asked for specific timelines such as when the paper went to bed, where it was printed, who might have access to it before it hit the newsstands, etc. He wanted specific times as to when the general public would get its first glimpse.

The suspense was killing me. I decided to play a card and asked, "Totally off the record, Duncan, does this involve budget balancing?"

"Yes, and I didn't say that! I'll be in touch tomorrow morning."

Duncan called a little after noon the next day, and said they were preparing to send a fax and would I please be the one who took it off the fax machine.

A veil of secrecy shrouded the *Eagle* offices for the remainder of the day. Those with a need to know were quickly briefed and jubilation was written on many faces.

The following morning, the *Elgin Eagle* broke a national story as one of the most important pieces of legislation in the last ten years was announced – in our paper and, of course, in much of the national media that follows legislation. The news release from the senator's office said that yesterday the senator had unveiled a comprehensive budget-balancing agenda following an extensive interview with the *Elgin* (NH) *Eagle*.

By noon the street in front of our office was filled with news media folk from all over. We gave a full story to the AP early, which shielded us from having to repeat the same thing over and over. Everyone on the staff who entered or left the building was interviewed. Unlike the plane crash story, which was basically a regional story, this news had national appeal. And just as quickly as the Elgin activity erupted it died down, as numerous scribes returned to Washington or to whatever presidential campaign they were following.

Months later, after Senator Sparkell's presidential campaign had ended, I met Duncan at the National Press Club and he took me through the step-by-step journey that led from our interview with the senator to their releasing the news five days later. The strategy was to let it bubble up with a small paper in New Hampshire and then, after the initial shock value had diminished, to treat it like any other news release. They felt confident using us as the introductory news vehicle because they had seen that we understood the issue. And the budget story that they released was exactly what we had been driving for during our interview. The senator had immediately picked up on that. He also knew that we knew a lot of the backstory, and that any comments we made after the story broke would not muddy the water.

The senator, of course, could not immediately be reached for comment when the story broke in our newspaper. After all, he was somewhere in the wilds of New Hampshire. But sympathetic members of Congress were, conveniently, very available for comment. Thus various nationwide constituencies were introduced to the pending legislation, and helpful local spin around the country would also enter the process.

The story that Dennis, John and Karen wrote was a masterful blending of the news release from the senator's office plus our own interview. Friday night we assembled the entire staff and the two economics professors at The Pizza Joint (no kidding) for pizza and budget beer. God, I love this business.

Suddenly many other candidates felt it would be beneficial to meet with the *Elgin Eagle* reporters to trumpet their unique grasp of the issue, some for Sparkell's position, some against. Over the next month or two, five or six additional candidates visited our paper and they all redirected some of their print-advertising budget to us. We weren't running stories in order to get ads, but where an ad is placed does, to some degree, reflect on the advertiser.

As candidates vied for slots to visit with the *Eagle*, we crafted an approach that gave them an opportunity to bloviate on the Sparkell bill and also ushered them into our candidate template, thus assuring that all candidates were treated equally.

The second bunch of candidates who were trying to latch on to the Sparkell bill were not coming to some run-of-the-mill small town newspaper. When Dennis opened up the discussion on the budget issue, several ran headfirst into the buzz saw. They weren't prepared to have their budget talking points vetted the way our team did. It wasn't a case of arguing with them so much as drilling down through some superficial responses and uncovering the fact that there was nothing left to find. All of that preparation for the initial Sparkell interview was yielding results, and my only regret was that perhaps as few as thirty percent of our readers were tuned in.

* * *

Penny and Alek Hallitus had been publishing the *Addison American* for more than forty years. They were the third generation to publish the paper and were ideal for the task. Alek had always been helpful when we needed something, such as a spare part for one of our typesetter machines, or a camera-ready ad from an advertiser, but what was constantly on his mind was that the *Eagle* was always on the counter of the Addison Drugstore. "We've been here for over a hundred years but your paper is on the counter while we're over in the corner with all the other newspapers," he lamented time and again. "I can't figure it out."

Addison was a fast-growing town about twenty-two miles southwest of Elgin. We really didn't cover it, because no one over our way gave a hoot about what was happening in Addison. But Addison had expanded into quite a commercial hub and many of our readers had begun trekking over to shop at its specialty shops. Sadly, a couple of big box stores had weaseled their way onto the Addison commercial palette and the rural veil that once defined Addison was permanently pierced.

But small and large stores alike need to advertise, and many of Addison's retail stores were on our radar. Conversely, Penny's sales force, known to us as Penny's Rangers, were frequently observed trolling shops in Elgin hoping to grab a piece of the ad budget.

Although the logic was indisputable, getting a retailer twenty-two miles away to advertise in a non-local paper was a heavy lift. Over the years, our ad team was able to hone the argument down to a few very simple sentences, but getting a retailer to grasp it was another story.

Just to make a lesson fun, we often did play-acting with our sales team.

"I'm talking to Holland's Men's Clothing store," said Rosemary, our ad manager, "and I only have a few minutes. How do I package this to get his attention?"

The sales team knew the answer, but Rosemary's rhetorical question led off to the answer.

"Here's the pitch," she said. She got up from her desk, flipped her hair back, and stood before the team. "Our newspaper has a circulation of just about seven thousand. Double that number when you include pass-along readership. So close to fourteen thousand people each week are consuming the award-winning *Elgin Eagle* because we are delivering a huge amount of news that they can't get anywhere else. Do we cover news of Addison? Of course not, that's the job of the *American*, and they do a great job of it. But Mr. Retailer, Elgin doesn't have a men's clothing store, so people have to look elsewhere. They can drive over the horizon on a ninety-mile round trip to one of the big shopping malls and find a store or two once they recover from the traffic and the trauma of finding a parking space. Or they can drive just twenty-two miles down the road to Holland's. But they're not going to come if you don't tell them you're here. So you should consider devoting some of your ad budget to prospecting our readership. I would also guess that half of our readers are much closer to Addison than twenty-two miles. The bottom line is that fourteen thousand Eagle readers need to know what Holland's has to offer."

It was Rosemary's idea that having the *Eagle* on the drugstore counter of the Addison Drugstore was important. Many businesses owners in Addison would see the paper, which would reinforce that we were an option. So each week when Walter would drop off the papers at the drugstore, and calculate what the store owed us for papers sold the previous week, he concluded the transaction by handing store owner Derek Fogg a five-dollar bill for positioning the paper on the counter. Win/win!

Rosemary was a natural-born sales genius. She had a wonderful ability to see the union of seller and buyer from both perspectives, and often from standpoints that neither side contemplated. She was adroit at pointing out obvious, but often overlooked, sales techniques that went beyond the basic sales approach. "Know what is the best time to call on someone. Be flexible – you may have to come back in fifteen minutes. What is your Plan B if you suddenly have fifteen minutes? Your time is valuable. Look professional. When you are showing advertisers a newspaper with their ad in it, double check beforehand to make sure that the print job on that page is perfect, open to that very page, because you want them focused on their ad and nothing else. If they don't have an ad in the paper, you should leaf through to show them how well it is laid out. Make sure you know if one of their competitors has an ad in that issue, if so, make sure they see it – you won't have to point it out, they will see it. All the time you want to be talking about page after page of news, much of which can only be found right here. Because of that, our readers consume our paper and in the process we lead them to your ad."

"Tell Anita and Peggy the story about the oriental rug ad, Rosemary," said Vickie.

"What oriental rug ad?" inquired Rosemary.

"You know," said Vickie. She brought both arms up alongside her body with palms pointed up.

"Oh, yes," said Rosemary. "Oh, yes!"

We had tried for years to get an oriental rug merchant who was located in one of the major cities to run an occasional ad with us, she explained. He spent a huge amount of money advertising his product in his town, and we finally convinced him to try an ad with us, "We got him to go with a two-week combination rate," said Rosemary. "The ad came in camera ready so all we had to do was paste it into place. But the fun was just beginning."

Pages that have everything ready and pasted into position are placed under a large camera that photographs the page, and that leads to the final step, making the actual printing plate for the page. As the pasted-up page is placed under the camera lens, a glass cover is lowered over the page and locked into place to form an airtight seal in the box containing the artwork. A vacuum is then turned on and all the air is extracted from the box, drawing the glass cover tightly against the page. This assures that everything is on the same focal plane before the camera shoots. The vacuum reaches its limit, shuts off, and the camera clicks.

"So, we have this guy's first-ever ad in our paper and Thursday morning we turn to his ad and ..." Rosemary pauses for effect and Vickie can't stifle her laugher. "A fly had apparently buzzed into the vacuum box just before it was closed and the ad showed this crushed fly desperately peering out right in the corner of his ad!"

"It was funny and sad," said Vickie, giggling.

"What did you do with the client?" asked Peggy, who had joined us about a month earlier.

"I called him and told him we had a printing problem with his ad and that we would run a make-good ad for one additional week at no charge," she said.

"Just one make-good?" said Peggy.

"Absolutely," said Rosemary. "Once you start throwing in all sorts of freebies, it does two things. First, it basically cheapens the value of the paper. It says that we have all sorts of space and can easily throw in this or that."

"And the second thing?" inquired Peggy.

"Once you give something away without a good solid explanation, it quickly becomes an expectation. The advertiser starts thinking like a car buyer and wants to cut a deal every time you walk through the door."

"The *Banner* is always cutting deals," said Vickie. "At first it was tough to sell against that. But now most of our advertisers know that we don't cut deals, so they can calculate exactly what they are spending vs. their competition."

"And many advertisers are now chewing the *Banner* to shreds because they won't run an ad in the *Banner* without some sort of deal," added Rosemary.

"What kind of deals?" asked Peggy who, by now, was totally into the discussion.

"They promise rates that are way off their rate card. They give away spot color in ads, they give away position in the paper, they make up deals on the spot. In short, they are now being gnawed to death by advertisers who know the *Banner* rate card is meaningless," said Rosemary. "And that has severely cheapened the product."

We, like any other business, can, and do, have periodic sales or specials, she explained. "Ed is adamant about the fact that every sale or special we offer *must* have a clearly defined beginning and end. That establishes the finish line, and most retailers understand that because it is exactly what they do."

What about advertisers who continually try to play the *Eagle* against the *Banner* in search of a deal? Our response is always, "The *Banner* knows what their product is worth. And you, Mr. Advertiser will never know who got the best deal, you or your competitor."

"That argument doesn't always win," injected Rosemary, "but by standing firm, we eventually bring them in. Concurrently, the *Banner* is seeing its sales revenues dwindle, down eight percent two years ago and another eleven percent last year."

"But there are some really stubborn advertisers out there," said Anita, "bastards who refuse to advertise without a deal." She went into a sixty-second tirade about Harold's Hobby Shop. And her voice grew louder and louder and the harangue ended with a very vocal "the son-of-a-bitch!"

At that point, the entire editorial staff on the other side of the room burst into applause and Anita stepped forward and executed a charming curtsy.

"That poor little fly," said Peggy, "trying to escape from that vacuum box."

Chapter Twelve

Whenever we traveled to a national press association meeting, fellow publishers from around the country asked about the economic boost the New Hampshire Primary gave the newspaper. They assumed that candidates were flooding us with advertising. The candidate advertising train had pulled out of the station years ago, and most weekly newspapers were not on board. Television had replaced print as the favored message carrier, and New Hampshire and Boston television stations were overwhelmed with ad schedules that often started six to eight months before the election and flooded the airwaves until the polls closed.

We probably got more Primary print advertising than any other New Hampshire weekly newspaper because of two things: a) We had a reputation of being a creditable and knowledgeable source of information about much of the process and b) Madison Avenue had taught me how the media buyers worked. But the campaign ad well was quickly going dry.

Gene Rowley, who was running a campaign for a Midwestern governor who awoke one morning and saw a future president in his shaving mirror, called me one afternoon to pick my brain. For many years Gene and I had served together on a UNICEF committee in New York. Gene wasn't your usual political hack. He worked only for candidates who were in lockstep with his political beliefs. He never had to go out and scrounge for work; everyone wanted his expertise. And Gene had a very high political and ethical bar.

"We need to print up a political flyer to insert in several newspapers in New Hampshire. Is this something you can do?" asked Gene. "We want to keep it totally under wraps until the very last minute."

We could help with it, I told Gene, but we weren't a printer. "We can certainly prepare the piece for you, Gene, and we can connect you with our printer."

He wanted a list of newspapers in the state where the insert should run. I felt I was getting too close to his campaign. "Suggest some papers and I'll be happy to give you my opinion," I said. He rattled off three dailies and two weeklies, one of which was the *Eagle*. "Those are all good newspapers, Gene, and I'm certain they will work with you to keep it quiet until it runs."

I asked him why he wanted this printed up here instead of in DC. He wanted it printed locally so it could say that it was printed locally and didn't look like something dragged in by a bunch of carpetbaggers. "Printed in NH" was the tagline he wanted and I had to break the news that our paper was actually printed in Massachusetts. He quickly regrouped. "How about 'Proudly Printed in New England?'"

"'Proudly printed in New England' it shall be."

I suggested that Gene should do all the prep work in his own shop and send the camera-ready artwork directly to the printer. I agreed to follow up with Patrick Press to make sure that the artwork arrived and the print job was going forward.

Gene certainly could have used the "Printed in NH" line regardless of where the piece was printed, but that kind of deception was not in Gene's genes.

Despite occasional scathing letters about how we were favoring one candidate over another, I was very attuned to keeping myself and our paper firmly on politically neutral terra firma. I often personally supported my favorite candidate after the primary, if he was still running, but I never wanted our paper to be seen as favoring one party over another. We weren't the least bit hesitant about endorsing someone in the final issue before the election, but observant readers knew, I hoped, that that endorsement was based on solid one-on-one conversations with the candidates.

Placing advertising in media all over the country was usually done by using the research of SRDS (Standard Rate and Data Service) out of Chicago. They published a huge volume of data about every newspaper and magazine in the country, including prices, sizes, deadlines, contacts and so forth. It was the media buyers bible. When I purchased the *Eagle*, I quickly bought a small ad in the New Hampshire section of SRDS. Probably ninety-nine percent of all weekly newspapers never use SRDS, which is geared toward major media buyers looking at large metro demographics. For that reason, weekly newspapers that show up in the listing jump right off the page. Over the years our presence in SRDS got several major accounts.

"Somebody from Gran and Drizzle," said Lana. "Line two." Our phones never stopped ringing on Monday morning, and four lights on the phone were constantly illuminated as the deadline window was rapidly closing.

Gran and Drizzle? Who in the hell were they? It had to be some law firm with a legal ad. I picked up the phone.

"Hello, this is Ed Remington," I said.

"Hello Ed, this is Jim Graham with Graham and Driscoll, we're an ad agency in Washington."

I asked him to repeat the name of the firm. "Graham and Driscoll," he said.

I burst out laughing and told him what I heard was Gran and Drizzle. That bit of levity perched that conversation on the right set of rails.

Graham was calling to inform me that they had sent us a full-page ad for one of the presidential candidates and wanted to know if it had arrived. I was just about to tell him no when I glanced over at Lana's desk just as she was pulling the ad out of a long mailing tube.

"It's just arrived, Jim," I said, gesturing wildly at Lana to see if it had shown up with a cashier's check. Ads from political candidates and restaurants must be prepaid, we'd learned over the years. Without payment up front, there was a good chance that we'd never see it. Lana, bless her heart, had already stitched together where I was in my conversation. She had noted Graham and Driscoll on the return address and she knew that my first question was going to be, "Did they send a cashier's check?" She was racing toward my office with the ad in one hand, the check in another, and her coffee cup clinched between her teeth.

"That will run on Thursday, right?" said Graham.

"Correct, Jim, and thanks so much. How did you hear about our paper?" I asked.

"Standard Rate and Data," he said. He then volunteered that they had never done a political campaign before and he picked my brain about some timing issues. We also connected on a couple of mutual friends and the call was over. Wow, pre-paid full-page ad completely out of the blue, what a great way to start a week.

I had heard of the man featured in the ad, a fringe candidate with zero chance of winning. But the money was green and we were probably the only paper that was going to get that ad, because we were in SRDS.

I refilled my coffee and spread out the ad to acquaint myself with the candidate. It was a crisp ad, very well laid out and easy to read. But suddenly the easy read became a difficult read. The ad had the usual sprinkling of jingoistic jerky, you know, truth, justice and the American way, but it then stepped right off the cliff. The ad was peppered with multiple anti-Semitic references. These weren't crafty wordplay jabs, they were blatant accusations. I read and reread the ad to see if perhaps these were some sort of typographic or production errors. They weren't. This guy was about as anti-Semitic as they come. The decision about whether or not to run that ad was an easy one, but before I rejected it outright I wanted Lana and Karen to look it over. I told Lana to hold the cashier's check and asked if she could come to my office. She came right over. "Please look at this ad and give me your opinion," I said.

When she finished reading, she stood up, shot her right hand outward and said, "Holy shit! Is this for real?"

"I think so, and we have the check to prove it. The agency is real and I guess this candidate is too." I began to wonder what this guy was trying to prove.

Karen had much the same reaction as Lana. I told her that the ad would never see the light of day, but I was going to call the agency and see what was up.

I called Graham and Driscoll. Jim was out of the office until after lunch. Great, I had two hours to stew over this, and that is exactly what I did.

Jim returned my call. "Kind of different, isn't it, Ed?" I went off the deep end. When I calmed down Jim and I had a nice conversation about the candidate and the ad. Jim had balked when the ad copy came in but the principals at the agency eventually concluded that the best thing they could do was to take the guy's money and watch him disappear. I wondered why the agency didn't just resign the account on the spot, but decided that my mission wasn't to reform those with poor judgment. I did, however, suggest two or three tweaks to the ad that would make it acceptable. Jim confessed that they had already tried that.

"I can't run the ad as it is, Jim, so I will return your check and that will be that," I said. I'm sure my voice cracked when I mentioned returning the check.

"Shall I throw the ad in the woodstove?" said Lana.

"No, keep it," I answered, although I had no idea why.

However, the following week the ad was printed in the *Banner*. And the week after that, it ran for a second time. It set off a brief barrage of letters in the *Banner* from incensed readers. But because their paper was so full of nothing, not a whole lot of people ever saw the ad.

In our shop, only three of us knew the back story about that ad. But on Dec. 22 the ad was hung on the wall at our Christmas party and staffers won quarters for their dart hitting the photo of the candidate between the eyes. It was sort of a Waring blender moment with people celebrating Christmas with an anti-Semitic ad in the center ring.

He finished right at the bottom of the pack.

* * *

"Your goddam paper isn't worth a shit!" The shout reverberated throughout the building. "You cost Kitsy the title, you bastards." The enraged woman hurled a handful of torn paper into the air.

"Whoa," said Lana, cool as a cucumber. "What are we talking about here?"

"The Little Miss Hancock County Contest," echoed the woman, "You made her lose! I'll never forgive you."

I crossed the room to take this banshee off of Lana's morning menu.

"Hello, I'm –"

"I know who the hell you are and you probably think it's great that you broke a little girl's heart, you bastard," bleated the virago without making eye contact.

"Why don't you come over to my office and we'll get this all sorted out?" I gestured toward my corner.

She pirouetted and headed for my office. With her back turned, it was safe for Lana to shoot her the finger, which launched a snicker from the other four or five people who were already in the office that early Monday morning.

In my office, she plopped herself down in a chair. I asked if I could get her some coffee.

"Hell, no!" she snapped, followed by, "Well, OK."

We had been down this road several times, I knew exactly why she was there. I also knew that the only way to depressurize this woman was to slowly open the valve and let her vent. So I pulled my chair alongside my desk so as to establish a more conversational setting without being separated by four feet of timber.

Vickie delivered the coffee accompanied by a small pitcher of cream and some sugar packets. "Vickie, you are amazing," I said to myself.

The woman, Elizabeth O'Shannessy, tried to tell me the story of the "Little Miss Hancock County" pageant, which is a hoax that turns up every few years. In years when it isn't functioning, we might see "Little Miss Adams County," or who knows what. These bogus pageants go on all the time, targeting kids from four to twelve or thirteen. Actually, they don't target the kids, they target the mothers.

The scam goes something like this: Parents pay an entry fee of fifty to a hundred bucks for their little cherub to be entered. They then pay a modest twelve-dollar fee for the official contest head shot, and additional copies can be purchased for only three dollars each. Of course, the mother needs an eight-by-ten photo of the cherub with the words "Little Miss Hancock County Pageant" emblazoned across the bottom for Aunt Polly, Aunt Kristie, Grandma one, and Grandma two, and a few others and suddenly the modest twelve-dollar photo fee has doubled.

Then comes the coup de grâce, the pageant program. Each contestant is required to sell at least $250 worth of ads in the pageant program. The ads are priced at $20, $30 and $40 each. Advertisers can purchase a full page in the program for $150. Once the contestant has sold the ads and collected the payment for them, any additional ads are bonus points. The contest hasn't even started and it's already off-script in that it is awarding points toward the win, based not on looks or personality but on sales ability. While not a single one of the hundred contestants has yet to hit the runway, each has already ponied up almost $375. And the fun has just begun.

I told Elizabeth to take me through the whole contest experience, hoping that as she heard her own words, if that was possible, that maybe some reality would begin to sink in.

While Elizabeth vented for several minutes, I debated as to whether or not I should just get to the point and tell her that she was a victim of a well-oiled scam that preys on stage mothers. As she unveiled each step in the process, I inquired about the cost, and other details that might snap on the reality switch. When she got to the bit about the ads, I knew we were getting close to the magic moment for her visit.

"So, when Kitsy sold her required ads, she was –" I interrupted her. "She was to notify the local paper and the paper would print the names of the advertisers who were backing Kitsy."

"*Yes*," she said, "exactly. How did you know that?"

"We've been down this well-worn road many times, Elizabeth. Did Kitsy get more points when the newspaper printed her list?" I asked. I knew what the answer was going to be. I also knew that the reality ghost still hadn't made contact with Elizabeth.

"Absolutely, there are bonus points – in fact, this was triple points. And when you ignored us, you cost us those points, and those points probably cost Kitsy the title," she complained. Her hand trembled, her face got beet red, and her voice cracked.

Usually when I see a reaction like that, I offer some words of sympathy, but I have a difficult time doling out sympathy for pure stupidity or ignorance. I held my tongue and let Elizabeth continue with her saga.

But that was the end of the story for Elizabeth. The fact that we had failed to publish Kitsy's list of advertisers was the reason she had lost – case closed.

Kitsy was certainly in line for some serious bonus points; she'd sold almost seven hundred dollars worth of ads for the contest organizers. Little Kitsy O'Shannessy of Elgin, New Hampshire had handed over more than one thousand dollars to the organizers and she had yet to don her tutu!

By using the carrot of getting the names of advertisers published in newspapers, the contest organizers knew that it was going to make the contest more creditable. And it also would make next year's ad sales that much easier. "Look, Mr. Businessman, you're getting additional publicity in the local newspaper for supporting this little girl."

Lost in the translation was that the *Elgin Eagle* was the one who was doing the heavy lifting. Running a list of people who run ads in a bogus contest is not news; it is of zero interest to anyone other than the contestant, the organizers of the scam, and the advertisers who were roped in. Every now and then we might run a cute picture of some little contestant all decked out in her pageant outfit, but no one is going to read a story about who ran ads in a program. Even publishing an anemic story like that is damaging to every other ad in the paper because it gives readers a reason to quit reading. Could I make Elizabeth understand that? I didn't think so, but now that she'd crossed the finish line I wanted to lead her out of pageantland and back to reality.

"Just got two dozen glazed doughnuts from Freda's," said Vickie as she thrust the box through the door of my office. "Help yourself." She handed Elizabeth a napkin. Vickie had taken on the role of floor nurse and her timing was perfect.

Elizabeth was quick to take her up on her doughnut offer. "This is the last thing I need, but I love Freda's doughnuts," she said.

"We all do, Elizabeth," I said grabbing one too.

Over the years I've learned that silence is the strongest stance during confrontational moments. Once I learned to subdue my combative DNA and just let an envelope of silence settle over the situation, things happened. And this was one of those moments. Silence was going to be my next step, aided and abetted by the fact that we both had a mouthful of dough-nut.

I made eye contact with Elizabeth and waited her out. The silence stretched out for perhaps five seconds, but for Elizabeth it probably seemed like five minutes. Finally, she was compelled to fill the void. Previous encounters like this pretty well dictated what she was going to say next, she was going to apologize.

"Mr. Remington, I'm sorry for the way I burst in here today. That's not who I am and it was a bad thing to do," she said.

Hold that silence, there's more to come.

"I was just so frustrated, and so upset over the way the pageant went that I wanted someone to blame. And your paper was it," she said, as more white sugar powder graced her lapels. "But your paper wasn't to blame," she added.

"I think you're right, Elizabeth, and I agree," I said. "The facts that you have laid out this morning pretty well make that case."

I knew that Elizabeth now wanted the confessional door to be slid wide open, but I had neither the time, inclination, nor the proper vestments to hear a full confession. This had been a traumatic three days for Elizabeth and I flipped on the silence switch again. Elizabeth was ready to pour it all out.

Then the fickle finger of fate intervened. From the other side of the office, a verbal outburst had erupted as an irate women was yapping at Lana. The woman glanced around and saw Elizabeth in my office.

"Hi, Elizabeth. What are you doing here?"

"The same thing as you, Meredith," said Elizabeth who had surely heard the outburst, "We need to talk."

"I will in a little while, but right now I have some things I want to get off my chest," huffed Meredith.

"That's what you and I need to discuss, but not here. Please, Meredith, listen to me. Let's go over to Freda's and have a talk. Then you can come back here if you want. Please," begged Elizabeth.

"OK, let's go," said Meredith. She hoisted what looked like an eighty-pound purse over her shoulder and the two of them headed for the door. Lana unclenched her fist from under her desk and with index finger extended began to make circles with her hand alongside her head.

As they got to the door, Elizabeth ushered Meredith through first and then, as Elizabeth entered the doorway, she turned and looked right at me and brought her thumb and forefinger together and flashed a big smile.

A week or so later, Elizabeth and Meredith asked for a meeting. They wanted to tell their story about the Little Miss Hancock County pageant fraud. I told them that we would be more than happy to tell the story, but the fraud accusation was going to have to be a conclusion that the reader would come to. There appeared to be nothing illegal about what the contest organizers were doing. They were legally vacuuming up significant amounts of money brought forth by overanxious parents who left their powers of observation and common sense at the stage door.

Karen assigned the story to Deborah. We had several meetings about how to approach the story without making Elizabeth and Meredith look like fools and also to make sure that we didn't run into a legal skirmish with the Little Miss Hancock County organizers.

Deborah brought in another four sets of parents of princess wannabes, two of them willing to admit they'd been had and two still embarrassed, but wanted to tell all. The story expanded from the Little Miss Hancock County pageant to two others. As it turned out, Elizabeth's fleecing was mild compared with some of the add-ons that others experienced.

In addition to the usual registration, photos and ads, one of the pageants sold pageant attire. With the mention of attire being for sale, it was also quietly revealed to parents that one of the judges was the designer of some of the attire. Others sold seats for the pageant. The pageants were held at the Holiday or Ramada Inn, and the pitch was that the contestants responded much better when they saw familiar faces in the crowd. With that helpful hint, stage parents lapped up a half-dozen premium seats at ten bucks a whack – the pageant "family rate." Guest rooms at the facility were also available at the pageant family rate that the organizers had painstakingly negotiated on behalf of contestants. No cameras were allowed during the pageant lest they distract from the proceedings. But fortunately, organizers had a photographer whose pictures could be purchased.

All of this fun and games was laid out in Deborah's story, and while no accusations were leveled at the pageant organizers, it was caveat emptor for our readers.

After the story about the bogus contests ran, the demands from stage mothers of future Little Miss Hancock County contestants didn't dwindle a bit. As the saying goes, "There is a sucker born every minute." And we always made sure to be stocked up on coffee and glazed doughnuts following such contests, because the waltz was about to repeat.

* * *

I would bet serious money that *Yankee* magazine could instantly confirm this, but I believe ninety-nine percent of all conversations in New England start with comments about the weather. In fact, it is probably a universal conversation fuse everywhere in the world. Past, current, and future weather is a topic of core interest to all.

Naturally, we can't compete with the electronic media when it comes to informing people about current and future weather, but at one staff meeting we discussed reporting past weather trends. "People find something heroic about surviving a fierce thunderstorm," said Dave Harrison. "I don't know why, but I think that is a common response."

"'Mine is bigger than yours' is almost always the direction that is taken when discussing ...," John paused to allow the laughter to rise and fall ... "snowfall amounts."

"But is yesterday's abnormal weather really news other than for gardeners or farmers?" Karen said, in an effort to try to take the discussion to a little deeper level.

"There may be instances where a report on past weather is stitched together with another story in the same edition," said Dave. "For instance, a street fair on Saturday that endured off-and-on rain showers. If there had been torrential rains, that would certainly have been part of the story, but off-and-on showers might not have been reported. People could couple the poor results at the fair with the report on the rain."

"I doubt that many people do that kind of meteorological research," said John. "Yesterday's weather is yesterday's weather. It's gone, and no one gives a hoot."

It was a good discussion, skillfully facilitated by Karen. She led it into a writing lesson. The weather often is a bit player in a story that can inject useful information into the larger picture, she said. Not all stories need a line about the weather, but it ought to go into the writer's consideration hopper.

Weather did become a big issue in our area one Saturday night when a teenager was killed after his car shot off the highway during a rainstorm at 11 p.m. Chris Bourbon arrived on the scene just as the first police car arrived. Chris was on his way home from a party and feeling no pain. He pulled over and ran toward the cluster of people who had just extracted the kid from the car. Halfway across the road, Chris's feet went out from under him and he slid for ten or twelve feet.

"I got out and made it over to the scene to see what I could do. One look and I could tell there was nothing anyone could do," he recounted.

After the victim had been removed, the police asked Chris if he could take some photos of the scene.

"By this time I had pretty much sobered up," said Chris, "but taking accident photos at night on a rain-slicked highway is next to impossible even when you're stone-cold sober. The police wanted the photos for accident investigation purposes, but under those conditions, photos weren't going to reveal a whole hell of lot."

Then it dawned on Chris that he hadn't seen anyone else "bust their ass on the highway like I had done."

"I think I was the only person who had encountered ice," he said. "I relayed that to the state cop in charge, but for some reason it didn't resonate with him. All he wanted was pictures of crumpled tin and damaged guardrails and the tree that administered the fatal blow."

Fortunately, John Hammond, the local road agent, was one of the people who had gathered at the scene and Chris's "busted ass" story got John's instant attention. He had a chat with the state cop and suggested that there might be another significant piece of the story. All traffic was cleared from the highway for at least a quarter mile each direction. Only five cars and a few rescue vehicles had actually made it to the scene, only two of which had approached the scene from the same direction as the victim.

For about an hour, police and rescue personnel walked the lanes and centerline of the highway. They found random patches of ice that had formed over parts of the road. None of them was wider than four or five feet, but they were difficult to see and difficult to find because there was no pattern to them.

Chris photographed the whole episode from the moments after the crash until all responders left the scene at approximately 3:30 a.m. The accident team benefited hugely from his presence to record a vital visual record. The accident team pretty much pinpointed the exact spot where the victim's car hit an icy patch and that, coupled with speed, was the fatal cocktail. The following morning, a second team arrived and John, the road agent, called Chris at home to let him know.

"With four hours of sleep and one hell of hangover, I responded to John's plea to get back out there with my camera," said Chris.

"How come you had a hangover after being out there all night?" asked Deborah.

"Because when I got home I refilled," said Chris.

Ken got the story because he was the only reporter Karen could reach the following morning. Word of the accident had been broadcast over the police scanners, but the rescue was so fast that there was very little chatter to suggest that it was anything exceptional. One code 10-79 went out, a code to notify the medical examiner, which suggested a fatality. That was followed by a 10-21, which was a request for the medical examiner to use the telephone and not the radio. The last thing anyone wanted was a gaggle of spectators. Ken had heard it but it was twenty miles away from him so he let it go, knowing that three or four other staffers lived much closer.

When Ken arrived at the scene and linked up with Chris, a new accident investigation team had just arrived. John told them that Chris had photographed the scene extensively the night before, and Chris played a card that might prove helpful to all.

"What would be the chance of getting a large front end loader down here right now?" Chris asked John.

"For what reason?" John responded.

"Because I think with about eight or ten feet of elevation, I can get a photo that will show exactly what happened."

Everyone knew pretty much what had happened, why it happened, and where it happened, but Chris was suggesting that one photo could tell the entire story. John instantly jumped on the suggestion. "I can have my maintenance chief bring one down. How soon do you need it?" he asked.

"As soon as possible. Because in about forty-five minutes the sun is going to highlight that fatal ice patch, and five minutes later that ice will be gone," said Chris. "But even if the ice patch is gone, the photo will still tell the story, and we can use some traffic cones to outline the location of the ice patch."

The lead investigator from the State Police investigation team listened to the exchange and then mentioned that they would like to outline the perimeter of the ice sheet before it disappeared. Chris knew that a photo showing a white line around it would be powerful, but Chris knew that a bare bones photo showing the road without added markings would make a sober impression. He negotiated an agreement that, if need be, they could outline the icy patch whenever they felt it was necessary.

John, using the mobile telephone in his car lit a fuse under his maintenance supervisor, Charlie Gallus, who, twenty minutes later, arrived on the scene with the loader. They positioned it according to Chris's wishes, and he climbed into the bucket and they raised it as high as it would go. Chris, being the perfectionist that he is, told them to lower it and reposition it about four feet more to one side.

"I couldn't believe it," said Ken, "Chris was the guy in charge, telling cops where stand, what to do. It was a hoot."

"Where to stand?" asked Karen when the story was being retold in a staff meeting.

"No," said Ken, "poor choice of words. Where *not* to stand."

Chris knew that his shot was going to disappear any instant and once the loader bucket was at altitude, there were several responders in the frame.

"I wanted a clean, stark shot," said Chris, "so I asked them to please get out of the shot."

"You weren't that polite, Chris, but they got the message."

The shot said it all. It clearly showed the ice patch, the skid marks, the crumpled roadside barrier, and the fatal tree. It needed no explanation.

With the help of John Hammond, Ken really got into this story. They researched how many accidents had occurred along that stretch of road and convinced the state to post a lower speed limit through the area. John even convinced Chief Harley to run more radar through there. The state cops also responded with increased radar. With that intensive surveillance, amped up by repeated stories in the *Eagle*, that section of road was reduced from a kill zone to an accident-free zone – almost.

But writing more speeding tickets was just the frosting, the real cake underneath was carefully baked by John, aided by a strong and vivid portfolio of *Elgin Eagle* pictures. John built a bulletproof case that the stretch of road was poorly designed and invited accidents. Eventually, the state rebuilt the whole section of road in the largest regional road construction project in the preceding fifty years. In the interim, on cold nights, state highway vehicles unloaded huge amounts of sand and road salt along that stretch of highway – much to the delight of area body shops, which thrived as salt gnawed away at auto undercarriages.

* * *

We didn't want to surrender all weather stories to the electronic media gang, so we decided to publish a weekly photo of the weather monitor chart that someone donated to us. This device had a central drum that looked like a soup can, around which was mounted the paper sheet to capture the movements of the temperature bar, a long bar hooked up to a temperature sensor. At the end of the bar was a tiny pen that marked the weather on the chart for one week. It was somewhat interesting, but was anyone reading it? I doubted it.

So after a year we ditched it, and the uproar from readers was significant. "What happened to the weather chart?" fifteen or twenty people demanded. When fifteen or twenty readers respond, that is a fairly significant sample. The weather chart feature was quickly revived.

The instructions for placement of the weather chart machine advised that the sensor be ten to fifteen above ground so as not to be influenced by warm roads or sidewalks. The wire from the temperature sensor to the actual machine was all of three feet long. We had no second story in our building so there was no good place to put the machine. But right across the street was an old feed store that hadn't had a retail establishment in it for twenty years. It was owned by a couple of spinster daughters of the now-deceased owner of the building. Over the years, everyone and his dog had tried to purchase the building from the two women, who lived in upstate New York, but they never wanted to discuss it. They put just enough money in it to keep it structurally sufficient and visually acceptable. And a local architect and a stationery shop had worked out some sort of rental agreement to store records in the building.

The two women, Marge and Elsie, really liked Ellen because they had seen her on Broadway. So Ellen was sent on a mission to convince them to allow us to perch this tiny device on an inside second-story windowsill and have a little sensor slipped under the closed window.

Ellen took the "girls," as the locals had dubbed them, to lunch. They then visited the building and Ellen explained how it all would work. She showed them the machine and the sensor and after much fussing, they concluded that it was a safe thing to do. The following week I went over and plopped the machine on the sill, opened the window, tacked the probe on the outside and added a twenty-five-foot extension cord to get power to the unit.

Once a week, Lana would wander over to the building and remove the old chart and affix a new one. Every other month or so she would refill the ink reservoir and that was about it.

Five or six months after the weather station was installed, the "girls" returned to town and walked through their building. They then marched across the street and informed me that they were unaware that the machine was electrical. I tried to explain that the amount of electricity required to move a needle up and down a half an inch and revolve a drum every seven days was insignificant, but they wanted to make sure of that.

I told them that I would check it out and see what the cost was and if we owed them any money for the time we had already occupied their space we would certainly reimburse them.

I wrote a letter to the local electric utility giving the mechanical specifications that were included with the weather station. Several days later I got a call from an engineer at the utility asking how formal his response letter should be. I told him this was really serious business for the "girls," so be as clear and concise as possible.

The engineer's letter arrived and I forwarded it to Marge and Elsie in New York. The utility company's letter included all the math they had used to arrive at the conclusion that the *Elgin Eagle* weather station was most likely consuming three cents of electricity per year. Given that we'd already been running the machine for about five months, we owed the girls somewhere between one and one and one half cents. I was about to suggest that we just round it up to two cents, and prepay for another full year and glue a nickel on to the page. But I wasn't one hundred percent confident that levity would go over here.

Ellen followed up with a phone call to the girls and all enjoyed a good laugh. Ellen included a one-year complimentary subscription to the *Eagle*, and the weather station kept on turning.

Many readers receive our newspaper via the U.S. Postal Service. Postal subscriptions have a significant upside and a small downside. It is good for the homebound subscriber, and it is good for us because it's a sure sale every week. But it requires a lot of work to serve that group of readers, which is approximately twenty percent of our total readership.

We went through a long process of moving from using the Addressograph machine to imprint addresses, to a computer-based system that was supposed to simplify the process. We printed labels every week, and a few months later our printer acquired a machine that allowed us to just deliver a multi-folded stack of green bar computer printout of the labels that were electronically cut up and glued onto copies to be mailed. All postal copies were then placed in individual mail sacks for each town. We also devoted considerable effort to get the mail to each town's post office in time to make that day's delivery.

It was extremely important that our Thursday newspaper be received on Thursday.

A stack of newspapers being dropped off on the steps of a rural post office at 4:00 a.m. is also bundled according to postal route, assuring that the rural carrier can grab the bundle and hustle out the door and deliver the papers that morning. The burden is on us to keep those postal routes current. Most postmasters are very helpful, because attention to detail at our end makes their jobs run smoothly. There were, however, a couple of curmudgeon postmasters who didn't seem to grasp that without patrons, they'd be shut down.

One little post office that was in the back of a general store was in the postal service shutdown crosshairs. We joined the squawking from the locals and actually amplified it when our story was picked up by the *Boston Globe*, and the general store post office survived. Picking up the morning mail was a town ritual – most of the world's problems were addressed and solved in those get-togethers.

However, in dealing with fourteen separate post offices, you always had one postmaster who knew all the rules and insisted that they be followed to the hilt.

Warren Fushardt was the postmaster in Tucker, one of the smaller towns on the fringe of our readership. Lana nicknamed him Warren Fuzzyfart, and he was a royal pain in the ass. Every postal rule had to be followed to the letter, which elevated him from postmaster to being a postal inspector and enforcer. One week, he refused to deliver the papers until the following day because our driver had left them on the wrong loading dock. There were two loading docks at the back of that facility and they were side by side! One side, apparently, was for arrivals and the other, ten feet away, was for departures.

When the Tucker subscribers didn't get their papers that week, Fushardt told them that the screw-up was with the *Eagle*. One or two episodes like that could be enough for a subscriber to cancel his or her subscription and go back to getting the paper at the local store. Instead of getting the paper fifty-two times a year, he might drop down to forty-eight or fifty. It doesn't sound like much, but every week, X number of loyal readers simply don't get around to reading the paper and that impacts the effectiveness of ads in the paper. It's not a huge impact, but given the tiny profit margins that many of our advertisers work with, one sale could move the needle. Besides, it's a compact between the advertiser and the paper that I was determined to honor.

I went to Tucker to find out why so many Tucker readers had called our office looking for their *Eagle*. It took a while to get the specifics about the papers being left on the wrong side of the dock and when it was revealed, I blew my top. What a pompous son-of-a-bitch, I thought, or maybe I said it aloud. It was time for a drive down Spaulding Orchard Road to settle down and not widen the gulf between us and the bastard Tucker postmaster.

But Fuzzyfart soon surfaced again, and this time we rolled the dice and won.

He called me one day to inform me that the weekly ad for one of the local parochial schools was against the law; a postal regulation prohibited advertising that promoted gambling. And Fuzzyfart was dialed in on the ad for the Blessed Sacrament School that told readers about the weekly Friday night bingo game.

He informed me that we were breaking the law by running that ad.

The school was in Ralston, the next town up from Tucker. That whole segment of our readership, I'm certain, had more Catholics per square mile than anywhere else. Blessed Sacrament was fading fast and those bingo games were a major player on their balance sheet. I knew this because I had written a story about the Friday night bingo games and got to know several of the sisters who ran the school.

The bingo games were an event, and they were attended by people from all over the region. The school gymnasium was packed with bingo players, each one holding court over six to twelve bingo cards. Adjacent to the spread of cards in front of many players were a few lucky charms to entice the bingo gnomes to do the right thing. It was serious business for the players and vital business for the school. And you could cut the smoke in the hall with a knife. There must be an unwritten rule that you need to chain smoke to play bingo.

As the bingo games' popularity grew the school added a remote flashboard that enabled fifteen additional player tables to be set up in a long hallway allowing room for another hundred players. On any given Friday night, approximately three to four hundred people flocked to Blessed Sacrament school to try their luck. It helped finance the school, but it wasn't going to save it. The school had been struggling for years and the sisters who ran it kept doubling and redoubling their efforts. We dropped off a bundle of twelve complimentary newspapers each week and two or three times a year we got a sweet thank you note.

Now this postmaster had decided that he was going to prohibit the school from announcing this lifeline to its very survival.

"Mr. Fushardt," I said, "Bingo game ads from parochial schools run all over this state, and no one except you is objecting. That bingo game is the very life blood of that school. I don't give a damn what your rule book says, those ads weren't in the mind of the rule book writers."

"It's gambling pure and simple," answered the officious twit.

"Here's next week's headline, Mr. Fushardt," I said before he could continue, *"Tucker Postmaster Shuts Down Blessed Sacrament Bingo Games."* He started to speak and I cut him off and barked, "The week after that news breaks, Mr. Fushardt, the headline is going to be something like, *'Tucker Postmaster Found Dead In Woods,'* because everyone associated with that school knows how important those weekly games are to the school and how important that school is to the entire region. So if you want to call in your postal Gestapo, Mr. Fushardt, you go right ahead, but that ad will be in the *Elgin Eagle* next week and for as long as they want to run it."

I drew in a breath and added, "If you want us to run a story about how you feel about the ads, we'll consider it. I don't think such a story would accomplish much of anything other than to draw crosshairs on your forehead, but if you'd like us to inform readers of your diligence in reading and interpreting the postal rule book, we would consider such a story. In fact, maybe it would be of interest to our readers."

I figured that by now, Fuzzyfart could either see the edge of the cliff, or maybe he was a true masochist. "It's against the rules," he huffed, "but I'm not going to push it."

Bingo!

Every few years, an aggressive group of U.S. Congress folk would encourage the Postal Rate Commission to kill the subsidy for second-class mailings. This would launch a series of phone calls and meetings with various members of Congress to make their voice heard and defend the ability of newspapers to be delivered to rural customers. Quotes such as "A popular Government, without popular information, or the means of acquiring it, is but a Prologue to a Farce or a tragedy; or, perhaps both," [James Madison, 1822] would be appended to the appeals. When the dust had settled, the second-class rates might have inched up a little, but they were still in place.

The more I got into the issue, the more fervent became my concern. We were a very rural area with several months of horrendous weather that often made travel impossible for elderly subscribers. So the postman, charging through snow, rain, heat, or gloom of night, was quite often their main connection with the outside world. And the *Eagle* delivered that connection in a nice bundle every week.

Because we were using the postal service, the *Eagle* was treated as mail and was always put inside the rural postal box rather than shoved into an open tube, like the *Globe* and the *Arnett Messenger*.

We had one customer who did receive his newspaper in a newspaper tube.

Charlie Cornman was an eighty-plus-year-old veteran of World War I. He and I had become good friends over the years. His health was deteriorating and he was basically confined to his house which was barely heated. The local Rotary Club built a ramp that allowed him to be wheeled outside on occasion, but those excursions were few and far between. As the years passed, so did a lot of Charlie's friends, and those who were still around couldn't get to his little shack. Inside his house he was fairly self-sufficient, able to cook, bathe, and carry on with a well-honed routine, and concerned neighbors checked in on him from time to time. Dan Caldwell, one of our drivers, was one of Charlie's chums. They often shared army stories and Dan would occasionally be called in to adjust the rabbit ears on the TV so Charlie could watch the Sox game. Dan, who raised and trained dogs before he retired, had given Charlie a huge golden retriever named Rufus, who occupied half the space in the shack. Charlie and Rufus were inseparable.

One day Dan stopped by my office to tell me about an inventive device he'd created for Charlie – and Rufus. He mounted a spring-loaded "door" on one end of an eighteen-inch-long piece of six-inch diameter plastic pipe to make a tube for the newspaper. He attached the tube under the mailbox, and every week while doing his *Eagle* run he swung by Charlie's and put a copy of the *Eagle* wrapped in plastic and tied with some dayglow surveyors tape, into the tube. The tube was mounted at a slight angle, allowing the tail of the surveyors tape to hang out of the open end. When Charlie heard a triple toot of Dan's horn, he opened the door and Rufus tore down the driveway, grabbed the protruding tape, and proudly carried the newspaper back to the house firmly in the grasp of his enormous mouth. I thought about that moment every Thursday and so did many others, because when the little dayglow tail of surveyors tape vanished each Thursday, it was a sign that Charlie was alive and well. Many staffers routinely reported in, "Charlie got his paper – the *Eagle* has landed."

Our weekly cartoon came from a national news syndicate. They were particularly proud of the *Elgin Eagle* because weekly newspapers rarely, if ever, signed on with national syndicates. There were many reasons for this, foremost of which was the cost. Syndicates that offer cartoons generally cater to the large metro dailies. The syndicates send them a weekly package of seven or more cartoons. A weekly will only run one cartoon a week, but the syndicate isn't in a position to decide which one to send. So they could either send the entire package of seven or more, a cost that no weekly could afford, or else just cater to dailies.

At a National Newspaper Association meeting I met Bill Simpson, the representative for American News Syndicate (ANS), the premier news syndicate in the U.S. Virtually all dailies in the country subscribed to some of ANS's services, whether it was filler material, cartoons, columns, crossword puzzles, or pictures. Bill and I worked over a bottle of Dewars one night in a saloon in Kansas City and between us we crafted a way that the *Eagle* could receive the weekly cartoon package at a ridiculously low rate. I loved the cartoons and Bill thought having them in an award-winning weekly might open up a new opportunity for ANS.

So cartoons arrived every Friday afternoon and we had the privilege of selecting one from the smorgasbord of seven to twelve offerings. As a bonus, ANS sent me a box of eight Omaha Steak filets each Christmas. Ellen would carefully tuck steaks into the back of our home freezer awaiting just the right circumstance to share them. The end result was that the steaks, through multiple freeze/defrost cycles, gradually became something akin to old Bean boots. Even Typo, our dog, treated them as low-grade carrion and buried them in the woods hoping that some area coyote would find them and haul them away. Once, when we presented the freezer-burned stuff to Typo, he walked to the edge of our cantilevered deck and pitched them over the side one at a time. In addition to the steaks, we had enough Omaha Steaks Styrofoam shipping boxes to built a multi-room igloo.

But the Omaha Steaks and a bottle or two of booze from our printer were the only gifts that we accepted. Most respectable newspapers followed the same pattern, but we probably carried it to extremes. When we did restaurant reviews, we tried to arrive incognito and always paid for the meal. When we sent a reporter out to review a play, we always paid for the ticket. Any gifts sent to us were promptly returned to the sender with a polite note. This policy was discussed in depth with all of our staff and they were happy to be free to do a guilt-free story.

Privately and good-naturedly, fellow publishers complained to me about the policy. Every four or five months I had morning coffee with each of the fellow publishers from around the area to share common problems and find out what was new in the rapidly changing world of newspaper production. Our policy of purchasing our own tickets brought some good-natured condemnation from Alek Hallitus, publisher of the *Addison American*. "We feel like a bunch of cheap beggars," he said. I tried to soften the blow by commenting that we had dug ourselves into a hole and now it was impossible to extricate ourselves. "We can't suddenly declare that hereafter we want free tickets, meals, or whatever," I said. "We don't publicize our policy, so quit fretting, Alek – you cheap bastard." He loved it.

We also went out of our way to try to keep personal friendships out of the mission. This was difficult, given the small size of our staff, but we encouraged any reporter not to worry about declining a story due to a personal friendship. This also held true for reporting on anything in which the reporter had an interest. I never filed a story on any organization of which I was a member. When a member of one of those organizations approached me, I always responded that one of our reporters would be in touch with him. That, of course, didn't insulate me from either the glee or the glum once a story was printed. But that is the nature of the news business.

On one occasion, due to a hostile news source, I intentionally violated my own rule. A large company in Arnett was going to be acquired by a company in a another state. I went to the press event where the company management made the announcement, and their rationale for the sale made no sense to me. This story was a natural for the *Arnett Messenger*, the daily in the town where the company was located. At the news conference, in addition to myself there were reporters from the *Messenger*, the *Banner*, and another paper. There were also two "reporters" from a couple of area radio stations. Radio stations in our area were populated by disk jockeys, not reporters with notepads. As company management extolled the benefits of the sale, the press gaggle were all busy taking notes. I had a lot of questions, but I didn't want to ask them with the other reporters in the room. If someone else thought of the same question, great, but I wasn't going to spoon feed a daily and radio stations who, by virtue of their news cycles, were going to be able to scoop us by forty-eight hours in this case.

One young reporter from the *Messenger* actually got off a couple of good questions, but the company spokesmen's verbose answers didn't address the question. The kid tried a follow-up, but the spokesman was getting irritated and let everyone in the room know it. Part of me wanted to defend the kid and smack down the surly vice-president who was enjoying being the center of attention. But I held my tongue. The *Eagle*'s mission is "to give our readers local information that they couldn't get anywhere else," and I was confident that given a few moments alone with the company executive, I could add a lot of backstory that thus far hadn't been part of the discussion.

While the rest of the media shuffled out of the room I engaged some of the company personnel in some blather about nothing until the room had cleared. Once the room had emptied, I uncorked my question, which concerned current salaries of company management. I suspected that this sale was basically a massive unfurling of golden parachutes for the top brass, and to hell with the local workers. The spokesman said that he didn't have that information at hand. I asked him if he could find a copy of their latest 10k filing with the Securities and Exchange Commission. That report would have all salary information. He hemmed and hawed and finally dismissed me by saying they didn't have a copy.

Bullshit!

I was boiling mad and returned to the office and called a broker friend in New York. A couple of minutes later, I was the proud owner of one share in the company and was entitled to lots of information. The share cost $13.10 and the sales commission cost $7.70! I probably could have gotten the information without going the stockholder route, but I wanted some additional standing.

Thus, after that purchase I was *technically* reporting on something in which I had an interest, but the company's sleazy approach left me no other choice. So I retained the services of Steve Carroll, a retired writer for the *Wall Street Journal*.

This distanced me from direct involvement as I let Steve follow the trail, often using my status as a stockholder to extract information from company management. Most requests were for information that was already public, but the stockholder status speeded up the responses. We could see some massive self-enrichment on the part of company officers and the employees were going to be left twisting in the wind. We couldn't talk about intent, of course, but the facts spoke for themselves. And we stood on that soapbox alone; for many months no other paper joined our chorus. But the company's employees got the message and their reaction was loud, heartfelt, and totally dismissive of their management that was totally dismissive of them. Within twelve months following the sale, company management slowly disappeared into the night.

Three hundred and fifty-six people lost their jobs in Arnett because the company was moved to Alabama. All existing stockholders were encouraged to surrender their stock certificates for new ones. But my certificate was more than just a piece of paper. It still hangs, framed, on my wall.

Chapter Thirteen

When a community newspaper office is located in or near the retail hub of a town, it often serves as a de facto information bureau for both locals and visitors. Our location was perfectly sited for that role.

"A *what*?" inquired Lana. She held the phone several inches from her ear due to the caller's excitement. "I don't understand. What's a japonabike, some sort of flower?"

A brief silence followed, and then Lana threw her head back and covered her face with her forearm to stifle a laugh.

"Where again?" she said. "OK, thanks so much!" She put down the phone and buried her head in her folded arms. "I can't believe how dumb I am," she cried. Tears ran down her face and her distinctive cackling laughter reverberated through the office.

Karen had already made her way across the room to help sort out whatever needed to be sorted out, and five or six staffers who were there also suspended whatever individual tasks were at hand until the suspense was revealed.

Lana kept her head buried in her arms, occasionally raising it to gasp for air. An outer ring had formed around Lana's desk comprised of everyone else in the room as Karen bent over Lana and gradually extracted the story.

A reader had called in about a possible story, but the way the caller framed it just didn't come across to Lana.

When Lana heard "japonabike," she went one way while the caller continued straight ahead. Eventually she heard the caller saying there was a "Jap on a bike" out on the highway and he was crossing the country from east to west.

Before the laughter died down, and even though it was 5:00 p.m. every reporter in the room begged Karen for the story, but calm, cool Karen had two criteria that needed to be met before giving out the assignment. She mentally brought up the manifest for the next issue, who had what and where it stood. She also wanted to make certain that whoever got the story, *got* the story. Was this more than just a bike trip? Was there another purpose, message, or mission?

Just then, Chris Bourbon came in and announced that he had just run across a young Japanese guy who was biking across the country.

Such coincidences as this were not unusual for our newsroom. Due partly to the fact that we were a perceived information hub and partly due to location, we won by default.

Just a few months before, Ken Taft, a member of the Boston Red Sox, stopped at Freda's for a late breakfast. No one recognized him given the sunglasses and lack of any Red Sox logo anywhere, but Joe Spitalli, one of the short-order cooks, spotted him the moment he walked through the door. He immediately called our sports editor, John Sedlak, who was one of his teammates on a local slo-pitch team. John rushed over to Freda's and took the booth next to the incognito guest. John wrote a little note on a placemat saying, "Ken, I know it's your day off and you don't need any interruptions but if you could spare me three minutes after the meal, we could meet outside and no one will know you were here until next Thursday. Thanks! John Sedlak, sports editor, *Elgin Eagle*."

Ken turned around and said, "No problem, John, and thanks for understanding."

After the meal, John and Ken met at the back of Freda's kitchen and John got off a few questions and a little inside baseball chat. It was a thrill for John, but the best part was the picture that Freda shot with John's camera. It showed Ken and John talking and just behind them was Joe Spitalli, the grinning short order cook. He was wielding a spatula trying to look busy, but it was clearly visible that the skillet was completely empty.

Karen assigned Sally to catch up with the young cycler. Peggy, one of our ad sales people, asked to go along. Everyone sort of paused for a moment at this attempted blending of ad sales and reporting, two ingredients that we tried to keep from going into the same bowl. Before anyone could even think, "What?" Peggy explained, "We lived in Japan for almost four years and I speak very good Japanese."

"Let's go," said Sally amidst a few shouts of *sayonara* and one audible *sake*. The two words emptied the entire Japanese-language vault of the *Elgin Eagle*.

This is the fun part of the news business, it is almost totally in the *now*. News doesn't just happen from eight to five or only Monday through Friday. The news cycle is never ending and fitting in stories such as a random Japanese cyclist with an ongoing story about a town that is putting the final touches on its annual budget is the challenge, the mission, and the fun. Orchestrating these static and random pieces was what kept my heart beating. Distributing the unexpected, over-the-transom news stories was a skill that made Karen such an important part of our team. She had a limitless mental data bank of who had handled what stories and was able to dole out assignments so that everyone felt they had gotten exactly what they wanted.

Another layer was always in play in our newsroom. Not all news stories start with an assignment. Some just happen when a reporter is close by. Had a reporter spotted the

Japanese cyclist first, it would have been his or her story. However, there still would have been a personal moment when that reporter would have graciously handed that story over to someone else if there was any possibility that he was intruding on someone else's turf or beat.

Most of our reporters were using the *Elgin Eagle* as a stepping stone to more prestigious and profitable journalistic destinations. An important goal of their *Eagle* tenure was to build the resume, the clip file. A good clip file would show a wide variety of stories including breaking news, routine news, feature writing and interviews. Our interview process wasn't any different from that of dailies. In addition to writing skills, we also looked at the breadth of stories and the ability of the writer to tell a story in a manner that could hold the reader's interest, even when the subject matter was flaccid.

"Takayuki Muro, this is my boss, Ed Remington," said Sally, presenting the nineteen-year-old Japanese student who was hoping to cross the U.S. by bicycle over the summer.

"Konnichiwa," I said, which I knew was a safe "hello" in Japanese. I quickly switched to English to get the conversation going in a direction where I could be a participant. "Where do you live in Japan?" I asked, mindful that any answer would resonate about as strongly with me as would a listing of bird species found in Tanzania.

"Sapporo," said Takayuki. "Do you know it?" Well, he speaks English, I thought. That will help us get to the core of his story.

"Oh, yes, the winter Olympics," I said. "A very pretty part of the country."

We chatted for a few minutes, with Vickie occasionally stepping in to get the language train back on the rails. Night was coming on, and Takayuki would soon head down the road to find a desolate place to spend the night. Sally was hinting that she would like to take him home, sort of like a stuffed bear that she had won at a carnival, but she also knew that it wasn't a real professional move. I called Ellen and explained the situation and an hour later, Takayuki was sharing dinner at our house along with Karen, Sally and Vickie. His English improved as the night wore on, and he tore into Ellen's grilled rib eyes like a starving dog.

He had been on the road for over a month, starting in Washington, DC, then north to Boston before heading west. He apparently opted for the New Hampshire route to avoid traffic. We learned that he was an only child and his father had died in an industrial accident four years earlier. He was studying mechanical engineering at a Japanese university, but wanted to take a year off to do the U.S. bike trip.

"When was the last time you talked with your mother?" asked Ellen. On the day he left DC, more than a month ago, he told her. "Well, let's call her. What time would it be in Sapporo right now?"

"She will be eating breakfast right now," replied the young man.

A helpful international operator stitched the call together and we all left the room while Takayuki and his mother caught up on things, and then she asked to talk with me. I took the phone and motioned for Takayuki to share the earpiece with me. The mother was so overcome with hearing her son's voice that she could barely speak, but she laced the next few seconds with multiple thanks. She then wanted to talk with Ellen, and that conversation reached another level that resulted in tears flowing down the faces of both Ellen and Takayuki. While they were both pressed up to the phone earpiece, I took a couple of photos. Those pictures were a big part of a half-page spread that Sally wrote for the *Eagle*.

The sooner we got Takayuki into a shower, Ellen and I agreed, the happier everyone would be. Public showers for cross-country cyclers are not common, particularly along the back roads. We finally convinced him that a shower would be a good idea and we washed all his clothes. Early the next morning, after a quick review of his maps, I loaded his bike into the back of the car and dropped him off at the exact spot where we had picked him up some fourteen hours earlier. I had him address a manila envelope to his mother so I could send her copies of Sally's story. I gave him two stamped, self-addressed postcards and asked him to send us one from any-place in the Midwest and the other when he completed the journey. We never received either, and "Japonabike" became another closed chapter in *Eagle* lore.

Everyone talked about the story for two weeks and then it was bumped by a family who had driven an oxcart all the way to New Hampshire from Kansas. They too were adopted by the *Eagle* family. This time Dave Harrison, who rented a small cabin at Hickory Hill Farm just outside of town, was the host. The owners of the farm were thrilled with the prospect of host-ing an ox-drawn wagon, and we had another feature story that was beyond the expectations of our readers. Word of the team spread among ox-team owners around the area and at least three people stopped by the farm that night to talk ox with the Kansas family. Several months later, the family concluded their journey at Lubec, Maine. One of the people who vis-ited them in Elgin bought the oxen, and a potato farmer from Aroostook County, Maine bought the wagon. For two or three years thereafter, the ox team would show up in various area parades sporting a sign that read, "The Oxen Who Walked Across America." Well, only half of America, but why quib-ble? The family hopped a plane from Boston to Kansas, and everyone lived happily ever after.

One addendum to the ox story demonstrates the intercon-nectivity of everything around us and why we in the media need to stay focused on that reality. When the various ox owners made their way down to the Hickory Hill Farm to talk with the Kansas family, Dave Harrison was sort of the official greeter. He followed up the Kansas story with a separate story about ox teams in the area. That story had a pretty vertical appeal, of interest to a smaller segment of readers. One ox mentioned in the story became a local celebrity. Sargent (named for the John Singer Sargent painting *Shoeing the Ox*), suddenly found himself a regional folk hero following a story Dave wrote.

Sargent and Tailore (I think it meant 'golden tail'), the dog on the farm where Sargent lived, were the best of friends. If Tailore was present, Sargent was a magnificent draft animal, capable of pulling mammoth loads of fallen timber out of the forest. On the other side of Sargent's yoke was Singer, who'd do his daily chores regardless of the presence of Tailore. But Sargent wouldn't budge if Tailore wasn't nearby. Dave presented this relationship between an ox and a dog in a wonderfully written piece that he worked on for weeks. A local writer picked up the story and within a few months, a children's book was published with a sweet storyline about the two friends, featuring eighteen incredible watercolor pictures. That led to a small segment on a national morning news show, and Dave was given credit for launching the whole thing.

When one is at the crossroads of day-to-day activity, there is a natural tendency to try to fit the pieces together into something real or rational. All newspapers receive far more information than any single person or entity. It is also the landing zone for far more information than it can use. There is a nonstop process of sifting through that daily load of information in search of news, perhaps an additional or missing piece to an ongoing story or a glowing ember for a completely new one. Dozens of offshoots shine light into the recesses of daily life and allow us to present to our readers some of the wonders that are right around them.

It all comes down to people interacting with people.
Whether they're driving an oxcart, pedaling a bike across
the country, or arguing about a town budget, people are the
very core of the news business. And that's what makes it the
best job in the world.

* * *

Late one fall afternoon, a call came across the police scanner
announcing that an elderly patient was missing from a local
nursing home. I heard the call, and decided to swing by and
see what was being done. As I stopped in front of the facility,
Dennis pulled in right behind me. As we were headed toward
the building we both noticed Chief Harley, who lived one block
over, strutting down the sidewalk.

It was a Saturday afternoon and the chief wasn't in uniform – in fact he looked, and walked, as though he had just
left some Oktoberfest celebration. There was no sense of urgency in his gait; he was there to be seen and take charge. One
of the younger cops was already on the scene, as were several
members of the fire department. This was a recipe for disas-
ter, because police and fire personnel are like oil and water.
That was the divide in all small towns, an inherent competition between red and blue.

However, in those emergency situations when both departments were involved, there was usually something on fire. In
that case, the top fire official was in charge of the scene and the
police force knew enough to resign themselves to traffic control and stay out of the way. But a missing person emergency
requires lots of people to begin an organized search. And the
chief immediately stepped in to be the major domo, in spite
of the fact that his breath could have cleaned a carpet. He
asked very few questions of the nursing-home personnel, then
dispatched a large search team to sweep the area from the
nursing home down to the river, about a quarter mile away.

It was all woodland, but easily traversed. He conjectured that the missing man, Robert McClennan, might be headed to the main road out of town, so he dispatched another team to sweep that route. Dennis made notes of the chief's orders, and we took some pictures of local volunteers wandering aimlessly in and out of the adjacent woods. We asked the nursing-home director to get us a good picture of McClennan, and offered to print up extra copies if other papers wanted to run the photo in an attempt to locate him.

Over the next several days, posters went up in every shop window and soon state television channels were periodically showing pictures of the missing person. Five days later, Robert McClennan had still not been found.

The chief then arranged for dragging operations to take place in the river and a massive leafleting effort papered both sides of all roads leading to and from town. The chief guessed that McClennan's destination might be his home in Ohio, and the entire search took on a Horace Greeley look as the focus headed west.

Three weeks after McClennan vanished, his story dropped from the news cycle. The chief discontinued his periodic news sessions and the world moved on.

A year later, a young boy in a local park got lost. After fifteen or twenty minutes he showed up at the home of Dan and Susan Dimperio. In his brief sojourn through the woods, the boy had come across a metal bracelet bearing the name and blood type of one Robert McClennan. The kid put it in his pocket, and several minutes later wandered into the Dimperio's back yard, weeping in relief as he realized that he wouldn't have to spend the night alone in the woods. After a few minutes, he showed Susan what he had found. She immediately stitched it together and called the police station. They informed her that it was dinnertime and someone would be out shortly. She was infuriated.

I had known Susan for years ever since she chaired a committee to get sidewalks installed around the local grade school. There was nothing shrill about her, but she had a great determination that was infectious to all around her. She established a committee, all moms, and in no time the sidewalk expansion also included increased areas around the grade school *and* the middle school as well.

Being blown off by a hungry cop was not something that sat well with Susan Dimperio. She informed him that she was going to call the *Eagle*, and she did.

Karen got the call and summoned Dennis, who had covered McClennan's disappearance a year before. It was five-thirty on a Wednesday afternoon and the paper was pretty much laid out. We were crunching out the final galley proofs of various stories and completing the weekly jigsaw puzzle of piecing it all together. Dennis and Karen came into my office and told me what Susan had said. This was obviously a huge story, and it raised as many questions as it answered. McClennan's medical bracelet was found, but where was McClennan? Had he taken off the bracelet, was it stolen from his room, were his remains nearby? And the side story might be the lackadaisical police response to Susan's call.

Dennis and I took off for the Dimperio's, five minutes away. When we got there one of the younger town cops, Steve Hill, was also pulling up. Apparently Susan's threat to call the *Eagle* caused someone in the police department to forsake the pork chop in favor of the police cruiser. We stood by as Officer Hill interrogated Susan and the scared kid. Hill was new to the force, straight out of the police academy – idealistic, sincere, and clueless. And sadly, through no fault of his own, he was unaware of the whole McClennan story. One thing was clear almost instantly – there were two young people in the Dimperio backyard who were both without answers, the kid who found the bracelet and a young cop looking like he was taking his police academy final. A few minutes into the interrogation, Hill's coded language was saying, "If anyone can help me here, I am all for it." Ever so slowly, Dennis skillfully fed the officer questions, and before long everyone knew that the kid wasn't going to be a big help. He had no idea where he'd found the bracelet.

When Chief Harley showed up, Hill gave him a briefing. The chief never acknowledged Hill's effort or asked him a single question, or the kid, or the Dimperios. It was show time and the chief called for a search party. That seemed to be a good move, but while that party was arriving, the chief never asked any questions of anyone.

Within twenty minutes, some twenty people, mostly volunteer fire personnel, were ready to fan out through the woods near the Dimperio house. As the group spread out and headed into the woods, a young reporter from the *Banner* showed up. Harley gave him a sanitized briefing emphasizing that he, the chief, had everything under control. He stated that an "item" had been found that "may or may not have belonged to Robert McClennan."

"May or may not?" For Christ's sake, it had the man's name on it!

The *Banner* reporter seemed to be satisfied. He shot a couple of photos of police cruisers and left.

Dennis and I hung around for the next five or ten minutes, then went back to the office to put together a story with what we knew at the moment, along with an historical echo of the Robert McClennan disappearance a year earlier.

As we walked in, Karen was putting the final touches on what she knew would be the historical context part of the story. This would mean that Dennis could focus totally on the now.

Chris quickly processed the film from my camera and Dennis's, and we selected a shot of the search team heading down into the woods. It was 8:15 p.m., forty-five minutes away from launch and Karen was still rearranging four or five pages in order to push in this late-breaking story.

At 8:20 p.m. the police scanner squawked and a calm voice announced that a missing item had been found. The announcement was so low key that many in our newsroom let it roll in one ear and out the other. Hell, we were on deadline, no time for any more police chatter. But Karen heard the 10-79 mention in the announcement. A 10-79 call meant that the medical examiner had been summoned and Karen instantly knew that Robert McClennan had been found. If the address for where the 10-79 was destined was part of the radio transmission, we missed it. But we surmised it would either be the Dimperio residence or the nursing home where McClennan had lived.

Dennis tore out the door along with Chris, who was armed with our Speed Graphic camera and its Polaroid adapter. Karen smiled over to me as she symbolically showed she was tearing her hair out. We both knew that we were sitting on a potentially big story. If we didn't break it tonight, by our next edition a week later it would be old, old news.

As Dennis and Chris went by the Dimperio house they saw the chief just getting into his car. Three or four other cars belonging to searchers were going to have to be moved before the chief could exit down the steep narrow driveway. We floored it and screamed down to the nursing home, which also was sporting a police car and a few rescue personnel. The police officer was Hill, the youngster who had interrogated the Boy Scout earlier in the day, when Dennis had been an immense help to him. It was time to reciprocate.

Dennis and Chris piled out of Dennis's car. "Where's the action?" they asked Hill.

"Right over there," said Hill, "but I don't know if I can let you in."

"It will be all right," said Chris. "We may be able to get you some photos to help with your investigation."

Chris and Dennis had to get in and out before the chief got there. Harley would throw a police line around the whole damn forest if it would keep the *Eagle* from getting a story.

They tore off into the woods and quickly came upon a couple of volunteer firemen who were standing over a mass of fabric and bone, the probable remains of Robert McClennan. This wasn't a picture Chris wanted to take, but he grabbed two shots. The rescuers showed them another mass of gnawed bone. "This was where the kid found the bracelet."

"How do you know that?" asked Dennis.

"Because he told us," said Phil Corbin, a local volunteer fireman who was on the same slo-pitch softball team as Chris. Apparently the kid and his father had been at the nursing home just a short while ago, and while they were there the large mass of remains was found. This created some excitement and when the kid and his father approached, it all came back to the kid and he showed the rescuers where he found the bracelet, less than fifty feet away from the first mass.

Dennis and Chris got a picture of Hill and volunteers stringing yellow tape around the woods, then piled into Dennis's car and were heading down the road when the chief drove past in his cruiser.

We contacted the printer and asked them to hold the press for fifteen minutes. Adding this new bit of information to the story was the easy part, but we needed to make room for the new headline and eyebrow – a little additional line that is tucked in just above and to the left of the main headline.

The following day, page one of the *Banner* blared out: "*Item Found, May Be McClennan.*"

The *Eagle* headline said, "*Remains of McClennan Found*" and the eyebrow added, "*300 ft. from Nursing Home.*"

Our staff was elated that we had broken this story, and the gulf between the *Banner* headline and ours was front and center. When I scooted into Freda's for a quick breakfast, the usuals also commented on the two headlines. I smiled and gave them a quick wave and headed back to the office. The feedback from the Freda's gang made my day.

Later that afternoon, Dennis and I went back through the whole McClennan story. We revisited the initial search and all the other aspects surrounding this tragic episode and concluded that we would never be able to fully develop what a lousy bit of police work this had been. There was no great public interest in or affection for Robert McClennan. He was someone who had been dropped off by his family at the nursing home, and how or when he died was of little interest to anyone except possibly some Midwestern relatives.

The tragedy of the McClennan story played itself out again a few years later, however, when an Alzheimer's patient disappeared and the search crews combed the countryside for two or three days and came up empty. This patient was found a week later within five hundred feet of the facility.

After that we made some noise about how searches were conducted. We found ample evidence to validate our position that a search technique that created concentric circles was a very effective approach. The local fire department signed onto our call and soon they had a completely revamped search-and-rescue procedure. It started with concentric circles of searchers, tightly spaced, circling clockwise around the starting point. After expanding the search for a radius of five hundred feet all searchers were brought back to the center. A second concentric-circle search was launched over the same area, but this time those who had been on the outer rings were brought into the center, and the center-ring searchers went to the outer rings. Research had shown that someone overlooking a clue on one pass was likely to repeat the error. By

giving all searchers some different real estate to search, one of
the two people who traversed a given point would notice something. To add a different perspective, the second circle search
had the searchers going counterclockwise. The Elgin Fire Department put the whole procedure into a manual and a local
bank financed its publication. Copies of the search manual
were sent, free of charge, to all fire departments in the state.
The search technique was called "the McClennan Circle."

Chapter Fourteen

The whole sad McClennan episode lit an emotional fire under Dennis. Determined to sort out the Chief Harley drug story, he redoubled his efforts to chase down Donna Lemoine, the mysterious Donna L. He caught up with her just in time; her court date was eight days away.

But she wasn't going to say anything because she had no idea whether the person on the other end of the line was a real reporter, or some law-enforcement type posing as a reporter. In a savvy bit of investigative reporting know-how, Dennis arranged to meet her in a public place in Lowell where he could allow her to confirm his identity.

The meeting took place and Donna unloaded the whole story involving drug sales and Chief Harley, plus some vague info regarding Boston connections. The agreement for giving Dennis this info was that she would not be named as a source regardless of the circumstances. This was a huge risk, not only for her but for Dennis and the paper as well.

Did we trust her? Not really, but in the course of the conversation with Dennis she let it be known that she had no love for Chief Harley, who had used her as a go-between on a drug sale but refused to pay her cut. He claimed that he had not yet been paid the full amount and that was what was delaying his sharing with her. However, the egotistical chief had also bragged to another cop that now that he had the Boston contact, he didn't need Donna L anymore and had no intention of paying her. That cop, a new recruit to the world of law enforcement, soon played that conversation back to someone along the pipeline. It quickly made its way to Donna and the fuse was lit.

The real bombshell was when Donna told Dennis that another deal involving the chief was ready to go down. Ironically, it was scheduled just two days before her trial. She had found out because in a conversation with the Boston contact, he assumed that she had knowledge of the deal. She didn't, but she played along. At the conclusion of the conversation, Donna uncovered that Harley was striking off on his own, and she knew a drop was in the works.

"We're in over our heads," I told Dennis. He readily agreed. It was time to link up with the *Boston Globe* crime reporter. I thought about giving our attorney a call, but knew that her knowledge of something like this was going to be nil, and guarded. You have an attorney to keep you out of jam or get you out, but not this time.

Chief Harley swam right into the net like bass chasing a minnow. The behind-the-scenes work that preceded the actual takedown must have been significant. I'm certain we weren't given all the various steps, but roughly it went something like this:

Dennis had a long discussion with the *Globe* reporter, who then brought in another reporter who knew even more about how this might go down. They took it all to the law enforcement in Suffolk County, because Suffolk was Boston's county and the deal was going to go down in Boston. It then became known that in this forthcoming exchange, the chief was the buyer and not the supplier. The seller was Hammy McKinney, a mid-level drug dealer who was well known to law enforcement throughout New England but elusive as hell. McKinney wasn't known for megadeals, but he was one of the most active drug dealers in New England. The volume of McKinney deals was substantial.

Unbeknownst to McKinney, or any of us, a Grand Jury had indicted him the week before, but he hadn't yet been arrested. The day before the deal was to go down, law enforcement snatched him coming out of a doughnut shop. It happened in the blink of an eye and no one in or around the doughnut joint saw it go down.

They took McKinney to a local precinct and he smarted off to them that they had nothing on him. At that point they produced the indictment and informed him that it contained enough to easily lock him up for thirty to forty years. However, there was a chance to redeem himself and maybe cut that time in half. Armed with the indictment, the Boston police, aided by federal officials, were in a perfect position to squeeze McKinney.

He was suddenly most cooperative, and even more so when they told him that they were aware of the deal that was scheduled to go down the next night. He not only gave up a list of names but agreed to go through with the deal with Chief Harley and a second buyer. His only condition was that during the actual exchange, the cops would rough him up in front of Harley and the other buyer to add some authenticity and a bit a theater for the benefit of the chief and any other watchful eyes in the neighborhood. When he walked through those prison gates, McKinney didn't want to be branded as a snitch.

Neither the *Globe* team nor Dennis were allowed to be anywhere around when the deal went down, but they were told that the takedown was going to occur at 10:00 p.m. The newshounds hoped that the gendarmes would arrange a mini-perp walk while they were booking Harley, but the possibility was never mentioned.

Dennis was wound up tighter than a hoarder at a yard sale.

"Where's it going down?" I asked Dennis.

"Across from the Copp's Hill Burying Ground on Hull Street in the North End," said Dennis. "I'll bet I know exactly where it will be," he said as his mental Boston roadmap played out.

"How do you know the time and place?" I asked.

"I know," said Dennis, and I dropped it. Dennis was not only protecting me, but also probably honoring information that Donna, the *Globe* reporter, or maybe even a cop or attorney might have shared. One thing was certain, if Dennis felt confident about anything, you could bet on it!

Tuesday evening, Dennis was camped out at the Boston PD headquarters. The deal was to go down at 10:00 p.m. and at 10:45 up came a cruiser. The police conveniently unloaded McKinney and Chief Harley and another guy at the very side door where Dennis and other media types were stationed, cameras at the ready. The three photographers were all on one side so as not to shoot flashes into each other's cameras. Even two Boston TV channels were on hand as the subjects arrived – some aspect of this super-secret sting had obviously found its way to the media. Yes, police like to be recognized, and will often make that happen.

McKinney had been down this road before and immediately pulled his jacket up to cover his face. But Chief Harley wasn't as quick on the draw and Dennis nailed him.

The only downside to the entire episode was that the *Globe* and Boston TV got the scoop. We had to wait an additional day before we ran the story, which became known as the "Chief" story. We had a tremendous unattributed picture of our crooked chief on page one looking like he'd just been hit with a cattle prod. People picked up on our photo of the chief on his perp walk. We explained that we got it courtesy of some Boston media and let it go at that. But we remained silent as to our role in the entire event. It would be optimum for us to stay out of it from here on out.

At the trial eight months later, an abridged version of our participation in the investigation was part of the discussion and Dennis's work was selectively rolled out. His story was recognized the following January as the runner-up for the Best Investigative Story by the nation's largest weekly newspaper association. I'm positive that it would have won the category had the full extent of our involvement been submitted, but we all agreed that given the cast of characters, discretion was the better course of action.

The chief only got eight years because he ratted out on some other minor players. After five and a half years he was granted probation. He was prohibited from holding a law-enforcement job ever again. The last we heard, he was living in Arkansas and working as (are you ready?) a part-time police officer.

On Thursdays, the day the paper comes out, I was usually still running on the adrenaline that started dripping seven days earlier. It pretty much hits its peak when the paper goes out the door to the printer on Wednesday night, but the detox from that rush doesn't always dissipate overnight. In fact, an adrenaline booster often occurred in the middle of the night, as concerns about a headline, a misspelled name, an omission, or a misdirected jump churned through my weary head. Worrying about such things is like worrying about the weather, because there isn't a thing you can do about it. But that was my micro-detail m.o., and it made Wednesday night slumber a sometime thing.

On Thursday mornings, I was up at 5:00 a.m. because I wanted to be at the office when the paper arrived from the printer. Our drivers knew the routine, and my presence wasn't needed, but that was my moment of closure for a given edition; and it's also a great time of day. Once all the drivers were properly dispatched, I would head over to Freda's for my one and only sit-down breakfast of the week. By the time I arrived, the clientele had already practically digested the latest edition of the *Eagle*. I would be met by a barrage of poorly crafted one-liners about its stories.

On the day the chief takedown story was published, the locals still hadn't pieced together our involvement. They had all read the *Globe* story the previous morning, but the *Eagle* story went into considerable detail that wasn't in the *Globe*. But because they didn't have both stories in front of them, they weren't quite sure what they had read in which paper.

On this morning the usual Freda's forum was lacking. That was just fine with me, because we were intent on keeping a low profile and not revealing anything more than what we had published. Our profile, though, was sky high when the three papers were compared side by side. In the *Globe*, the photo showed a picture of McKinney, the drug dealer, trying to pull his coat up over his head, another drug dealer with his head down, and Chief Harley out of focus in the background, as the three were being hustled into the police station. Our Page One photo showed Chief Harley looking almost right at the camera, clear as a bell. When the *Globe* photographer got off the shot of McKinney it caused the chief to raise his handcuffed arms to escape the flash, Dennis said. "But because of the way the press was deployed along the perp walk, I was in a perfect position to get the chief's face before he tucked his chin into his raised arms. That's also why he never knew I was there," said Dennis, "All he saw was flash."

The *Banner* carried the *Globe* picture, and a confusing remix of the *Globe* story.

As I was standing at the cash register at Freda's, ready to pay my bill, Norm Jones, a senior attorney in Elgin, leaned forward and whispered, "You guys are really good." I didn't turn around and acknowledge the remark because I figured that Norm wanted to keep his remark private between the two of us. I simply raised by right hand just above my shoulder and flashed him the "V" for victory. I felt a gentle nudge in the small of my back and I knew all was well in Elgin.

Elgin was suddenly without a police chief. By this time Bill Sauer had risen to the rank of deputy chief, and he was next in line for the job. There was nothing but good in Sauer's record and appointing him as chief would seem to be automatic, pending various database checks, etc.

But the Elgin town fathers decided to enact their own Genesis moment: "Let there be a problem, and there was a problem." Without even discussing the merits of promoting Bill Sauer, they decided to conduct some sort of search. They were going to advertise the position around New England just to see "who's out there." They tried to sooth Sauer by saying, "Of course, we encourage you to apply."

I didn't think this was intended to be a slap in Sauer's face, but more because the selectmen, were clueless about how to proceed and wanted to buy some time. But it couldn't have been a worse move.

What in the hell were they searching for? Someone well trained, who'd be around for some time, who had a spotless record, who communicated well and who would be readily accepted by the community. Another important piece of the equation, leadership skills, is often one of the most difficult skill sets to find. The leadership piece, if found, is usually pretty thin, given the salary range that a town like Elgin can offer. Experienced police officers with proven leadership skills were vacuumed up by larger cities, with the smaller towns often being the incubators for up-and-coming metro cops. But Sauer's qualifications were already highly demonstrated on our own soil.

Dave Harrison and Sandra Garrett attended the selectmen's meeting where the search was announced. Fortunately, the board didn't vote on it, but asked the town administrator to round up everything he could about the search process. Dave reported that Bill Sauer sat stone-faced, staring at the broken clock hanging on the town office wall, never saying a word or expressing an emotion.

My heart said to tell Sauer that we were going to do everything possible to derail the selectmen's search idea, but I didn't want to get that close to someone who could be the next police chief. It was only two days before our next edition was to come out and I decided to let the *Eagle* fly headlong into this nonsense. But I was concerned that Sauer might be so humiliated by the selectmen's actions that he would bolt, so I asked Dave to tell Sauer that the newspaper was not in favor of what had been proposed and was going to do whatever it could to end it.

As our Thursday edition emerged, the news about the "search" was first made known to readers. So we were in a bind where we couldn't rally significant public opinion before the next select board meeting. Thus we had the difficult task of using our editorial page, usually page four, to inform our readers about a story they might have read about minutes before on page one. Connecting dots that quickly is not easy.

Rather than turn it into a huge battle where the selectmen would have to defend themselves, we decided to report their decision as something that they were considering but hadn't adopted, which was exactly the situation. We then fed in more of that intended action until it swallowed itself. We used our editorial page to compliment the selectmen on their desire to find the best candidate and added demonstrated facts showing that Bill Sauer was their man.

In a companion news story we dug out some statistics on the cost of conducting a search. Those numbers alone would put the fear of God into the penny-pinching board. It was an easy story to write, because it all made so much sense. In the editorial we treated the appointment of Bill Sauer as the next police chief of Elgin as a foregone conclusion.

The select board met on the following Monday. The police chief succession was barely mentioned and discussion was postponed when the town administrator asked for another week to gather more data.

By now local opinion was starting to gel. We received twenty-four letters to the editor supporting Sauer as the next chief. This was an incredibly high number, showing that the community was tuned in. Several of the letters were critical of the select board, and all were positive about a Sauer appointment. We made space for a dozen letters, and while we could have sculpted the impact by selecting only the best letters, we decided to take the first twelve that we drew out of a hat, actually a Jack Daniels liquor box. A couple of letters were too long and never made it into the box. Of the twelve that were selected, two criticized the select board and ten were pro-Sauer and pro-saving money.

Several of the same letters also appeared in the *Banner*. One of them talked about the expense of a search: "After reading your report on the cost of ...." We hated it when people quoted our work in other papers without proper attribution.

The public pressure and the pure common sense of the issue prevailed and the search ended at the ensuing select board meeting. Rogers William Sauer was named the new police chief, subject to a favorable review by the state agency that oversees law enforcement. A sizeable crowd showed up and extra chairs were set up in the hallway.

Dave and Sandra were still on the story and I went to the meeting just as a concerned citizen. I stood along the side wall of the room, along with two dozen others. The local cable TV camera was focused on the selectmen, which offered viewers, if any, no sense of what was going on. Dave and Sandra sat on separate sides of the room, talking with attendees and taking copious notes. Officer Hill stood at the back of the room, not as an attendee but as an on-duty officer. There was an understanding between the police department and the town that a uniformed officer would be present at any public meeting that could become contentious. Sauer, wisely, was not in attendance.

It is illegal for selectmen to meet before a meeting; everything is supposed to be done in public. That said, well before the meeting even a dead man could have felt the widespread public interest in the issue. Two of the selectmen entered looking like kids walking out of a candy store with a Snickers bar hidden under their jacket. With the appearance of an overflow crowd, the board clearly got the message. By law the selectmen had to allow anyone present to weigh in on the issue. Every comment was pro-Sauer, and only two were critical of the board.

Luther Burgoyne, who lived in Elgin but drove a truck for a huge dairy operation in Glossop, was one who couldn't pass up a live microphone. When Luther spoke, no mic was needed, as his bellowing voice could be heard in any neighboring state. "Usually in error, but never in doubt," Luther loved to hear himself. His pontifications made perfect sense to Luther, but everyone else would look at each other in puzzlement – and their body language would wonder, "What in the hell did he just say?" Luther gave his speech and ended by pulling up just short of spelling out where the selectmen's heads would be should they fail to name Office Sauer. He got his sought-after laugh.

The other anti-selectmen board mention came from Gerald Rutledge, the town's designated "aginner." Whatever the issue, Rutledge always found a way to be against it.

The other speakers were all pro-Sauer, and they generally kept their remarks short. The selectmen finally voted 3 to 0 for Sauer. When the vote concluded everyone in the room and adjacent hallway burst into applause and a few cheers. Within two minutes, the room had emptied and the select board continued with their meeting.

I returned to the office and called Karen with the results. She could have tuned in on the local cable channel, but there was the built-in delay of transferring the tape from one location to another and Karen knew that my call would be faster than the TV broadcast. Also, Karen didn't have the right DNA to plop down in front of a TV and watch any local government meeting where a fixed camera was in play. We reviewed our game plan for handling the announcement. Karen was disappointed that there was no picture of Sauer at the meeting. We had already pulled together a pretty good background story, which included a picture of a four-year-old Billy Sauer dressed up as a fireman. The photo would launch a lot of good-natured exchange between the police and fire departments, but unlike Harley, Sauer could handle it with humor and respect.

* * *

For years we had been besieged by area citizens who wanted Elgin High School to start a football program. There was an active Pop Warner league in town, but no program in the schools. Starting a football program was going to cost money, and this is New England, where the thought of new taxes results in the trashing of Boston Harbor.

The football planets aligned one summer night when a pair of local doctors asked me what the chances were of a football program being adopted at Elgin High. Anything was possible, I told them, but it would take a strong and sustained effort on the part of the public to move it forward. I added that if we detected the emergence of such a group the *Eagle* would be most supportive.

"We have a strong beginning for such a group Ed, and what we wanted to hear was what you just said," remarked Dr. Al Rotch.

They had a core group of eighteen people from all corners of the local population and they were fully cognizant of the fact that the support of the *Eagle* was going to be a key component.

"We've had three meetings so far," said Dr. Jake Cary, a dentist, "and I think we'll probably have a couple dozen people in attendance at the next meeting."

"Give me some names," I said. They rattled off an impressive lineup of locals, most of whom were movers and shakers. I was heartened that the list included three or four women. A football program should include the whole school, whether students are playing on the gridiron, leading cheers, or participating in a pep squad or a marching band.

The *Eagle* had raised the issue of a local football program several times in the past, but we were basically trolling to see if there was any interest. It always generated a call or two, but then faded away.

There is almost a precast rhythm to the issues of football and kindergarten. Every year or so, there is a public stirring about the need for one or the other. Unfortunately, these outcries were usually spearheaded by parents of soon-to-be kindergarteners or football players. Once that short window closed, so did the interest. But the majority of the committee that the docs had assembled had kids who had graduated from the local school system years ago. This committee was driven by people who had seen the effect that a solid sports program can have on a school. That knowledge was paired with the reality that Elgin's high school kids were not offered a lot of social outlets, places where they could gather and have fun.

The two docs were bringing forward something that I felt had a reasonable chance to succeed and I reiterated that the *Eagle* would be right there with them.

It took eighteen months and dozens of meetings, events, and information sessions before the program was finally adopted at the school district meeting in March. The meeting approved funding for converting one of the two school soccer fields into a gridiron. Perimeter fencing was included, as was partial payment for uniforms. Seating at the field was left to a yet-to-be-formed booster club. All games would be day games because there was no funding for lights.

John Sedlak, our sports reporter, was beside himself. John had played varsity football at Dartmouth, and he was like a kid with a new toy.

"They need a press box," he said.

I told him that was probably a few years down the road.

A couple of weeks later, John came into my office with Edmund Schlitt, who owned the local lumberyard and hardware center. He was about six feet four inches tall and had hands that looked as though they could crush steel. He had agreed to donate all the materials to build a six-by-sixteen-foot press box with approximately five feet reserved for the press, five for home coaches and five for opponents. The whole thing would be covered, but not enclosed. It didn't hurt that Schlitt's nephew was just starting at Elgin High and had gone out for football.

"How are coaches in the press box going to communicate with coaches on the sidelines?" I asked.

"Telephones," Schlitt answered, "although it will probably require that both teams share the side of the field closest to the press box."

"Who's going to build it?" I inquired. "This has to be a safe, substantial structure."

"No problem, I assure you! I already have a half-dozen volunteers and there are lots of other nail knockers out there who will be more than willing to be a part of this," Edmund said.

"It's got to be a substantial structure, a safe structure," I injected again.

"I know that," said Schlitt, "and we have huge sub-grade footings in the plan and more than enough anchoring for the whole structure. On top of that, Dan Lloyd, the architect, has a structural engineer who has already signed off on the plans — even called them overkill."

Within two years, the Elgin Bobcats were a formidable opponent in our part of the state. In year five, they won the state championship in their division.

John Sedlak had moved on to writing sports for a daily in New York, but a small plaque at the base of the stairway leading up to the now twenty-four foot-long, fully enclosed press box read, JOHN SEDLAK PRESS BOX.

The football program also had some downsides. As the team got better the school started to actively recruit a new coach, someone with a good reputation who was ready to put in a few years in Elgin before stepping up to an A-league team. They found their guy in Earnest Knight, a dynamic personality with a great command of English. Ernie could persuade a vulture to jump off a gut wagon. He quickly pulled together a team of assistants and volunteers and molded them into a single, cohesive unit. The team started winning consistently, and the town loved it. But there were rumblings that there was a side of Ernie that was the opposite of a fun-loving, successful coach.

Our sports editor, Mike Meehan, was a local favorite thanks to his exciting writing style and his attention to detail. Mike had been a sports reporter for a western Massachusetts daily for almost a decade, but when his wife got a fantastic career opportunity in our area, Mike traded in his notepad for stay-at-home-dad status. Once their child was in school, Mike again felt the printer's ink flowing in his veins, and he stopped by our office shortly before John Sedlak left. Great timing.

Mike had found some software compatible with our little TRS-80 computers that could track every possible kind of statistic. Football fanatics can't get enough statistics. Mike's software tracked yards gained, running attempts, passing attempts, passing yardage, tackles made, time of possession and lots more. It produced a visual x-ray of the game that replicated game stats one would expect from the *Boston Globe*. The problem was that someone needed to capture those stats during the game in order to enter them into the program; and that's were Mike showed his professional ingenuity.

He pitched the concept of an assistant sports reporter to a group of Elgin High students. At each game, he explained, the person would be granted access to the press box and would capture all the statistics, then enter the data into Mike's software. Before writing his story, Mike would consult with his assistant and sometimes he'd assign the youngster to write a companion story. The side bar stories usually concerned something that was occurring in or around the football program that wasn't necessarily a part of the game.

Assistant sports reporter wannabes clambered for the job. His backups had backups, and the reporting for Elgin Bobcat games was unmatched in New England. At the Regional Newspaper Awards competition, Mike won Best Sports Story for his ongoing reporting of game stats and accompanying stories. And on his own, Mike had a trophy shop in Boston make up individual awards for each assistant who had contributed.

Mike and his den of assistants were well wired with the team and it soon became clear that Coach Knight was all about winning. He began playing favorites with his players, meting out punishments (laps, pushups, bench time) for players he thought weren't carrying their weight. Personal harassment and belittling became more the rule than the exception.

One night he smacked a kid alongside his head, Mike told me the next morning. "Knocked him right on his ass."

"Did the kid have a helmet on?"

"Nope," said Mike.

"Who else saw it?"

"Most of the team, I would guess, and those who didn't see the smack certainly saw Billy Yadon lying on the ground in a fetal position with his hand over his ear."

"We're turning him in," I said.

"It's time," echoed Mike, "but this is going to be ugly."

"I know that, Mike, but there are witnesses, lots of them, and this guy is out of control."

"I agree."

That decision was easy to make, but I was keenly aware of the potential ramifications.

We didn't want to leap off the cliff until the local gendarmes had an opportunity to dig into the assault. Mike had a visit with Chief Sauer, and within a few days the chief had statements from half a dozen team members, the victim, his father, and of course, Mike.

"None of the players wanted to say anything at first," said Sauer, "because they knew that they would be the next Ernie target." But Sauer told them that there wouldn't *be* any more Coach Ernie, because striking a sixteen-year-old kid was not an offense that would be overlooked.

The chief brought in the coach, laid out the evidence, and described the ensuing charges. In an odd sense of entitlement, the coach suggested that he might fight the charges. He was apparently going to test his popularity. Two days later we ran the story. Mike's first-person description of what had happened was central to our story, and we also used our editorial page to ask for the instant removal of the coach.

As soon as the paper came out, phones started ringing. Elgin and the adjacent towns that were part of the school district were immensely proud of the Bobcat football team. And their admiration for Coach Knight was also intense. The local reaction to our story and editorial stance was shrill and ugly.

It started with a smattering of hang-up phone calls wherein we were labeled pansies, spoilers, bullshitters, and even communists. Threats to kick our ass were made as were the usual declarations that the caller would "never buy your goddam paper again."

Lana grabbed a ringing phone and in her usual professional-sounding voice said, "Good morning, *Elgin Eagle*."

"Fuck you," said the female caller.

"Thank you for calling," said Lana. She slowly pulled the phone away from her ear and returned it to the cradle with a slow, wide sweeping arc. "Well!" she said. "Time for more coffee."

We also had calls from people livid at the coach's action.

Our job is to report the news, all of it, and sometimes that means reporting on things that the public may not like. President Kennedy said:

"… our press is protected by the First Amendment – the only business in America specifically protected by the Constitution – not primarily to amuse and entertain, not to emphasize the trivial and the sentimental, not to simply 'give the public what it wants' – but to inform, to arouse, to reflect, to state our dangers and our opportunities, to indicate our crises and our choices, to lead, mold, educate and sometimes even anger public opinion."

I knew there would be a reaction to the Knight story, but I never thought it would rise to this level of anger, hostility, and downright insanity. I don't know what bothered me more, the actual reaction, or the fact that such a defenseless stance was showing up in our corner of the world. I'd always felt that kindness, civility, and respect were givens in our area.

The hostility subsided as the day wore on, and the following day the only obscene calls were those left on the answering machine the night before. There were eighteen calls on the machine and four of them came from the same guy. We knew because we could hear the ambient noise in the background of each of his calls. It sounded like a pack of dogs howling to a country and western song that was playing at the wrong speed. Our answering machine only recorded the calls and the time they were made, but not the callers' numbers. This guy was hitting our machine about every half hour. It was obvious that he was going through several six-packs of suds at the same time, and each call became more obscene and slurred. The fourth and final call was the gem. First he was upset because the automated voice that had answered his call wasn't responding. He then went into some sort of tirade about the Green Bay Packers. Getting those three words, Green Bay Packers, was quite a vocal hurdle for him, but he finally got them in the right order. Then he was ready to announce the purpose of his call and after several stabs blurted into the phone that he couldn't remember why he called, before ending it with a "thank you." Another tape preserved for the *Elgin Eagle* Christmas party.

There was only one hit on the answering machine on Saturday, but Sunday was not a day of rest for those who were furious at the *Eagle*, and the answering machine fielded half a dozen complaints, mostly mild. All of those, we noted, arrived after church.

I also got a call from Harry Coleman, a fellow publisher in the northern part of the state who had received his complimentary copy of the *Eagle* in Saturday's mail. His paper had been through almost the same drill, he said, but their coach wasn't smacking kids – he was making untoward advances.

"The creep was fondling kids and still people wanted to keep him around," said Harry. "But that kind of rabid reaction lasted only a few days, and that's probably what'll happen in Elgin. If you need to get out of town and hide out for awhile, you're welcome up here. I can always use a good reporter or delivery man."

"How about someone to split some firewood?"

"That too, Ed. Stay tough," chuckled Harry. I love the fraternity of publishers.

On Monday, the letters to the editor started to come in. I expected a torrent, but there were only a dozen or so. Like most newspapers, we required that all letters carry a name, address, and phone number. We always called the number to confirm that there was a real person at the other end. Three of these letters were from anonymous senders. Three others were in favor of the coach being dismissed. The remaining letters tried to argue that smacking a kid, while bad, wasn't the end of the world, or that the coach deserved a second chance.

"This isn't a second chance scenario," said Karen, "this is a felony. I wonder how many readers understand that?"

A few minutes later, our entire editorial staff was in our conference room for a hastily called Monday morning meeting. Karen laid out everything that had transpired. She wanted to hear any personal feedback that any of our reporters had encountered. Several people had received some blowback from the story reflecting a diverse range of opinion from supporting our stance, to no opinion, but nothing negative. I asked Lana and the advertising representatives to join the meeting and share any reactions they had experienced. Lana said that on Friday her phone was glowing red, but now it had mostly calmed down. The ad team only revealed one advertiser who was upset with the story.

"Did he threaten to pull his ads?" asked Dennis.

"No," said Vickie, "we pulled them for him. He's ninety days overdue on his account."

That was the levity we all needed. I used the opening to remind them that we're only doing our job. We don't pick and choose the news – it happens and we report it. I assured them that as the magnitude of this story finally took root, the "glowing phone" would return to its exquisite midnight black.

The meeting broke up and everyone was totally on board with our effort.

Our next edition published the letters. The only news story about the incident was that the school board was going to hold a special meeting. The coach's action ignited the school board, and a couple of the members weren't shy about sharing their views.

"I can't believe what some of those school board members were spouting off about the coach," said Mike, who had been in the news business long enough to know when the libel or slander ice is getting thin. "It was a lynch mob mentality at Freda's this morning. Mather and Brannon were 'educating' the customers about what happened."

"Dumb," I said. "This is still a personnel issue and I can't believe those two are so inept that they'd open the school board up to a lawsuit by the coach."

"Were they on the board when Knight was hired?" asked Mike. He sensed a mission in their madness.

"Mather was the chairman of the board and I think Brannon was on the search committee," I said.

"So it's cover-your-ass time for them."

"I would guess that's the bottom line here," I said, "and getting this to a special meeting can't happen soon enough."

The board members were prepared to can the coach, but Knight beat them to it and resigned. He was probably hanging around to see what he could milk out of the school board before he left, but a couple of meetings with lawyers from both sides convinced him that it was time to punt. The incident that we had reported on turned out to be incident number six. As the police expanded their investigation to other players, the dike burst and Knight's brutality emerged.

So the coach left with some unused paid vacation time. The board debated about whether to remove team pictures from the school that included the coach and it was decided to let them remain.

Our story was picked up by several of the dailies around the state; even the *Boston Globe* ran a small piece. This wasn't the spotlight that Elgin wanted, but the fact that it was quickly resolved recovered any lost PR turf the town may have surrendered.

A few weeks after the coach quit I had a cup of coffee with Chief Sauer and complimented him on the quick, firm way that he took the reins when the story was brought to him. "It was the *Eagle* who flew in with those reins," he reminded me. Our first person account made it a much easier case to handle, he said, because it allowed the kids to come forward. "If the kids had clammed up, it would have taken longer, but this was black and white."

"Just like a newspaper," I said, feeling guilty for overpowering the verbal softball that the chief had inadvertently thrown my way.

A popular assistant coach took control of the Elgin Bobcats team and they won three of their final four games, tying for second in the league. A playoff game was required pitting the Bobcats against the Coastal Academy Gulls, a public high school team that was defending its championship. Sharon Mullin was the owner and publisher of the Gulls' hometown paper, the *Elizabeth Echo*, and I had known her for many years. We met for lunch at a Holiday Inn restaurant midway between Elgin and Elizabeth and exchanged photos of the teams and provided any other information that could improve the pregame coverage for both papers. We also decided to spice up the rivalry with a side bet between the two of us. If the Bobcats won, Sharon would give us four quarts of Chubbuck's Clam Chowder that was made in Elizabeth. If the Gulls won, I'd give Sharon a gallon of maple syrup from Eva and Bill's Sugar House.

We announced that wager utilizing sort of a double-pump technique where the item is mentioned in one story and expanded upon in another. Experience had taught us that whenever a town was in any sort of competitive situation, whether it be a firemen's muster or a wager between two newspapers, there were readers who wanted to be in on the competition. So we mentioned the bet in the main story about the game that kicked off our sports section. Generally, about thirty-five to forty percent of readers read the sports section. The rest either skipped it entirely or skimmed it for a picture or mention of someone they knew. That meant that more than two-thirds of our readers wouldn't know of the wager and thus not be in on the friendly rivalry involving their town. So Sally crafted a more detailed story, which we placed in the first section in a spot where we tried to present "happy" news. The wager story instantly became the most talked-about story of the week. For three days we heard nothing but, "You gonna share that chowder with your readers?" and the like.

Walking the narrow line separating entertainment from news from opinion is sometimes difficult. A news organization has access to a lot more information than the general public. So obvious conclusions or acceptable outcomes that are quite apparent to us often require that we put that ball into the court of readers in a cogent crafting that allows them to reach an informed conclusion.

In a ceremony a week before the game, a flip of a coin gave Elgin the home-field advantage. On game day, the place was packed. By now the school had bleachers running down both sides of the field, and one side was given over to the opponents. Both teams had large cheerleading squads and marching bands. Though the bands would be in attendance, it was agreed that there would be no halftime marching, so the game could end a little earlier and seacoast fans could begin their two-hour trek home. That was a great decision because the

marching ability of the Elgin band was, to put it gently, dis-
jointed. It mostly performed for night games and because of
the low-profile bleachers, no spectators were high enough to
get a broad overview of the proceedings, so the band's freestyle
frolic was pretty much unnoticed by the crowd.

Newt Treir, the band director, was a graduate of the University of Illinois. There, in the heart of the Big Ten, marching
bands were an integral part of the athletic program and hundreds of musicians took to the field at halftime. Newt wanted
to replicate that in Elgin. His fifty-five-member band wasn't
going to be performing any intricate marching maneuvers, but
that didn't stop Newt from trying. One night they formed up in
one end zone and started playing "Around the World in Eighty
Days," as they attempted to march the length of the field in
a round formation to signify the world. Just after midfield,
the entire southern hemisphere of the band went astray and
by the time the band reached the other end zone, the formation had morphed into something close to an ant colony. They
then reversed direction and the second field-long march was
supposed to resemble a hot-air balloon. It never really got off
the ground. Three-quarters of the way down the field the formation resembled a string of sausages. The crowd went wild
and the band members soaked up the spontaneity and exuber-
ance.

It was a cold fall evening, perfect football weather, and the
crowd was really into it. Mike was camped out in the press box
with his assistant and Sally was roving both sidelines doing
some mini-interviews with fans from both schools. Chris had
so many cameras slung around his neck that it was a wonder
he could remain upright. We also had an Elgin High senior
doing a sidebar story on what happens in and around the concession stands. The Elgin field had two concession outlets.
One was permanent in its own little shed and it was run by
the school booster club for the benefit of Elgin athletics. Ad-

jacent to the school shed was a mobile concession wagon run by a former Elgin graduate, Andy Hostetler. There was no overlap between the offerings of the two – the mobile unit sold only pizza. It was called "Basic Kneads" and the pizza was prepared on site. Andy's donation to the school-run stand was that he refrained from selling anything other than pizza. If a customer wanted a soft drink to go with the pizza, it had to be purchased at the booster club stand.

Andy's pizza truck had a great on-site sales technique. On the top of his truck he perched a small bracket holding a sign which read, "Hello –" followed by the visiting team's name. For this game, the sign read "Hello Gulls." A small light illuminating the sign would come on every two or three minutes. Because the sign was high up on the cab of his wagon, and because it was pointed at the crowd on the opposite side of the field, it wasn't of any concern to Elgin fans. But the sign more or less granted the opposing fans permission to make their way over to the friendly pizza wagon and Andy sold a lot of pizza at Elgin games – a true equal-opportunity peddler.

The game was a tie until the final four minutes. Elgin scored, but a big lumbering tackle from the Gulls managed to break through and barely deflect the extra-point attempt by the Bobcats. Final score 27-26, and the season was over.

Sharon and I had announced in our newspapers that the bet between us would be settled right after the game. And shortly after the Gull's celebration died down, the PA announcer explained what was about to happen.

Our sports reporter, Mike Meehan was there with his six-year-old little blonde daughter, Denise. We arranged that she would be the one to walk out to midfield and deliver the gallon jug of syrup to Sharon. However, late in the fourth quarter, little Denise was shivering and I took off my topcoat and then wrapped her in my brown corduroy sport jacket. The jacket fit right over her parka. So out on the field ran this little cannonball of fleece and down, lugging a huge jug of maple syrup. About twenty feet onto the field, she dropped the jug and spent about fifteen seconds fumbling with the removal of her mittens in order to be able to grab it. Then one of the mittens found its way to the turf, and that led to putting down the jug in order to retrieve the runaway mitten. But little Denise had a plan, she took off both mittens and stuffed them in her mouth, then ran the rest of the way to the center to meet Sharon and deliver the heavy jug. Photographers from both papers caught shots of the little girl, in a jacket that was dragging on the ground, two mittens shoved in her mouth, and her eyes fixed squarely on Sharon's face as she handed over the syrup. A perfect ending to a perfect season. As a bonus, when I finally got to my car, there on the front seat sat four quarts of Chubbuck's Clam Chowder.

* * *

Some newspapers do yearly April Fool's Day spoofs, but we found it much more effective to wait until April 1 actually fell on a Thursday, the day we came out. We also ran a full-blown Halloween edition only when the holiday coincided with our publication date. We covered Halloween every year, of course, but when the holiday and publication stars were aligned, we went the extra mile.

The April 1 edition was always the most fun because we also made it a big event for our staff. New England winters are long and cold and usually we hadn't escaped winter's clutches even in mid-March. It was a good time for a staff brain-storming party to develop some content for the April 1 edition. We rented out a local hall, brought in a bartender and sometimes hired a small band. The whole staff plus spouses, full-timers, part-timers, drivers, and significant others were invited.

The main draw was a competition for the best April Fool's hoax idea. It had to be something that was remotely believable, could be illustrated with some sort of art or photo, didn't embarrass anyone, and clean. All ideas were submitted anonymously and there were usually a couple of dozen four-by-six-inch cards posted on a board for people to vote on. These were whittled down to the top ten and eventually the whole staff chose a winner. The prize was a twenty-five-dollar gift certificate from Len's Grocery Store – we supported those who supported us.

At the beginning we tried to protect the anonymity of whoever was submitting an idea. Once we had selected the top ten, submitters were encouraged to advocate for their creations. Everyone knew that considerable backroom politicking took place prior to the event.

Chris Bourbon was hyperexcited about his airport idea. "We can superimpose Air Force One landing at the airport," he said. "It's somewhat plausible because they have that huge runway."

Everyone enjoyed John's idea for a story about plans to build a tunnel under the local highway. He wanted to write about a half-mile-long tunnel that would replace the existing Elmwood Road underpass. "It would have a lighted bike path along one side," said John as he popped another beer. The fun part of that story was the fact that the existing Elmwood Road underpass led to a subdivision that was never built, so the existing underpass probably saw a dozen cars a year, principally teenagers looking for a remote setting. The developer had built it prior to the start of construction, but his financing fell apart and Elmwood Road was a true "road to nowhere."

Vickie wanted to go with a story that Elgin was going to prohibit on-street parking for foreign-made automobiles. Yes, almost all the auto dealers who advertised with us sold domestic cars. Anita wanted to announce that the local police would periodically give awards to people carrying local grocery bags. Ah, the ad girls, always on point!

Peggy Bleyler, another of our ad gang, won the award with her idea for the town to install hitching posts for horses. She refined the concept to allow for posts to be mounted at every third parking space. Any horse tethered to a post would be held to the same parking requirements as a vehicle. In addition, the horse owner would be responsible for removal of any droppings.

Peggy, who owned horses, said she and her husband could bring a few horses into town and we could arrange a photo with some of the selectmen.

By this time, we had a great select board and all of them had a good sense of humor, so we knew we could count on their help.

The gift certificate went to the Bleylers and on Monday, Dave pitched the idea to the selectmen, who loved it. Getting the photo without the public connecting the dots was a real Houdini act, but Chief Sauer closed off a street or two for ten minutes and we pulled it off.

On April 1, the front page of the *Elgin Eagle* had a headline that read, "SELECTMEN AGREE TO HITCHING POSTS" and the eyebrow above the headline read, "SOME MERCHANTS SAY NEIGH."

A picture showed the three selectmen looking on as Dan Bleyler, dressed in chaps, plaid shirt, and Stetson tied up his horse to a hitching post just down the street from the town hall.

Dave's accompanying story explained that such a move "may be needed someday." The first phase, he wrote, would cost about $8,500. Quotes from selectmen detailed that the sanitary issues had been fully studied, and announced that they were close to concluding a plan for a small corral area to be cut into a corner of the little downtown park. "A local business has agreed to donate half of the $20,000 cost for the new corral," they finished.

As we were putting the paper together the night before the April Fool's edition hit the streets, the laughter in our office could have been heard in the next county. Everyone knew what we were going to do, but as it all came together it got even funnier.

I couldn't wait to get to Freda's the next morning. The spoof had hit pay dirt. As I entered, a guy who worked for a local real estate company demanded, "Is this for real?"

Before I could answer, Harry Winterstein and someone else said, "Of course it's real, and it's long overdue."

The body language of those within earshot showed that the issue was equally divided between the credulous and the sane.

Harry went into an extended listing of the benefits of hitching posts and others began to throw in their thoughts as well. Others stayed on the sidelines.

By the time I got back to the office, Lana was doubled over with laughter as she recounted the phone calls that she had received. Most were complimentary of the hoax, but a few wanted more details. We didn't have time to continue with the hoax so Lana would ask them to go to the top of page one and read the first words in the upper left-hand corner. Most caught on when they read the April 1 dateline. They loved it. No one felt they had been betrayed and they signed on to the fun.

A couple of local merchants posted signs welcoming horse riders, and at three o'clock a mounted group headed by Dan and Peggy Bleyler and six friends, cantered down Main Street. The sight acted like a human magnet and drew people out of every store and office to celebrate April 1.

Karen had suggested that we increase the pressrun for the issue, but I didn't think it was necessary. She persisted, and I upped the run by three hundred copies. Karen was right, the issue sold out. People will always respond to well-crafted creativity, whether it be in a music hall, an art gallery, a Broadway theater, or a weekly newspaper in Elgin, NH.

Bravo, staff!

Chapter Fifteen

"It's called a mouse," said Gene Henneke, a local business consultant who commuted to Boston for three days each week. Gene was totally caught up in the computer revolution, and had helped me debug our system on many occasions. But the day he hauled in his Macintosh computer and showed me the mouse, I was speechless. He was so caught up in what he was showing me that the words all blended together and I had no idea what he was saying. All I knew was that I was looking at something that could reshape the capabilities of businesses like ours.

All hell had broken loose in the technology trenches since that first session with Gene. Newspapers left and right were acquiring the latest computer gadgets, many of which were obsolete before they were installed. While they definitely improved productivity in our operation, they also were enabling a new form of competition that was cancerous.

"Upham's Lawn and Garden is going to run every other month instead of every month," announced Anita, slamming her folders down on her desk. "How dumb can you get?" She swept around and accidentally hit Rosemary's coffee cup, which began a crop-dusting maneuver down the side wall of the building. None of us grasped that what Anita was complaining about was probably going to be one of the biggest contributors to the decline of community newspapers in America.

I let Anita, assisted by Rosemary and others, mop up the aftermath of her tirade (it's amazing how much liquid is in a fourteen-ounce coffee cup). When things settled down I asked Anita and Rosemary to come over to my office. As they entered, I made a point of picking up my coffee mug and moving it out of range of Anita. That little ice breaker helped the last bit of steam to be expelled and paved the way for a productive talk rather than a rehash.

"I gather Upham's upset you," I said.

"They're cutting their ad schedule from once a month to every other month," she said. "Guess why?"

"There could be dozens of reasons," I said. "Business slowdown, crippled cash flow, a different ad mix, lack of —"

"Ad mix is it, Ed," said Anita. "And about as dumb as you can get."

"Who's benefiting from the new ad mix?" I said. "The *Messenger*?" I was referring to the daily newspaper in Arnett that sold a few copies in Ossett, where Upham's was located.

"No," said Anita, "even dumber than that. The *Ossett News*."

"The *Ossett News*! What's the *Ossett News*?" I asked.

"There's a guy in Ossett who has a little computer and printer and he's started a monthly paper called the *Ossett News*," said Anita rolling her eyes and clenching her fist.

"Tell me more," I said, not yet fully grasping the sea change that I was encountering for the first time.

This guy was going to publish a monthly newspaper in Ossett, Anita explained. Actually it was more of a newsletter printed in an eleven-by-seventeen-inch format. It would contain local news about Ossett and maybe some tidbits from surrounding towns. The entrepreneur was going to charge Upham's $200 for a little less than three quarters of a page of advertising, compared to our charge of $220 for just under one quarter of a page.

"Upham's thinks they're getting a great deal," said Anita. "They're oblivious about circulation!"

Anita's statement was the salient point that so many small businesses overlooked. In their quest for a low rate, they often ignored the two main parts of the goalposts: Circulation and readership.

Throwaway newspapers, which are mailed or distributed without charge, often have significant circulation, but lousy readership. If people aren't reading the thing, your ad is a lonely critter tucked somewhere into the freebie. Other papers that offer low rates, often don't have the circulation from which readership may emerge. Again, your ad is going to be the best-kept secret in the county.

Upham's Lawn and Garden was a niche business. There weren't many garden centers in the area, and there was considerable competition among the few that existed. So their advertising needed to reach people in many different locations. By going with the local guy with his monthly news report, they were forgoing circulation in favor of cost. On top of that, the news piece in the monthly newsletter wasn't going to tell readers much that they hadn't already read in the *Eagle*, so readership isn't going to be significant.

But Upham was probably focused on the fact that his advertising bill for the year was now going to be $120 less than it had been the year before and his ads were going to look really big.

The common sense in arguing circulation and readership seems easy to comprehend, but it often trails in the consideration of cost. "How much is it gonna cost?" was the most popular refrain our sales force heard.

A week or two after the Upham's decision to move from the *Eagle* to a locally published newsletter, I began to stitch together a direction that didn't portend good things for small community newspapers.

Advances in printing technology have made producing a weekly newspaper much easier than it was twenty years earlier. Production of a newspaper has many facets, but for simplicity's sake it can be divided in half. The front end is what we do, from gathering the news all the way to getting it to the printer. The back end is the actual printing of the paper. Very few weeklies own their own press, and those that do hang on to them forever because of the huge investment combined with a mega-load of nostalgia and affection for that old baby in the back room.

With the arrival of desktop computers, much of the front end can be handled by one single person. Every now and then a local news option would pop up and a few local advertisers would adjust their ad schedules to include the new entry. It never amounted to a huge amount of lost revenue, at least on an individual basis, but with two or three scattered around in various small towns, it nibbled away financial margins that are pretty thin to begin with. Upham's decision would erase $1,320 from our annual sales revenue.

Fortunately, we had the ongoing advertising seminar in place that educated merchants about their advertising in our paper. The seminar had always been a hit because it was truly helpful, and it was the only one of its kind, at least in our locality. With the sudden and unexpected arrival of the *Ossett News*, we decided to ramp up the seminar and include a heavier emphasis about getting ads into a paper that brings readers content that they can't get anywhere else.

The Upham's decision ushered in a new discussion and I wanted an organic response from our sales force. If the ad gang understood what might be going on with Upham's, they'd be in a much better position to develop a meaningful response. I was sure that their thoughts would also help me grasp the larger issue more fully.

I suggested a Saturday morning breakfast meeting at the office. I lured them in with the offer of a catered breakfast of blueberry pancakes and sausage from Freda's and I promised a 9:00 a.m. start and an 11:00 conclusion. Everyone showed up, but I don't think the breakfast was really needed. They were already reading between the lines.

"Let me take a swipe at it, Ed," said Rosemary, our ad manager. "I think I can make a compelling story as to why the *Elgin Eagle* gets the advertiser the most bang for his buck."

I had some definite thoughts on the subject, but I promised myself that I'd remain silent in the hope that my ideas would correspond to those of the ad team.

The name "Upham's'" soon became the shorthand, the code, for any advertiser who wandered into newsletter hell.

"You kill the Uphams with reach," said Vickie. "The Ossett rag reaches Ossett, on a good day, but that's it. What about the Harlows, Bartlettsvilles, and Addisons of the world?"

"People who pick up the newsletter wouldn't find anything new," Anita quickly added. "We're beating them four to one."

"Huh?" said Rosemary.

"We have four issues of the *Eagle* each month to this guy's one newsletter. He's selling stale fish," said Anita.

Peggy brought up the issue of prestige. "I think the consumers make some sort of judgment based on where they heard about a company. There has to be more credibility to your ad appearing in a real newspaper than in a homegrown newsletter."

"I think that's a valid point," said Rosemary, "but it's probably something that should obliquely be mentioned, not put into the advertiser's face."

"You mean I can't say, 'Your customers are wondering why you are having to advertise in this cheap little rag rather than a real newspaper,'" joked Anita, as she rolled another pancake around a sausage.

"Actually, the public isn't keeping score," said Rosemary. "They're oblivious as to how many ads run with whom or where. But *we* know, and Peggy's point is valid."

I took exception to some of that conclusion but decided to keep quiet, it wasn't a big deal. But readers do indeed have some sense about which newspapers have ads and which ones don't. A newspaper that is continually lacking ads appears to be stranded on the reef, and usually that signals that the incoming tide will wipe things clean.

It was still too early to be able to define the makeup of the *Ossett News*, but the sense of our group was that Upham's Lawn and Garden was going to be the exception. The newsletter might pick up some little ads from home-based businesses and a few local storefronts, but advertisers needing a broader customer base would hold back. "Upham's is momentarily blinded by the light," screamed Peggy as she popped up from her desk and launched a bad Manfred Mann chorus. She was joined by the rest of the group and that was followed by a quick discussion about "douche vs. deuce."

Getting Upham's or any other advertiser to attend another advertising seminar was going to be a heavy lift and we agreed that we needed a different approach. We decided to do an after-hours wine and cheese event. The unwritten criteria for receiving an invitation was the volume of advertising that an individual outfit did with the *Eagle*. We picked a financial threshold that would scoop up Upham's. When we ran a printout to create that list, we found that we had thirty-five local advertisers whose annual advertising expenditures with us were greater than Upham's. And inviting that number of people wasn't going to allow us any time to deliver a message.

"Of course, some won't make it," said Vickie, "but it's a roll of the dice."

"The optimum number would be something in the neighborhood of fifteen," I said. "Twenty at the most."

We decided to roll the dice and invite all top thirty-five advertisers to the new and improved *Elgin Eagle* Advertising Seminar, "Your Advertising Outreach Going Forward."

As Rosemary and I developed the seminar, Anita, Vickie and Peggy started priming the pump with potential attendees. They pitched it as "exclusive" and by "invitation only."

Twenty-four, including Upham's, accepted the invitation and we had a great two hours with them. Following forty-five minutes of wine and cheese and chitchat, we presented a twenty-minute slide show about circulation, readership and ad preparation. The sections for circulation and readership were augmented by recent studies conducted by two separate national newspaper organizations. They showed the effect that television advertising was having on daily newspapers, but the weekly papers were still immune to electronic media. And no impact from desktop publishing was on the radar — yet.

We concluded the slide presentation with our mission statement, which was that we were delivering information that our readers couldn't get elsewhere. We didn't promise 24 or 28 or 32 pages of virgin news, but we could clearly demonstrate that we were a unique conduit for informing the citizens in and around Elgin, New Hampshire of the day-to-day happenings in their world.

"We leave the Red Sox to the *Globe*," I told them, "but we scoop the *Globe* every single week when we report on the athletic teams at Elgin High, or the planning board in Ripley, or the missing horse in Wells."

On that note, we thanked them for coming and reopened the bar for anyone who wanted to hang around. They all did! The feedback from attendees was extremely positive. We had presented the case for circulation and readership in a short, easy-to-grasp manner, and it was accepted. The only downside to the event was that despite a positive RSVP, Lyle Upham was a no-show.

There was a happy ending to the Upham's bolt, however. Two months into his adventure with the *Ossett News*, he returned to his monthly schedule with the *Eagle*. The *News* had quickly morphed into a monthly collection of recipes and a listing of birthdays, anniversaries and atrocious poetry. Its regular advertisers were Pauline's Christian Hair Salon, Jack's Knife Sharpening Service and the Ossett Mini Mart.

When Dennis saw the name Pauline's Christian Hair Salon, he asked what that was all about. "It's a hair salon that plays gospel music for its patrons," Vickie informed him.

"Was that some sort of punishment for their patrons?" said Chris.

It turned out that Pauline was the sister-in-law of Beau Caldwell, the owner of the *Ossett News*. "And Pauline's son is Jack, the Knife," said Vickie.

"Who?" inquired Sally.

"Jack, the knife-sharpening guy."

"All the incestuous news that's fit to print," added Christopher, looping a Freda donut around his middle finger.

Several months after Gene Henneke introduced me to a mouse, I was at a computer show in Boston and my head was spinning. The first guy I ran into at the turnstiles going into the exhibit hall had a white shirt with a plastic pocket protector. My mind flashed back to college when we would watch the engineering students come into the student union with that hallmark attire. I hung around for three hours and even attended a short thirty-minute presentation put on by Apple, but I still didn't even know how to frame my approach to this technological explosion. I'd seen enough, however, to know that the *Eagle* was going to have to fledge from its existing front-end pattern and join this new whatever.

When I returned to Elgin I called Henneke and told him that I needed some guidance. He told me to call Bruce Carlisle, who he said knew as much about computers as anyone.

Ironically, Bruce had worked as an intern for us during his senior year in high school and his freshman year in college. In high school he did some sports reporting for us and the following summer he produced some feature stories and covered some routine town boards. He knew the deadline discipline that was so important, and he was a true perfectionist.

Bruce had just graduated from Carnegie Mellon University in Pittsburgh, and he was a self-declared "computer geek." Even though he placed that label on himself, I was uncomfortable using the term for a year or so.

I arranged a meeting and when we met I couldn't even frame the purpose for the meeting. "This whole technology thing has got my attention," I told Bruce, "but I feel like I'm on a carousel with everything going around and around and up and down. My sense is that we'd better climb up on a horse quickly before we get thrown off through pure inertia."

Bruce grasped exactly what I was trying to say, or at least said that he did, and we worked out a consulting arrangement whereby he would steer us into the world of computers. The first thing we did was to decide that there would be two separate systems, one dedicated to the business and writing end of the *Eagle* and the other to production. The result was one system with a Macintosh core and the other with a Microsoft (MSDOS) center.

Part of the business and editorial system handled circulation, financials (payables and receivables), payroll, and similar items. For years we had farmed out our payroll services because of the inordinate amount of time that it took to process it each week. We elected to continue with that service, and all we had to do at our end was input the hours for hourly employees and the commissions for the sales group.

We also had a separate entry for those moments each month when, if needed, we would recapture any commissions paid to sales people whose customers had failed to pay their bills for ninety days. We had a solid front-end agreement requiring payment within ten days from the receipt of monthly statements. When an advertiser was thirty days late we added a service charge and sent a listing to each member of our sales force with notification that so-and-so is now thirty days overdue. At that point, no commissions were recaptured from the sales account executive, but notice had been given. The hope was that she would begin to hound the client to pay up.

Of course no one liked to do that, but without putting that assignment right in their lap, there was little incentive for them to make the customers pay – just keep selling them advertising.

Other papers paid commissions only when payment was made, but that caused a turbulent cash flow for our sales reps and required a hell of a lot of extra bookkeeping. So we paid a salary and a commission each week, but we could recapture that commission if need be. The non-and slow-paying accounts were always the same fifteen or twenty, and the promptness of their payment often reflected their own seasonal retail revenue curve.

So we cut our advertisers a lot of slack – "too much," said Ginny Laven, our seventy-five-year-old bookkeeper. Ginny had lived in Elgin her entire life. She knew every single business and had been a bookkeeper for many of them over the years. She knew where all the skeletons were hidden. "He'll never pay you until you completely cut him off," she would say. "Call him during lunch. He won't be there but his wife will, and she'll make sure he pays up."

Ginny "retired" from a local department store at age sixty-five. I went to her retirement party and ended her retirement that same evening. She loved coming to work at the *Eagle*. "It's such an easy-going, fun atmosphere," she said one day. "Without this, I'd be long gone."

The circulation piece of the software that Bruce found was spectacular and gave us a crystal-clear overview of our subscribers and newsstands. It was the first time that all of our financials were in one integrated system, and it allowed for a wide range of "what-if" scenarios.

None of the writing software was new, but Bruce tweaked it so that many of the repetitive keystrokes could be handled with just a couple of keys. Things like quote boxes and headlines would require a keystroke or two rather than minutes designating fonts, widths and attributes. And all of this continual tracking of a given story gave Karen and me an instantaneous readout as to where things stood at any given moment.

The new kids on the block were parked in the production area of the newsroom – two huge Macintosh terminals with drive-in-size screens. The price tag for those dual behemoths was through the roof and neither was worth a damn until another load of money was thrown at the necessary software.

It wasn't simply a matter of moving in the new production computers and hauling out the old typesetting machines. There was a long learning curve, requiring that both the old and the new systems were operational in the small production area. It also resulted in electrical fuses being blown left and right. That was remedied by Matt Smith, a local electrician who had become our unofficial resident plug-and-wire guy. "You don't need to rewire anything," Matt said. "Just string a couple of extension cords from other circuits and live with it for several weeks or months." He pointed out that we would soon be getting rid of the big-power using typesetting machines and could "roll up the orange." That's why Matt's little two-inch weekly ad always ran at half price – sort of our family rate.

It was a really exciting time for the *Eagle* as we sprinted into the digital age. We were the first weekly newspaper in the state to go to totally digital typesetting and layout. We hosted a regional press association workshop for any newspaper that wanted to attend. Naturally, the day of that workshop our laser printer decided to roll over and die, so we couldn't show the attendees the output, but they got the drift. I used that opportunity to underscore that such glitches were more traumatic because there were so few people trained and ready to come and fix it.

* * *

"A damn dead moose hanging from a tree in his goddam front yard," said Ken as the editorial meeting convened.

"Slow down," said Karen in her most motherly tone. "Let's go through this again. Exactly what did you see, and where?"

"A dead moose strung up in this guy's front yard, right there on Main Street in Mount Ralston. Hanging upside down with its chest slashed open and dried blood around its nose and mouth. Right there on Main Street, greeting all the school kids on their way to school!"

Everyone in the meeting recoiled, and applauded Ken for his passion.

"Did you get a picture?" asked Karen.

"Are you kidding me?" said Ken. "If I had I'd probably be the next one in the tree."

Everyone's laughter was chopped off when Chris said, "I got a picture."

"We should run it," said Ken.

"Why?" asked Karen.

"Because it's unusual, and there's probably going to be considerable public reaction."

"Are you comfortable doing the story?" said Karen. "Can you rein in your obvious disgust and write a well-rounded story?"

"No problem," said Ken, "my life insurance is paid up."

Ken filed a great story, with interviews from a half-dozen people in Mount Ralston as well as the moose hanger himself. He encountered no problem from the guy until he asked why he used that particular tree when there we many more all along the back end of his driveway. "He got real defensive when I asked that question."

"What was his reason?" said Sally. "I didn't see that in the story."

"He said it was as good a tree as any, and judging from his reaction to my question, I just decided to let it go," said Ken.

The fact that we did a story featuring a dead moose hanging from a tree on a main street quickly was interpreted by some as an anti-hunting piece. Actually it wasn't the story itself, but the public reaction to the story that opened up Pandora's box *of shells*. And the three villains, in order of venom spewed, were the *Eagle*, Ken, and the moose hanger. Ken spent a lot of time in Mount Ralston gathering opinions. The women in the community were, for the most part, appalled at the Main Street moose. Men were either ambivalent or OK with the display. The three women didn't object to being identified, but two of the three men wanted to remain anonymous.

Two days after the story came out, I got a call from fellow publisher Harry Coleman who had become my unsolicited but most welcome shrink. Harry was there for the coach story and he knew that the road ahead for the *Eagle* was also going to have some bumps.

"It's real-world stuff," said Harry, "but you're going to take a lot of flak from people on both sides. It will be intense for a week or so, and then disappear."

"How can you be so sure?" I said.

"I've been down this road several times. We run lots of bait and bullet stories, because lots of people up here in the north are into it. But every now and then someone will think they see a hidden anti-hunting agenda in a given story, and that often opens the box."

"Has it ever gotten violent?" I asked.

"Just twice," he said. He waited through an appropriate pregnant pause, then added, "Naw, never violent, just some name calling."

"And threats to never read your goddam paper again?"

"Oh, for sure!" said Harry, with a chuckle.

We did get letters accusing us of being sensational, anti-hunting, insensitive, invaders of someone's privacy, and Communists. One letter accused us of being disrespectful of the moose – Christmas-party material. Another, noting Chris's byline on the photo, accused him of being some sort of pervert. At the next editorial meeting, everyone, on cue, got up and moved their chairs away from Chris.

"I've been unmasked," he moaned, dropping his chin onto his chest and covering his face with his hands. Then he popped upright and announced that immediately after the meeting, everyone was invited to the darkroom to see his 'best material'.

Harry's prediction of the uproar disappearing quickly didn't come true. A segment of the hunting community had whipped themselves into a lather and the *Eagle* was the target. They were convinced that we were taking an anti-hunting stance. We countered with a calm and sane editorial about community standards, and never got into the gun issue. They interpreted the omission as some sort of admission that we were truly against hunting.

A turgid Boston radio talk show got wind of the back and forth and pretty soon the *Eagle* was their target, painting us as the paper that couldn't stand the sight of a dead animal. They called one morning and asked for an interview, but I declined. I had learned over the years that radio interviews emanating from the blathering radio talk shows are totally in the control of the interviewer, who has his hand on the mike switch. He'll open your microphone when he feels like it and he'll shut you off in mid-sentence. Objectivity and fairness aren't part of the equation, it's all about sensationalism and ratings. A response just prolongs the conversation that has already run off the tracks.

* * *

"A guy just called and said there's a bomb in your building," Sally told me over the intercom.

"A what, Sally? A bomb?" I asked.

"Yes," she said, just as calm as could be. I asked her to come over to my office and repeat exactly what was said.

"He said, 'I came up there this morning and put a bomb in your building,'" said Sally. "And I, like you, said 'a bomb?' and he responded, 'a bomb' and hung up."

"What else, Sally? Did he sound young, old, accent, anything?" I asked.

I didn't want to create a panic among the five or six staffers who were in the building at the moment, but this wasn't a gamble I was going to take. I was ninety-nine percent confident that no one could put a bomb *in* our building, but I was going to yield to that unknown one percent. I asked Sally one more time, "did he say *in* your building?"

"Yes," said Sally. "I came up there this morning and put a bomb *in* your building."

OK, time to act. I hollered for everyone to come over to my office right now. Everyone headed over except for Allison, who was pounding away in the production area.

"Allison, I need you here right now," I said, trying not to sound ultra urgent.

"Just a few minutes, Ed," she responded.

"*Now*," I barked as I glared across the room at her.

Allison came over immediately, looking like a scolded puppy.

"We just got a call that someone has placed a bomb in the building," I said as calmly as possible. "Turn off your computers, gather up your stuff, and get the hell out of here until we get this sorted out."

It's impossible to describe the various looks on their faces. Dave Harrison wanted to talk it through, and I told him to wait until we are all across the street. Shutting down the darkroom was a little more complicated than just turning off a computer, so I told Chris not to worry about it and just be the first one out the door. I also told everyone not to discuss this with anyone.

Within sixty seconds the building was empty. I called the Elgin PD. The dispatcher said she'd send someone right over. I suggested that the vehicle arrive without lights and sirens.

About four minutes later a local gendarme arrived and I could tell from his body language that this was a first for him. He was soon joined by a second cop and they stared at each other for a few moments, then wandered around the building searching. Their collective bomb experience had probably been garnered watching Road Runner cartoons and I was chuckling to myself as I thought they were looking for something fizzling.

After poking around for a few moments, they both came back to me and one of them asked a good question: "Do you know of anyone who might want to do this to the *Eagle*?"

By this time I had stitched together three pieces that might be related. First, we had recently run a story about a guy in Tucker who had been charged with fleecing elderly customers who bought wood from him. Second, John Wilbanks, the guilty business owner, was livid that we had covered the court case in detail. He had called me with the standard "I'm gonna sue your ass" threats. And the third piece of my mental mosaic was that to get to Elgin one had to come "up" from Tucker – as in "I came *up* there this morning and put a bomb in your building." In addition to Wilbanks, there were two other characters from that neck of the woods who had expressed some extremely vocal issues with our paper in the past.

So when I was asked if I knew anyone who might want to do this, I answered "Yes. Three in fact."

"OK," said the cop, and that was the end of the discussion.

A few minutes later we concluded that the building was safe and I motioned for the staff to return.

A mention of the bomb scare was included in the police log the following week with no other details. When I was in a local dry goods store a couple of days later, Bill Birch, the store owner, commented on it. Bill was one of the first people I met when I arrived in the area and we had become good friends, often acting as private and confidential sounding boards for each other.

"Do you know who made the threat?" Bill asked.

"Not yet, Bill. We'll probably never know."

"I'll bet you a hundred bucks that it was John Wilbanks," said Bill.

Wow, Bill had fingered my prime suspect. And Bill knew nothing about the "I came *up* there" threat.

I tried to look calm but felt my poker face melting fast.

Bill then pulled together the recent stories concerning Wilbanks's crooked business shenanigans, and the fact that the *Eagle* had reported it in detail, while the *Banner* ignored it. Then he laughed and said this was exactly the kind of thing Wilbanks would do.

"What do you mean by that?"

"He blew up a neighbor's fence years ago because it was on his property, like about one foot. And he accidentally on purpose hit a loaded boat trailer that had gotten in his way at Lake Carlisle."

"He hit a loaded boat trailer?" I said incredulously.

"Sent the trailer and boat right down the ramp. The whole mess tipped off the side of the ramp, overturned, and the boat and trailer gulped down five hundred gallons of water." He laughed, "Claimed it was an accident and there were no eye-witnesses, but people on the scene said that the chocks under the boat trailer suggested that the tongue of the trailer had been swung a good fifteen feet. The guy is a ticking time-bomb." Then Bill heard his words and choked on his coffee.

I knew better than to join the discussion with Bill because I didn't want to lock horns with Wilbanks, even though he was the prime suspect in my mind. And I was probably influenced by the response of "OK" from the police on the day of the bomb threat when I told them I had three suspects. Pursuing this any farther could open a long and torturous journey that had an exceptionally high probability of leading to nowhere.

Chapter Sixteen

Ellen gave me a shove and said, "The fire whistle is going off," as she turned on the scanner.

I pulled myself upright as the scanner came to life and I caught just the last bit of a transmission: "… Dublin Street, Elgin."

"Damn," I thought. "Where on Dublin Street? It's a long street."

As I headed for the bathroom Ellen turned up the scanner full blast and the address on Dublin Street was broadcast, but the number meant nothing to me. The dispatcher then added the needed locator: "the *Banner* building."

"Holy cripes, the *Banner* is on fire!" We scrambled to get dressed, grab cameras and car keys, and head out the door. It was 3:16 a.m., a fact we got from the fire marshal the following day.

We decided to go in one car, knowing that we could always find a ride if one of us left before the other.

Ellen drove. Her planned route was designed to end-run any roadblocks thrown up by the police; not that there were a lot of police around at that hour. She also was calculating that if the fire was significant, and more fire companies were called in, she wanted to be in a position where we could get out.

The temperature was close to zero, and the area had just dug out of a twelve-inch snowstorm, the third large snowfall in the past two weeks. The snow berms lining the streets were ahead of the snow-removal crews, providing an added obstacle to any emergency response.

We saw the glow of the fire when we hit the main highway. Fortunately, we were coming in from a direction that would not be the route for many first responders, not at this stage of the game at least. But then the scanner dispatcher came on and called two additional volunteer fire departments to the scene. This meant that someone knowledgeable had already gotten to the scene and determined that all of Elgin's fire resources would not be adequate to deal with this fire.

I knew of an approach that wasn't on any map. It entailed going around LaForce's Mini Mart. Behind the store they had a couple of dumpsters and a dirt road, maybe seventy-five feet long that led from there to a little dead-end street behind the store. No one used it except the trash-removal folks because there were no homes that far down on the dead-end street. As we headed toward the glow, Ellen unveiled her approach plan. She knew about the little road because last spring she had taken a picture of a family of raccoons that had set up shop inside one of the dumpsters.

She pulled to a stop, "Got film?" she asked.

"Just two rolls," I said, "and you?"

"Lots," she said with a confident smile. This was going to be a defining moment for Ellen. She had recently attended a photographic workshop in Boston that dealt with nighttime photography.

She described the workshop attendees as "wall-to-wall sports photographers trying to figure out how to get a great action shot in night conditions." But Ellen teased out of the two instructors some extensive know-how about shooting other things at night, specifically structure fires.

The *Banner* building didn't belong to the *Banner*, but they were the largest tenant. There was also The Pizza Joint, a beauty salon and a fabric shop. The upstairs had some additional *Banner* offices and a couple of additional spaces that were rented out from time to time. The original *Banner* building, the one owned by the Calloway family, was a stately old church that had been converted into an office complex. For years, the Calloway family printed the *Banner* in what was once the sanctuary – the "real news" replacing the "good news." After the Calloways sold the paper, the St. Louis owners decided that they didn't need all that space. The paper was no longer being printed on site, and they just didn't grasp the wonderful historical aura that surrounded the building. So they relocated to Dublin Street and did a nice job of tailoring it into a functioning newspaper office. Their old Goss press was dismantled and sold to a weekly newspaper in northern New Hampshire.

We sprinted toward the fire. "Should we split up?" asked Ellen.

"Good idea," I said. "Which side do you want for openers?" I knew that Ellen would have a preference and she was much more adept at getting these photos than I was.

"I'll start at the pizza end," she said, "but let's work fast. This is a narrow playing field and they may be sweeping us out of here very quickly."

"OK, you start on the north," I reconfirmed.

"I don't know which end is north," she shouted. "All I know is I'm starting at the end with The Pizza Joint." She shot down the street, laughing. She was right – five minutes later the cops and fire personnel began directing the twenty or so people who had already shown up back down the street. From that vantage point, the scope and ferocity of the fire were severely subdued. The enforcers might have been reticent to come down real heavy on a woman, so Ellen got a couple of extra minutes. That's when she got the money shot.

When she joined the throng, which had grown to about thirty-five or forty, she gave me a thumbs up. She was so excited that she could hardly get her words out. "If the exposures are right, I got some great shots!"

"Is there some doubt?" I said, knowing full well what the response would be.

"No doubt at all," she said "but the best shot was fast and I just hope the focus was correct." She was reloading film on the fly. "No," she said, "I got it."

I, too, had gotten off a couple of shots that looked pretty good, at least through the viewfinder, but I had also been busy talking with people on the scene.

Soon the crowd had swelled to over fifty people, many with their winter coats on and their pajama bottoms covering their Bean boots. Additional firefighting apparatus was rolling in from adjacent towns and hoses were being unrolled in all directions. The fire, which had apparently started in the *Banner* office, had migrated through the beauty salon and was gnawing away at The Pizza Joint. In about sixty seconds it burst into the pizza space like a gaggle of teenagers armed with free pizza passes.

The place literally exploded, blowing out the front window and sending an audible gasp through the onlookers. "I told you the place was a grease pit," came a voice out of the dark, "but the pizza was good."

The stairwell inside the *Banner* offices was the perfect chimney to take the fire up to the second floor. Within minutes, sections of the second floor were hurtling down into the first floor space. This in turn created more upward drafting and served as a shortcut for the fire to fully engulf the second floor.

Within ninety minutes the excitement was over. No bright flames were lighting the winter sky and without that visual warmth, the crowd became aware of how cold it actually was and quickly faded into the night.

Deborah and Mike from our staff had found Ellen and me, and we jointly concluded that we had probably done as much as we could. We agreed that we would deal with the follow-up in the morning. After all, it was Thursday night, and we had six days to get this story into the *Eagle*.

Ellen and I started retracing our steps to our car, the route now ankle deep in water that was rapidly turning to ice. Rounding out the obstacle course, lots of fire hoses were concealed under the water. We were stopped by Tim Bailey, a young cop that had been on the force for about a year. When he saw it was us he said, "Hi, Mr. and Mrs. Remington." I explained where our car was parked and that was our destination. He walked with us until we got across the street, aiding us with his flashlight. Tim was the only person on the Elgin police force who was an Elgin native. He had been on one of the youth soccer teams that the *Eagle* sponsored each fall, and I always tried to get to a game or two just to add support. While everything around me at that moment concerned the fire and our story, I had a momentary mind shift as I remembered that at the soccer games the kids always called me Ed. Now that this one had grown up, I'd become "Mr. Remington."

We reached our car and Ellen flipped me the keys. "You drive," she said. "I don't think my hands can grip the wheel."

The car cranked a couple of times, but finally turned over. We sat there for a minute hoping that the heater might begin to earn its keep, then carefully threaded our way down the little dead-end road. On the way to the car we had jointly agreed upon the exit route so as to not be caught up with blocked streets, and our plan worked perfectly until the last turn. The street was blocked, but there was just enough room for us to skirt around the pumper truck. As I was executing that mobile pirouette, we saw someone coming up from the fire and recognized Arnold Stripe, the publisher of the *Banner*.

"I have to talk to him," I said to Ellen. "It won't be long."

"I'm fine now that the heater is working," she said.

I intercepted Arnold in the middle of the intersection. The noise from a nearby pumper was deafening and I motioned for him to go over to another side of the street. "A hell of a way to spend a winter night," he said. "I wonder what started it?"

"My first guess would have been The Pizza Joint," I said, "but there was no fire in their kitchen when we arrived."

"No, it started in our shop, but I can't figure out how," he said. I sensed he was still in a state of shock or denial or perhaps just freezing cold.

I put my arm around his shoulder and said something to the effect that tomorrow begins a whole new set of experiences and "he'd get through it."

It was a weird bit of camaraderie. There had been little interaction between Arnie and me since he'd been posted in Elgin a year earlier. He was another of the St. Louis parent company's stable of roving publishers. The tenure in Elgin was merely an assignment, a stepping stone that hopefully led to something bigger and grander. Arnie, his predecessor, and the woman before that were all cogs in a larger wheel, and that top-down form of corporate management will never work with a community-centric business like a weekly newspaper. But at this moment my heart went out to Arnie, or if not Arnie, for the *Banner* and the Calloway legacy.

"Tomorrow or Saturday, when you finally assemble your troops, bring them over to our office and we'll make sure that the *Banner* publishes an edition next week," I said. I buried any immediate thought as to how we were going to accomplish that.

"Excuse me, Ed, but what did you say?" said Arnie. He squared around and looked directly at me.

I repeated my offer. "Thanks, Ed, that's very kind of you," Arnie replied. "We may take you up on that." He too was probably wondering how that could be accomplished.

I knew that any decision from Arnie would have to be approved by the corporate suits in St. Louis, and that was going to muddy the waters. I had a strong feeling that getting an issue out the following week was not only important for the *Banner*, but that the *Eagle* was being given a special moment to make a meaningful gesture inside of the Fourth Estate.

Friday morning came earlier than usual, but I was still running on the adrenaline of the night before. A note on the refrigerator from Ellen announced that she was at the paper developing film. I knew she was anxious to see the results of her subzero shoot, and so was I.

On the way into the office, I stopped by Freda's, where the fire was the one and only topic. As I was waiting for coffee, I suddenly had sort of a survivor's guilt because my newspaper was not the one that had burned to the ground. "How stupid," I thought. As soon as I was away from Freda's, that insipid guilt vanished.

As I was getting out of my car at the office, a guy approached me and identified himself as being with the AP. He wanted my reaction to the fire and I told him that any fire was sad and this one had a particular poignant overlay because it was a newspaper. I talked about how well the fire was contained, never mind that all that remained was the cellar hole. And I commented on the fact that no one was hurt. Fortunately, he didn't get into the last-newspaper-standing scenario because I would have probably had a reaction that wouldn't have been printable.

The mask of gloom and doom was dispelled the minute I walked in the office. There stood Ellen holding up a contact sheet and a loupe, a small magnifying device that one uses in order to look at individual images. "Check out the second and third pictures on the left end of the third row," she said. I set my coffee down on Lana's desk, switched on the desk lamp, and bent over the contact sheet.

"Well?" said Ellen. "I told you, no doubt!"

"There's a lot of smoke in the frame, but I can see what you were going for," I said.

Ellen stepped closer and grabbed my hand with the loupe. "*This* row, Bozo!"

"Oops!" I said. "I get detention." Then I saw what Ellen was so excited about.

Just as the fire was whittling away the front wall of the building, the entire multi-framed front window had been reduced to a wide gaping opening rather than a stack of ten-over-ten glass panes. This opening was totally surrounded in fire and inside the building was the original sign that hung in front of the *Banner*'s old building when the Calloways owned it. It was a one-word sign, *BANNER*, and was in the original font that the family had used, a modified Old English blackletter typeface that mimicked the *New York Times*. The tweaking of the typeface had been done by someone in the Calloway family long ago. As the fire swirled around the sign, the word *BANNER* seemed to call out and writhe in agony.

"That photo sums up the entire story," said Karen in awe.

Friday came and went and there was no call from Arnie. I didn't write a lot of significance into that silence; the whole *Banner* world had been turned on its head and decisions numbered in the hundreds as input from Elgin and St. Louis was being wrought into an action plan.

I told our staff that I'd volunteered the space for the *Banner* to get out their next edition. Our whole gang jumped in and within an hour a tentative work plan was hashed out that could, we hoped, deal with two separate trains coming down the same track.

Arnie called me at home Saturday morning and asked if I could join him and a couple of people from their St. Louis office for breakfast. I agreed, and suggested that we meet somewhere other than in Elgin. Diane MacIntosh, who, with her husband Bob, owned a great little B&B about three miles from Elgin, would gladly turn over her dining room or parlor, I told him, and also whip up a breakfast. He agreed. I called Diane, she was thrilled, and the meeting was on for 10:30 at the Up Country Inn.

Arnie introduced me to Jim Doss, the president of Western Media, Inc., and Stan Wandress, their corporate counsel. I told them how sorry we were about the fire and volunteered copies of every photo we had shot should they need them for insurance purposes. I was startled to find out how little grasp they had regarding the *Banner*. Their offsite subscription list, essentially a backup to what was in Elgin, wasn't current. There was no individual listing of current accounts, just monthly totals. Even archives of old issues were not routinely sent off premise. In short, the fire had obliterated the operation from top to bottom. As this was unfolding, I found myself throwing out idea after idea as to how they might overcome various problems.

They were hesitant at first, about why we had offered to allow the *Banner* staff to use our facility to produce their next issue, but they quickly understood that there were a lot of historical and institutional ghosts floating around in Elgin that would never show up on a monthly status report or balance sheet.

The next five days were the busiest I had ever had since I purchased the paper, and they were among the most enjoyable. Both staffs understood the mission, but the *Eagle* staff was dumbfounded with our visitors' plodding pace. By Monday afternoon, *Eagle* staff were writing *Banner* stories and we shared some of our fire photos with them. Everyone tried to respect the others' independence and publishing privacy, but by Tuesday morning there was considerable collaboration on the fire story and each organization was trying to give its readers something that wouldn't be duplicated in the other paper.

We drove that approach because we had covered the fire with four people to their one. Ellen gave up one of her best photos for their page one. Wendy Beaumont, the editor of the *Banner*, insisted that Ellen's byline accompany it, but Ellen gave her a firm No.

Their ad sales ability was shattered and it was decided that their sales team would call local merchants and invite them to run in the *Banner*, the same ad that they were preparing to run in the *Eagle*. They hawked the ads at half price and sold enough to demonstrate an ad-to-editorial ratio of about 35/65. Financially it didn't amount to anything, but having the ads was going to enhance the look of the edition.

Wednesday morning, Doss and Wandress called and asked if we could reconvene our meeting at the Up Country Inn.

I told them I was right on deadline and it was a little different this week with two newspapers to produce. I asked if we could postpone the meeting until the following morning. "Certainly," said Doss. "Ed, the topic of conversation is going to be the sale of the *Banner*," he added.

I didn't respond other than to tell him that the topic would go no farther than me. He appreciated that.

The sale of the *Banner*? I couldn't take it in at the moment. We were giving birth to twin newspapers and we had just a few hours left. I told the printer that layouts for both papers would arrive together and that the *Eagle* driver would bring both papers back to Elgin.

The grand plan worked exceptionally well until the *Eagle* truck arrived in the morning and delivery people from both newspapers got into the mix. In our haste to produce two separate newspapers, we had neglected the delivery piece of the equation. On a dark, sleety Thursday morning, our delivery truck rolled up to our office ninety minutes later than usual due to the combined print run. But no one there had been fully briefed as to what was going to whom and to where. If ever there was to be a turf war between the two papers, this would be the moment. I doubt anyone waiting in the cold was aware that the two editorial staffs had been working side by side for the previous five days. But any ill feeling was apparently freeze-dried by the cold.

The bundles were identified, but the markings were tiny three-inch labels that were hard to read in the winter morning light. Because of the ninety-minute delay, the early news outlets were empty. A steady stream of people soon began appearing at the office to purchase a paper on site – everyone wanted to see the fire story. Our delivery people and the *Banner* delivery people were suddenly given the task of selling single copies and making change for each sale. When the quarters, nickels, and dimes ran out they were hearing, "Keep the change." This could have started a whole new cottage industry of curbside sales.

The problem was that there was no one in charge, and delivery of both papers was anywhere from one to two hours late. Had it been just one newspaper's delivery team, it would have instantly worked itself out. But each team had developed rigid procedures over the years, and anything that would upset their routines threw a wrench into the gears.

I had been awake since four and Ellen and I had laid in bed in the dark discussing the sale of the *Banner*. It was now 5:15 and we were sipping coffee and trying to find a handle so we could get on board with the idea of the *Banner* being sold. We kept coming back to the Calloways and to the *Banner* staff, but neither was compelling enough to make us want to purchase a paper that was basically not there.

"There's nothing to buy except a name," I said, "and outside of sentimental and historical reasons, what's the purpose?"

I had called Missy a few hours earlier. If we decided to bid on the paper, she advised me, we should make sure that any and all liabilities remained with Western Media. That was standard procedure and, according to Missy, was easily done in the sales documents. But we agreed that the *Banner* was basically dead.

Ellen and I also reached that conclusion and I was off to my meeting at the Up Country Inn.

I had decided to make our decision known to Jim and Stan right up front. We had no interest in pursuing this at any price and I didn't want to waste their time or mine. They had a plateful of issues with which to deal, and there was no point in dragging things out.

Bob MacIntosh brought in a pot of coffee, a bowl of scrambled eggs, and a platter of blueberry pancakes. On a separate platter was a pile of bacon and link sausages. As he left, I decided to get right to the heart of the discussion, but Jim Doss spoke first. "Yesterday when we talked, Ed, I believe I said the topic was the sale of the *Banner*, or something close to that, right?"

"Verbatim," I said.

"It was a poor choice of words," he said.

Dozens of scenarios shot through my sleep-deprived mind, but before any of them took root, Doss continued, "We're closing it down." He drew a breath, "I'll bet you didn't expect that, did you?" he said.

I had a moment of complete mental paralysis. This had not been a talking point for me and Ellen, and I was wondering if this was a business discussion or a wake. Buying time, I rearranged the sausages on the platter. "How soon?" I asked.

"It's over – as of now," said Stan. "We already have board approval." That was a funny statement, because I knew that their board was populated with one controlling family.

I wanted to choose my words carefully but I didn't have time to massage the message. In another delaying tactic, now that I had the sausages in a row, I asked Stan to slide over the coffee creamer. "I think it is a solid decision, and a sad one, too,"

I said. "But the *Banner* is one of many community newspapers across America that are closing their doors. There are many reasons and theories, in addition to fires, as to why this is happening. But it is happening and most papers, such as the *Banner*, have gone down fighting."

"We owned twelve weekly newspapers two years ago, Ed, and four dailies. Today we have seven weeklies and two dailies," said Jim. "Cable TV, the Internet, email, desktop publishing, they are all chipping away — not to mention papers like the *Elgin Eagle*," he said with a laugh. "Your paper was, is, as solid as they come, and competing against you was a mission impossible."

I thanked him for the compliment and then let my softer side get into the discussion. First I asked if they had any intention of publishing a final edition. They weren't sure, and I dug in, "There has to be an end, a goodbye, a look back and a look forward." I told them that now that we'd been down the road of producing both papers simultaneously, that a second time around would be much simpler. They agreed on condition that we let them pay.

I asked about the *Banner* staff. "It's working out pretty well," said Stan. "Arnold and Wendy are already reassigned to some of our other properties. The young reporter they just hired has quit, and the other reporter, the girl from UNH, is going to join a magazine that Bob's family owns in Boston."

"We could probably pick up one of their local people," I said slowly.

"All the locals are part-timers," said Stan.

Well, I thought, I'm sure we can fold some of those part-timers into our weekly routine.

We weren't going to be able to rescue them all, because I foresaw a marginal increase in business now that the *Banner* was out of the picture. But we had a lot of part-time people doing jobs from proofreading to cleaning. We could shuffle them in and out to give everyone some work time.

Jim and Stan accepted my suggestion for a final edition of the *Banner* and we got it out the following week. It wasn't really special, because the hearts of its creators weren't in it. That week, the *Eagle* had a feature story about the *Banner* and a farewell editorial with a picture of the founding Calloways that we dug out of the local historical society.

As I wrote that editorial I felt I was writing a eulogy, and I guess I was doing exactly that. I tried to keep it positive and dwell on the history rather than the present; but the present was very much on my mind. The one question that hung over the piece was, "How much longer?"

There will always be a place in American communities for a communications source that reports, explains, analyses, and discusses the surrounding world. What format that vehicle will take is evolving, but people will always be closely connected with their communities, and the community newspaper is the perfect voice. That envelope stuffed with clippings is going to outlast the password-protected digital device.

I finished the editorial about thirty minutes before the paper was due to head out the door to the printer. "Was this a tough one to write?" Karen asked.

"It was tough," I said. She gave me a huge hug, stepped back, and we stood there staring into each other's eyes. We were both aware that there was a recurring rumble along the community newspaper fault lines, but right now the printer was waiting.

A moment later Gene Baker, our driver, called and said that he had to take a kid to the hospital. "Took a tumble on the basketball court," Gene informed me, "But he's gonna be OK."

"I agree with taking him in for a check, Gene, don't worry. We'll get it handled at this end. Give me a call tomorrow with a medical update," I said.

Finding the replacement driver was easy; it would be me. I needed alone time on the road, at the printer, and on the road again.

As our paper was flying off the web press, I reflected that just an hour before, on that same press, the final edition of the *Banner* had been printed. It was already loaded into our truck. It would be offloaded after we had offloaded the *Eagle*.

Our press run was completed. The *Eagle*'s pallets were ushered into the truck by a forklift, and I headed toward Elgin. I turned off the radio and let the quiet take over. Thirty minutes later, as I approached the state line, my headlights illuminated the new signs for Jack Harris's auto dealership. Jack had retired about six months earlier and I knew that today's edition carried a story announcing that his son, Eric was taking over – the third generation! Harris Auto was a regular weekly advertiser with the *Eagle*, and the Harrises were friends.

I pulled into their lot, dug out a business card and wrote a congratulatory note to Eric. I clipped it to a paper and pushed it through the mail slot of their office.

God, I love this job!

-30-

Acknowledgements

Special thanks to the hundreds of persons who worked side by side with me in all the newspaper ventures. Our success was always rooted in hiring the best people we could find, understanding our mission, and moving forward – as a team.

The episodes in this book, while fictional, are very reflective of the daily occurrences at any weekly newspaper. The difference is how you handle them.

A special thank you to Anne Lunt, a copy editor who leaves no stone unturned, and Melanie Bertoni, whose proofing and research skills are without equal. Gyaki Bonsu-Anane pulled the cover together. The encouragement department included Liz Thomas, Jim and Peggy Howard, Paul Hertneky, and many others. And this would never have been completed were it not for the patience and encouragement from my wife Beverly, who listened each day as the words built up and with an ever so slight tilt of the head could convey a message about what she had just heard.

But, again, thanks to all who shared the deadline discipline with me – it was one tremendous ride.

about the cover

This 1980 bronze sculpture by Derek Wernher is located at the Brookgreen Gardens in Myrtle Beach, SC. It depicts a weekly ritual of "Len Ganeway," the pen name used by former *County Press* owner Bob Myers. Photo was shot on 7/12/2006 by Gordon Shecket. http://gordon.shecket.org/

Contents